PRAISE FOR LISA TAWN BERGREN'S *THE CAPTAIN'S BRIDE*
BOOK ONE IN THE NORTHERN LIGHTS SERIES

"I found myself immediately involved in the stories of Elsa and Peder, Kaatje and her wayward husband, Soren, Tora and her quest for wealth and power, and a host of other people who sailed with them to America to fulfill their dreams. Lisa Tawn Bergren has a straightforward, evocative style of writing that makes her characters breathe. They walk right across the page and straight into your heart."

—*Francine Rivers,* author

"Pick of the month. 4½ stars! Lisa Tawn Bergren is a rare talent in historical fiction, writing with exquisite style as she immerses lucky readers in the powerful emotions of her full-bodied characters. Stay tuned for the next book to continue this exciting trilogy."
—*Romantic Times*

"Bergren at her very best! What an incredible tale of adventure, from Norway's sparkling fjords to the high seas of Cape Horn, to the rocky shores and plains of America in the 1880s. Even with such a panoramic backdrop, *The Captain's Bride* keeps its spyglass trained on the lives of people you'll care about deeply, from first page to last, as they wrestle with all the temptations of spirit and flesh we all know too well. Lisa Tawn Bergren's writing talents unfurl in this historical page-turner—I loved it!"

—*Liz Curtis Higgs,* author

"Lisa Tawn Bergren has skillfully entwined the lives of the immigrants as they face opportunity and disaster in their adopted country. The characters capture the heart and parade through the imagination long after the book has been closed. *The Captain's Bride* rides the swells of history into the reader's imagination! Elsa is an independent-minded heroine worthy of imitation today. A triumphant saga!"

—*The Literary Times*

"*The Captain's Bride* is one of those rare pleasures…a terrific tale, told with extraordinary straightforwardness, honesty, and insight. In this, her first historical novel, Lisa Tawn Bergren, a remarkably gifted writer and student of human nature, has created a landscape filled with living, breathing characters. God's compassion and grace illuminate each page."

—*Diane Noble,* author

DEEP HARBOR

DEEP HARBOR

LISA TAWN BERGREN

WATERBROOK
PRESS

DEEP HARBOR
PUBLISHED BY WATERBROOK PRESS
5446 North Academy Boulevard, Suite 200
Colorado Springs, Colorado 80918
A division of Random House, Inc.

The characters and events in this book are fictional,
and any resemblance to actual persons or events is coincidental.

ISBN 1-57856-045-4

Printed in the United States of America
1999

10 9 8 7 6 5 4 3

To all who know the Deep seeks them
and who, in turn, dive right in.

Acknowledgments

I'd like to thank my readers who made sure this was a decent book before even my editor saw it: Tricia Goyer, Joanna Weaver, Maria Hansen, Rebecca Price, and my husband, Tim (who is forced to read everything I write and swears each one is the best, God bless him). Joe O'Meara essentially wrote the section on chess, since I've never played and would have to be dragged, kicking and screaming, to learn. Brian Shouers, the reference historian at the Montana Historical Society Library, sent me invaluable information on Helena in 1886. And my editor, Traci DePree, made this a much better book with her insight and suggestions. To all of you, thanks.

Author's Note

I've had many people ask me how to pronounce "Kaatje," and I thought I'd answer before you got into Book 2. I've heard guesses from "Katie" to "Cootie" to "Catgee." It's "Kaaatya." Isn't that pretty? Sorry to make you struggle. My handy-dandy name book showed pronunciations!

c o n t e n t s

p r o l o g u e

June 1886

*T*ora Anders strolled down the wooden sidewalk of Helena, Montana, with purpose. She walked everywhere with purpose these days, but today was special. Trent Storm was in town again. And he had invited her out for supper. She needed to get back to her fine Queen Anne style home—the pride of Helena—to bathe and change. Tonight would be different; she was sure of it. Tonight Trent would propose at last. Hadn't she waited four years for this day?

She nodded at two towering cowboys who dipped their heads appreciatively, touching fingertips to hat brims, and then at two women she did not know. Tora had been in Helena for a little over a year. Having built her last roadhouses for Storm Enterprises in the vicinity, she decided it was time to make some semblance of a home for herself. And in the process, she hoped to entice Trent west by her blatant refusal to return east.

This hard, energetic place was rife with trouble as well as opportunity, and it fit Tora to a tee. She loved the gently sloping mountains in the distance, the rolling hills that gave way to plains. Montana was Tora Anders territory if she had ever seen it. Surely Trent would fall in love with it just as he had fallen in love with her. In the distance she heard the train whistle, and she quickened her step. She doubted that

1

Trent would come early. It was more likely that he would take care of some business and visit Helena's Storm Roadhouse—one of the finest restaurants Tora had set up for him—before coming to call.

There was little to fear from his examination of the roadhouse. Tora had become a difficult perfectionist of a boss. She made frequent impromptu inspections of the facilities and was meticulous about every detail. If a table was not set with pristine linens or the utensils were not placed just so, she was known to take hold of the cloth and pull the whole table setting to the floor, even firing the manager on the spot. Consequently the roadhouses she had begun for Trent—sixteen over the last four years along the tracks of the Northern Pacific—had the best reputation of them all. She smiled, feeling smug for a moment. With any luck at all, Trent had heard the critics' reports just as she had. At twenty-two years of age, Tora Anders was already a force to contend with. And her fame as the "Storm Roadhouse Maven" was rivaling her sister Elsa Ramstad's fame as the "Heroine of the Horn."

She laughed under her breath, thinking of her father and what he would have thought had he read the American papers. Had he lived. *The old bird probably would have been scandalized,* she thought. *He never really did embrace what America was all about: freedom and opportunity.* Certainly his two younger daughters, Elsa and Tora, had not turned out as they had been raised to be. Carina, the eldest, was the only one to do as their parents had planned; only she stayed at home in Bergen, Norway, married a Bergenser, Garth Ramstad, and raised children.

Tora frowned as she thought of her own daughter, Jessie, then banished the memory from her mind. It had been a long time since she had allowed herself to think of the child, and she quickly decided it would be a long time before she thought of her again. It was a tad more pleasant to think of her sister Elsa's son, Kristian, who had to be about two or three by now. Perhaps there was another one on the way. It was difficult to know, since she had not corresponded with Elsa for over four years and had only found out about her nephew by reading Elsa's popular column in the *New York Times*.

She turned off the sidewalk, onto an intricately laid brick pathway, and walked through the ornate iron gate in front of her home. Walking up the steps, she peeled off her white lace gloves and pulled at the wide ribbon that held her French straw hat on her head. It was warm for June, but the heat felt right somehow.

Her maidservant, Sasha—one of three in the huge house—opened the door as if she had been waiting for her. This pleased Tora to no end. "Good afternoon, Sasha," she said primly, stepping through the massive doorway. The tall ceilings and thick mahogany paneling kept the place darker and thus cooler than out-of-doors. Tora handed Sasha her gloves and hat. "I trust you completed your task of oiling the staircase woodwork today?"

"Yes, Miss Anders," Sasha said with a deferential curtsey. She was short in stature, had drab brown hair, and spoke with a slight Russian accent. In a town full of Chinese and Irish, it had been difficult to find the right servants, Tora mused. But Sasha was one of the best. An excellent maid, and none of Tora's gentlemen callers would look her way twice. *Perfect.*

"I did the paneling in the dining room as well," the maid added hastily as Tora walked to the staircase and peered closely at the hand-carved balustrade, looking for traces of dust. But Sasha had done an impeccable job. All the way up the grand, sweeping staircase—which Tora hoped to descend soon in a fine French wedding gown—there was not one speck of dust to be found.

"Good," she muttered, heading at once to the dining room. Tora loved this room. After the heavy, dark paneling of the foyer and hallway, entering the dining room was like entering dawn. Everything was different. The panels were outlined in white-painted wood, their interiors covered in coordinating velvet that was padded from behind. Tora likened eating in the room to dining on a massive bed fit for a queen, and the guests she entertained around the enormous, ostentatious table often agreed.

Absentmindedly, Tora walked around the perimeter of the room,

3

thinking of the many admirers who had sat at the table, gazing at her longingly. In the West, women were scarce, and women of quality and wealth were treasured like gold from the mountains. Men came to the Montana territory to farm the rich soil, help lay the tracks, or mine the high hills in the distance. The capital bustled as people entered and exited daily for other parts of the territory, leaving their money in the townspeople's hands as they went through. Yes, it was a fine place for a woman to make her way, and men far and wide admired her for her tenacity. Gentlemen came to call at all hours of the day, and her maidservants turned many away without an excuse.

Because Tora's heart belonged to one man: Trent Storm.

He was the man who had made her the woman she was today.

She was the woman who would make him a man of true power in the future.

And it would all begin tonight.

Trent Storm made his way through the throngs of people at the train station, not surprised that Tora was absent rather than there to greet him. It was not their pattern to have a cheerful reunion at the station. Instead, Tora would want him to come to her, in her corner, so to speak, giving her the advantage. She would be dressed to the hilt and smelling of her intoxicating cologne—a mix of jasmine from the Orient and vanilla—and smiling at him in that way that melted his heart. What he wouldn't give to see her in a plain dress like the simple farm women around him! He yearned for the chance to slip his hands into her hair and release the pins, setting free those thick, chestnut waves to cascade down past her shoulders. They would frame her face and those incredible blue eyes, and it would take every bit of his control not to kiss her…

"Mr. Trent!" the porter said again, clearly irritated. "Your valise! You forgot this back there."

"Oh, thank you. I don't know where my mind is," he started lamely, fishing in his pocket for two bits for the man's trouble. Of course he knew exactly where his mind was. And it was time to clear it. He had spent four years waiting for Tora Anders to be honest with him, to reveal the reason she had made up the story of her family's death on the high Atlantic seas, and the reason for her lies since then. He couldn't understand why she would hide a perfectly respectable past. His private detective had discovered that she had a mother and sister alive in Bergen, Norway, and another sister who was married to a prosperous sea captain named Ramstad. The "Heroine of the Horn" they called her. Trent often found himself spellbound by the stories she wrote for the *Times* and the exquisite drawings she included. Apparently Tora had come to America with Elsa; however, curiously her name was not on the *Herald's* manifest. Was that the reason for her secrecy? he wondered for the thousandth time. Had she stowed away?

For a brief time she had been the housekeeper for a shipmate of Ramstad's, caring for his two sons. Then she had come to Minnesota and sought Trent's employ. But why the duplicity? The questions drove him nearly mad.

And as attracted as he was to Tora on the outside, he was disappointed with how she had degenerated on the inside. What were once guts and gumption now seemed greed and gall.

All in all, his relationship with Tora had soured. And it was time to end it. Tonight. Tonight he would expose the truth he had held within for four long years and demand an explanation. If she was honest, he might give her a chance. But if she tried her old games with him, it was over. At forty-five, he was too old to live life in such a manner.

"Trent!" Karl Martensen called, trying to shout above the din of the crowd. "Trent Storm! Storm!" Trent did not pause, obviously deep in thought. Karl dipped and turned through the throngs, hastening his steps across the platform to reach Trent. What was he doing here in the wilds of Montana? The answer came to Karl a moment later. Of course. The reputation of the roadhouse that Tora Anders had set up for Storm Enterprises last year was the talk of the line. Curiously, Tora had stopped here in Helena, electing to build a home and make some investments of her own. Trent had obviously rewarded her generously for work well done. Was there still something between the two of them?

Karl could not imagine letting one's heart wander so far as Tora Anders. Having grown up with her in Bergen, and seeing what she was capable of in America, he knew she was dangerous. Perhaps the affair had faded as so many others had for Tora. Perhaps Trent was the conquest of the past. Now, with some gold in the bank, Karl was sure she had set her sights higher than even Trent Storm would ever reach. What would appease that girl? *Nothing,* he answered himself sourly.

"Trent! Trent Storm!" At last the man turned, his eyes searching the crowd for the one who had called his name. His hair had gone more gray at the sides but was still full and wavy on top. He was a distinguished gentleman through and through, Karl thought, admiring the cut of his clothes and the way Trent held himself. Everything was just right on the man, except…except for the slight slump of his shoulders. Was he aging? Weary from the trip? Karl doubted that. Trent owned one of the most extravagant of the Pullman railroad cars and traveled alone in it. It was as close to the lap of luxury through Dakota as one could find.

"Martensen!" Trent smiled sincerely and stretched out his hand as soon as he spotted Karl.

"Whew!" Karl said, shaking his hand heartily. "This town is certainly getting busy."

"Statehood's in the wind," Trent said, looking around as if he himself had discovered the place. "It's a fine land with plenty of opportunity. Unfortunately we are not the only businessmen to have found her."

"Ah well, I think she's big enough for all of us. Especially since we are two of the first. The gold's pretty well tapped out, but there's more to this land's riches."

Trent smiled with him and then gestured toward a hired coach. "Need a ride? Where are you heading?"

"Oh, I'm waiting here for the next train from the Washington Territory. Bradford Bresley's due in on the four-forty."

"Bresley? Glad to know you're still doing business with the man."

"Exclusively. When John Hall and I parted ways four years ago, it was a natural thing to develop a partnership with Brad."

"You are fortunate," Trent said. "I always wished there had been a man I could trust as friend as well as partner."

"The railroads are a tough place to find such an animal," Karl said with a laugh. "Say, are you in town for long? We should talk about a couple of things Brad and I have rolling."

"I'd be glad to. Staying at the Cosmopolitan Hotel for a couple of days, then it's back to Minnesota. Look me up there tomorrow."

"I will." Karl gestured as if he had just thought of something. "Oh, and are you going to see Tora Anders by chance?"

Trent nodded once, his face inscrutable.

"Give her my best, will you?"

Trent stared him in the eye for a moment, then nodded once again. "Tomorrow, Martensen. And bring Bresley along with you. Let's talk over dinner, shall we?"

"Sounds fine."

Karl watched as Trent stepped into the cab and tapped on the coach's roof, the driver setting off at once. Judging from the hard look in his eye, whatever business Trent had with Tora was apparently not of the heart. And as Brad would say, something was definitely rotten in Denmark.

Elsa laughed as Kristian bent down and buried his face in a jasmine bush full of white, fragrant blossoms, sniffing theatrically. "Look, Mama," he said. "I smell."

"Yes, you do," she said with a giggle. Elsa picked up his squirming body and buried her face in his neck for a kiss. "You smell just like the flowers!"

"Down, Mama! I want down!"

"Kristian, we must hurry. Can you find your papa? He's right up there, at the corner." She knelt and pointed, hoping to distract the toddler from the intoxicating Hawaiian flora and fauna. She had just extracted him from a fissure in a rock, trying to get at a gecko lizard, and now he was entranced by the flowers! It would be impossible to get him all the way through town without carrying him, kicking and screaming.

Elsa looked ahead at Peder, hoping he could help with Kristian. Her husband was gazing across the busy dirt road at the mercantile, his expression intent. Did he see someone he knew? As she watched, he took a step back, into the shadow of the porch above the sidewalk.

"Go, Kristian! I'll race you!" Elsa whispered. Kristian spotted Peder at last and took off in his direction. She smiled at his delighted giggle and followed along at a leisurely pace. Elsa winced as Kristian squeezed between two natives and shoved aside a little girl in his efforts, then smiled again as he reached his father, embracing the tall man's leg. It was a glorious day to be in port at Honolulu, and she reveled in the chance to smell the fragrant flowers with her child and to gaze up at the green Koolau Mountains to the towering extinct volcano west of Koko Head at the point. What an exotic, idyllic place!

The people in town were native Hawaiians, imported plantation workers from China and Polynesia, and merchants, plus a few trailing whalers. The whalers spent half of their year in the vicinity, harpooning their kill and taking the cargo home to Japan, America, or even Russia. Soon the last of them would be leaving for distant shores, as the migrating whales had done months before. It would be nice to visit the place during the quiet that the natives usually enjoyed. Elsa grinned at the thought of a lazy day on the beach, combing the sand with Kristian for sand dollars and seashells and cuddling with her husband in a hammock for a nap beneath the palms.

Her smile faded as Peder grabbed up the child and looked for her anxiously. She reached him a moment later. "What? What is it?"

Peder took a step in front of her, as if posturing himself as protector, and nodded toward the mercantile. "There, just inside the window. Do you see that man?"

Elsa studied his profile, slightly obscured by the reflection of the glass. He was in uniform, a British uniform, to judge by the color and stripes. He stepped closer to the glass and bent to pick up a jar from the front window display. Elsa gasped. She edged closer to Peder, unable to believe her eyes.

Mason Dutton. The pirate who had threatened her life and nearly burned the Ramstads' first ship to the waterline.

A pirate, by anyone's account. The horrible memories filled her mind.

"But," she mumbled softly, "he is in uniform!"

"Come. I'm getting you out of here." Peder took her arm firmly and led the way down the rough-hewn sidewalk toward the wharf.

Elsa hazarded one more glance over her shoulder toward the mercantile.

And Mason was staring right back at her.

Mason Dutton let a slow smile crawl up his face as he watched Elsa Ramstad hurry away with her husband. It had been years, but as soon as he saw her, that moment he had first seen her in the West Indies came hurtling back to him. She was more beautiful now than that nymph he remembered, who had been swimming with the sailors of Peder Ramstad's ship. He could still see her slim legs, kicking in the crystalline waters as her skirts billowed about her. Her full lips as she defiantly looked back at him.

Mason had almost had her husband's ship, as well as her. They were one of the few crews ever to fend off his forces in his years of piracy, and the knowledge burned within him. He was not one to take defeat easily; if he could have another opportunity to make the fair

Elsa Ramstad his own, he would seize the challenge. There would be no greater satisfaction than seeing Peder Ramstad's ship burn once and for all.

Had they recognized him? Elsa's big eyes, perfect for her sculpted face, had held recognition and fear. It pleased him to think he frightened her. *I should.* They would be even more unnerved had they heard of his new reputation in these waters. "Run, mouse, run," he whispered. "The cat is in the house." He admired her slim waist and noted the child in Peder's arms with interest. Mason had kept up with the Heroine of the Horn through the newspaper articles in the years since they had crossed paths, admiring her obvious tenacity and talent. *All that and beautiful too. Yes, Mrs. Ramstad, someday you and I will again exchange words, and perhaps something more.*

Peder pulled her around a corner, ending Mason's lustful imaginings. Had it not been for Ramstad and his louse of a first mate, Karl Martensen, Mason was sure things would have ended differently. The fact that the two men and their crew had foiled his efforts brought a grudging respect, but also a burning desire to set things to rights, to get even and claim what was his. And what wasn't his these days? he asked himself with a low chuckle in his throat.

Mason set down the jar with a clunk that made the shopkeeper scowl in his direction, then quickly look away upon seeing the perpetrator. Mason Dutton owned the people in Honolulu and the surrounding waters of the Hawaiian Islands. They were his people, he their king. Or dictator. If he chose to strike, he did so. If he chose to ignore them, they breathed a sigh of relief. Most steered clear of him, paying the required dues to exist under his "protection." And he liked the sense of power it gave him.

He waved at a man whose stolen British uniform bulged at the seams, and the man immediately lumbered over. "Captain Peder Ramstad is in town," Mason said quietly. "Find out the name of his ship, their cargo, and when they intend to set sail."

Kaatje blinked, her eyes stinging from the salty sweat of her brow, and eased her horse to a stop. With the back of her hand, she wiped her forehead and looked around for Christina and Jessie. They were near the house, making mud pies as they had been doing for over an hour. She smiled. *The industry of small children.* If only she could sell their wares for money! On the stone wall that bordered the well were pie after pie, testimony of the girls' busy morning.

All in all, life was good here in the Skagit Valley of the Washington Territory. The soil was more dense than in Dakota, and thus heavier to clear and plow, but richer for growing. Here, they didn't have the problem of drought that the dryland farmers of Dakota battled; instead, they contended with rot. Still, it was easier to bring in a crop here, and Kaatje was glad for her move. In the four years since their arrival, she had managed—with the help of her dear Bergenser friends—to build some semblance of a home for her daughters in the one-room shanty and bring in enough of a crop to sustain them through each year. With God's help, they would do it again in 1886.

If only it could be a bit easier, she thought to herself. Her neighbors had expanded their farms and their homes since arriving, whereas Kaatje found herself barely able to sustain what she and her friends had begun. She closed her eyes. *Forgive me, Lord. I am thankful for what we have been given. I'm just so tired. Ease my weariness.* Slowly, she unhooked the harness of the plow from her waist and chest and then released her horse. Her shoulders and back ached from the work, and she winced as the fabric of her dress moved over her back, made raw from the leather straps. She paused and gave in to her exhaustion for a moment, hand on neck, eyes closed, sweaty cheek to the slight breeze from the west.

"Mama! Mama!" yelled her girls in unison, glad Kaatje was taking a break for lunch. They hauled a tin bucket of water, and Nels, the draft horse, whinnied and took a step forward as if they were bringing refreshment to him instead.

"Poor Nels," Kaatje soothed, stroking his giant sweaty neck. He was of good stock and had served them well here in the Skagit Valley. Certainly without Nels's help Kaatje would have accomplished little on this land.

When the girls reached her, Kaatje smiled broadly, invigorated simply by being near them as they chatted about business as if mud pies were a booming industry. "Give me a cup, child," she said to Jessie, who offered up the tin scoop. Kaatje drank deeply, dipped for another, and then nodded at Nels. "Give the rest to him, please. He must be very thirsty on such a day as this."

"Yes, Mama," Jessie said, happy to treat her big friend she had named after a fellow Bergenser. Jessie had a natural way with animals. Someday, Jessie had announced the other evening, she wanted to be a shepherd like Jesus, caring for her sheep on the hills that surrounded the Skagit Valley. She often begged to accompany Birger Nelson when he herded his flock to new pastures high in the hills. On the other hand, Kaatje's older child, Christina, seemed to fear the horse and preferred chores that did not entail caring for Nels or their hog and sheep.

If they were different in their personalities, they were even more dissimilar in their outward appearance. Christina was short for her age, with dark blond hair that waved a bit, and she had Kaatje's gray eyes. In comparison, Jessie was fast approaching her older sibling's height, and her dark hair held the same tight coil that Soren's once had, making it wild and unruly but, at the same time, wonderful. Her eyes were a remarkable summer-sky blue, reminding Kaatje daily of her husband long absent, and of his indiscretions.

It pained her a bit, when she thought of it, that there was nothing that resembled Kaatje in the girl—which only made sense because she was not her biological mother—but Kaatje often felt her heart did not make sense when it came to Jessie. She loved the girl so much that somehow Kaatje felt God should imprint her own image on the child, much as he had on Christina. She longed to erase any hint of Tora Anders in Jessie. She wanted to erase all the ugliness of the past, all the memories of Soren's affairs with Tora and the others, and only view the hope of their future.

Kaatje walked to the shanty, eager to enter the shade and protection of their small home and rest a bit before returning to the field. She wanted to sit in her rocker and close her eyes, but instead pulled bread from the basket on the sideboard and directed Christina to get last night's leftover beef from the tiny icebox. As she placed forks and knives on the table with napkins and plates, the weariness overcame her. A blinding pain shot through her head, making her wince, and she stumbled toward her bed.

"Mama?" Jessie said, rushing over to her. "What is it? Are you ill?"

"No, child," Kaatje struggled to convince her. "Just very tired. Eat your lunch with Christina, and let your mother rest. I will be fine in a moment."

She awakened an hour later to both girls, settled by her bed, studying her intently.

"Mama! Are you all right?" Christina said, clearly frightened.

"Do you need Doc Warner?" Jessie asked, sounding like a small adult.

"No, children. I am fine." Pressing away the pain that racked her body from head to toe, Kaatje sat up. "I'm simply tired. It is not normal for women to do such work in the field."

"Because Papa is gone," Jessie said forlornly.

"If only he would come back!" Christina wished aloud.

"If he could find us," Jessie added.

If he's alive, Kaatje thought to herself. After hearing nothing about him in the last four years, she assumed the worst. Soon, she would find the gumption to discover the truth. But not yet. Right now, she still held the tiniest hope that Soren was alive. That he would return to them and make things right after all these years. That Kaatje would have the chance to rant and rave and let him know how difficult life had been without him, and watch as he groveled for her forgiveness. That was all she wanted. A chance to let out all the fury that boiled beneath the surface. A moment of vindication. The day when all the things that were wrong in her life became right.

"All in God's time," she told her daughters. "Someday it will all be made right. In God's time." She closed her eyes, willing her body to rise. For her children, who gazed at her in such distress. For herself. The world would not beat Kaatje Janssen. She had too much to live for.

section one

Broken Cisterns

o n e

When the knock at the door sounded twice, sure, quick, Tora's heart jumped. She swallowed and resettled herself in the chair, making sure the best side of her face was toward Trent and the flounce of her polonaise that fell to the floor was "just so." She could feel his presence before he came into view, and she wondered at this thing inside her heart, this thing that would not die, that stirred for him more than any other. What was it about Trent Storm?

He entered the room as if he owned it, looking elegant in new attire. He peeled off his gloves and coolly perused her. "Tora," he said with a nod and then a slight smile. There was something hopeful in his eyes, and Tora was glad for it.

"Trent!" she said in a surprised tone, as if she had forgotten he was coming, and went to him. He bent over her hand and kissed it, then held it in his warm, strong fingers as they stared at each other. After a long, intense moment Tora squirmed. "It has been a while, Trent."

"Yes, well, things at home have kept me quite busy. Helena is a few miles from Duluth, mind you."

"Please sit down," she said with a grand gesture, hoping he would notice the neorococo furniture just in from France. He sat without hesitation. "Yes, but we haven't seen each other for what? Five months?"

"Counting, darling?"

Tora frowned. His eyes were alive with challenge, and the air was suddenly charged with energy. "No, not at all. I simply was commenting. I've certainly been busy enough establishing new roadhouses—I've not had time to count the hours until seeing you again." She hoped the edge of sarcasm in her voice would deflate whatever dangerous balloon was rising between them.

"Quite. The facilities here are quite impressive. Not to mention this house." He glanced around. "Very nice. I trust you did this with only your own funds."

Tora scowled. This was not going at all as she had planned. "Of course, Trent," she said, hating the defensiveness in her tone. "I wanted to build a house in which I could entertain important guests, but moreover, a *home*. I had to borrow a certain sum from the bank, but they were happy to assist such a prominent—"

"A home?" Trent interrupted, rising and walking to a window that stretched from the floor to the twelve-foot ceiling. He parted the velvet drapes and looked outside. "Hmm. A home. Something that reminds you of Bergen?"

Tora felt the blood drain from her face. "Bergen? Why, it has been years since I've thought of Norway. No, I was thinking of someplace—"

"Like Camden?"

"Camden-by-the-Sea?" she managed to ask without her voice rising an octave. Where was he going with this? "No, what I started to say was—"

"That you needed a home," he put in.

"Yes," she said, staring back into his eyes when he studied her.

"A sense of place."

"Yes, I suppose so."

"A place where you know who you are, and others do as well.

That's the reason for this grand showcase of a home, correct? The three-story, overdone, showy Queen Anne of the Storm Roadhouse Maven?"

Tora rose, thoroughly alarmed now. "Trent, whatever is wrong with you? I had so hoped you would like it, so treasured the idea you might want—"

"What? To live here?" He shook his head once, decisively. "No, Tora. I do not even know who the Storm Roadhouse Maven is. You have not allowed it. How could I marry you? How could I come and make a home with you? You have grown more distant in the time I've known you, wrapped up in your own vision of the future and a very tangled net of lies."

"Of...of lies?"

Trent pulled a yellowed paper from the inside pocket of his jacket and quietly unfolded it. "The Heroine of the Horn," he read aloud. He stared down at her. "Elsa Anders Ramstad. Your long-lost sister. Here's the amusing part, though. She apparently does not remember being lost. In fact, she seems to have a very solid idea of who she is and where she has come from."

"You...you spoke to her?"

He ignored her question. "You told me she was dead. Do you think that she claims the same of you?"

Tora sat down, hard. "Perhaps in some sense she does," she muttered, half to herself.

"That is the first honest thing I've heard from you in a long time."

Tora sighed and stared toward the window. She knew it was the end; this was the reason for Trent's growing distance. He knew. He'd known for a long time. And her secrecy had driven him further and further away, even as she sought to draw him closer. "How did you find out?"

"Some detective work. I so wanted you to confide in me, Tora." He spoke as if he were talking about someone else, a distant relation. "Why didn't you tell me? Why the secrecy? Was I untrustworthy?

What is so humiliating in your past that you could not simply tell the truth? Not enough drama for you? Tora Anders," he said with a shake of his head and a sigh, "you could have been a star on the stage. You've put on quite a performance these last four years. For a while, I told myself it didn't matter, that you must have your reasons. Probably a silly pride thing, or whatnot. But it kept eating at me, and I couldn't let it go. Last month, I decided enough was enough. If you couldn't be honest with me, we certainly had little hope for a future." He turned to her, his voice full of anguish. "Why, Tora? Why did you not tell me?"

She could feel his stare but could not find it within herself to meet his gaze. "Tell you? When we first met, you were my employer! It was easier, cleaner if I came to you as an orphan. And as to Camden, and the baby, I couldn't tell you all of that. *Trent Storm* would never have hired an unwed mother."

When he did not respond, Tora quickly looked at him. The stricken expression on his face spoke volumes—he hadn't known! He hadn't known *all* of it! Looking suddenly ten years older, Trent sat down hard on the settee. Tora rose and went to him, kneeling at his feet and resting her face on his thigh. "Oh, Trent!" Tears came unbidden. "Trent, I did it to survive. If you had known I was less than the wholesome woman you hired to work in your facilities, would you ever have employed me, much less courted me? I had to do it! I wanted to do something important with my life. To do this," she said, waving about her. "And soon I was doing it as much for you as I was for me."

"At the expense of a child," he said numbly. "Where, Tora? Where did you leave your baby?"

"In a good home," she said simply.

"Look at me," he said sharply, raising her chin forcefully. "The child lives?"

"I hope so," she whispered. For the first time in years, Tora felt a sense of relief in sharing the burden of her secret with another.

"You feel sorrow over your decision?" His eyes never wavered.

"Occasionally. But not for some time. There's so much more to my life now—"

Trent laughed a mirthless laugh and rose, as if brushing her off. "Do you realize how heartless you sound? God wants a different woman for me, Tora. A woman with heart and passion. Not perfect. I am far from a sinless man myself. But I fancy that I face up to my mistakes. I expect nothing less of a woman I would love."

So that was what this was all about? Some overblown sense of judgment? Why, he didn't know her! He didn't know what she had gone through to get to this station.

"You are dead to me, Tora Anders," Trent said simply, walking to the door with heavy footsteps. "You are fired and no longer associated with Storm Enterprises."

Tora's mouth dropped, and her heart thudded dully. "I—I—"

"You are on your own," he said, walking to the doorway. He turned back once. "I sincerely hope, Tora, that one day you will find your way home."

And with that he was gone.

Karl was not sure why, but after supper that evening he decided on a walk. Casually, he asked directions toward Tora Anders's home, and gradually made his way there. She sat by herself in the front garden, sipping from a tall crystal glass and looking morose. It stunned him to see her again. She was as lovely as ever, her dark hair done up on top in an elaborate knot, her clothing impeccably fine. *What does it cost to find dresses like that in the Montana territory?* he wondered briefly.

He stood at her iron gate, transported in time to their voyage six years before when he discovered Tora had stowed away aboard the *Herald*. She was an imp of perhaps sixteen then; now she was a grown woman. His mind flickered to her older sister—the woman he had longed for who had ultimately cost him his best friend. Had Elsa grown in beauty as her younger sister had? Quickly he pushed the thought from his mind. He had seen Tora at social events on Trent

Storm's arm in years past, but something was different about her tonight. She looked somehow lost, troubled.

Karl chastised himself at the protectiveness that rose in his breast. Whatever sadness she felt, Tora probably brought on herself. He cleared his throat.

Tora looked up at once and a small smile raised the corners of her perfect mouth. "Why, Karl Martensen. Here in Montana!" She rose and waved him in. "Please, join me. Would you care for some lemonade?"

It sounded like an uncommon luxury to Karl, having citrus in a mountain town, and he nodded quickly. "Tora," he said in greeting, bowing his head as he took off his hat and hugged it to his chest. He did as she bid and sat beside her on the garden bench, while Tora told a maidservant to bring more lemonade.

"I'm pleased to see you, Karl," she said, a note of weariness in her voice. "It has been a most unpleasant day."

"I am sorry to hear that."

"Yes. Perhaps you can take my mind off it. I refuse to dwell on the unpleasant! Tell me of you! It has been what? Three years?"

"Four, at least," Karl responded. "I've seen your work along the Northern Pacific. Our paths, surprisingly, have not crossed, although your reputation and expertise have not escaped me."

"Yes, well, apparently my reputation and expertise are not enough for Trent Storm."

"Oh?"

"He saw fit to sever our business relationship this afternoon."

"Ah," said Karl, understanding at once why Tora was less than her normal self. "And your personal relationship?"

"It was dead long ago. I had a schoolgirl's dream of what it could be. Trent let life interfere."

"Life?" Karl asked carefully.

Tora glanced at him sharply. "Yes. I told him the truth, and he could not handle it."

"About your daughter."

"Yes. He just cast me away like so much riffraff." She pulled a handkerchief from somewhere in the folds of her dress and dabbed at her eyes. "Can you imagine?"

Karl fought a smile. Here was the Tora Anders he remembered, manipulative to the end. "I can," he said softly. "You must have hurt him deeply. What was it?"

Tora sniffed, as if offended, then sagged a bit. "Well, to secure a job with Storm Enterprises I had to present myself as a woman with no ties. Free to do as they bid. As Trent bid."

"No ties. No child?"

"As well as other things."

Karl let her comment slide. "I see. So he just found out about your baby?"

"Yes. I do not see what difference it makes! She isn't a part of my life. He would have no responsibility for her!"

"Perhaps that is just what he wanted."

Tora laughed, laughed as if it was a tremendous relief to do so, then soon sobered. "You think Trent *wants* a family?"

"I know few men who don't. Maybe he was simply waiting all these years for you to be honest with him, to show him who you really are, rather than who you want to be."

Tora rose, color flaming on her cheeks. "Who are you to presume to judge me? You know nothing of who I am, let alone who I will be."

Karl stood beside her, sensing their time together was already at an end. He silently lamented not having the chance to sip lemonade, to catch up with a woman who shared some of his history. He laughed at himself. He was apparently so lonely that he even felt led to reach out to Tora Anders! "I beg to differ, Tora. I know who you are. I've known you all your life." He brushed a tendril of dark hair from her eyes as she shied away, clearly irritated at his overly familiar gesture. "On the other hand, I do not know who you will be."

"Oh. And who are you now, Karl Martensen? Still the philanderer in sad pursuit of my married sister?"

Karl winced at the truth of her comment and forced himself to stare back into her eyes. "I made a fool of myself and wasted some of the best friendships I ever made. I made a mistake and then I walked away before apologizing. Are you letting Trent do the same?" Bile rose in his throat. How long would he be haunted by past sins? He seemed unable to recapture any sense of peace in his life. Even Tora could see it, use it.

She ignored his question. "I think you should go."

"I will." He turned to depart, then looked back at her. "What will you do?"

"I'll be fine," she said, as if miffed that he dared question her. "I have investments, and ideas of my own about what to do along the railroad."

"You intend to compete with Trent?"

"Did I say that? I said I had plans of my own." She smiled in feline fashion, and Karl knew that it was exactly what she was scheming.

"Trent would be furious. Believe me, you don't want an enemy like him on the line."

"Like Hall?" she baited him, reminding Karl of his infamous past employer.

"You'll note that I found it prudent to develop my own business along the Northern Pacific, rather than the Great Northern. Villard has gone broke again," he said, referring to the chief financier behind the Northern Pacific, "so who knows what will transpire along this route. It might be wise to consider moving, and for reasons beyond Trent."

"And leave all this?" she asked, her eyebrows raised in surprise. "Never. Helena is my home, and a perfect base of operations along the Northern Pacific."

Karl cocked one eyebrow and pursed his lips. "It is your decision, obviously. I'm simply saying it's always wise to diversify." He turned to go and was at the gate when she called out to him, her tone hesitant.

"Karl! Tell me…have you heard from my sister or Peder?"

He gave her a small smile. "Not for years. Peder and I had a parting of the ways. Last I heard, they had built a second home in Seattle. Running lumber from the Washington Territory back east. You should write. I bet Elsa would appreciate hearing from you."

Tora sniffed and shrugged her shoulders a bit. "Perhaps. I have heard of things more crazy than that."

"Good-bye, Tora."

"Karl," she responded with a stiff nod. He closed the gate behind him and strode down the dusty street, the long dusk of northern nights holding firmly to the light around him. And suddenly, it was as clear as day to him that Tora Anders was only as lost as he was in the world.

Still feeling listless and at odds the next evening, Trent forced himself to rise from his bed and dress for his dinner with Karl Martensen and Bradford Bresley. He had actually slept through the hot summer afternoon, something he had not done since he was a child. But he had had little choice. The weariness overcame him and sleep came as a blessed relief. Now, drowsy, he buttoned his shirt and tucked it into his trousers as he gazed at his image in the mirror.

He was not unattractive, he decided, looking at one side of his face and then the other. The years had left him with deepening lines about the mouth and eyes and graying hair, but there was no sign of jowls or a paunch about his waist. He could have had his pick of women in the years since his beloved wife had died. Why had it been Tora Anders who stole his heart?

He regretted his decision to cut her off from Storm Enterprises—she had done a fine job in setting up the last sixteen roadhouses. But how could he go on loving, let alone working with, a dishonest woman? A woman who would desert her own child? Who knew when her questionable morals would end up affecting his business? No, it was time that Tora Anders was on her own to prove just what she was made of.

Shaking his head as if to remove thoughts of her, he donned a bowler hat and left the hot room. Downstairs it was cooler, and he greeted Karl and Brad in the lobby. In minutes, they were seated in the hotel dining room, menus in their hands, and shortly thereafter, the waiter came and retrieved their orders.

"Saw John Hall last week," Trent said casually, studying Karl carefully. He knew little of what had happened between the men other than that Karl had broken off his engagement to Hall's daughter, Alicia, and had left John's employ at the same time. He had long suspected John of unscrupulous business dealings, and had since cut off his own relations with the man.

"You did?" Karl asked with an upraised brow. "I try not to."

"As do I," Bradford put in.

"How do you manage?" Trent asked. "This is a big territory, but John Hall is everywhere."

"We've met up a few times, but I always try to steer clear. I have found that there are some battles worth waging, and others best avoided. Besides, I like to think that time and distance heal many wounds. It's been four years since I broke my engagement with Alicia, and Hall, apparently, has bigger fish to fry. I think he'd just as soon not see me either."

Trent nodded. "I would not want to wage war with Hall—I think you are prudent. But do not ever think that John Hall will forget; he has the memory of an elephant and a dark side once encountered. I've met many a man who was broken by him. I'm glad you escaped unharmed."

"Yes, sir," Bradford said. "That's why I recruited him as my business partner. Prudent and fast as a hare," he chuckled, bringing the other two into his laughter. "And we've done well for ourselves. Despite a few losses to Hall, as you said, this is a big territory. Everywhere we look these days, we see new opportunities. Perhaps Storm Enterprises would like to hear about a few of our ideas."

Trent looked from Bradford to Karl and smiled. He was approached weekly to help finance new "opportunities." But there was something about these two young men he liked. He immediately trusted them. And after his last exchange with Tora, he felt like a hungry trout ready to pounce on a fat worm. This was just what he needed, the chance to jump into something with both feet, the opportunity to feel genuinely good about something. And these men were good at heart—he could sense it in his gut.

"Gentlemen," he said, "I'm interested. Tell me what you have seen, and what you would like to do."

t w o

July 1886

*E*ven weeks after their hasty departure from Honolulu, Elsa could not get Mason Dutton out of her mind. As Kristian napped, she took her accustomed position over the captain's cabin and began sketching his face in the merchant window, hoping to eradicate his image once and for all. For Elsa, there was something about getting an image on paper that allowed her to move on to other ideas, thoughts, images. She had been avoiding drawing his haunting image, fearing what Peder would say, when genius struck.

What if, for the *New York Times,* she wrote of her initial encounter with Mason, and then their brief encounter in Hawaii? She'd always heard the pen was mightier than the sword. Perhaps some American diplomat would read of their plight and investigate. Who knew? Mason might be an impostor or might have been wrongly awarded a British military position, his government not aware that they employed a pirate. Imagine! A pirate in His Majesty's Royal Navy! Why, they'd be appalled, and likely grateful to the American who uncovered such an unsavory scheme.

With a smile on her face that melted away the worry lines in her forehead for the first time in weeks, Elsa sketched madly, recreating the man's image as she'd seen it in the store window in uniform, as she originally saw him in street clothes, and in profile. The detail she could conjure up surprised even Elsa, for it had been years since their first encounter, and their meeting in Honolulu was brief and distant. But his eyes, his cold, penetrating eyes, had pierced her soul and made her tremble if she thought too much about them. He was clearly a man with a vendetta. And Elsa had to strike first.

When Kristian awoke, Elsa climbed downstairs and comforted her sleepy, grumpy tot with a quick cuddle and a story. Then she walked hand in hand with him, leading her son to Cook, who usually looked after him for an hour or so before beginning dinner preparations. She smiled at Peder as she exited the galley, proud of her handsome husband at the wheel shouting orders to the crew to raise more sails to take advantage of the trade winds.

Memories of departing Hawaii at a mad pace clouded her vision. The crew had stared at Peder in wonder as he ordered all aboard within the hour, those not reporting left behind. Afterward, they were even more surprised as their captain ordered all sails set in dangerous winds. Why, they had nearly capsized in Peder's effort to put miles between Mason and his family. For the first time in a long while, Elsa was genuinely afraid. Because Peder was frightened. She ducked into their cabin before Peder could detect any change in her mood. He had said little to her about Mason, dismissing the suggestion that they report him to the authorities, claiming that they'd never see him again anyway. Elsa decided he was unnerved by the uniform, unsure what power Mason might wield now, and what he could use that power to do to an innocent man. No, best to steer clear of him entirely, he obviously thought. Elsa disagreed. She would see to it that Mason was dealt with from afar, accomplishing both their purposes.

But first, she would tell a tale that would thrill her Victorian audiences at home, longing for adventure from their armchairs by cozy fires, and indignant that such an animal might endanger their beloved Heroine of the Horn. Her editor, Alexander Martin, would be thrilled.

She was just finishing her tale, written in her personal style—as if to family instead of the thousands of *Times* readers—when Peder came in, pulling off his cap. His hair was longer and had a delightful wave to it that Elsa found wonderful. Many mornings as he slept, she would pull a curl from his temple until it was straight and then smile as it coiled back into place. His cheeks were ruddy from the wind, his skin tanned a golden brown. All in all, she thought herself very fortunate, for her husband was not only attractive but affectionate as well. After six years of marriage, they were more in love than ever.

Elsa started chattering about her afternoon, the weather, Cook's plans for supper, anything as she quickly shoved her just-dry sheets of paper under a nautical map book. Peder took off his coat and hung it beside his hat on the rack by the door and turned to his wife, watching her carefully. "And when I heard Cook planned to serve us salt beef again, I felt I simply had to put my foot down," she continued, a bit unnerved beneath his stare. "After all, we're but a week from Japan, and it's high time we had some decent food. What is he waiting for? Oh, I cannot wait for a crisp piece of celery, a nice beefsteak, or some wonderful, juicy fruits, just picked!"

Peder sat down on the settee and continued staring at her, a small grin on his face. "What is it, Elsa?"

"What?"

"What is eating at you?"

"I don't know of what you speak."

"You do. You always get chatty when you don't want to dwell on something…or talk about something." At that thought, his eyes narrowed a bit. "Tell me."

Elsa squirmed, irritated at how well he knew her. Desperately, she cast about for something to say. She rose and walked to the window, her hand trailing on the desk to buy her time, as if she were contemplating what to say. "I have been thinking."

"That is obvious. Of what, love?"

Outside the window, Cook turned the corner with Kristian in hand. Elsa smiled. "I would so dearly like another child." It was true; another child had been on her mind for months. There would be time enough to tell Peder of her article for the *Times,* she rationalized.

Peder chuckled lowly and rose to embrace her from behind. "It has not been for lack of trying," he said in her ear, and Elsa felt herself blush. "But I will see what I can do."

Elsa turned in his arms to kiss him soundly before Cook tapped on the door. "I do love you, Peder Ramstad," she said, hoping her eyes conveyed all the passion she felt for this man.

"And I you," he said softly, bending to give her another quick kiss as the knock sounded at the door.

From the other side they could hear Kristian yelling, "Mama! Papa! Are you in there?" They laughed together as Peder opened the door and their child ran in for a hug as if they had been away for weeks.

An hour later, the Ramstads sat down at their dinner table with Riley. Cook entered, glanced meaningfully at Elsa, then nodded at Peder. "Stewed chicken," he announced curtly.

"That smells delightful, Cook," Elsa enthused, stowing a small smile as he haughtily exited the room for the remaining side dishes.

"I'll say," Riley agreed, in his thick Cockney accent. "Had me fill of salt beef 'bout a week ago. It will be all right to be ashore this time."

"I'd like to make better time lightering the case oil than last time," Peder said, referring to discharging their load of kerosene.

"Good luck, Cap'n. Japan is notorious for their slowness."

"I just don't understand it. How can we load twenty thousand cases in three days, and it takes them twenty days to unload it? Are they lazy?"

"Not as I understand it, Cap'n. Just cautious."

Peder grumbled as they passed the chicken. "It still grates on me. An idle ship is a ship not making money."

"You'll be busy with customs, paperwork, and the agents, anyway. You should take advantage of the time—take the missus and Kristian out on a holiday. Enjoy yourself."

"Let's pray!" Kristian said, folding his hands and looking at everyone else expectantly.

Elsa smiled and Riley said, "The little mite's on the right track, I'd say."

"Good idea, son," Peder said, and proceeded to give thanks for the food.

"Amen!" Kristian echoed the adults, clearly as proud of himself as they were.

As they began to eat, Elsa ventured, "It would be lovely to see some of the sights, Peder. I've been reading Keeling's guide, and he describes some wonderful excursions."

"Perhaps," Peder said noncommittally. "As Riley said, I'll have my hands full for some days with the ship's business."

"I do wish you would hire an agent for some of that work sometimes," Elsa said.

"And hand off five percent of my profit?" Peder shook his head. "Ramstad Yard is doing fine. Why not enjoy some of the exotic ports we visit? And your family? It would be good for Kristian to see them too."

"We will see."

His tone irritated Elsa. "You will see to our business, husband, as always. But I will see to our son and myself. I want to at least see greater Yokohama. It sounds too delightful to pass up."

Peder looked up at her sharply, his fork poised in mid-bite. "You will not go alone."

Riley shifted in his chair. Elsa willed herself not to do the same under Peder's gaze. She hated when he took the captain's tone with her. "I will hire a guide."

Peder continued to stare at her. "We will see. I am uncomfortable thinking whom you might meet."

Elsa frowned, confused. "The Japanese are purported to be some of the most respectable, genteel people on earth."

"No. I am uncomfortable with whom you might meet." The repetition of his sentence finally caught her attention.

"Surely, you don't believe that Mason Dutton—"

"Would follow us here? Why not? I—"

"Mason Dutton!" Riley exploded. "Where did you see that scum o' the earth?"

"Hawaii," Peder said briefly.

"That explains all sails set," Riley said, chewing thoughtfully. "You might've let me—"

"Peder," Elsa interrupted, "we cannot live in fear of the man. It is one thing to avoid Dutton, another to run from him. Let us go to the authorities."

"I am still mulling it over. I'm not afraid to tell you that the uniform throws me off. Now, he might be an impostor, or he might be the genuine article. Perhaps he's even a decorated officer. This far from home, who would the authorities listen to?"

"Well, at least we three could identify him. Why not take him on? It is unlike you to run from a fight." The words were out before she could stop them.

"I cannot explain it. I could find no peace over the idea of staying in Hawaii and confronting the…" he paused, glancing at Kristian, "and all I could think of was how I nearly lost you to his henchmen on that island, and how I now have *two* of you to protect."

Elsa was silent, considering his dilemma. The drama of that West Indies night when Mason Dutton and his men attacked the *Herald* came flooding back. Mason Dutton and his crew had swarmed the *Herald*, weapons drawn, in a brazen attempt to take over the ship and kidnap Elsa. Peder had indeed nearly lost her; he *had* lost his best friend, Karl Martensen, in the process. She could understand Peder's urge to flee rather than fight in Hawaii. But how long would it haunt them?

"What do you think he has up his sleeve? Do you believe he was an officer five years back?" Riley was asking Peder.

"I have no idea. I am all at sea," he said, using the common sailor's expression for *confused*. "If he was an officer for the Royal Navy, why were he and his entire crew in civilian clothes?"

"On leave?" Riley asked.

"Perhaps. But for what period of time could he manage that? And his ship was not Navy issue."

"So he became an officer since that time."

"It might be." Peder took a bite and chewed thoughtfully. "For a man like Mason, it would increase the stakes. He likes the game, more than anything. It's all like a grand chess match."

"Mama, I want more beans," Kristian said, ignoring the conversation around him.

Elsa served him, resisting the urge to encourage the child to say "please." "I still think we should confront Dutton if we see him again. This cannot go on forever. And what purpose would it serve for him to come after us? He tried before and lost. Why would he not go after easier prey?" Elsa put in.

"Because the pot got sweeter," Riley said, staring into Peder's eyes as if understanding what he was thinking. "Forgive me, ma'am, for saying it this way, but there's you, a grand fish that got away, and then there's Peder, who made Dutton turn tail and run. Neither sits well with a man."

"We didn't exactly defeat him. He left us wounded and got away!"

"There is no pride in that," Peder said. "There is pride only in victory for such a man as he."

Elsa sighed and set down her fork. "I refuse to run from him."

"We will run until I decide what to do," Peder said firmly.

"There are ways—" Riley began.

"None of which are appropriate to our ways," Peder interrupted. "I appreciate your impulse, Riley," he said more gently, "for I would like to throttle him myself. But I need to wait on the Lord for his way in this."

Fearful once again, Elsa bowed her head and stared at her plate. In all the time she had known Peder, there were few times when he was not confident about his next move. As much as she hated arguing with him—oftentimes finding him bullheaded and unwilling to consider her viewpoint—it gave her confidence to see such assuredness in his own mind. To see her husband falter made her heart skip a beat.

She glanced over at Peder's desk, at the nautical book, knowing her hidden article about Mason was beneath. Perhaps it was just the answer for them. If they could not take on Mason Dutton themselves, the public could do it for them.

Days later, confident in her decision, Elsa finished her article on Mason Dutton. Perhaps now she could put the scoundrel out of her mind for good. Peder would be furious with her at first, but it would be months before the article appeared, and probably weeks after that before Peder would get wind of it. By then, Elsa hoped the authorities would have taken appropriate action to bring the man to justice—and save her marriage from too much strife. Why, this was exactly the reason that Peder still lobbied to keep her and Kristian ashore. She would not back down now!

She smiled as she tucked Kristian in for the night and donned her cloak for a stroll on deck. They had made land way down west that afternoon, and she hoped for another glimpse of Japan by moonlight. She was not disappointed.

Riley joined her at the lee bow rail. "That point there," he said, raising a finger to the horizon, "that's Omae Saki."

"*Saki* means cape, correct?"

"Aye," Riley said, a note of pride in his voice. "Been studying the language, ma'am?"

"A few words in *Japanese Words and Phrases for the Use of Strangers.*"

"A good resource," Riley said. "Still thinkin' about traveling about a bit?"

"Perhaps," she said noncommittally. "Oh, Riley," she said, gripping his arm. "Look at that!" She pointed at a reflection in the sky, like a cloud of smoke with fire glowing in the midst of it. "Is it a volcano?"

Riley chuckled. "Fusi Yama. It's still 'bout a hundred miles off. But she's a sight. Half of her is crowned in snow. I think it's but the moonlight reflecting off of that snow, not fire."

"I can see why the Japanese carve its image on everything possible." She had seen it on the many pieces of furniture and curios that Peder had brought back in years past. "She must be quite a sight by morning light."

"She's quite a sight now," Riley said. He brought fingertips to his cap brim and nodded once at her. "G'night, ma'am."

"Good night, Riley."

"Ma'am." Riley hesitated a moment. "If you wish to take an excursion while we're here, I'd be happy to escort you if the cap'n isn't available."

"Thank you, Riley." As Riley left, she stared off at Fusi Yama, considering her article and drawings in their room, already packaged and ready to post. If only God could send the northern lights here, to this foreign land, as a sign that all was right with her decision! That she wasn't causing more trouble for Peder. All at once, she longed for her father, for home, for the secure. To be able to trust in his wisdom instead of her own. But she was an adult now. And while she missed the security of her father's protection, she also knew she was a woman who wasn't afraid to take risks, to find new adventures. She thrilled at the sight of a land never seen before, waiting to be explored. And explore it she would.

In typical Victorian fashion, Elsa attacked exploration like a new business venture. She had read many books that had exhorted their readers to work at the experience, to truly study the people and places, and come away richer for it. So her sketch book was constantly out as she captured one scene after another. She considered herself fortunate that Kuma, her Japanese guide, was as adept at entertaining Kristian as she was at helping Elsa discover new and fanciful corners of the city. By week's end, she had seen much of Yokohama, and had made several important new friends. One family had even invited her and Peder to stay with them at their mountain home.

She was just completing an article for the *Times* when Peder came in, sighing heavily. "Seven weeks!" he said, obviously disgruntled. "How can it possibly take seven weeks for a vessel to discharge her cargo?" He sat down at his desk and opened his logbook, obviously disgusted. "I do not wish to trade here too often," he said.

Elsa set aside her lap desk and went over to him, placing her arms around his neck. She kissed his ear. "You need to get away. Off this ship. Come with us. We've been invited to a lovely mountain home by a fine family. It will do you good."

"I cannot, Elsa. Who will see to the business at hand?"

Rebuffed, Elsa let her arms slide away and stood up stiffly. "Riley. Your first mate. You remember, the man who should be taking care of such things while his captain embraces life with his family? He works for you, Peder. Why not let him do his job? It must drive him crazy, having you in the midst of it all, meddling."

Peder was silent for a moment, and Elsa took a breath, wondering if she had overstepped her bounds. But then his shoulders began to shake and laughter followed. He turned and smiled at her, then rose to take her in his arms. "Elsa, Elsa. What would I do without you?"

Kristian emerged from his room, wiping his eyes as he struggled to awake from his nap. He ran to them and Peder picked him up, nestling the boy between them. "Hi, Papa," was all he said.

"I hear we're taking a trip together," Peder said, looking Elsa in the eye.

"To the mountains?" Kristian asked, wide-eyed.

"To the mountains," Elsa said, smiling.

They left the following day. Elsa waited in an open carriage with Kristian as she watched Peder giving Riley last-minute instructions in apparent detail. She could tell that Riley struggled to remain patient with his captain as Peder went on and on. She pulled out the pocket watch from his coat on the seat beside her and called to him. "Peder!"

He glanced her direction and, seeing the watch, nodded once. Thank goodness they needed to catch a train to Tokyo, or Peder would talk all day. She exchanged a glance with Kuma, who struggled to keep Kristian in the carriage. "Peder!" she called again.

He turned away from Riley a moment later and hurried down the gangplank. "All right, all right," he said, climbing in and taking a delighted Kristian to his knee. "Let us get to the train station!" It seemed to Elsa that time rushed by as they boarded for their short one-hour train ride and then their journey on the jinrikishas up the bumpy path of Mount Atago. How good it felt to be away from the water and with her family! Even Peder seemed to relax as the hours and miles melted away thoughts of the case oil, still languishing in the hold.

"We are here," Kuma said over the edge of her jinrikisha to Elsa and Peder as they turned off the main road and down a thickly wooded path. The girl was not more than twenty, and dressed in the common kimono, rather than the more popular Western dress. Elsa appreciated that although Kuma had been educated and earned a good wage as translator and guide, she had not rejected her Japanese heritage.

The Saitos were a wealthy family, and their mountain home sat amid impeccably kept grounds. A lush lawn set off groomed trees as the forest grudgingly gave way to the property's borders of precisely placed stones in a wall of about three feet in height. Here and there the hot pinks of lotus blossoms in bloom and the deep purple of another flower caught Elsa's eye. As they drew closer to the house, the garden became more dense and sculpted, with waterfalls cascading into delicate pools and tiny plantings. Peder smiled at Elsa and nodded. "Incredible."

She could only nod in agreement.

"I would wager you're thinking about your canvas and oils."

"Or at least my sketch book. Oh, Peder, I could spend days here."

He smiled and placed an arm around her. "We'll stay as long as we are welcome."

The Saitos were gracious hosts, attending to the Ramstads' every need: taking their shoes when Elsa, Peder, and Kristian entered their beautiful home; offering countless cups of tea; and giving them a detailed tour of the estate, explaining through their translator not only the uses and names of the things they saw but the fascinating history of their ancestral home. By early evening, Elsa and Peder felt at home. After a traditional Japanese dinner, and stilted but eager conversation through Kuma, the families said their good nights.

Mrs. Saito's final gift to Elsa that evening was a nod toward the bathhouse. Urged by her gentle gesticulations, Elsa slid open the surprisingly sturdy door of rice paper, and followed a rounded stone path through a heavily shrouded garden. There, in the midst of a smaller private garden, surrounded by high walls covered in fragrant flowering vines, was a tall redwood tub, steaming in dusk's waning light. Four servants emptied their last offerings to the tub and bowed toward Elsa, excusing themselves.

One waited until the others left, and then gestured toward a changing screen and a silk robe hanging over its edge. Unable to deny herself the luxury, Elsa eagerly moved forward and accepted the woman's help in removing her gown and corset. She hoped Peder and Kristian would not miss her. Just a half-hour in the steaming water would do her a world of good, she thought. The smoke from the train, the dust from the mountain road, sweat from the excessive heat over the last days—all would melt away in that wonderful tub!

She expected the servant to disappear when she moved toward the redwood tub, but instead she moved to pick up lush towels from a nearby bench and place them on the edge. Then, ceremoniously, she lit three candles in delicate torches, casting a soft glow across the sanctuary. Lastly, she raised a bottle and sprinkled five droplets of a rich, fragrant oil into the tub. Only then did she nod at Elsa and excuse herself. Smiling, Elsa moved forward, disrobing and sliding into the hot cauldron. How long it had been since she had had the opportunity to bathe in such luxury! Shipboard, they were reduced to sponge baths and, when she could manage it, perhaps a basin of two inches. This, this was heaven.

She did not know how long she soaked there, letting the warm waters soothe away aches and pains, when she heard a snap and crackle of leaves underfoot. Her eyes widened, and she whirled in the tub, terrified that Mr. Saito or some servant might unknowingly enter the bathing garden and embarrass them both. Out of the shadows came a man, and Elsa's heart stopped momentarily.

It was Peder. A slow smile spread across his face, his teeth white in the glow of the lanterns. "I knew I was right to let you talk me into this," he said softly.

Elsa smiled back, feeling mischievous. "You'll probably want to bathe too."

"Already done it. While you were escorted here, and Kristian to his bunk, Mr. Saito and I shared a pipe and then a steam bath. A brisk splash in the stream finished our manly bathing task." He drew nearer, picking up a bar of soap from the bench. "Your hair?"

Elsa smiled again. "That would be divine. The perfect end to the perfect day." She settled back against the side of the tub as Peder soaped up his hands and then scrubbed her scalp until there was a thick lather. Then he let his fingers massage the long tendrils, working his way out to the ends and letting the bubbles drop into the water in thick globs. For fifteen minutes he worked on her hair, almost putting his wife to sleep. She breathed deeply, just thinking about the pleasure of giving in to dreams right then and there, when he dunked her.

She came up, sputtering. "Well, thank you very much."

"Needed a rinse. Oh. Still some more." He dunked her again.

This time she came up splashing. He laughed, wiping the water from his face. "I suppose I deserve that." He leaned closer to her, resting his chin on his hands as he stared over the edge into her eyes. "I do love you, Elsa Ramstad."

"And I you, Peder Ramstad."

"You are the finest thing I have ever been given in life. I treasure you. You know that, right?"

"Most of the time," she said. "When you are not obsessing over the ship."

"I will try not to obsess too often." He leaned closer and gave her a long, tender kiss. It was a moment Elsa knew she would never forget.

"As long as you steal away with me to mountain cottages once in a while," she said, still closing her eyes, relishing the memory of their kiss, "you may obsess once in a while."

"That's good to know," he said, smiling. He rose and opened up a towel. "Now, shall we retire?"

"I suppose," she said reluctantly. "As enticing as you are, husband, it is tough to leave this bath. Do you think we could bring it aboard?"

"Right," Peder said. "I can just see Riley's face now."

Elsa giggled. "Or Cook's. Can you imagine how many pots he would have to boil to fill this up?"

"I'm afraid it will have to be a fond memory. Come now. I'll brush out your hair."

His promise brought her out of the water, and Peder surrounded her with the huge towel. "I think it's Egyptian," he commented, fingering the lush cotton.

"A Norwegian woman in an Egyptian towel, surrounded by an exotic Japanese mountain bath. Quite the globetrotters we are."

"Aye. Come, wife. We might be far from home, but my mind is on hearthside matters."

Elsa smiled. "Coming, husband."

three

Kaatje kissed her sleeping girls and pulled the rough wool blanket to their chins. Despite the heat of the summer days, the night temperature dipped and grew chilly, oftentimes enough to warrant a fire in the hearth. Tonight Kaatje could have gone either way with the fire, but she was feeling lonely and wanted the cheery crack and snap, as well as the light, to keep her company. She sat staring into the flames for a long time, thinking about Soren, remembering the tilt of his nose, the sparkle in his blue eyes. What had become of him?

Glancing at her slumbering girls, Kaatje rose and walked to the kitchen sideboard. Behind the sacks of flour and sugar, and beneath a loose board, she pulled out her last letter from Soren, cradling it to her chest as if it were he, instead, in her arms. She did not know why she hid it from her daughters, only that it was hers and hers alone. Her last connection with the husband she had lost long ago. Her daughters had yet to learn how to read, but regardless, she wanted it all to herself.

Sighing, she sat down in her rocker and straightened the two sheets of paper she held in her hand. One was from Soren, crumpled and yellowed with age and handling. It had been forwarded by the postmaster in Dakota to the Skagit Valley postmistress. The other page was smaller, a note from the proprietor at a place called Kokrine's Trading Post, Yukon River, Alaska.

She straightened out the first and read the words, words she could have recited from memory. But seeing his fast, elaborate scrawl was like touching the man. So she read it yet again.

18 December 1881
Darling Kaatje,

I am alive and well in the interior of Alaska. This is a fine land and I have found my way, making my living as a trader, and eventually, I will do so as a miner. The railroads had no future for a man like me, so I moved on after we got through Montana. I was so close to Alaska, with winter soon upon us, I could not see the wisdom in returning to Dakota, knowing our friends would see to your and Christina's safety and well-being.

There is word of gold strikes all around me, and I am confident that soon I will find the perfect place in which to stake a claim and make us rich. You and Christina will be able to join me, in a grand house here, or I will come home to you a wealthy man. This is what I was born to do, Kaatje. I know that now. Farming has no end to it. I am willing to roll up my sleeves and work like any other man, but for what? Farming is endless in its strain and hardship. Mining, a man works, and then a man sits back and enjoys. This is what I want for us.

Already gold has been discovered on the Kenai Peninsula, Kasaan, Sitka, and near Juneau. You see? I am surrounded! Truly, it is only a matter of time. I will write again soon.

> *Always,*
> *Soren*

Blinking back a tear, Kaatje stared into the fire for a while, then turned her attention back to the other, shorter note in her hands.

5 February 1882
Mrs. Janssen,

I am sory to report that yur husband has not ben seen around these parts in some time. Last we saw, he was hedin to Fortymile and hasn't ben herd from sinse. I will keep yur letter in case he comes this way agin soon.

Cordilly,
Malcolm Heffner
Kokrine's Trading Post

She had heard, of course, nothing since then, despite the fact that she had sent numerous letters to any address she obtained rumored to have gold in Alaska. Someday, perhaps one of those letters would be answered. Until that day, she didn't know what else she could do.

You could go.

The Voice in her heart startled her. She shook her head at such nonsense. Go to Alaska? What would she do with the girls? The farm?

Rent the farm to others. Take the girls.

Kaatje's heart pounded at such preposterous thoughts. This was not of God! It was wishful thinking, fanciful dreams of reuniting with her husband. She grew angry at herself. Why, they had not even been happy when they were together. Soren was a philanderer through and through. What would happen to the man when he became rich on gold and sat idle? Nothing good, that was sure.

She rose and walked to the door, pulling it open angrily and striding to the well outside. Hauling up a bucket of fresh, cold water, she splashed her face again and again, even as the tears came. Kaatje braced her hands on the stone facing of the well, gasping for breath. Why did she put herself through this? Why did she repeatedly read those letters? It never made her feel any better, simply lost and angry and sorrowful. She threw the bucket down the shaft with all the strength she could muster, finding only mild satisfaction at the splash far below.

Turning and leaning against the well wall, she dried her tears and studied the cabin—looking warm and cozy in the night—her breath frosting in the cool evening air, and the stars high above it. She spotted the North Star at the end of the Little Dipper and stared.

You could go.

"And do what?" she cried aloud, shaking her fist at the sky. "Wander around, looking for my lout of a husband? He does not deserve it!"

You need to know.

"I need to know nothing of the kind! I need to know my children are well and fed. How would I know that on a road in Alaska?"

You could go.

Kaatje sank to her knees and sobbed, so suddenly overwhelmed and weary that she sank to the cold, damp grass as she wept. "I cannot, Father. Do not ask it of me. I can't. I can't. I can't."

She did not hear the Voice again. Only silence.

It had been a very wet spring and early summer, and that day at the church potluck, Kaatje found herself grinning.

"You think this is funny? Struggling with rot here in this soggy land?" Einar grumbled at her as she set a plate of lefse before him.

"I do," she giggled. "Just think. When we first got to the Dakota Territory, all we did was complain about the dry land, the lack of rain. But here we get too much!"

The table of men and women laughed too, and Kaatje's smile grew. These people were her family, her security. They had been her stronghold when Soren left, filling the hole that his absence created. What would she have ever done without them?

"It is good to see you laugh, joke, Kaatje," Nora said, a toddler on one hip.

"It is good to have a reason," she said as they walked back to the kitchen. The Gustavsons' home, one of the largest in the area, had a huge dining room that could seat eighteen. Consequently, they often hosted church suppers and the like. Their house felt like a second home to Kaatje.

"You're a quiet one today," Nora said.

"You mean when I am not making people laugh?"

"Yes. Is something bothering you?" She handed Kaatje another steaming dish.

Kaatje grimaced as she looked at the plate. "Yes. Lutefisk. Ish!"

Nora laughed through her nose. "Ah well, then, I suppose you'll tell me when you are ready. Just know I have a listening ear for you."

Kaatje gave her a tender smile. "I know, friend. Thank you. This is something I need to wrestle with myself first. When I'm ready to burden another with my troubles, you'll be the first to know!"

"I'll be waiting." Kaatje felt Nora's warmth and caring. Her friend would be the perfect teacher for the valley's children, once her own were old enough to attend school. Knowing Einar, he would build a special schoolhouse for his wife, and they would have one of the best schools in the Washington Territory. The closest school was now an hour away by wagon.

Kaatje sauntered over to the window and stared out at the verdant valley. God had surely brought her here. To raise her children. To protect them. Why would he want her to go away again? To some place that might endanger them all?

f o u r

July 1886

*T*hree weeks after Trent had disappeared from her life for good, Tora sat staring in her looking glass, wondering at the woman's image reflected there. She was still beautiful, perhaps more beautiful than the day Trent hired her on at Storm Enterprises. But there was a hint of sorrow around her eyes, the first she had ever noted in her face. Grim, she drew her ivory-handled brush through her long, dark hair and pinned the last coil on top of her head. She would not be sad forever, she knew. She had a life to lead, and it would be a fine one, with or without Trent Storm.

Sasha knocked on her bedroom door and peeked in. "Mistress? Mr. Aston is here to escort you."

"Fine. Tell him I will be down directly." Sasha disappeared from Tora's mirror image and she powdered her face once more. Standing, she smoothed the lace frills at her waist and fingered those at her plunging neckline. She affixed a small hat—trimmed with ribbons and feathers—atop her elaborate hairdo, dabbed some more coloring on her lower lip, and pulled on long gloves. *Trent would have liked this feminine finery.* Making a small sound of disgust, she willfully banished all thoughts of the man.

She had done nothing but cry for those first days after his

departure. Now she was simply angry and anxious to get back at him. Tora gave her reflection a small smile. Plans were already afoot to preempt his next roadhouse in Spokane. The world would see what would happen to a man when he dared spurn Tora Anders.

Tora grabbed a small beaded purse from her bed and went to the top of the stairs. She grinned when she saw Andrew Aston, dapper this evening in a sharp-looking suit and hat. His coat had the fashionable bound edges of the day, rounded at the bottom, and he carried a distinguished walking cane. Andrew's curled mustache completed the ensemble, Tora decided, and the delightfully mischievous spark in his eye as he looked her over from head to toe made him all the more daring. Yes, he would serve her purpose, as her escort as well as her banker. She simply had to play her cards right.

"Why, Mr. Aston, don't you look fine?"

"Not as fine as you, Miss Anders, I dare say," he said, placing his bowler back on his head and offering his arm. "Did you have a wrap?"

"No," she said with a flirtatious smile. "I was hoping you could keep me warm—dancing this evening—so I'd have no need of it."

He stared right back into her eyes, and for the first time, Tora noted they were a dark chocolate brown, like his hair. He smiled broadly and offered her his arm. "I'll do my best. Shall we?"

They took Aston's carriage to Mount Helena, the city park on the southwest edge of town. From there, they would be able to see the entire city and all of the fireworks that private citizens were sure to set off. It was a delightful, warm summer night, and for the first time in years, there was no threat of rain on this Fourth of July celebration to spoil the planned Chinese fireworks display. Tora still could not get over how her fellow Americans, many of them newly transplanted from other countries, went so wild over this holiday.

As they passed along the city street, it seemed to Tora that every window on it was hung with red, white, and blue swags of fabric. When they reached Mount Helena, little boys ran around with sparklers, giving the night a warm, magical aura. A band was playing the "Battle Hymn of the Republic" in the gazebo, and couples of all ages strolled the boardwalk paths, chatting and laughing. At one end of the park, a crowd of men gathered, shouting, cursing, and shooting their guns in the air on occasion. The sheriff and his deputies were nearby on horseback, keeping the riffraff from the respectable crowd, and watching the men with an air of indifference.

"I can't tell you what it means to me to escort you this evening, Miss Anders," Andrew said, pulling her hand into the crook of his elbow. "I have thought about this evening for an entire year, it seems."

"Yes, well, I appreciate your persistence. It just so happens that your invitation arrived on the same day my heart was freed from another."

"Trent Storm, I presume."

"Yes. We've decided it was time to end our personal relationship."

"And your business relationship?" Andrew asked delicately.

Tora knew the import of his question. Andrew's bank had lent her a tidy sum for two mining investments, as well as the beginnings of her new roadhouse in Spokane. If she let on that Trent had fired her, it would only be a matter of time before the bank called her note. "That remains to be seen," she said vaguely.

"Ah. I see." He paused and cleared his throat, bringing them to a stop. "But you are receiving income from Mr. Storm?" He laughed uneasily. "I cannot imagine him cutting you off without a dime. After all, you're the Storm Roadhouse Maven!"

Tora laughed and eased him forward, back into their languid walking pace. "That would be something," she said, pleased that he had set himself up and there was no need for a lie. "And suddenly, I am free to cavort with handsome devils like yourself," she said.

Andrew glanced at her quickly, obviously taken aback by her forwardness. "And I do consider myself a lucky devil."

"Mr. Aston, I believe we are on the edge of something delightful," she flirted.

Andrew guided her back toward the center of the park, where the mayor was speaking of America's many attributes, and the import of keeping the country free. *Yes, free for me to make my way, with or without Trent Storm,* Tora thought. He spoke of how America was made up of the brave who fought for her, gave their lives for her. *And I will give my life to get what I want.* He spoke of her future, glorious and bright. *And I will ride her future like the crest of a wave.*

Cutting a ribbon, the mayor officially opened the evening games. There were three-legged races by torchlight, a pie-eating contest, juggling clowns, and a carousel, brought in at tremendous cost from Minneapolis via train. Children squealed and pushed their way through the crowd to be the first to ride the fantastic machine, while parents looked on and laughed. The music, once begun, was a delight to the ears, and the gaslights were indeed a sight. Tora smiled, feeling suddenly a child again herself.

"Would you care for a ride?" Andrew asked, smiling down at her.

"Oh no. Let the children go first. I will have my turn later."

"Indeed. I'll make sure of it. Would you care for some lemonade?"

"That sounds divine."

"I'll be back directly." Tora watched him as he edged through the crowd toward the lemonade stand, shrugging at her when he noticed there was a line. Tora laughed. There was no doubt about it, Andrew Aston was the most desirable bachelor in town, and his attention was flattering. But he failed to move her deep down, as Trent had done. Had Trent killed her capacity for love, desire? She frowned at the thought. No, surely, it would simply be a matter of time before she could conjure up those feelings for someone else.

Yet she knew with absolute certainty that Andrew was merely a pawn in her game. She needed him, at least for the time being. And when she was done with him, she would discard him as she had others, waiting for the next man who could stir her. She would wait for love, and a man worthy of her desire. In the meantime, Andrew was a pleasant distraction.

"Well, boys," a deep voice said behind her. "Ain't she the picture of Venus di-my-lo?"

Tora glanced over her shoulder, unwilling to give the rabble-rousers who had obviously breached the sheriff's boundaries more than a cursory glance.

"That's Tora Anders," one whispered loudly to the first. "Storm's girl. Best steer clear of her."

"That's a shame," said the first. "But she's not with Storm tonight. Maybe she's available."

"You can bet I would never be seen with you," she said primly, turning to face the man. He towered over her, but she refused to cower, facing his dark gaze without flinching. "I suggest you gentlemen move on." He stood well over six feet tall, with the broad shoulders of a man accustomed to physical labor, and a face laden with scars.

"Well ain't you the haughty-taughty type? I'd like to take you down a couple o' notches."

Tora could feel his rakish gaze as he looked her over. She stood still, silent, unwilling to give him any edge.

"Come on, Brice," said his companion, "I wanna work come Monday, and I won't if Storm finds out about this." *They must be cowboys,* Tora surmised, *employed on one of Trent's ranches along the railroad lines.*

"Maybe she won't always be Storm's girl," Brice said.

Tora turned away from them, as if they were merely pesky flies she could ignore, when she saw Andrew approach, tossing the glasses of lemonade to the grass and reaching inside his jacket as if for a sidearm.

Brice, apparently spotting him too, said softly in Tora's ear, "Ahh, the banker. Best be goin'. Evenin', ma'am."

"Miss Anders, are you all right?" Andrew asked, stepping between her and the retreating men, his hand still inside his breast pocket.

"I am fine. Don't be silly. They were just a bunch of bored cowboys."

"They will not bother this fine crowd anymore tonight." He walked away, heading toward a deputy and speaking with him, using wild gestures.

"He'll have them in jail, I suppose," Tora whispered to herself. She reached inside her bag for a handkerchief, feeling suddenly weak. Her hand trembled, and it surprised her. She hadn't realized how afraid she was until then. After a few moments, she regrouped, telling herself that Tora Anders needed no one's protection, certainly not Andrew Aston's, or Trent Storm's.

As she searched for the linen handkerchief, Andrew returned to her and the fireworks display began, the crowd shouting in delight. In the dim light of a green-gold explosion, Tora looked up at Andrew and leaned closer to his chest, silently beseeching him to kiss her.

All at once, she needed to know she was desired, and protected, and close to another, if but for a moment.

And Andrew happily complied.

A thousand miles away, Trent stared out his window over the Mississippi River and watched Duluth's own fireworks display. Never in his life had he felt so miserable. He needed to know how Tora was, what she was up to. Even if she could not belong to him. A knock sounded at his door.

"Enter," he said curtly, taking another sip of his drink. He glanced over his shoulder. "Ah, Joseph." He perused the short, stocky detective and waved at the crystal decanter.

Joseph declined. "You wished to see me at once?"

"I did. Sorry to disrupt your Fourth of July celebration, but I have a proposition for you, Campbell. Please, sit down."

The detective sat down on the edge of his chair, hat in hand, as if ready to spring.

"I need you to follow Tora Anders."

"I see," he replied without comment. "For how long?"

"Six months. Maybe a year. I want to know what she's up to, how she's faring. I want you to be nearby at all times, ready to help if she needs it."

Joseph laughed. "If you'll permit me, Tora Anders does not strike me as a woman who needs a rescuer."

His words struck Trent to the core. A rescuer? He shook his head. "Call me a fool. I want her followed. I don't trust her or her judgment these days—she's a woman scorned. Doesn't always make for the best decisions. Find out everything you can."

"And the pay?" Joseph asked carefully.

"Double your normal rate, plus room and board. She was still in Helena, last I knew. But knowing Tora, it won't be long before she moves on. She'll have something up her sleeve; you can count on it."

"Understood. I take it you want me to leave immediately?"

"As soon as possible."

"I'll need to tie up some loose ends, with my family and my business."

"Why not take your family along? Rent a house in Helena. It would help you fit in better."

"A good idea. I'll run it past the missus. The kids would kill for the chance to see the Montana territory and get out of this humidity for the summer."

"Very well." Trent stood. He shook the shorter man's hand, dismissing him. "One other thing. Find out what you can about Tora's child. The one she gave up before arriving here."

Joseph grimaced. "I will do my best, sir. I'm afraid I failed you in not ascertaining the child's mere existence before. Makes it hard for a man to promise he can find the child."

Trent nodded sadly. "Do what you can. And send me weekly updates, will you?"

"Certainly. Good day, Mr. Storm."

"Godspeed." Trent turned toward the window as Joseph exited, thankful for the detective's discretion. Not once did he question going, nor why Trent wished to know of the woman he had left behind. No trace of emotion was visible on his face. Perhaps that was why he was so good at what he did. He was able to blend in, fade out, and no one ever knew he was there.

He was the antithesis of Tora Anders.

Tora walked through the newly constructed walls of her soon-to-be roadhouse, savoring the smell of fresh-hewn wood and sawdust. It was a glorious August day in Spokane, Washington Territory, and her new hotel was coming along famously. Another month and she would be ready to receive her first customers. Getting to this place had taken some doing, but it was all working out just fine. She smiled as she envisioned writing out a check to Trent Storm, reimbursing him for the "loans" she had taken from Storm Enterprises. She had worried that he might cut her off someday and had been wise to "prepare."

"Tora! Tora Anders!" a man called. The voice was familiar, but Tora could not place it. Frowning, she walked down the steps to what would eventually be the main lobby, when Andrew Aston caught up with her.

"Why, Andrew! What are you doing here?" she asked in wonder, going to him for a quick kiss. Her gladness was fleeting, however, as he turned to allow her lips to touch his cheek, but nothing else. "What? What is it?"

"I have some urgent business to discuss with you, Tora," he said, his face remaining hard. Dark shadows hinted that he probably hadn't slept in days.

"Certainly," she replied, dread edging her voice. "This way. There is a bench in the back where we might find a bit of privacy." She led the way through the carpenters, ignoring the fact that all workers had stopped to listen in. She took a deep breath, trying to slow her heart to its normal pace, unwilling to panic until she found out what Andrew had to say.

As they sat down, Andrew pulled off his bowler hat, dusty from the road. He twisted it, round and round, in his hands. "I have some bad news, Tora."

"Oh?"

"I need to call in your loan. Board of directors is demanding it."

"What? On what basis?"

"On the basis that it appears you have used funds taken from Storm Enterprises without permission." He whistled and cocked his head a bit, then glanced at Tora in wonder. "Trent Storm is involved in too many businesses in Montana and elsewhere to not have very long fingers. It's been made clear that you're no longer in his employ. You haven't been since June." His eyes narrowed as he stared at her.

Tora shifted uncomfortably under his gaze. "I told you we had had a parting of ways. I don't see what import that has. This is my new building, made primarily with the loan I took out with your institution. As long as I make my payments, what do you care how I obtain the funds?"

"If only it were so simple." Andrew rose and paced. "They know, Tora."

"Know what?"

"You've used Storm's name for more credit here. You told people it was for the Storm Roadhouse, when it was in your name, not his. That's how you've obtained the money you've needed for rock, lumber, nails, and labor. Our money went solely toward the real estate."

"I don't know where you've gotten your information, Andrew. But have you looked at my location? Just a block from the railroad station, closer than Trent's! I'll beat him here! I'll own this town!"

"Is that what this is all about? Beating Storm?"

"Certainly not," she said, raising her chin. "This is about Tora Anders coming into her own."

"On Storm's credit. It'll shame him, blacken his name. He'll be furious."

"By the time he finds out, I'll write him a check and all will be well. I am aware that this is big business, and surely you yourself have seen things done in a more…roundabout fashion."

"I beg to differ. Trent deals in a straightforward manner. And he already knows of your…indiscretions. He was the one who wired the board of directors."

Tora stilled, chilled to the bone. How? How on earth had he found out? She had been so careful! She cleared her throat, determined to gain control of the situation again. Tora smiled up at Andrew. "Surely you don't believe all this. Why, Andrew, I don't know what I'll do if your bank cuts me off! Look at this!" she said, waving about her. "It's going to be glorious! A fine investment!"

"One we can't afford to make," Andrew said, meeting her eyes. He reached inside his pocket and drew out a paper, handing it to her. "Your loan is due in fourteen days."

Tora whipped the paper from his hands, angry now. "You will be speaking with my attorney shortly."

Andrew nodded once and placed his bowler hat back on his head. "Very well. Tora…I…I'm sorry about this."

"As well you should be. Good day, Mr. Aston," she said haughtily, walking quickly toward the hotel. "I'll thank you for leaving *my* property immediately."

It took two weeks for Tora to understand the depth of her difficulties. In Spokane, she could feel the squeeze of Storm Enterprises' long arm. Word was spreading that she had double-crossed Trent, a leading employer and investor in the new, growing region. When she returned to Helena, things worsened. Where once she was the leading socialite in town, in two short weeks she had become an outcast. No one came to call; no one answered her pleas for help. Worse, news arrived that her mining investments were failing—the first had had a major cave-in and would be weeks in recovering; the other had yet to yield more than a pittance in silver.

With payments on her house, carriage, mining investments, and roadhouse property loans coming due at once, Tora was suddenly in a panic. She had no savings account, and her extravagant lifestyle had eaten up any extra cash she had. That morning, she had let two of her maidservants go, holding on to Sasha in one last, desperate measure. She refused to let Sasha go! She refused!

Angrily, she pulled on her white lace gloves and hat and left the house for Andrew's bank. He would see her side of things and fight for her. She would make sure of it.

Even if she had to propose marriage herself.

five

$\mathcal{K}$arl leaned out the stagecoach window, ignoring the August dust. He was too excited to let anything upset him today. In a sense, he was coming home. Even the dust smelled clean, honest. After receiving a letter from Kristoffer, forwarded to him in Helena, Karl looked for the first opportunity to come to the Washington Territory. It was here in the Skagit Valley that his fellow Bergensers had moved. Here he would see old friends for the first time in over five years!

He gazed around at the thickly wooded hills that protected the verdant valley. From edge to edge were healthy crops of peas, wheat, and potatoes. Karl smiled. God had favored the Bergenser farmers at last. His thoughts went from the valley farmers to the shipbuilders in Camden, and back to Norway and his family. He felt the smile fade from his face as the image of Karl's father came to mind. They had not parted well. Karl felt a tug of guilt. In many ways his father's words—though spoken in anger—had proven prophetic. He had been right about his son way back in 1880; he had seen the sin within Karl, the hypocrisy. Even though he wouldn't have admitted his lust for Elsa, his father had seen it plainly. And he had called himself a Christian. He wasn't worthy of the name. Was he even worthy to see these old friends?

It was too late now. The stagecoach driver brought the rig into town so fast that Karl wondered how he would stop without hurting someone. He needn't have worried. "Whoa!" the driver yelled at his team, as the passengers around Karl scrambled for a handhold to keep them from joining the others on the far bench. The coach came to an abrupt halt, jostling all the passengers.

Karl was the first out. "Kind of reckless, don't you think, coming in like that?" he asked, leveling a reprimanding gaze at the driver.

The driver merely glanced at him and then turned to toss down his satchel. "Move along, mister. You do your job, and I'll do mine. Don't like how I do my job, don't ride on my coach."

"I'll consider the wisdom of that," Karl said, turning toward the crowd down the street. Apparently, there was some sort of festival going on, judging from the number of people, the noise, and the banner across the street. Small towns like these thrived on festivals—a chance to see neighbors and make merry—as a good remedy to summer boredom. He had seen such events countless times before, in countless small towns he traversed, looking for the next business opportunity.

Karl had just spotted the small two-story hotel across the street when someone screeched out his name. "Karl! Karl Martensen!" Out of the crowd came Nora Gustavson, lugging in either hand a boy of about four and a girl barely old enough to walk. Her eyes wide in surprise, she let go of their small hands and covered her mouth, and shook her head as if Karl were a vision.

Karl laughed heartily, the first laugh of its kind in quite a while. It was so good to see his old friends. Yes, this was like coming home. "Karl! Hey, everyone! It's Karl Martensen!" Out of the crowd came familiar faces: Birger and Eira Nelson, Nora's husband Einar, Nels, and Mathias—rechristened "Matthew" upon arrival in America—proudly bringing his homely bride forward to meet Karl. Finally, Kaatje and her two small girls emerged. He embraced or shook hands with them one by one, exchanging small talk with each as he went, finally ending with Kaatje. He gave her a gentle hug and then crouched to solemnly shake hands with each of the girls.

"Where's Soren?" he asked, as he rose and the crowd dissipated. Nora and Einar left them for a moment to retrieve refreshments.

"He is away," Kaatje said, her face inscrutable.

"I see," he said, deciding to leave it at that. "Well, I had better get cleaned up or you are liable to disown me. I'm just going to check into a room over there," he said, nodding at the hotel.

"Oh, there's no need for that," Kaatje said, hands on her hips. "Come and stay in our hayloft."

"That's very kind of you, Kaatje," he said gently. "But with your husband away, it might not look proper."

She nodded, flustered when she realized her invitation was inappropriate.

"But I would take you up on dinner."

"That would be fine," she said, looking pleased. "About six?"

"I'll be there. Just give me the directions before you leave town."

Einar Gustavson gripped him at the shoulder, distracting him from Kaatje. "Martensen, what brings a seaman like you to town?"

"Well, I'll tell you, Einar, I've been away from the oceans for some time. I've been building steamship businesses along the riverways. Mostly along the Northern Pacific route. Facilitating loading, passengers, that sort of thing."

"Ah, I see," Einar said, nodding sagely. "Sounds fine. You and Peder parted ways, then?"

"Yes," Karl said, looking away into the distance so as not to betray too much. "Some time ago. I hear his shipyard has been a great success." He paused, then changed subjects. "It was a letter from Kristoffer that let me know where you all had settled. Thought I'd come up for a visit since I was in this part of the territory."

"Well, it's good to see you, man. Come out and share a meal with us before you leave."

"For sure, Einar." He glanced up to see Pastor Konur Lien approach. "And I'll have to get a church service in too," he said with a grin, shaking the pastor's hand.

"You had *better* intend to do so," Konur said. "It's so good to see another Bergenser's face!"

"For you? Think about me! You're surrounded. Why, you have half a congregation from Bergen here, pastor."

"And the other half is from the community. God has been gracious."

"I'm glad to hear it. Dakota Territory didn't work out, I take it."

"Hard going, there. Dry soil. Just when we got decent crops to harvest, the locusts came. I took it as a sign from God. So far, it has been a wise decision to come here. Going on four years now. And we're all alive and healthy. Many of our people have growing farms."

"I'm pleased to know it is so," Karl said. "Now I had better secure a room for the night. I'll be by to catch up with you and Amalia, pastor. As well as for Sunday services."

"Good enough, Karl. God bless you."

Karl paused a moment as Konur left his side. It struck him that it had been years since he had set foot inside a Christian sanctuary, and again, his father's warning rang in his ears. When he had left Peder, it was as if he had forgotten about God too. He hadn't prayed or sought out God's guidance as he once had. How hypocritical of him—to greet his old pastor as if nothing had changed!

When everything had. When he had.

After renting a gentle, strong mare from the local stables, Karl rode out Main Street dead east, as Kaatje had directed. He had bathed that afternoon in lukewarm water and secured his belongings in a decent room, if a bit run-down. Better than the pleasure of being clean again was the comfort of a small town, a small town where friends surrounded him. It was a picturesque evening, with long, warm streaks of sunlight edging through the plants and grain as if direct from heaven. And for the first time in a long while Karl felt some sense of peace.

When he reached the Janssens' farm and turned onto their lane, the girls ran out to greet him, barefoot, but with their Sunday dresses on, if he guessed right. They gave him bright smiles, and Karl was a bit startled at the physical differences in the two. He hadn't noticed how dissimilar the two sisters were when he had seen them in town. It puzzled him. But both were cute as buttons and sweet as honey, as Brad would say.

"Is this the Janssen farm?" he asked, when they arrived at his side, a bit breathless. He pretended not to recognize them as they nodded madly, their eyes big. "Well, I was a bit confused when I saw such pretty young ladies come to greet me. Here I thought you were just two little mites!"

"No, sir," Christina said. "I'm almost six years old."

"Six! Why that's practically ancient. Have you heard of the great pyramids?"

Christina shook her head in confusion.

"Well, they're what we consider *old*. But they can't be more than a few years older than you."

"How old are *you?*" Jessie asked.

Karl laughed. How long had it been since he had stopped to think about how old he was? Birthdays had come and gone, with little or no recognition from him or any of his friends. "Almost thirty, I believe."

"Thirty!" Jessie cried.

"No, don't be so surprised," he said, nodding at Kaatje as she came to the front door. "Why, I'd bet your mother was almost that age."

"Mama, are you thirty?" Christina asked. She ran to her and took her hand.

"I hope not. No, I think I have a couple of years."

Karl dismounted, tied the reins of his horse outside the house, and walked toward Kaatje. "Interesting how someone's age is vital when you're young, and not so interesting once you're old."

"Tell me about it. Come. Come in, Karl. I have some coffee on."

"Sounds great," he said, following her inside, ducking as he came through the doorway. "It's beautiful out here, Kaatje. And it looks like you have a good little farm going. How long is Soren away?"

Kaatje paused before answering, and Karl, for the first time, wondered what was going on. Why did a farmer leave in the middle of growing season? "He's been away for some time. Sit. Sit down, Karl."

"Oh? How long?"

"Four years."

"Four years!" He could feel himself blush as the girls stared at him intently. He sat down at the table and forced himself to soften his tone, to carefully choose his words. "That's an awful long time to be without your man. So…so you've been bringing in the crops yourself?"

She sat across from him and passed him a tin mug of steaming coffee. "And clearing, planting, weeding, watering, fertilizing…Not without the help of the other Bergensers, of course."

"But still, they had their own crops. I take it that the bulk of the work has been left to you."

"We help make pies," Christina volunteered.

"Mud pies," Kaatje said with a small smile.

"And I take care of Nels and Hans and the chickens," Jessie said.

"Our horse and hog," Kaatje explained.

"Well," Karl said, "that about covers things, doesn't it? Good thing your mother has done so well in the fields while you two were minding the house."

Both girls nodded solemnly. Karl stifled the desire to ask where Soren had gone, and how he could do such a thing to Kaatje, to his children. There was no sense in bringing up the unpleasant memories in front of the girls. Besides, who knew what Kaatje had told them? He would find out later, after they had gone to bed, and figure out some way to help them.

"Are you hungry, Mr. Martensen?" Jessie asked.

"Starved," he admitted. At once, all three of his hostesses jumped up to serve the meal. In short order, there was a thick beef stew, lefse, and a fresh apple cut in fours on the table.

"Haven't seen food like this in ages," Karl said.

"Would you bless it for us?" Kaatje asked.

Karl hesitated, reminded once again that he had no right to ask anything of God. Then he said, "Sure. Heavenly Father, we ask you to bless this family, and this food to our bodies. Amen." He figured God could not say no to that—who was more worthy than these three?

Later that night, Kaatje returned to the main room after tucking the girls into bed in the back room. Karl sat in the rocker, a mug of tea in his hands, staring into the fire. Warm, flickering light reflected on his face, and Kaatje felt content to have her old friend here. He apparently enjoyed it too, judging from the two hours they had all lingered at the dinner table, and the hours since. It had been good to have an adult to talk to, someone who cared about her as a dear friend. Did he miss having a family as much as they all missed having a man about the house?

"Well, they're all tucked in and fast asleep."

"They probably were out as soon as their heads hit the pillows. Their eyes were drooping for the last hour."

"They enjoyed themselves," she said, pouring herself a mug of tea and joining him by the fire in another chair. "I have not heard them giggle like that in a long time." She hesitated and then looked up at him gratefully. "I haven't had that much fun in some time, either."

"Nor I," he said softly. He looked at her endearingly, and Kaatje felt safe, known, loved. "As one childhood friend to another, may I ask you a question?"

Kaatje nodded, half dreading what was to come.

"Why did Soren leave?"

She paused, then said, "Wanderlust, I suppose. Originally it was to work on the railroad, to get some extra cash for the farm. I think that the farther he got from home, the more free he felt. He loved me and Christina," she rushed on. "I am sure of it. But his desire to see other places, to get his hands on the wealth 'just around the corner' got to him. He's always believed he could be rich. And he's always looked for the easy way to that wealth."

Karl was silent, as if considering her words. "It's a trap," he said at last. "I take it he's mining, then?"

"Along with half the territory's men, I think," Kaatje said. "Last I heard, he was in Alaska."

"They say that's where the next big strike will be."

"And if they keep saying that, Soren will stay put. He was trapping and trading to make his way in the meantime."

"He sends home some support?" Karl asked carefully.

Kaatje smiled gently. "Karl, I have not heard from him in over four years. I'm not even sure if he's alive. Lately, I've had this wild idea…" Her voice trailed off.

"Wild idea?"

"It's nothing."

"What?"

"I…I just have been thinking about going."

"To Alaska?"

"Crazy, is it not?"

"Why?"

"To try and find Soren, I guess. But there is something else. It's as if God is urging me to go."

"With two small children?"

"I said it was crazy."

Karl studied her, and Kaatje squirmed under his gaze. "All my life, I've thought of you as one of the most sensible people I know, Kaatje. If God is directing you there, maybe you should listen. I hear if you're good with a gun, have a trade to take with you, and bring decent supplies, you can make a go of it up there." His words of encouragement stunned her. But they were soon followed by: "That isn't to say I love the idea of you going alone. It is rough territory, Kaatje, rougher than you've ever known." His expression grew more concerned the longer he thought about it.

Kaatje laughed it off. "And where is God leading *you* these days?"

"Changing the subject, are you?" Karl paused, thoughtful yet somehow sad. "God…it's been as long since I heard from him as since you last heard from Soren."

So that was it. Despite his bravado and ease in making them all laugh, Kaatje had noticed the lonely look in his eye. It was as if he were exhausted, searching. "Oh?" she asked softly. "Haven't heard or haven't been listening?"

"Perhaps both," he said wearily. "I haven't exactly felt worthy of talking with him." He shifted in his seat as she remained silent. "I did something terrible years ago, Kaatje. Something that God couldn't forgive."

"There is nothing that God can't forgive," Kaatje said gently.

Karl stood, obviously agitated, and leaned one arm against the mantel, staring into the fire. "I was in love with Elsa," he said softly. "I kissed her."

"Oh," Kaatje said, remembering that Elsa had told her in a letter that Peder and Karl had parted ways. "And she…"

"Made it clear I had made a terrible mistake. I made some excuse to Peder and jumped ship. He still hasn't forgiven me. At least I don't think so. He never wrote back to me after I wrote him, asking his forgiveness."

"And you think that God cannot forgive you for that? Go to Peder, ask his forgiveness face to face, like a man, then ask God the same. Have you forgotten the Christ? Karl, man, this is what he died for! Your greater sin is pride for not going to him!" Kaatje surprised herself with her vehemence. But wasn't this exactly what she feared kept Soren from returning home to her and the girls? Fear that she wouldn't forgive him?

Karl looked up at her, obviously startled by her straightforward words, then back at the fire. "I suppose you're right. I wrote once—"

"It is not enough. It's still eating you alive and keeping you from the Lord. From Peder. Go to him. Go to him, Karl. They're just south of us! In Seattle. I think they're due home in the next month or two. Settle it, once and for all."

"Perhaps you're right," he said, sighing and sitting back down in his chair. "This is why I came to the valley, Kaatje. Only here do friends know me well enough to yell at me."

Kaatje smiled. "What are friends for?"

"I've missed you, Kaatje. I've missed all of you." There was no hint of flirtation in his voice, merely kinship. "I wish I could find a fine woman like yourself or…"

"Elsa?" she finished for him.

"Or Elsa," he said, as if testing out the words. "There are no finer women than you."

"There is a woman out there for you," Kaatje said with utter confidence. She felt she must make it clear that she intended to honor her marriage. And it was obvious to her heart that Karl would never be anything more to her than a dear friend. "I know it. But you have to clean out your trunk first. You're carrying an awful weight."

"I agree," he said gently. "Well, I've made more than a nuisance of myself, staying so late. I'd best be off."

"It was a pleasure, Karl. Please, come again before you leave."

"You can be sure of it," he said with a smile, placing his hat on his head and pulling on his coat.

Kaatje grabbed a shawl and followed him out the door. "You'll be able to find town? There's but a sliver of a moon."

"I'll find it." He hesitated, then moved closer to kiss her softly on the cheek. He mounted his horse and nodded once at her, then reined the mare into a trot off down the lane, and Kaatje listened until she could no longer hear hoofbeats. In the silence of the night, after such a full evening of talking, laughing, and companionship, Kaatje suddenly felt bereft.

She touched her cheek, remembering the soft scratch of Karl's beard and how Soren's cheek once felt against hers. How long had it been since a man had kissed her? Since Soren had held her in his arms? She ached for the feel of being held again, for the warmth of a man's body enveloping her own. To be with her husband. To *belong* again.

Where was he? What would it take to find him if she went to Alaska? "Please, Father," she said, sinking to her knees and beseeching the skies with outstretched arms. "Please, Jesus. Send me word. Let me know if he's dead or alive. Let me know if I should keep hoping. Please, Father. I beg of you! I beg of you!"

There was no response as she continued to stare for some time up at the black night sky alive with a million stars. Slowly, her arms sank to her sides. But she had no tears to weep tonight. She felt empty, and utterly alone.

You could go, came the Voice. *You could go.*

Karl rode back to town, thinking of Peder, Kaatje, Elsa—a deluge of thoughts coursed through his head at once. It had been a long time since he had felt so stimulated, invigorated by honest conversation and laughter. Bradford Bresley, his business partner, often did that for him, but their work kept them apart. Brad had married Virginia Parker and settled down in Butte, Montana, concentrating on their efforts in the Midwest and the mountains, while he, the single man, volunteered to go farther west and see what enterprises he could drum up there.

It had been years since he had spent more than a day or two with the Bresleys, and then conversation was mostly about business. When he thought about it, Karl had isolated himself from those who truly knew him, anyone who could ask the questions that mattered. It was little wonder that he felt lonely and hollow.

Karl raised his head and breathed deeply. The land smelled good, of damp peat and grain heated by the afternoon sun and then cooled by the evening breeze. He knew this valley could do so much more. To the north was a wide, shallow bay, in which barges came to load up the farmers' harvest and ship it down to Seattle. But the railroad was inefficient in getting the crops there, and Karl began visualizing how he and Brad could improve shipping and, in turn, help his fellow Bergensers prosper. It was not an enterprise of charity; they would no doubt find a handsome profit for their labors. But it was too broad an enterprise for their resources. He would need to contact some investors to find the cash necessary to accomplish such goals. Trent Storm immediately came to mind. It was just the sort of thing they had discussed in Helena.

He would spend the next months surveying and researching the project. But tomorrow he would wire Brad and Trent. From the profits, he would easily be able to help Kaatje and the girls. They needed so much—a new barn, an addition to the tiny house. More animals to help them make it through the winter. He knew Kaatje would be too proud to accept such grandiose charity from another. So Karl would just have to find a way to do it anonymously.

He frowned as he thought of her words once more. *Soren loved Christina and me.* What about Jessie? How could the man have left any of them? Kaatje with her red cheeks and kind, gray eyes? Christina with her blond curls and fast way of speaking? Vivacious Jessie with her all-consuming love for animals? Kaatje had not heard from him in four years; why, he had probably never even met his second daughter! Once again he wanted to throttle the man for his idiocy, for his lack of responsibility.

Then Karl laughed at himself. Soren wasn't the only one who had run from those who cared about him. Soon Karl would have to face his own responsibility. Kaatje had been right. Since Peder had not contacted him, he needed to go to his old friend. And beg his forgiveness. On his knees if he had to. His resolve made him feel more free than he had in years.

six

August 1886

They had been at sea more than two weeks, heading straight for Washington Territory and their newest home, confident that the Japanese wares they purchased in Yokohama would sell better there than in the waning markets of San Francisco or New York. Besides, it would get them home by late August and give Peder a chance to see how his employees and projects fared at their new sawmill in Seaport. From there, Peder would take a load of lumber to the East Coast, check on their shipyard in Camden-by-the-Sea, and they all might be able to get back to Seattle in time for Christmas—their first in the West.

More and more Peder allowed his ships to travel through the winter months, their hulls sufficiently reinforced to handle the more inclement weather. But he still hesitated to take his wife and child along, especially with Elsa expecting again. Either way, Elsa decided, she would be happy; in her new home in the delightful Washington Territory, or in her cozy home in Camden, near dear old friends.

It was with these happy thoughts that Elsa put paint to canvas, blowing up a small daguerreotype of Peder and Kristian in samurai costume to a much larger, colorful format. Her intent was to ship it to the Ramstads in Bergen for Christmas. She was just painting Kristian's wooden sword, a miniature version of his father's, when Peder entered the study and placed his arms around her shoulders. He kissed her cheek and studied the painting. "I cannot believe you talked me into doing that, or that you intend to send it to my parents."

His tone held none of the disgust of his words. "You loved it. Admit it," she said, dipping her brush in a deep gray for emphasis along Peder's sleeve.

"I did it for you."

"And your son. He still plays with that sword, threatening his stuffed bear with dire consequences if he doesn't obey."

"Every man needs another to command. Luckily, I have a crew, since my wife won't listen to me." He rose and walked to his desk.

Elsa smiled. "Come now. Your parents will adore this painting. Not only do they get to see their son and grandson, but they get to show you off to their friends and neighbors as obvious world travelers. These photographs are all the rage. Few have an oil painting, to boot."

Peder guffawed, but Elsa knew he was secretly pleased. She smiled again at the photo at the edge of her canvas. Father and son looked remarkably alike, and she knew one day Kristian would be just as handsome as his papa. Would he sweep some girl off her feet as Peder had done to her? What would he do? Captain a ship for Ramstad Yard? Or something entirely different? Her heart leapt at the thought of seeing him go as their own parents had watched them leave Norway. Certainly, it had been difficult enough to leave on the *Herald* for America—but what would it feel like to be the aging parent left behind?

Her thoughts returned to her mother, her sister Carina, and the burial plot of her father she had yet to visit. "Peder," she said carefully, "what if we delivered this painting in person? What if we went to Bergen for the winter?" She turned on her stool, getting excited at the idea. "Think of it! How grand it would be to introduce Kristian to his grandparents, his cousins! To see Carina and Garth *married*. I'm dying to see my mother—"

Peder's face squelched any further words. "I'm sorry, love. It's impossible. Maybe next year."

"How often have we said that?" Elsa asked, irritated. "Next year, next year. Always next year. My mother might be dead before I get home again." She turned back to the painting, but did not lift her brush.

Peder approached and placed one hand on her shoulder. "I am sorry to disappoint you again, love. It's just that we barely have time to get home, unload our cargo, and get to Camden to see to business. Add a trip to Bergen and I'm afraid we're risking heavy winter seas. I won't risk it. Especially with you expecting again."

"So we're back to the old argument."

"Yes, we are. Are you not a bit afraid? If not for yourself, then for our children?"

"I could have the baby in Bergen. What it would mean to my mother!"

Peder's hand left her shoulder. "*If* we made it to Bergen. I will not risk it, Elsa. I will not risk you and my children. We will winter somewhere safe and consider a trip in the new year."

"But, Peder, with the new hulls, the new ships Kristoffer is turning out—"

"No!" he said, then lifted a hand as if to soften an unintendedly harsh tone. "No, Elsa. Do not ask it of me. I could not bear it if anything happened to you, or Kristian, or this new babe. I want our lives together to be long. Can't you understand?"

She looked up into his eyes, noting for the first time the sweat upon his brow. Elsa rose and entered his embrace, staying there for a long time. "I understand, Peder. Perhaps you are right." She pulled away and looked into his eyes. His face was pale and he looked ill. "You didn't tell me."

"I thought I could beat it. Surely these fevers are nearly over."

"It could be years, the doctors said." Malaria had struck Peder years before; but still every few months he suffered through recurrent fevers.

"I hate it. It weakens me."

"It will end someday. Come. Come to bed, love." She tenderly helped him undress and slide under the cool cotton sheets. Grateful, Peder said nothing but merely acquiesced to his wife's ministrations. She poured a basin full of water and rinsed a cloth in it, then placed it on his brow. Within minutes, he was breathing in the heavy, steady rhythms of sleep.

Several evenings later, Elsa coaxed herself to sleep, trying to drive from her mind that Peder was once again delirious with malaria's fever and that Riley had earlier that day muttered darkly, "Red sky at morning, sailors take warning." Something dire fast approached. And Elsa knew she needed to be rested to handle it.

She was awakened by the increasing climb and crash of the *Eagle's* hull. Lighting a lamp, she looked behind her at Peder, who was soaked in sweat and obviously unconscious. In the corner, swinging in a hammock as calmly as King Neptune, Kristian remained fast asleep, oblivious to the dangers just outside their cabin. Grimly, Elsa pulled on a pair of dungarees and Peder's oilskin jacket and pants, rolling them up at the bottom. The jacket was huge on her, but it gave her a better chance of remaining somewhat dry as she helped Riley and the crew.

Over the years, as Peder grudgingly taught her about the art of sailing, Elsa had become more and more proficient. She learned everything from tarring the ropes to reefing the sails to charting a course. Elsa found her education thrilling, and delightful fodder to send home via the *Times*. Her audience was alternately aghast and delighted to hear of her hanging from the topmast or sliding down the edge of a sail, not to mention a woman donning trousers to safely go where men usually went.

Together, she and Peder had weathered storm after storm, many worse than this one, and her confidence had grown. Were she to round the Horn again at the helm, she could stand there as proudly as any sailor aboard the *Eagle*. Especially with Riley beside her.

She supposed it was he at the wheel, if her eyes did not deceive her. It was dreadfully dark outside, and from the feel of things, the *Eagle* was sailing close hauled upon the wind, lying over. If they leaned much farther, they'd be upon their beam ends in no time. Determined to help, Elsa stepped outside.

She squinted against the stinging spray of rain pelting her face and hesitated as everything in her told her to go back inside. Sailors raced about, no doubt following orders to take in sail. The heavy seas beat against the *Eagle*'s bow with all the gentleness of a sawyer's ax, making it sound as if she were about to splinter apart. Above Elsa, topsail halyards had been let go, and the great sails were filling out and backing against the masts with a noise that competed with the storm's own thunder. Sailors were still climbing aloft to furl more sails before their ship capsized.

Without another thought, Elsa joined them, never once speaking to Riley at the wheel. He was busy shouting orders into the wind that none of his men could hear. But instinctively, they all knew what must be done. Never had Elsa climbed aloft in such heavy seas. She grunted and clung to the mast as the newest wave sent a shudder through the schooner, and then determinedly moved onward as soon as it passed. Sails at the course and topsail lanyards had been furled, but the upper topgallants and royals remained reefed, still catching enough wind to be dangerous. That was where the others had climbed, awaiting sufficient help to begin the process of hauling in the buntlines, leech lines, and clew lines and gathering the canvas to be lashed securely.

Her stomach lurched, for the higher she climbed, the more susceptible she was to the rock and roll of the ship. It seemed impossible that the men had made it to the top royals without falling immediately to their deaths. Gritting her teeth, she went higher, just getting her feet in place and a tether around her ankles before they began the process. Over the lanyard she leaned with the others, hauling in sail as fast as she could and securing it, thinking only of returning to the deck far, far below them all. *If we aren't all shaken out of the nest first,* she thought grimly. They completed their task in record time.

The wind had pulled and loosened her hat, sending it careening away on the wind, and now it worked on her hair. If it hadn't been for the rain that plastered it to her head, Elsa might've been blinded by the freed tendrils. Blinking to clear her eyes, she headed toward the main mast, anxious to get down to the relative safety on deck. A young sailor winced when he saw her, quickly gesturing for her to go down first. None of the others had yet noticed that the captain's wife was among their number.

Carefully choosing her handholds and footholds, Elsa made her way down as fast as possible. Huge waves had begun to sweep the deck, like no other storm she had seen before. Crazily, the seas rose and burst over the ship from all sides. It reminded her of the times when she had been swept across the planks and nearly overboard, of Karl's saving presence, of Peder's near demise when a similar wave had taken him. With the sails furled, she hoped Riley would send the less experienced men down the hatch. But there was no need.

"Cyclone!" screamed a sailor near her, barely audible over the wind. Elsa looked about. Men scrambled to the fo'c's'le, the galley, the stern, anywhere there might be refuge. There was nothing to be done on deck now that the sails had been reefed, and every man knew that survival lay behind a protective wall and fervent prayer.

Elsa decided to seek out Riley. She needed to see his face, know this was yet another storm they would make it through. But it was not Riley at the wheel.

"The mate! Where's the first mate?" she screamed over the banshee wind at Finch, their second mate.

Finch looked at her for a moment in stunned disbelief, then nodded around the corner.

That was when Elsa noticed the captain's cabin door, swinging open, back and forth. *Kristian.*

"Kristian!" she screamed, suddenly envisioning the toddler awake and wandering these dangerous decks looking for his mother. He would not have a chance. "*Kristian!*"

With painstaking slowness, she made her way to the door and pulled herself inside. It was dark, the lamp apparently extinguished. The noise of the storm was substantially lessened in the cabin, but still loud. "Kristian!" she yelled. "Peder, are you awake?"

No one answered.

Elsa stumbled as another wave swept past, sending her tumbling over a trunk that had slid from its place, water cascading in around her. Disoriented, she blindly made her way to what she thought was Kristian's corner and hammock. "Kristian!" she said, quieter this time, more desperation in her voice.

"Mama?" came a sleepy reply. He started to cry, groggy and sleepy.

Oh, thank you, Father, Elsa prayed silently. *Thank you, thank you, thank you.* "It's okay, sweetheart. Mama's here." She found his form in the dark, and bent over to kiss his forehead. "We have a little storm on our hands. Go back to sleep."

"Okay," Kristian said, obviously falling right back into deep slumber.

Another wave passed, sending a gushing spurt into the cabin. Elsa was on her way to close the door when a man's form appeared in the doorway. "Elsa!" It was Riley.

"Riley. I wanted—"

"Elsa! The cap'n! 'Ave you seen him?"

The note of panic in his voice sent an icy shiver down her spine. She turned back toward the bed in confusion. "Peder? Peder is in—"

"I saw him around the cabin a minute ago! I can't find him!"

No. No, it isn't possible! Peder had not been out of bed for nearly a week. He didn't have the legs for a storm such as this! "No!" she shouted. She shoved Riley aside, with one thought on her mind: *Find Peder.*

"Mama!" came a frightened voice from the corner.

Elsa paused, looked at Riley, and back over her shoulder. "Get a man in here to stay with him before you leave this doorway," she ordered.

"Elsa—"

"Do it!"

She could barely discern a nod from the man, but left him there, confident that he would not leave his post, or her son, without doing as she bid. "Peder!" she screamed into the wind, wanting to curse the rain that blinded her. Never had she felt so helpless. "Peder!" Another wave came over the side, crashing into the back of her knees and sending her sliding. She didn't go far, however, and was soon on her feet again.

"Peder!" she screamed, so loud she could feel the strain in her throat. "Peder!" She rounded the corner of the cabin, heading astern. A man came by and Elsa reached out to grab his arm. "The captain! Have you seen the captain?"

"No, ma'am!"

She did the same with the next, and the next, until she had covered all the men beyond the cabin. Her legs trembled and Elsa shook with cold. She willed herself not to panic. Perhaps he had gone around and then toward the bow. That thought brought little comfort. At the bow, the sea had the fiercest power. It could take a grown man who was well, let alone an ailing man. "Peder!" she cried, sure he was nowhere near her, but wanting to do something, anything.

Within minutes, she was at the bow, tethering herself to the foremast before the next watery enemy swept over her. "Peder!" she cried, once it passed. *Please, Father, let him be all right. Please.* It was no use; she could see nothing, and there were no men at this end of the ship to ask about him. Slowly, she moved about the railing, calling his name. *If he was here, he's dead for sure,* she thought, emerging from another wave. Without the tether, it would have pulled her overboard too. *Please, Father. Dear God in heaven—*

"Elsa!" Riley said, startling her at his sudden proximity. "I said he was back astern!"

"I know!" she yelled, following him across the deck. At least the rain was lessening. Perhaps they were almost through the worst of it. "I can't find him! Thought I'd check the bow!"

"You intent on killin' yourself?" he yelled.

"Peder! We must find him!" She ignored Riley's anger. He was only trying to protect her. But the panic in her breast was getting harder and harder to contain. Where was he? Where was Peder? She refused to even think that he might already be gone. That was when she heard the first hint of a song on the wind. Slowly, she looked up.

Dimly, she could just make out a figure in a nightshirt on the end of a lanyard, not twenty feet above them, almost over the edge of the ship. He was singing boisterously, and Elsa was sure it was Peder, delirious from fever, reefing an imaginary sail that had been hauled in hours before. Riley followed her gaze and swore profusely. Elsa was paralyzed with fear, but Riley immediately set into action, climbing the mast toward his captain.

All Elsa could do was make her mouth form one word, one single word of prayer: *Please.*

She blinked, trying to keep track of Riley's progress, when she saw Peder falter. It was as if the wind had hit him for the first time. He leaned forward, then back, overcompensating.

No.

It seemed to take him forever to fall. Elsa watched in stunned disbelief, her eyes opening and closing as the wind sent sheets of rain her way, freezing images of his descent in her mind, blocking out others. He hit the starboard railing, no sound audible over the storm. One of the few sailors present dived for him, obviously hoping to catch an arm, a sleeve, anything.

But Peder was overboard less than a second before he got there.

"No!" Elsa screamed, her voice finding its way out of her paralyzed body. "Peder!" She ran to the side as best she could against the storm's fierce waves and peered over the rail. "Peder!" she screamed. "Man overboard! *Man overboard!*"

Riley set about the business of trying to slow their progress, to keep them near the same spot. But in the howling wind and waves, it would take little time for man and ship to be separated. Nets were thrown, hoping to catch him before they went too far. Sails were set to counter their progress, yet not catch the ship aback. Still, they moved onward.

"A lifeboat!" Elsa screamed. "The lifeboat!" Men looked at her helplessly, knowing that a lifeboat would surely capsize before it reached the water. It would be a futile effort only endangering the others involved.

Elsa turned back to the water, strangled by her helplessness.

Peder did not reemerge. It was as if he hit the water and sank, so fast did it happen. Elsa made as if to go after him herself, hooking a leg over the railing.

Men on either side of her gripped her firmly. One bellowed, "You can't, ma'am! Think o' your son!"

Thoughts of Kristian were the only thing that kept her aboard that night, when the one thing she desired was to save her husband, or join him in death.

Peder was gone.

Forever.

Even two days later, Elsa still could not believe that her beloved was dead. That he would not appear around some corner of the ship, out of some hatch, and wonder at her excitement of seeing him. *Well, of course I'm here, darling,* he would say. *Where'd you think I was?* How could such a vital person be alive one second and gone to eternity the next? It was beyond her comprehension.

When Kristian had asked her that next morning where his papa was, all she could mutter was, "Dead. Dead, dead, dead." She knew the boy was confused, and frightened by her manner, but it seemed to Elsa that she was not herself. That she was unable to control her mouth or mind. Quietly, Cook had spirited the boy away, giving Elsa some time alone. She felt like a bird in the sky, watching the preparations for her husband's funeral below. A funeral with no body. How could God have done it? How could he? Without even a chance to say good-bye, one more opportunity to say, "I love you"? Other than utter loss and devastation, the one emotion she could find within herself was anger.

God had failed her. He had failed Peder. He had failed Kristian. What was a boy to do without a father? And the child within her? A child who would never know the pleasure of a father's embrace or tender word. A child without Peder. Kristian without Peder. *Me without Peder.*

It was all too much. For hours she sat on her bed and rocked, ever so slightly, reliving Peder's fall, over and over. It was like a passage in a book that she kept rereading to try and understand something important missed—to get the action down, to understand the characters' thoughts, so the entire plot would make sense again.

What had Peder been thinking? He wasn't, of course. He was delirious with fever. What had she been thinking? How could she have left her husband and child? They had needed her, and she had failed them!

It was her fault he was dead. If she had remained inside the cabin, he would be emerging from malaria's hold about now. How could she have abandoned him?

But I thought he was unconscious! The men needed my help! she defended herself, feeling torn in two by her own inner argument. *He hadn't moved for days!*

Still, it was not a woman's place to be out on deck in such a storm, regardless of her experience. Even as the Heroine of the Horn. It was exactly that danger that Peder had feared. Yet she hadn't been the one to perish. It had been Peder Ramstad. Her husband. Her lover. Her friend. How, how, how on earth could he be gone? Her mind could not marry fact with fact. It was simply inconceivable. Once more, tears slipped down her cheeks as the ache grew in her throat.

Two weeks later, Elsa donned her black mourning dress once again. It was logical that women dressed in black for at least a year, she thought, since the color matched her mood. How could she wear anything else? The lavender Peder had purchased for her in New York? The pale yellow he had bought for her in England? Any other color was inappropriate, and the memories each one brought to mind were too much to bear. Peder had delighted in her figure, and when he finally had the funds to do so, dressed her in finery that brought a slight blush to her cheeks when she stopped to think of the expense. It was so deliciously intimate, however, that she had never stopped him from indulging in her.

Now, what was left? Years of memories and too many dresses to ever wear again. Especially since she intended to wear black forever. It was impossible to believe that she would ever find pleasure in any other color. That she would someday smile, laugh, swim, run, tickle Kristian, anything. All she wanted to do was curl up in the bed she had shared with Peder, inhale the musty scents of the sheets that still held a faint memory of his smell, and sleep until it was all right again.

Until the nightmare was over and Peder was home.

She assumed Riley was continuing their course to Seattle. Once there, she could leave this ship—this wretched ship that had cost Peder his life—and safely ensconce herself at home. Perhaps Kaatje would come to her. The idea brought her some measure of comfort, and her tears abated. Kaatje would know what to do, how to proceed. After all, she had ostensibly lost a husband herself. Just having her dear friend near would give Elsa strength. And the girls could look after Kristian, giving her a chance to rest and boosting his morale as well.

Elsa just needed to sleep. She was exhausted, unable to do more for her son than pull him to her on the bed, cradling his small body in the curve of her own. He would stay there with her for hours, seemingly aware that it was the best she could do, the most she could give him, then be off to bother Riley, Cook, or another of the crew.

Nights were the worst. After sleeping all day, she was awake come nightfall. And the dark always reminded Elsa of the storm. Back and forth she would pace in the cabin as Kristian snored softly in his hammock. Over and over again, she would peer through the window, sure that the man at the wheel was not Riley or Finch, but Peder. He would turn to her and smile, assuring her that, yes, it all had been a bad dream. But he never turned, never assured her with that brilliant smile of his. Elsa closed her eyes, remembering him in Bergen, at the altar, in Camden, at sea on their first vessel.

"O dear God," she whispered. "My dear Savior. How can it be possible that my husband be dead, when he lives inside of me?"

She heard no answer. Only the ongoing quiet *swish* of waves passing, the gentle rocking of the *Eagle*, the constant creak of the boards beneath her feet.

And Elsa found herself praying that another storm would come and take them all.

seven

❧

$\mathcal{F}$inding life intolerable that September in Helena, Tora saw no choice other than to move out. She had been shunned from the community, cut off from the important people around whom she thrived. Andrew Aston had made it clear that he was immovable and would not let her keep her loan, even when she used her feminine wiles on him. Without a roadhouse to oversee for Trent, she listed about the house, bored and worried. She laughed when she found herself actually quoting her father in a soft whisper, a man for whom she had had little respect: "Sitting around fretting will not resolve anything, Tora. Take a step. Sideways. Forward. Anywhere."

Begrudgingly, she admitted to herself that she had always taken Amund Anders's advice when it came to situations like this, and it had brought her far. It had taken her to America. To Minnesota. To Trent. She grimaced and stared out the window, not truly seeing the carriages and wagons that moved along the road. To be honest, her quest for more had also removed her from Trent's side. She had taken steps that, ultimately, landed her back where she had come from. But there were ways out. There had to be a way. She just had to find it.

A knock sounded at the door and Tora winced at the thought of opening it herself. She had let Sasha go a week prior, since she could no longer pay her wages. Sasha had stayed on another week, exchanging her services for a few of Tora's old dresses, but when it became clear that Tora's luck had not changed, she packed her bags and said a curt good-bye. Perhaps she hadn't been as fine a servant as Tora had thought. A truly loyal person would have given her at least another week.

She feared who the person might be on the other side of the door. Was it Andrew? Another of her creditors? Already the jackals had come and confiscated some of her finest new furniture. One of Sasha's last tasks had been to help her bring some of the older pieces from the basement to hide the vacant spots. It grated on Tora to look on them. *A step back,* she thought. *Now I need to take a step forward.*

Her visitor proved to be that step. She opened the door and looked over her shoulder, as if a bit bewildered. "Mrs. Hunter!" she exclaimed, fanning her face as the wave of heat from outdoors hit her. "I do not know where my maid is. Please excuse the delay in answering the door. Won't you come in?"

Mrs. Hunter nodded and gave Tora a demure smile, obviously knowing exactly where her maidservant was. "Thank you."

Tora shut the door and led the way to her sitting room. "Please join me in the parlor. Can I interest you in a refreshing glass of water? It's very warm outside."

"That would be fine," she said, taking a seat on the edge of the couch.

Tora left her to retrieve the glasses of water, wishing for the thousandth time that week for her customary lemonade. Why, she had become known for it! Mrs. Hunter would be blabbing the news all over town, no doubt, that Tora Anders could no longer afford lemons from California. The old biddies would take delight in the news! Oh, how they'd feast upon it! With an angry sigh, Tora pulled out two crystal glasses, retrieved some chips of ice from the cellar as fast as she could, and poured the water.

She paused. There was one lemon remaining in the icebox. If Mrs.

Hunter was thinking what she thought she was thinking, a slice of lemon in her water would squelch those malicious rumors immediately. Perhaps even take her down a notch, since she would think Tora had the lemons but did not deem her worthy of lemonade. Smiling for the first time in a week, she ran down the cellar steps again, returned, and put a nice, fat, picture-perfect slice on the edge of each glass. It looked rather elegant, actually.

Taking a moment to straighten her hair, she composed herself, casting away all her self-abasing thoughts, and strode down the hall and into the parlor. "No doubt you wonder why I asked you to drop by, Mrs. Hunter, so I'll get right to the point. I wish to lease this home for a while. I have business out west and will not be returning for some time. Of course, I'd like the house to go only to the finest family available. No children, please."

"None?" Mrs. Hunter asked, her look telling Tora that might be impossible.

"At least not under school age," she quickly amended. "I don't want any ragamuffins tearing up my fine furniture."

Mrs. Hunter nodded, obviously trying not to look about at the furniture which was of good quality, but nothing to fret over. "Very well. May I have a tour of the home so I may make some notes for possible clients?"

"Yes, of course. Please, follow me." She led the way through the three-story building, pointing out the finer aspects such as two indoor water closets with running water, gas lighting throughout the house, and decorating that only the finest citizens could fully appreciate. Tora dearly wanted someone who would take care of this house, to love it as she did, so that someday she could return. It was the first place she had felt was hers, hers alone, and she didn't want to lose it, nor did she wish anything damaged.

When they sat down again in the parlor, she paused to choose her words. "So, Mrs. Hunter, now that you've seen the house, can you give me some idea of what would be a fair monthly lease amount?"

"Do you anticipate keeping on your gardener and a maid?" Mrs. Hunter asked over the rim of her glass.

"I believe that the lady of the house would be more comfortable hiring her own help. It is such an individualized process, I find. Wouldn't you agree?"

Mrs. Hunter gave no suggestion that she doubted the sincerity behind Tora's words. "Yes. Of course. And the gas bill? It would be part of the lease?"

"I think it would be cleaner if we simply changed the name on the account to the leasing party. Then I do not have to fiddle with it from Washington Territory."

Mrs. Hunter glanced up at her quickly. "My goodness. You intend to go that far?"

Tora smiled demurely. "There was a day that I thought Montana sounded terribly far."

Mrs. Hunter returned her smile, nodding. "I too." She looked down at her notes, apparently in thought. "I do have a fine family in mind. A businessman, his wife, and their two sons. They've been at the Cosmopolitan Hotel for a month now, unable to find a home suitable for their needs. They enjoy entertaining, and from what I understand, have a home similar to this in Minnesota."

"Minnesota, you say? What part?"

"Minneapolis, I believe. Or perhaps it was Duluth…He doesn't intend to stay here forever. Probably an investor. I understood from him that it might be six months to a year."

Tora smiled. "That sounds perfect! Perhaps then…" She let her sentence drop, knowing she should play the game out to her best advantage. "May I meet them?"

"I could probably arrange that."

"And would they consent to a monthly correspondence, keeping me up to date on the house?" She laughed. "I assume it would be a short note. As mistress of your own home, I am sure you can understand my feelings. It is as if I'm giving away a ch-child." The words

were out before she knew what she was saying, and it made her
stumble. Quickly, she coughed, hoping to cover up her mistake.

Mrs. Hunter frowned a bit and then went on. "Certainly. I see no
harm in a monthly update. It might make you feel a bit less homesick.
Would you be available tomorrow afternoon, say, around three, for a
tour of the house and a chance to meet the family?"

Joseph Campbell escorted his wife up First Street, delighted at this
turn of events. Upon arriving in Helena, he had casually mentioned
Tora's house as an example of what he sought for his family. Now she
was renting it out, and with a monthly check due, as well as the desired "status note" she had requested, Joseph would be able to keep
tabs on the woman. He would know where she was, at least on the first
of every month. And his family could stay in one place while he followed Tora on her explorations. Who knew where she might go now?

It was not a surprise when Mrs. Hunter came calling. Joseph,
through some careful detective work, had discovered that Tora's mining investments were failing, and the checks from Storm Enterprises
had ended in June. He knew Tora had been living the high life for
some time, and she had to be nearly broke. In addition, after a few
covert interviews with some of the leading socialites in Helena, he discovered that Tora was on the outs with Helena's high society. A move
was clearly in her future, since Helena had turned its back on her.

Had she not been misusing his employer's name and credit, Joseph
might have felt sorry for her. As it was, he relished taking this, her
prized home, from her, even if it was temporarily. *How could such a
fine man as Trent Storm fall for a vixen like her?* he wondered for the
thousandth time.

Joseph pulled Mary closer as they drew near the gate. He was
thankful for his good, solid wife and the two delightful sons they
shared. Mrs. Hunter awaited them, just inside the gate.

"Right on time. Thank you. It's good to see you again, Mrs.
Campbell."

"Mrs. Hunter," Mary said with a nod.

As they went in the front door, Joseph tried not to stare too much at Tora. This was the first time he had seen her in close proximity. She was making introductions, when the banker Andrew Aston arrived, followed by five burly men.

"Why, Andrew," Tora sputtered, trying to close the door halfway. "I am afraid this is not a good time."

"No it is not," he said, pushing the door open again. He handed her a folded paper. "We are foreclosing on this house, Tora. You have five days in which to vacate. The furniture will have to go now."

Tora blushed a crimson red, and studiously looked at no one but the banker. "There must be some mistake—"

"Certainly not. You knew as well as I that this day was coming."

Joseph studied the two, instantly aware by their intense gaze that more had transpired between them than the typical banker-client relationship. Had she played this one as she played all men?

Tora took a deep breath as if to gather herself. Determinedly, she shut the door between Andrew and the men behind him, effectively cutting them off. "Andrew, can you wait here for a moment? Mrs. Hunter, Mr. and Mrs. Campbell, please excuse this incredible interruption. Obviously, I have something to straighten out. It should take no more than a moment. Won't you—"

"No!" Andrew exploded. "They must leave. There will be no more hostessing, Tora. It is time to get your affairs in order. We are taking your furniture today—"

"We had understood the house would be furnished," Mrs. Hunter said quietly.

"This morning," Andrew continued, "the Alberta mine closed. It was your last chance, Tora. I presume you are letting out your house to these fine people."

Tora sat down abruptly, obviously shocked by the news of the mine. Joseph knew exactly what it meant—the house might not even be enough to cover what she owed.

Andrew turned to the Campbells. "I am afraid that if you wish to lease this house, it will be from the Bank of Montana."

Joseph stepped forward and offered his hand. "Joseph Campbell," he said gently. "But as Mrs. Hunter stated, we understood the house would be furnished. If you take away the furniture, we will not be able to take it."

Andrew considered his words with a nod. "I suppose we could leave it in here for the time being, until we can get everything in order to hold an auction."

"Very well. We should come by to see you at the bank? Assuming, of course, that the house is up to the Campbells' standards," Mrs. Hunter asserted.

"Fine, fine. Tomorrow. Ten o'clock?"

Mrs. Hunter looked at Joseph. He nodded, then shifted uncomfortably, aware of how difficult this must be for Tora. They were talking about her home as if she were already gone.

"Very good. We will get out of your way, then. Good day, Mr. Aston, Miss Anders," Mrs. Hunter said. Joseph and the boys followed her out, but Joseph paused at the door, looking back.

Mary was with Tora, who sat in stunned disbelief. She touched Tora's head as if she were a grieving child, and then knelt before her, taking her hands. "We will take good care of the home, Tora," she said softly. "You have my word on it." She weaved in front of the younger woman, as if trying to gain eye contact. "Sometimes, the very worst thing in life turns out to be the best thing possible. Go with God, child." With that she rose and joined Joseph at the door.

Once outside, she took his arm and said softly, "She is the one, isn't she? The one you were sent to follow."

"How did you know?"

"A woman's intuition. Don't get too near her, Joseph. She is one of those women who can draw you in deeper than a whirlpool before you know it."

"I realize that."

"But there's something more. God is doing something within her. I can feel it."

Mary had an uncanny ability to ascertain such things, and Joseph filed the information away with all he had learned today about Tora Anders. He had a long report to write for Trent Storm tonight, and he had to pack. He was sure that Tora would soon be on the move again, with him along for the ride.

As they strolled to the hotel, the boys ran back to them to inquire what all the fuss was about, then ran ahead again, letting it roll off their shoulders as only children could. Joseph thought about what Mary had said. If God had something in store for Tora, perhaps she would soon be a different woman. Perhaps it was what Trent sensed too, and what made him want to keep an eye on her. With God, all things were possible. If he could move mountains, he could transform Tora Anders.

After a long day's train ride, Tora detrained in Spokane, happy for the sight and sounds of a fresh place, a place not yet entirely closed to her. At least there were a roof and walls on the hotel, which meant someplace for her to sleep for the night. She was down to her last dollar, as incredible as that seemed, unsure where the next would come from. If she could succeed in flattering the other banker in town, and her foreman, she'd be up and running in no time. She simply had to find a means to survive, just until the hotel opened. And then life would return to normal. She'd have her own source of income, a way to pay back Trent Storm the money she had "borrowed," and the cash to buy back her home in Helena.

She left her trunks at the train station, telling the manager she would return for them shortly, and walked the block to her hotel. Unable to believe her eyes, Tora dropped her valise in the middle of the road. Nothing had been accomplished on the shell of her hotel. There were no windows, no interior walls. On the frame of the front door was a simple sign: FORECLOSED.

She had thought the foreclosure would take time—that she had a few months to work things out. So much for the advice of flimflam lawyers. It was clear to her at last. She had been found out in Spokane as certainly as she had been in Helena. This was not her last chance. She was out of chances.

Feeling woozy, she began to reel, the sight before her fading in and out of focus. Carriages drove by, passengers staring at her in consternation. A cowboy walked up to her and said, "Ma'am? Are you all right?"

But all she could say was, "Fine, fine."

She stood there, staring for what seemed like hours, unable to do anything else. Suddenly, a small man was at her elbow, rousting her from her seated position and guiding her to the boardwalk on the far side of the street. "A shock for you, I'd gather, Miss Anders."

Tora looked at him for the first time. "Why, Mr. Campbell. What are you doing here?"

"I have some investments I needed to check on this way." He studied her for a moment. "I take it that building was yours?"

"Once," she muttered.

"Now, I'll not tread warily, Miss Anders. You and I both know you are facing dire circumstances. I insist on looking after you for the evening. I am happily married. This is not some ruse. I do this as a Christian and a gentleman. Please do not confuse the issue."

Tora looked at him, feeling as if she could not focus, let alone take advantage of the man. "Certainly," was all she could murmur.

He took her arm. "This way, Miss Anders. I will see that you have a decent meal, bath, and room for the night. Tomorrow, you are on your own."

Tora awakened late the next morning, feeling as if she had been drugged. It took her several minutes to remember where she was, and what she faced. What came to mind made her want to dive back under the covers. She did so for a bit, groaned, and then threw back the comforter. For better or worse, she had to face this day. She had to find a job, quickly, and the means to purchase food.

It grated on her nerves to remember Mr. Campbell's kindness the day before. In a stupor, she had not been able to do anything but accept his charity. It had felt heavenly, but now she owed him. *At least I know where he lives,* she thought grimly. As soon as she had the funds, she would wire him money to reimburse his expenses.

She quickly dressed and repacked her valise, for the first time remembering her trunks at the train station. Who knew if they still remained? The thought set her heart pounding, and she hurriedly made her way downstairs to the man at the lobby counter. "Pardon me. Can you tell me if you have seen Mr. Campbell this morning? I wish to speak to him."

"He checked out earlier, ma'am," the man said, using *ma'am* as if it were a derogatory word. No doubt he thought something unseemly had gone on between them, since Mr. Campbell had paid for her room and such intimacies as a bath and dinner. The clerk clearly did not recognize her as the Roadhouse Maven.

"I am sorry to hear that," she said graciously, ignoring his rude manner. "I will be checking out today as well. Tell me, I am in search of work. Do you know of anyone who is immediately hiring?"

"What's your experience?"

"Roadhouse work, for the most part. I have done everything from serve food to manage restaurants. I am willing to do whatever's set before me." Tora hoped she sounded dignified, not desperate.

"We're full up here at the restaurant. Only restaurant work around here was going to be…Why, you're the girl, aren't you?" He glanced down at his books. "Sure enough. Tora Anders! I'm sorry, ma'am, but you're out of luck in this town. Nobody's gonna hire the likes of you after what you did to Mr. Storm."

"Well, of all things—"

"Now before you go off in a huff, Mr. Campbell did do one last thing for you. He had your trunks transferred to my storage room. I'd appreciate if you'd get them out of there by day's end."

"I will do my best. It all depends on my finding employment today."

He pursed his lips, obviously considering her prospects. "Fine. Just be aware that if they're not out by the time the stage comes to town, they'll be sitting in the street. I have no room to store the luggage of no-accounts."

"Of all the rude…You haven't seen the last of me, mister. And next time you do, you had better find your manners."

"I'll take my chances," he said drolly as she walked out of the hotel and to the street.

Her situation was utterly humiliating. How could it all have come to this? How could Trent have cast her so far from him? This was more than a lovers' breakup; this was cruel spite. It was one thing to withdraw his company from her, but quite another to take away every shred of her dignity, everything she'd worked so hard for. Someone who loved her could never treat her so foully. Had there ever been a real love between them?

Angry now, Tora began entering every storefront in town, including the saloons. But it was as the hotel clerk had told her: the town was closed to Tora Anders. For the first time, she lamented taking on Trent Storm. And despite everything, she missed him all the more. Should she find her way back to Duluth? Try to talk to him once more? With a dollar in her pocket, how could she even make the trip?

After leaving the mercantile at the center of town, she collapsed on a bench just outside the door. No one was going to hire her. The only people who gave her a second glance were the barkeepers in the saloon, obviously thinking of less virtuous ways to make a dollar. The thought was preposterous. Never would she stoop to such levels!

As if on cue, her stomach rumbled, and she again considered her lack of funds. How was she to survive? Perhaps she should spend her last coins on a wire to Trent! As angry as he might be with her, surely he did not intend to turn her out on the streets…or perhaps he did. The thought made her genuinely sorry for her actions. She stared through a dust cloud kicked up by a passing stage, seeing only Trent's face as he had seen her off on her Montana adventure four years before. What could have changed between them? Why had her move driven him away, rather than straight into her arms as she'd planned?

She shook her head as if to shake out the image, and looked down the street to where the stagecoach had stopped in front of the hotel. True to his word, the hotel clerk had deposited her trunks on the street. "Of all the nerve!" she muttered angrily, rising to have a word with the man. But as she neared, Tora realized she had little to say, and shaky footing on which to stand. He was right; she had no call to assume he could keep her things. They belonged to her, and they were in his way. But how was she supposed to move all of these trunks? And to where?

She sat down dejectedly atop the largest, her head in her hands as she strained to find an answer. But none came, even as the sun set and the long arm of dusk enveloped the town. Fewer people remained on the street, and Tora became desperate. Where could she go? What would happen to her if she stayed out on the sidewalk for the night? Surely the whole town could not be as cruel as that! If only Mr. Campbell had remained!

Seeing no other choice, she approached the clerk again, asking to work for the night in his restaurant in exchange for a meal and a bed. He threatened to throw her out. With as much dignity as she could find, she walked out, head high, even as her heart sank to her toes.

Never in her life had she felt so lost, so afraid.

Tora vaguely heard the sound of creaking leather. Horror overtook her. Weak from hunger and exhaustion, she had fallen asleep among her baggage! Grimly, she opened her eyes to see a horse, and beyond him, a middle-aged man in a wagon who had paused beside her, peering at her through the darkness as if she were a vision. "Ma'am?" he tried tentatively. "You needin' some help?"

Tora fluttered her eyelashes, wondering at the proper response. At last! Someone who did not know her or of her reputation! "Oh yes, sir. I am afraid I've just arrived in town in search of work, and cannot find a soul who will consider employing me."

The man took off his hat and scratched his head. "Now that's funny. Thought there was more work in this town than there was workers. What kind of job are you seeking?"

"Well, most of my experience has been in running restaurants, but I am a good cook, and I have taken care of children in the past."

"Sound educated," he said softly, studying her eyes. His own were weary, sad.

"Quite a few years in Norway," she said, lifting her chin. "I learned English before I arrived in America, and tend to think I've done a good job in perfecting it."

"Know your numbers?"

"Very well."

He was silent, continuing to stare at her as if he could discern what she might not be telling him. It was as if she could hear his questions out loud. After all, if there were plenty of jobs in town, why had she not found a position? And what kind of woman took off to parts unknown without enough money to stay in a hotel until she was safely employed? Tora willed herself not to shift her position but rather to return his gaze as if unafraid that he, too, might leave her there on the street.

"Name's Owen Crosby," he said carefully. "You are…?"

"Tora Anders," she said without thinking, then held her breath to see if the name meant anything to the man.

"Got a spread about five miles from here. Got a schoolhouse in need of a schoolmarm immediately. Want to give it a try?"

A teacher? He wanted her to teach a bunch of children? "Oh, Mr. Crosby, I'm afraid I have no teaching experience."

"There's a shanty attached to the schoolhouse that's all your own. The missus could give you a hot meal tonight."

"I'll try it," she said a second later, unable to pass up the chance at a warm supper and a decent bed for the night. It wouldn't hurt to give it a try for a few days, and it would buy her time to decide on her next step. *Forward,* she told herself, *no longer backward.* She would show them, she coached herself with renewed vigor. They would all see who would win when it came down between Trent Storm and Tora Anders! "Now, Mr. Crosby, if you would be so kind as to help me with my luggage…"

Once they were loaded up, Mr. Crosby stopped at the mercantile, placing the merchandise he purchased in the back beside her trunks. As they drove off, Tora looked again at the window. For she was certain that she had glimpsed a man who looked exactly like Mr. Campbell. But then, she was so hungry, she supposed she could be hallucinating by now.

e i g h t

Early September 1886

lsa sat at the edge of her bed as Riley saw the *Eagle* to port. Kristian sat by her side, silent, as if aware of her anguish. For weeks she had longed to disembark, to get off this ship of memories and to her home. But now, with bags packed, the voyage over, she was reluctant to leave the last place she had shared with Peder and return to a home of other memories. A knock sounded at her door. "Enter," she said.

"Mrs. Ramstad," Riley said, hat in hand. He was a silhouette against the bright sunlight of one of Seattle's brilliant early fall days. "The ship's in, and I'm ready to see to her needs. I thought you and Kristian might like to take the first skiff to shore."

"Indeed," she said, standing at last. She turned around to glance at the room, the last room she would ever share with her husband. "You will see to our things?"

"We'll get 'em delivered to the house," he said gently. "You want me to clean out the cap'n's belongings as well?"

"Do whatever you think necessary, Riley." She moved forward, suddenly conscious of the tears ready to come. It had been weeks since she had cried, but clearly, her mourning had just begun. For to have Riley clear out Peder's things meant that another would captain his ship, another would inhabit their cabin.

What had become a way of life for Elsa was suddenly, irrevocably over.

"Come along, Kristian," she said, taking his small hand in hers. They walked out, and Elsa was surprised to see the entire crew on deck, hats in hands, waiting to see them off.

Finch stepped forward. "On behalf of myself and the crew, ma'am," he said, "we wanted you to know that we thought the cap'n a fine man."

Elsa nodded.

"Finer cap'n I've yet to see," called one from the back.

"Finer cap'n than we'll ever see," said another.

Elsa swallowed hard and tried to smile—it felt false on her face, and she wondered if it was obvious to them as well. "Thank you, men. Thank you for serving the *Eagle,* my husband, and me so well. God be with all of you."

"And you!" said several.

She turned and followed Kristian over the side and into the skiff. Never did she look back.

Dear Mrs. Hodge, their Seattle housekeeper, met them with open arms and the caring ministrations of a mother hen. Elsa did not know who had informed the short, stout woman of Peder's death, but as with many things, she seemed to have a sixth sense about how to remedy a situation. Before Elsa knew what was happening, she had a long, hot bath in her porcelain tub and, like a child, was put to bed by six. Mrs. Hodge had her niece, who was perhaps a year older than Kristian, over to play. She could hear them giggling outside her door, running through the halls, and it brought a measure of comfort to her. How long had it been since she had heard Kristian laugh? She couldn't remember.

Mrs. Hodge knocked and entered her room, carrying a tray of fruit, fresh bread, and hot tea. "It would do ya some good to eat, child," she said. Never had she referred to Elsa as "Mrs. Ramstad" or with the deferential tone that many demanded of their servants. But Elsa liked that. Mrs. Hodge was a good foot shorter than she, and rounder as well. But she was kind and honest and took excellent care of their home while they were away, and of them when they returned.

"Thank you, Mrs. Hodge. I have been so tired."

"Sure, sure. You deserve a good rest after what you've been through. But not for long," she said, her voice raised in warning. "Too much rest leads to the darkness. At some point you'll need to move, Elsa. Up and out and toward the future. You've had a hard blow, perhaps the hardest of your life. But remember that the Lord walks beside you."

Elsa nodded, feeling nothing of his presence but too weary to argue.

"Now eat some good, fresh food, drink your tea, and rest. Tomorrow is a new day."

"Thank you," she managed to murmur. But Mrs. Hodge was already gone. Elsa forced herself to nibble on the fresh peach, an uncommon delicacy, and the soft wheat bread that was still warm. It all tasted bland in her mouth. Would all of life taste bland to her forevermore? She hoped not. Taking a sip of tea, she nestled under the down comforter, then reached out to Peder's pillow, so perfectly puffed up, untouched. Even the sight of it dismayed her.

Elsa rolled on her back and looked past the four-poster to the plastered ceiling. "Dear God," she said, "how could I have fallen so deep? How could Peder leave?" Her questions went on and on, and she heard no answer in response to her railings. Then she fell asleep with yet another question on her lips: "How could you have let it happen?"

After two days of sleeping and resting in bed, she made herself rise, dress, and assess what needed to be done. Feeling as if she moved with shoes of lead, Elsa did the perfunctory tasks before her. She wrote to her mother, and then to Peder's parents in Bergen, Norway, weeping over her words. What sorrow they would suffer! Only they would come close to her own grief.

She looked once more at the painting of Peder and Kristian in their samurai costumes, touching Peder's image as if she were touching the man one final time. Elsa hated to let it go—to send it to the Ramstads as planned—but she also knew it would help assuage the pain of her news. Peder's parents would treasure the painting. Resolute, she wrapped it in brown paper and attached her letter, planning to have it boxed and sent on the next ship to Norway. Next she wrote to Kristoffer in Camden, explaining what had transpired and informing him that she was giving him a raise and a promotion. He was the official manager of their shipyard in Camden-by-the-Sea. After that, she wrote to her editor at the *Times,* requesting a hiatus during her time of mourning and that they put a brief notice in the paper.

Riley arrived as she finished her note. "You're looking better, ma'am," he ventured.

"Thank you, Riley. Please, sit down. What news have you?"

Smelling of the sea and out-of-doors, he took a seat in the armchair beside hers. It made Elsa aware of how pale she must look after being inside since arriving home. "The *Eagle* is nearly unloaded. I've arranged for all the goods to be sold a' market tomorrow."

"And then?"

He grimaced and ducked his head. "Then I wait to hear from you, ma'am, on what you're wantin' us to do."

Elsa sat back in her chair and sighed. "You, of course, Riley, are my choice for captain. Please obtain a load of lumber from our yard in Seaport and make a run to the East Coast with it. Check with our sources to see where you can get the best dollar for the load. Then you and Kristoffer decide on what to do next. I trust you both."

"Yes, ma'am." She could see by his eyes that he was glad for the promotion, but sorry for the means by which he'd received it. "If you don't mind, ma'am, I'd like t' stay for the funeral."

"Ah yes, the funeral." She dimly remembered the short, quiet service they'd held aboard ship. Then she recalled how she'd stood at the stern of the ship for days, looking, watching, waiting, hoping that somehow Peder would miraculously appear swimming behind them. She could not even remember what had been said or by whom at that seaside service. She hoped to have something more befitting of the man here in town—a service at church and a burial in the cemetery, despite the empty coffin. Elsa knew that Peder would have wanted a burial at sea, but *she* needed a place to go, to mourn, to remember. She needed a chance to honor her husband.

"It will be the day after tomorrow. Please, invite any of the crew who wish to attend too—and then push off for the East the day after."

Riley nodded, hesitating as if something was on his mind. "And you? What will you do?"

Elsa gave him a soft, small smile. "I will stay here for a while with Kristian. We need some time to adjust. Perhaps I'll return to the sea someday. Just not yet."

"You're welcome anytime on my ship."

"No, Riley, she's your ship. I'll captain my own should I return."

Riley's eyebrows shot up in surprise, but he said nothing. "Can I do anythin' else for you, Elsa? Do you need anythin'?"

Elsa reached over and took his hand. "Thank you, Riley. You have already done so much. I appreciate all that you do for me and Ramstad Yard. Just keep on as you have and I will be content."

He studied her for a second, his eyes moist. "Well, you just let me know, ma'am." He rose to leave, clearly uncomfortable with the intensity of the moment.

"I will. Good-bye, Riley," she said, feeling as if they were parting for a long while. *Yet another good-bye,* she thought wearily.

"Ma'am," he said with a nod, and left.

Elsa rose and walked to her desk. Quickly, she wrote out notes to the pastor in town, a basic obituary for the newspaper, and a brief correspondence to the principal people in Seattle who had known, respected, and liked Peder. They had made few friends here, having been away much more than at home, but many in the shipping community would wish to honor Peder as she did. She did not want anyone who wished to attend to miss it in the paper, although it wasn't likely. Even in a city the size of Seattle, word still spread fast.

She rose to take the stack of letters to Mrs. Hodge to deliver to the post office when an image of Karl took hold. He would want to know. Although Peder had never forgiven him, and Karl had never attempted to get in touch with them again, Elsa knew he would want to know about the death of his dearest friend. It made her sorrow that their friendship had never regained its foothold, and that she had been the cause. She sat down again, drew out a fresh sheet of stationery and dipped her pen in the ink.

> *10 September 1886*
> *Dear Karl,*
>
> *It is with a sorrowful heart that I inform you that my husband, and your friend, Peder, has died. On this last voyage, he again took ill with malaria, and during a storm, fell overboard. My sole comfort is that he was as ever a friend to Jesus, and is walking by his side right now. But mostly, I feel utterly lost in the midst of my grief. Please pray for me. Although you and Peder never rejoined as friends, take comfort in the fact that he always believed you were as close as a brother.*
>
> > *Always,*
> > *Elsa*

She hesitated, wondering where to send it. The last letter from him had been Saint Paul, but she had no record of his address. Shrugging her shoulders, she simply wrote "Saint Paul, Minnesota," and hoped it would get to its destination along with the rest of her mail.

Mrs. Hodge appeared at the door. "You care for some noon dinner?"

"A light snack, perhaps," Elsa said vaguely. "But first, could you see to this correspondence?"

Mrs. Hodge took the stack from her and peered at the addresses. "Certainly. I'll send my young nephew after it." As the eldest of ten children, Mrs. Hodge seemed to have an endless supply of nieces and nephews who were always at her beck and call. Peder had always said that they had not hired one woman; they had hired a family.

Elsa nodded. "Good."

"Elsa, Kristian has had a fine mornin' with my niece, but I'm thinkin' he needs some time with you. Are you ready to go outside? A walk might do you both some good. It's so glorious today! Soon the rain will be comin'."

"Oh, I have so much to do. The funeral to plan—"

"A walk would do you both good," she repeated. Although only fifteen years Elsa's senior, the woman talked to her as a mother to her child. It soothed Elsa's aching heart.

Elsa sighed. "Very well. Directly after lunch. Can we speak about the funeral plans now?"

"Yes, yes, let me just go tell the boy. He'll be so pleased."

As with so many things, Mrs. Hodge was right. Kristian eagerly took her hand as Elsa forced herself out the front door on Third Avenue. They lived in a fine section of town—just down the street from Sara and Henry Yesler's nearly completed, forty-room mansion—in a house for which Peder had proudly paid cash. Formerly owned by a mining millionaire, their two-story home was a classic, yet understated, Queen Anne with none of the showiness that some of Seattle's founders, like the Yeslers, had succumbed to. It fit Elsa perfectly, and she had been as excited as Peder to move in.

Just down the street was a city park, and Kristian pulled her hand, eager to get there and play on the seesaw or swings. He seemed thrilled that Elsa was moving, and willing to spend some time with him. A stab of guilt shot through her, and Elsa resolved to spend more time with her son, to force herself to be "alive," if only to him. Her grieving could take place at other times. Her son, and the child within her, needed her to take care of herself and give them all she could.

As they walked, they passed a cemetery, present in the city since its birth more than thirty years before. Many of the headstones had moss growing on them, and the lettering was difficult to read on others. Kristian pulled her hand to a stop and stared through the iron fence. "Bobby Francis says that Papa's name will be on one of those things," he said, pointing at the headstones, then looking up to Elsa as if asking her to deny it.

Elsa swallowed hard. She nodded once, staring out at the hundreds of headstones, testimonies to hundreds more who had grieved as she did—there was odd comfort in the fact. "Yes, Kristian. We are going to mark a grave with a headstone that would make your papa proud. We need a place to remember him, to honor him."

"Because he disappeared in the sea?"

Elsa paused, then said, "Yes. We have no body to hug one last time. We can't kiss him once more. But we can make a place that is his alone. A place where we can go and remember how special he was to us." She knew her words sounded mechanical, forced. But inside she felt as dead as Peder. She hoped her words would encourage her son, at least.

"What's it gonna look like?"

"The headstone?"

"Yes."

"I thought we'd put an anchor on it. Because he loved the sea. But he also loved Christ." She knelt down beside Kristian and spoke in his ear. "God is our anchor in the severest storms, Kristian. He keeps us safe. Always remember that. It would make your father proud."

Kristian nodded soberly. "Can we go to the park now?"

"Yes," Elsa said, raising her voice to make it sound lighter. "Let's go swing."

The funeral came and went as Elsa had planned it. She did not cry during the whole ordeal, and the ceremony itself brought little of the comfort she had hoped for. In retrospect, she thought the most crucial moment was when they shoveled dirt onto his empty casket. Inside her, she felt a door close at last. It was as if she finally believed it was real. Now she could stop imagining Peder miraculously pulled from the water by another ship; perhaps her dreams of him swimming to shore would end as well. She was at the edge of saying good-bye.

She could not do it during the service, nor at the house during the reception, nor in the receiving line as people left, murmuring their condolences. It was only that night, when she could not sleep, that she rose, dressed, lit a lantern in the downstairs hall, and made her way to the cemetery. The streets were ghostly in their quiet, the houses dark, their inhabitants long asleep. Yet Elsa felt no fear. She moved toward the cemetery as if she were meeting Peder again.

She opened the creaking iron gate and made her way to the freshly covered grave, visible from the street. In her hand she carried a single marigold, the only flowers left in the garden. Silently, she approached the grave, remembering a hundred moments when she had seen Peder at night. Working on the charts and the logbooks at his desk. Sipping tea and reading a book by lamplight in the sitting room so she and Kristian might sleep. Standing at the wheel of his ship, a rising moon on the sea beyond him, his hair waving in the breeze. How happy he had been! It brought a smile—the first sincere smile she could remember since his death—to her face. And tears.

Elsa knelt by his grave, staring at the anchor, freshly cut into the white granite. Beneath it were the words: PEDER LEIF RAMSTAD; APRIL 5, 1856–AUGUST 10, 1886; BELOVED FRIEND, FATHER, HUSBAND. She traced the words, feeling the rough cut on her fingertips and she remembered tracing his jawline as he slept, his beard's growth scratchy as well. She would never love another as she had loved Peder Ramstad. Love was over for her. She wiped her tears from her cheek and smiled at the stone, visualizing his face once more.

"I loved you, Peder. With all of my heart. You have taken a piece of me with you. But I would gladly trade it again for the time I spent with you." Sobs robbed her of speech for several minutes, until she could once again sigh, wipe her tears, and smile bravely at the stone. "Thank you, Father, for the time I had with this man. Help me to dwell on those happy memories rather than the grief I feel inside me now."

For the first time in a long while, Elsa felt a measure of comfort from her Lord. "Thank you," she whispered.

She stood, brushed the dirt from her skirts, and watched as it fell to the earth at her feet. "Good-bye, my love. I will always, always treasure the life I shared with you." Elsa wiped one last tear from her eye, picked up the lantern, and turned to go. She looked to the north as she departed the cemetery, and laughed at herself as she found the hope in her heart that she might see the northern lights. The visual reminder of the love God, her father, and Peder had had for her would have helped. But the sky was dark except for a few stars.

Still, she felt better than she had in days as she walked home, and she began to think about her future. What would she do with herself for the coming months? What would be constructive? Mrs. Hodge was right, there was a time to mourn, and a time to move forward. What would Peder have had her do? An image of Kaatje came to mind, and Elsa smiled. If only she and the girls had been able to come to the city! It would have helped so much to have her near.

Then an idea struck Elsa. She hadn't seen her dear friend in over a year, what with all their traveling. And the Skagit Valley was only a five-hour train ride away! She would pack up Kristian and go to her friend. Perhaps she could help bring in the harvest. Some good hard work would feel delightful, and she needed to see Kaatje and the other Bergensers. It would be the next best thing to going home.

She thought about wiring Kaatje with news of Peder's death, and of her intent to come for a visit. But then she thought better of it. No, it would be much better to surprise her dear old friend. And it would give Kaatje no chance to dissuade Elsa from the trip. What a delight it would be to see Kaatje's face light up in a smile, to feel her embrace once more! Elsa smiled and wiped her tears. She would go, just as soon as she could settle her affairs in Seattle.

nine

Late September 1886

Kaatje ignored her aching back and continued her work of cutting and shocking grain. She looked up over the field as she went on, again calculating how much more time it would take to complete her fields. As usual, the Bergensers were there en masse. Even Karl Martensen had come for the day.

Kaatje guiltily accepted their help, knowing that even though she would go to their farms to assist in the harvest, no woman could do the amount of work a man could. *Today, Alaska does not sound bad at all,* she thought ruefully.

Karl was next to her, securing a shock. "You never did tell me what you did after you left the Dakota Territory. The locusts took your crops; how did you all find the funds to travel west again?"

"Buffalo bones. Pastor Lien gathered us together, shook some sense into us, and set us about gathering. The railroads were paying nine dollars a ton; they sent them east to be made into fertilizer. We took a good thirty wagonloads to Bismarck, and somehow found our way out here. I think Pastor threatened the good train conductor with heavenly wrath if he did not let us on at a discounted rate."

Karl laughed, a good, hearty male laugh that made Kaatje stop for a moment. Soren used to laugh just like that—from the belly. She

113

shook off the memory. "So the poor bison who died on the range helped us Bergensers move farther along their old tracks."

Karl nodded. "Haven't seen more than a few bison at a time in years." He went on working, then said, "It was good you left when you did. The next year, the Dakota Territory saw some terrible flooding. Why, I saw a steamboat up on Third Street in Grand Forks!"

"You're joking!" she said, amazed at the image.

"No. Most of the Red River Valley was underwater. Snow melted too fast."

"We were farther away than that. Our land was so dry it probably has never seen a flood."

"Maybe. I still think this is good land, better land."

Kaatje smiled and nodded. "Me too. God has been gracious."

"And look at your crop! Surely enough to sustain you and the girls for another year!"

"Yes, and then some. It is good to have a little extra. I'm thinking that I had better have some work done on the barn or it's going to collapse on poor Hans and Nels."

"I've been thinking about that myself," Karl said, leaning his forearm on the top of his rake. "My company is almost done surveying, and I think our feeder railroad will come very near your land. It will be good for you during harvest, as well as your neighbors; you'll be able to load up your harvest right onto a railroad car and easily get top dollar. But we'll need some storage space for repair materials and the like out this way. Would you consider renting us a corner of a barn if we built you a new, bigger building?"

Kaatje gasped. "A bigger barn?" Already this summer had brought them two chickens as well as a hog that had *appeared* on the road. None of her neighbors had claimed it, so it was hers. They were desperate for space! A new barn would be a godsend. "Yes, yes. That would be wonderful. And you wouldn't have to rent the space. I'd give it to you, Karl, in exchange for the building itself." She sobered.

"But I'd want to own the building free and clear. No debts to your company?"

"No debts," Karl said, shaking his head as he continued gathering. "We'll write it out so it's clear."

"Fine!" Kaatje said, thrilled at this new turn. A good crop and a new barn! Perhaps she could use the surplus from this crop to improve their house in some way. Or maybe she could squirrel the cash away with the other meager dollars she'd managed to save, just in case…Just in case God didn't stop nudging her north.

For now, it was enough to save it.

Karl smiled to himself as Kaatje hummed beside him. His idea, in his opinion expertly planted, had obviously made her happy. She was clearly ecstatic, suddenly energized in her work. And if he planned it right, he could send out enough lumber and nails to build the barn, while conveniently overestimating enough to build Kaatje and the girls another room on their house. Kaatje deserved a room of her own. She had been through enough!

Karl was glad for her—and for himself. Business was rolling right along. Trent Storm had responded favorably to the plan he and Brad had submitted by wire to expand the freight service in the Skagit Valley, recognizing as he had the great potential of the land. The Bergensers, and others who had settled here, were only just beginning to tap into the wealth of this fertile valley. With better freight service, they could do perhaps twice what they were doing now, by moving the first crop faster and planting the second right away.

He wanted to rub his hands together, he was so excited. For the first time in years, he was doing something for others as much as for himself. And it felt good.

Ever since leaving John Hall's employ—and his former fiancée Alicia—Karl had felt driven to prove himself along the northern Pacific. At first, he wanted to show Hall that he could do business in an aboveboard manner, succeed as an honest businessman. Later he wanted the thrill of success to bolster his waning confidence.

While he had not run across Hall again in the succeeding years, he followed the man's triumphs and tragedies in the paper. Never would he amass the wealth his former employer had, but never would he be caught in the web they had tried to spin around him. Karl felt glad that he was out, yet he still felt largely empty. What was life all about? He had funds that could build Kaatje a huge mansion and increase her property tenfold, without even feeling the loss of it himself.

But since he had arrived in the Skagit Valley, he was acutely aware that it was not enough. Helping Kaatje like this was a step in the right direction; he knew it to be so. And Kaatje's suggestion that he go to Peder and Elsa and ask their forgiveness also felt right. He needed to clear the air, to right the wrongs of his past as best he could and get on with life. But he needed, more than anything, to be right with God. With each passing day here, he grew more sure that it was the underlying root of his depression, the cause of his listlessness and dissatisfaction no matter how much he achieved.

When Bradford Bresley and Trent Storm had arrived in Seattle last month, Karl had bared his soul. There were few men in his life with whom Karl could have taken such a risk. He decided it was God's way of helping him that two such men were present when he most needed them. He confessed his lack of peace and sense of aimlessness in his work. He even went so far as to tell them that he had lost touch with his Creator and felt utterly hopeless. They did not make him feel emasculated or lesser for his confession; Trent had even seemed to identify with his quandary. Karl had determined that it was the distance he felt from his Savior and his unrestored relationship with Peder that needed resolution.

He needed time away from work, and the pressures of business—though he was still working extra hours to find some way to get the Bergensers their railroad line. But that kind of work—more concerned with others than his own gain—did not drain his energies as his regular endeavors did. He needed space. He did not know where he would go or how he would go about the process, but it had to begin.

Brad, as ever, made light of Karl's serious intent, but assured his friend that the business would still be there when he returned, although ribbing him that Bradford Bresley would just be that much farther ahead. As if it mattered, Karl mused. There came a time when a man had all he would need for a great while. Then it was time to assess what really mattered. Perhaps that was why he had received such an understanding ear from Trent. The man had been in his shoes—perhaps had remained there for some time.

"Are you here to work, Martensen, or daydream?" boomed Einar, suddenly by his side. How long had he stood still, staring off into the distance? He could feel the heat rise on his neck.

"Well, you know, I've become somewhat a man of leisure lately. It's hard on an old man's back to do this work!" he said.

"Get this old man a cup of water and a new rake! He needs blisters on his hands again to remind him what a man's made of!"

"And a woman? What is a woman with blistered hands?" Kaatje asked, hands on hips, a smile on her lips.

"A queen!" Einar said, setting the others in the field laughing.

"And the woman who brings you water and cooks dinner for your hungry stomach?" Nora asked, pretending to be even more indignant than Kaatje.

"Empress!" Einar said quickly, kneeling at her feet. The men about them laughed harder than before and Karl joined them. How good it was to be with his countrymen! His family! Thoughts of his mother and father in Norway sobered him. His dear mother had passed away this last year of consumption, and his father was still unwilling to speak to him. It had been Gratia Anders who had notified Karl of his mother's death. His father had sent him away as a hypocrite, a charge he had largely been living up to these last six years, and which had kept him away. Where was his faith? Where was the faith that had come to him as he traveled with Peder, the faith that had ignited his heart with passion and belief? What had become of the man he had wanted to be?

It was time. It was time to face the sins of his past and move forward as a man serving Christ. And, he resolved, it would all begin today.

Elsa drove down the road east of town, as the stable master had directed. It felt good to be in the country, healing in a way, so opposite was it of city and sea. She smiled again to herself, nudging Kristian on the seat beside her in anticipation of seeing Kaatje again. It had been a year! A year! Having only just settled in Seattle, she had not had time to make the excursion north more than once. But she planned on staying in the Northwest for the winter; she and Kaatje would have plenty of time to catch up, to reconnect as the sisters they were born to be.

Her thoughts turned to her niece. What would Jessie look like by now? She would be five years of age, just a year older than Kristian. Did she look more like Tora? Or Soren? Or had the love of Kaatje so pervaded the child that physical resemblances would not matter? Elsa shook her head. Never had she understood Kaatje's graciousness in accepting her husband's misbegotten child from his lover's hands. Truly, her friend was a greater woman than she. Over the years, she had sent money to Kaatje to help buy Jessie clothing and food, but she had spent little time with her own flesh and blood. A stab of guilt shot through her.

"Look, Mama!" Kristian said excitedly. "A party!"

Elsa frowned as she noticed the many wagons beside what she assumed was Kaatje's house. In the warm light of dusk, the gathering seemed cozy, welcoming, festive. What could be going on? As they turned the corner, she saw the fields of cut and shocked grain standing to dry. It was harvest! She had missed it! And the group of neighbors were celebrating, no doubt eating a huge dinner after working so hard all day. Elsa faltered for the first time since leaving Seattle. What would it be like to enter such a gathering of neighbors? She felt like an interloper, an intruder.

There was no going back. A small girl spotted them on the road and went to the makeshift tables yelling, "Mother! Mother! Someone's here!" Then a dog ran out to greet them, barking incessantly.

A woman rose as they drew nearer, wiping her hands on an apron. Elsa could not see her face, but she recognized her stance, her way of moving. It was Kaatje. "Kaatje!" she yelled, suddenly unable to contain herself, her hesitation immediately forgotten. "Kaatje!" She pulled the horse to a halt and leaped down to the ground, trying not to run to her old friend, unable to do anything short of it.

Kaatje gasped, dumbstruck and standing still as if Elsa were an apparition. Then she opened her arms and laughed as Elsa reached her, pulling her into an embrace. "Elsa! Elsa!" she laughed. Kaatje pulled away to stare at her. "What are you doing here? Why didn't you send word?"

Elsa laughed and stared back at her. How she had changed! The year had been hard on her friend; she could see it around her eyes, her mouth. But to Elsa, there was not a more beautiful sight in the world.

Kaatje's smile faded as she stared down at Elsa's dress. "You're in black," she said softly. "What has happened?"

Abruptly, Elsa felt her smile fall too. For a moment, for one glorious moment, she had forgotten. Eager faces, dear old Bergenser faces, surrounded her in expectation. One by one, they each quieted, and their apprehension visibly grew too. Elsa swallowed hard and tried a brave smile. "First of all, this is my son, Kristian. Perhaps he could go and play with the children?"

Nora stepped forward and embraced Elsa quickly, looking into her eyes as if she understood. "Jessie, why don't you go and show Kristian and the others your new hog? Like a gift from heaven he was, showing up on the road like that." Eagerly, the children dispersed, off to the barn. *Jessie*, Elsa repeated her name in her head, following the girl with her eyes. *Jessie, my niece.*

Kaatje took her hands. "Would you like to sit down?"

Elsa nodded. "In a moment. First, you all should know how glad I am to see you. It's like being home!" Her eyes traveled around the group, noticing that nearly all of them were there, with a few men lingering back at the table. These were people who had celebrated with her and Peder in Bergen after their wedding; she supposed it was appropriate to grieve with them as well.

"I am afraid I have sad news. Terrible...terrible news. My Peder died, almost two months past." The women gasped and the men murmured, frowns upon all their faces. "We were at sea, in a storm, when he fell overboard. There was nothing—" Her voice cracked, keeping her from saying more. Surrounded by such love, such dear old friends, her grief bubbled to the surface once more.

"Come," Kaatje said, pulling her toward the small cabin. "Come inside, Elsa. You're with family now. We'll take care of you."

Karl walked around the corner of the house, pretending to stroll to the outhouse, unable to quite believe that Elsa was here. Since most of the people had gathered around her, few were left to notice his departure. He leaned against the side of the house and rubbed his face hard with shaking hands. She was here on the same day as his recommitment!

He knelt on the ground before him, staring up at the sky. Was this his first test? To be sure that he was ready to tread more holy ground? Behind him, through the thin walls, he heard a group enter the house. Slowly, he stood, willing himself to look through the window. Carefully, he edged nearer to stare inside. She was even more lovely than he remembered. But why was she in mourning black? Sorrow and weariness ringed her eyes with purple, but she was beautiful. Standing there, staring at her, he forced himself to search his heart. It pounded as he thought hard about Elsa, about what she had once meant to him, about what he had allowed himself to do.

After several long minutes, watching her as she spoke to the crowd about her, his heart slowed. No, this time it was different. There was something different now. What he felt were the stirrings of a gladness at seeing a long-lost friend, the same kinship he had felt with Kaatje. Had his lustful, dangerous desires at last abated? He found himself smiling, and ducked away from the window. It would not do to be caught, gazing into the window, staring at his friend's wife rather than joining the others inside.

"Thank you, Jesus," he whispered. How long had he prayed for such a relief to his wild dreams and desires? "Thank you, Father. Help this to be the way, for me to continue feeling this way." Braver by the minute, Karl rounded the corner to face Elsa in person. When some of their friends had departed and it was quieter, he took several more steps, considering what he would say, how he would say it. Then he wondered briefly where Peder was. Why wasn't he here with her?

He almost ran into Pastor Lien, out to fetch a pail of fresh water. The man was ghastly gray. "Pastor!" Karl exclaimed. "Here, let me help you."

Pastor Lien quietly handed him the tin pail, staring off at the last vestiges of sunset.

"What is wrong? Are you all right?"

Konur looked at him strangely. "You did not hear?"

"Hear what?"

"Elsa Ramstad arrived—"

"I know. I just saw her," Karl interrupted, unable to curb his sudden fear. "What? What is it?"

Konur gripped his shoulder. "It's Peder, man. Peder died two months past."

Karl dropped the pail and dropped to his knees beside it. Feeling as if Konur had punched him in the gut, he fought for breath. He couldn't believe it. Peder was dead. Peder was gone. There would be no forgiveness, no new phase of their lost friendship. It was all irrevocably over, and Karl struggled for comprehension, one thought repeating itself over and over in his head—*Peder is dead. Peder is dead. Peder is dead.*

section two

All Who Are Thirsty

t e n

Late September 1886

When the sad-eyed Owen Crosby called Tora's new home a "shanty," he had been generous. In Tora's estimation, it was little more than a lean-to, with cracks between the boards and a dirt floor. The only amenities were a clean straw tick and a small iron woodstove. It was little wonder that these people had trouble keeping a schoolteacher, Tora thought, since more snow would slip through the walls than stay out come winter. Hopefully October would not hold an early snowfall.

She had little time or energy to consider much else before hauling out a comforter and falling into a blissful sleep on the straw tick. Her belongings were neatly stacked against the south wall, taking up roughly half of the room. But Tora did not care. She had a roof over her head, food in her stomach, and tomorrow she would face what was to come. For now she was exhausted, weary from head to toe, and for the first time in as long as she could remember, Tora fell asleep in her bed fully dressed.

"Teacher," came a dreamy voice as Tora noticed a nip in the air for the first time since last night. "Teacher! Wake up!"

Groaning and a bit disoriented, Tora rubbed her eyes and sat up.

Before her were two girls, about six and eight years old, she guessed. She looked around the dreary shack, even more depressing by daylight. Could this be real? Could she have fallen so far as *this* in a few short weeks? *At least I have a home,* she chided herself, remembering her fear last night of sleeping in the streets as darkness fell on the town. *Now I have a job to do.*

"Teacher, the others will be here any minute!" said the eldest. Tora noted that both had neatly plaited, blond braids, reminding her of her sisters when they were young.

"All right. Give me a moment to get my bearings. I've only just arrived. You," she addressed the six-year-old. "I assume we have a water pump somewhere on the premises?"

She nodded.

"Good. Please go fill up my pail." The girl set to her task immediately, and Tora pressed back a small smile. Perhaps this wouldn't be the worst job in the world. The little urchins would at least do as she bid. Tora looked at the girl's older sister. "You have been a student here for a while, I take it?"

"Whenever there's a teacher."

"Good. You get the others to go inside the schoolhouse and write out their numbers and letters. It will be a start. Get an older boy—" She paused to squint at the girl until she nodded that yes, there was indeed an older boy. "Good, get him to build up a fire in the woodstove and warm up the room."

"Yes, ma'am."

"What is your name?"

"Fiona O'Meara, ma'am."

"Very well, Fiona O'Meara. Thank you."

She was off like a shot just as her sister entered with the pail of water. "Thank you," Tora said. "What's your name?"

"Gemma O'Meara."

"Good. I will see you inside the school, Gemma. I just need a moment to collect myself and freshen up."

With a nod, the younger girl left the shanty too. Tora shivered. Goodness, it was cold! She could see her breath! Grimacing, she cupped hands to the pail and splashed her face. It was freezing, but invigorating. Like her reflection in the pail as the water calmed, Tora's immediate future became clear to her. *I am a schoolteacher,* she repeated silently, trying to make it seem more real. *I am a schoolteacher.* Mrs. Segerstad in Bergen would have laughed herself silly over such a thought. Although bright, Tora had never been one to apply herself to her schooling. It was a daily battle. And here she was, a teacher!

She dried her skin with the edge of her skirt and rose to try and find another dress that might be suitable. After digging through several trunks, Tora realized that anything she had was too fancy for a schoolmarm. What would the mothers say if they saw her in Parisian-designed gowns?

Sighing, she turned back to one of her least favorite dresses, examined it with a critical eye, then proceeded to rip the ruffle off at the waist. It left a few hanging threads, but Tora decided that would be okay. Anyone who saw her would assume it was a cast-off from elsewhere, one donated to the poor schoolmarm. After today, Tora would make further alterations to her other dresses to make them suitable. But for now, she would only face today.

In minutes she was dressed. She was about to leave for the schoolroom when she spied a basket by the door, covered with a cloth. Peeking in, she saw three fresh rolls, obviously brought by the girls. For the first time, she noticed her rumbling stomach, and ate one as she left her room, and another on the way around to the schoolhouse door. Swallowing the last bit, and taking a deep breath for courage, she entered the schoolroom. About ten feet by eighteen, the house was built of clear pine boards, and held sixteen small desks. *More than most country schools,* she thought. There were a pair of four-paned windows on either wall, with a podium and desk at the front of the room, built up on a slightly raised platform. In one corner was a map of the United States, a bit outdated, she noted. In the other was a chalkboard.

Tora walked briskly to the front of the class, pasting on a smile and looking at each of the children. About twelve of the desks were filled, mostly with very young children. In the last row sat two boys of about fifteen years of age. They sat up straight when she turned to face them. "That's the prettiest schoolmarm I ever laid eyes on," one of the fifteen-year-olds said to the other, looking at her boldly. Tora ignored him, continuing to peruse the rest of the class.

Nine girls and five boys, she counted. One by one she took stock of what age she guessed each to be, and their demeanor. She felt overwhelmed—what did she know about dealing with children? But, she decided, they were simply small people, meant to be dealt with like small adults.

"I am Miss Anders," she announced lightly, still taking stock. "I am your new teacher." There was a redheaded boy of about ten, a brunette girl of about seven, and next to her, another brunette of about five or six. Tora's eyes rested on hers. With hair that gently curled to her shoulders, and dark summer-blue eyes that reminded her of…Tora stifled a gasp. Why, the girl was the spitting image of Soren! Of herself!

She sat down abruptly on the edge of her desk. Was this…was this Jessica? She could feel the blood drain from her face.

Swallowing hard and looking away from the girl, Tora fought to find her voice. "I would like you each to tell me your name, age, and how much you can do numbers, read, and write." Tora worked her way around to the other side of the desk on shaky legs. She sat down hard, trying to appear as if she were listening, all the while waiting for the children to be done and for the girl that looked like Jessica to speak. At last, her turn arrived.

She stood, and Tora noted her slender frame, yet tall height. Both she and Soren were tall. "My name is Letitia Conner," she said. She paused as Tora closed her eyes and put her head in her hands. "Miss Anders, are you feeling poorly?"

Letitia Conner, Tora repeated to herself. *Letitia Conner. She's not the girl! She's not my daughter.* Tora managed to look up and smile at her. "Yes, Letitia. I'm sorry, I have a headache. You look so familiar. What are your parents' names?"

"Mr. and Mrs. Edward Conner."

"Ah, yes," she said. "I'm sorry, I do not know them. Please go on."

The girl did so, but Tora was not listening. All she could think of was how the girl looked like Soren, like herself for that matter. The cut of her chin, the perky tilt of her nose, the bow of her mouth…It was all like Tora's. Did anyone else in the room notice? She glanced around. How foolish of her! She was in a classroom of children! Children did not notice such things. But her name…had Kaatje changed Jessica's name, as well as her own? Remarried? No doubt that louse Soren had moved on. Had Kaatje moved here from the Dakota Territory? Or had she given Tora's child up for adoption?

It was all too much to consider. As she pretended to listen to the other children as they stood to speak, the tears came unbidden. At first, Tora tried to hide them, pretending she was merely bothered by the dust, and she blew her nose, but she could not stop them. On and on they came until she gave in to the deep sobs that had been aching inside her chest ever since…ever since Letitia caught her eye.

She could hear the children hush in shock, then begin to scatter.

"She's loony," whispered one.

"We need to get my ma," said another.

Tora didn't care. It seemed all she could do was stay there and cry, cry as she hadn't cried in years. How long had it been since she had thought about Jessica? How long had she been missing her? For that was what struck her most; she had found her long-lost daughter, the daughter she had always missed.

A small hand rested on her shoulder. "Don't cry, Miss Anders," said a soft voice. "It will be all right."

But when Tora looked up, she just cried harder.

Letitia *was* Jessica. She had to be.

It was Mrs. Conner who came and retrieved her from the empty class-room and quietly led her to the shanty. Tucked under the comforter and given a sip of water, Tora looked at her rescuer for the first time. She was the spitting image of Letitia. The girl's mother. *She isn't Jessica.* Tora fought to find her voice, wondering at the disappointment that mingled with relief in her breast. "You…you are Letitia's mother?"

"I am." She stroked Tora's brow in a concerned fashion, obviously checking for fever. "Are you ill, miss?"

"A bit…overwhelmed." Tora's mind flew, trying to find a legiti-mate excuse for her breakdown. What would another woman under-stand, identify with, empathize with her for? For the first time in a long while, truth was her ally. "You see, I've lost everything. My home, my occupation, my love." She turned away as if it pained her to speak. And it surprised Tora that it actually did hurt to talk of such things.

"Poor girl," Mrs. Conner murmured. "And you lived where…?"

"Helena. I was in Helena." Tora thought fast, afraid that if she told too much of her story, these people could be affected by Trent Storm's long arm too and despise her as everyone else had. "I was in love with a man who cast me away like yesterday's bath water. Suddenly, I was lost. I had thought we would marry! I was employed by him, so then I was out of work too."

"Poor, poor girl!" Mrs. Conner said, obviously aghast at Tora's turn in fortune. "What brought you here?"

"I bought a train ticket with next to my last dollar. Mr. Crosby found me in town, looking for work, and mentioned you all needed a schoolteacher. No doubt you're thinking he made a huge mistake." She sat up and wiped away her tears. "I promise you, Mrs. Conner, this is truly unlike me. It was all just too much. I had just arrived—"

"That's right!" she interrupted. "Just last night! It was too much for any woman, let alone a woman who's been through what you have. You rest, dear. Get settled. Tomorrow's soon enough to begin school.

I'll speak to the other parents and explain. You just take care of your-self."

"Oh, thank you. You are too kind."

"Not at all. Let me know if you need anything. We're the closest farm, not a mile down the road to the east. I'll have my boy bring sup-per by for you."

"You needn't—"

"Nonsense," she said, pushing Tora's shoulders back until she lay down again. "You rest and let my boy know tonight if you're needing a thing."

"Thank you," Tora whispered as Mrs. Conner left the shanty qui-etly. "Thank you." She was so weary! With eyelids of stone, Tora gave in to the sleep that called her from deep within.

Tora did not usually dream. She could not remember the last time she had had a dream. But that day she had a dream so vivid that it was dif-ficult to shake. So when the Conner boy appeared at five with a knock on her shaky door, Tora struggled to wake. She shook her head, em-barrassed that she had slept all afternoon, and went to the door.

It was one of the older boys who had sat in the back. "You're a Conner?" she asked.

"Ross Conner," he said with a nod as he pushed a large basket toward her. "Mama sent this. I'll pick up the basket tomorrow at school. We're havin' school tomorrow?"

"Yes. Eight sharp. Do not be late."

He stood straighter when he heard the serious note in her tone, then shuffled his feet. "Mama wanted me to ask if you're needin' any-thing."

"No. Thank you. See you tomorrow morning."

"Bye!" he said, scooting away from her door as if she were the vil-lage witch, the relief in his walk visible.

Tora closed the door, still half lost in her dream. She sat back down on the bed, basket at her feet, trying to remember just how the dream went…There had been a girl, a girl that looked somewhat like Letitia, but not like her exactly. It was Jessica, she supposed. Did a mother have some supernatural power to discern what her baby would look like as a child? The last she had seen of Jessie, she was just an infant, chubby and cute, with eyes the color of cornflowers, and hair that curled up at the ends in little ringlets.

It was nonsense. All of it, Tora thought, suddenly angry. She stood and paced. Why, she hadn't thought of Jessica since that day she had left her in the road at Kaatje's feet, determined to go on with her life. It was all that rotten Soren's fault! If he had not gotten her pregnant, none of this would have happened! She could have gone to work for Trent immediately, they would have fallen in love, and no secrets from the past would have split them apart.

The anger dissipated as Tora once again thought of the child in her dream. When she had seen Jessica in her sleep, she had felt neither anger nor the weight of responsibility. Only the overpowering sense of lost time and guilt. What had she done? She sat down hard on the edge of her bed. Had she given up a child she had actually wanted? That was impossible! Her life held no place for a baby, a toddler, a girl. What Tora wanted excluded children. Once she and Trent had married and a suitable nanny was hired, then…

It was all too much, she concluded once again. Perhaps she was truly on the edge of hysteria. Who wouldn't be in her position? One of the greatest ladies in the West, now fighting it out as a schoolmarm in the Washington Territory! Next she'd be ambushed by Indians, the way her luck was running.

Wearily, she reached for the basket and unwrapped some roast beef, potatoes, and carrots on a plate. She picked at it for a few minutes then lay back down. Sleep overtook her immediately.

The next morning, she was up and ready for her students before they arrived. Determined to make things right—since she could see few options—she had built a fire in the school's woodstove and, after checking a student's primer, had written the alphabet on the board. Although she could speak English with almost no accent, she still had trouble remembering not to write her letters as she had as a child in Bergen, with crossed *o*'s and such.

She walked back to the woodstove, to see how her fire was faring. It sputtered and was a sorry excuse for heat, but at least Tora had tried. She'd assign Ross to see to it as soon as he got in. Today, she felt together, ready for this new challenge before her. One never knew. Perhaps her stint as a schoolteacher would lead her to other opportunities. Today after school she would go to Mr. Crosby and ask for a small advance on her salary in order to buy some food supplies. If the townspeople were to respect her, she needed to act respectable and stop assuming people would feed her. She felt a slight blush climb her neck at the thought. Imagine! Tora Anders relying on others for food! Not since she had stowed away on the *Herald* did she feel so on the edge, teetering between her dreams and disaster.

However, she felt much closer to disaster here, outside Spokane, than she had crossing the Atlantic. Perhaps it was because she had tasted success and failure, she thought to herself as she wiped off her dusty desk. And that taste of success had left her wanting more. No, this school would only be a place to rest, take stock, and then move on. She simply had to decide where she wanted to go. Back east? Farther west?

Thoughts of Elsa came to mind. She knew from the newspaper accounts that she and Peder were in Seattle. What would it be like to see her sister again? Perhaps she could go, packed with all her fine things, with the excuse that she wanted to reestablish their relationship. Tora shook her head. No, that would never do. Elsa drove her mad with her elder sibling ways, so condescending and self-righteous. And knowing Peder, he would probably sniff out the truth of her predicament, just as Trent had.

No, Tora Anders would make her own way in the world. One way or another.

e l e v e n

October 1886

It took Karl several days to work up the courage to return to Kaatje's farm. For hours he had paced the floor of his small hotel room, thinking about what he would say and how he would say it. Regardless that he only felt friendship with Elsa as he had stared inside at her, he doubted it would hold. For years he had drilled it into his mind and heart that she was married, that she belonged to another. And yet he had continued to love her. Now she was alone. Available. How could he talk to her, see her beautiful face without those old feelings of love and desire returning? That was the last thing she needed right now. Yet he so desperately needed to talk to her, to seek her absolution!

Disgusted with himself, he put his hat atop his head as he stared into the small, oval mirror. It had peeling gilt edges. Just like him, he mused. Once fine, now clearly needing some work. *Unfortunately for me,* he thought, *I need more work than a quick refinishing job.* No, he needed work from the inside out. He opened his door and left the room, inhaling the scents of stale beer and old food from the bar below. Between Elsa and his poor accommodations, it was tempting to head out of town immediately. He laughed under his breath. Even thinking of Elsa made his heart pound. What made him think that he could face her and honestly ask her forgiveness? Did his heart not need to be right before he could go to her? He turned back toward his room.

Go to her.

Karl stopped short and looked about the dim hallway to see if someone was there. No, he had been right. He was alone. Who had spoken?

You know the way. You know the path. Go to her.

Karl reached out to brace himself, a hand on either doorjamb. How long? How long had it been since he had heard his Lord's voice? Or was it the Lord's? What if it was the Evil One, trying to draw him back into temptation?

You know yourself. You know the path. Follow it.

No, it was him! It was him! "Lord God," Karl whispered, sweat suddenly pouring from his brow, "I do not know if I can. I don't know if I'm strong enough."

You are stronger than you think.

"She's alone and mourning. What place do I have there with her?"

Be her friend.

"And if I cannot leave it at that?"

Be her friend.

"But what if—"

Be her friend. Go.

As if physically turned, Karl pivoted on his heel and walked numbly to the stairway. He pulled a handkerchief from his pocket, dabbing at his brow.

"You okay there, Mr. Martensen?" the man at the front desk called.

"Sure," he mumbled. But inside, he felt anything but sure.

Kaatje answered the door, and Karl took the opportunity to breathe.

"I wondered when you'd work up the courage to come," she said, wiping her hands on her apron as if drying them.

"It took awhile," he admitted.

"She knows you're here," Kaatje said gently. "She's wanted to see you, if that helps any."

"It helps some. I was afraid—"

"Elsa is out with the children in the barn. Why don't you go say hello? And bring me back some milk," she said, handing him a pail.

Karl smiled down at his friend. How did she know so much? Was he so transparent? "Anything else? Want me to churn some butter while I'm at it?"

"Now that you mention it…"

"All right, all right, I'm going. No need to threaten me with additional chores." He turned toward the barn, feeling a bit better after bantering with Kaatje.

"Karl."

He turned back to her.

"She's very…tender. Her heart remains in Peder's hands, dead or alive."

Her words struck deep. Even Kaatje thought she must try to protect Elsa from him. He considered her a moment before answering. "I am here to be her friend, and only that. I wanted to leave, leave without ever seeing her. I doubt myself."

She nodded. "But God doesn't. He'll give you the strength, Karl. You know that, right?"

"Yes. For the first time in a long time, I'm sure of one small thing in my life. I'm heading in the right direction, and it all starts with your barn."

"My old, sad barn. Who knew it would have such import?"

Karl smiled. "We'll have to build you that new one in honor of such an occasion. I'd better go."

"Go, Karl. Go with God."

Still smiling, Karl turned again and headed toward the barn, feeling more sure with each step. Gradually, the trepidation within his heart eased, and his smile broadened. Truly, this was of God. He could feel him! He could feel him! How long had it been? The exhilaration of the Lord's presence almost made him want to jump and shout with joy, but as his hand met the roughened wood of the door, the joy fled. He was about to face his best friend's widow, a woman he had once coveted, a woman he would have tried to steal away if she had given him half a chance. "Help me, Lord," he prayed silently. "Help me to be as you asked. Her friend. Her friend only."

He pulled open the door, wincing at the creak that disrupted the quiet afternoon. It was dark and hazy inside, plumes of dust dancing through shafts of light from cracks in the ceiling. He passed through the tack room and through a narrow passageway to the main barn. There he saw her.

She was in the far corner, laughing with the girls and her son as they played with a baby pig. When she saw him, her smile faded and she stood immediately, absentmindedly brushing the straw from her skirt. Her eyes never left his. The children, as if sensing the importance of the moment, stayed silent. Karl almost forgot the children were there as he mentally told himself to put one foot in front of the other, going to her as she walked toward him.

Neither said a word, walking through shaft after shaft of light as if it were a dreamscape instead of reality. He dropped the bucket at his feet, then took her into his arms, holding her tenderly and backing up a bit to stare into her eyes. Bright tears in her eyes made him realize that he, too, was crying.

"I'm sorry, Elsa. I'm so sorry," he said simply.

She melted into his embrace again, her head against his chest. "I miss him, Karl."

An ache began in his throat, begging him to give in more fully to the sorrow he felt deep within. "I...I had just made plans to come see you and Peder—"

"Auntie Elsa," Christina interrupted, pulling them from their private universe. "We're going outside to play."

"Very well," Elsa said, clearly as flustered as Karl to realize they weren't alone. "Keep an eye on Kristian, will you?"

"Yes, ma'am."

Karl's eyes followed Kristian, studying the boy who belonged to Peder. He stood tall and proud already, reminding Karl of his old friend. His hair was a sandy blond, his eyes remarkably like Peder's mossy green. The three-year-old's eyes stopped Karl—they looked like the eyes of a much older child, reflecting pain, just beyond the immediate joy. *What would it be like to lose your father at such a tender age?* Karl wondered. As gruff as Gustav Martensen had been toward his son, at least he had always been there.

"Over here, Karl. There's a bench by the hay." Elsa led the way, a study in grace as she walked. Karl searched his heart, wondering at what he was feeling, but could not find anything but friendship. What relief! He wanted to sink to his knees and sing God's praises right then and there. But Elsa was waiting. "You got my letter, then. I sent it to Saint Paul, not knowing where you were—"

"No," he said softly. "I did not get your letter. I just happened to be here in the Skagit Valley and..."

"You were coming to Seattle?" she encouraged gently.

"Yes," he said, joining her on the rough-hewn bench. "I figured it had been long enough." He raised his eyes to meet hers. "I was coming to seek forgiveness. From you. From Peder."

Elsa looked away, as if visualizing another time, another land. "I was so sorry that what happened drove you and Peder apart."

"And you and Peder?" Karl asked, holding his breath.

"We had our moments, but eventually he forgave me."

Karl shook his head in frustration and moved to the ground in front of her, kneeling. He took her hand. "I was so wrong, Elsa. I'm sorry that what I did caused you any pain. I'm sorry that I robbed you and Peder of any time you had together. I know it must be hard, but can you find any way to forgive me?"

Elsa smiled and placed a gentle hand on his cheek. "Dear Karl. I forgave you long ago. Didn't you know it?"

"I had hoped..." He stood and paced away from her. He needed some distance to ask what he had to next. "And Peder?" He wondered if the words were even audible, it was so difficult for him to get them out.

Elsa looked down at her hands and then back at him. "Peder was more troubled. He forgave me, but I am afraid he never forgave you."

Karl turned, the hair on the back of his neck standing on end. Peder had died hating him! How was he to get past that? He looked up to the nearest shaft of light, silently studying it.

Gently, she laid a hand on his arm and looked up at him intently. He hadn't heard her approach. "Sometimes, Karl, I find that it is harder to forgive myself of a sin than to allow another, or God, to do so. Have you forgiven yourself?"

He shook off her hand and strode away. "How can I forgive myself?" he cried. "I never looked Peder in the eye. Never asked his forgiveness. When I think of how I would feel had the tables been turned—"

"Karl, Peder was wrong."

"What?"

"He was wrong to hold on to a grudge like that. You asked his forgiveness. You asked it in a letter."

"A letter!" Karl scoffed. "I wasn't man enough to face you both again."

"You did your best at the time. I forgave you then. It was enough for me."

"But not enough for Peder."

"And as I said, he was wrong. You know that. It is not our way. What if God held on to his anger at our sinfulness in the same manner?" She stepped forward, visibly trembling. "He was wrong, Karl. And I pray that God forgave him for his stubbornness. *He was wrong.*" She metered out the words, seemingly wanting to hammer them into his head.

Karl sighed and ran a hand through his hair.

Elsa smiled, catching him off guard.

"What?"

"Peder used to do the same thing when he was frustrated. You picked that up from each other as boys. I remember you both doing it in Bergen."

Karl allowed himself a small smile too. "I did a lot of things like Peder. Had it not been for him, I would never have gone to sea. Nor come to America. To say nothing of finding Christ."

"You were good for each other. It is tragic that your friendship ended as it did."

"Yes." He sat down again on the bench and Elsa joined him.

"He would have found it in his heart to forgive you, Karl. Eventually, he would have come around to it. Especially had you visited us as you planned. He might've been angry for a time, but then he would have worked it through. He would have seen the truth eventually and called himself pigheaded for waiting so long."

Karl glanced up at her. "You think so?"

She nodded once. "I know so. I knew my husband. And although he was terribly stubborn, he was also a fair man. And faithful. He missed you as much as you have missed him these years."

"Such a waste," Karl muttered.

"Truly a waste," Elsa murmured. She reached for Karl's hand, and again he was amazed at the wave of warmth that flooded through him. It was not of lust, but of friendship. "Don't let us part as strangers, Karl. Can you and I be friends? I need my friends," she said, her voice cracking a bit, "right now. I feel very alone."

Karl studied her eyes. "I am here to be your friend, Elsa. Above all else, I will always be your friend. Ask me, and I will help. Tell me what to do, and I will be there. Thank you for your forgiveness. For your words about Peder, even if they were painfully honest. Thank you for trusting me again."

He raised an arm and Elsa sank against his side. "Oh, Karl, I miss him so."

"Me too. Me too."

By the time Karl made it into Seattle from the train station, it was dark and raining periodically. The soft, soaking rain of winter matched Karl's mood. It was as if the skies wept for him, and for Peder. He stopped briefly at the hotel to drop off his luggage and considered waiting until morning to visit Peder's grave. It would be difficult to get a horse at this time of night, and the weather was not inviting. But like a penitent priest, Karl felt it was just as he deserved. *Why should this be easy, simple?*

He stopped at the front desk as he put on an oilskin hat and coat. "Where can I find a horse this time of night?"

The short, squat man with a mustache looked at him queerly and cocked his head to one side. "This time of night, no one in his right mind will be out, let alone letting out their stock."

Karl pulled a wad of bills from his pocket. "I'm sure I could convince someone to make the extra effort."

The man's eyebrows shot up in surprise. "Well sure. Now you're talkin'. I have a friend three blocks down. If you stop by the house—it has a pretty substantial porch, you'll find it sure. Foster'll take care of you."

"Thank you," Karl said, laying a bill down on the counter for the man's help.

"Anytime, mister, anytime. Be careful out there. It's liable to get a bit more wet."

Karl did not respond as he exited, feeling as if he were a man on a mission. He had obtained the Ramstads' address from Elsa. She had encouraged him to stay at their empty house, but he felt uncomfortable with the idea. No, his sole purpose in being here was to say his good-byes to Peder Ramstad, the closest friend he had ever had. The man he had wronged.

The more he thought about it, the more grim he became. He passed one saloon and considered entering it for a whiskey, then urged himself on. Before long, he had reached the stable master's home and knocked loudly on the door.

A woman's face peered at him from behind the window curtains, then disappeared. Then a man's face appeared. About fifty years of age, Foster was obviously displeased about being disturbed at this late hour. "What do you want?" asked his muffled voice.

"I need a horse."

"We're closed. Come back in the morning."

"I need it tonight."

"We're closed!"

"I'm willing to pay extra."

The man faced him more squarely from the other side of the door, obviously suspicious. "This some kind of emergency?"

"You could say that," Karl said, looking at him levelly.

The man sighed and nodded once. "I'll be out in a moment," he said, then disappeared behind the gingham curtains again. He went away, presumably to dress, and Karl paced the porch, ignoring the stable master's curious wife as she sneaked peeks at him from behind the curtain. The walls were thin, and he could hear them arguing.

"I don't care if he's the king of England!" she said. "No money's worth going out on a night like this! And what if the horse turns an ankle in this wet? Then what good will the man's extra dollar do for us?"

"Turns an ankle? Woman, my horses haven't known anything but rain since we moved here anyway."

"But it's dark, and we don't know the man."

"Says it's an emergency."

"Sure, sure," she said suspiciously. "He don't act like a man facing an emergency."

"What do you want me to do?"

"Turn him away. Tell him to come back come mornin' when you can see him better."

"I can't do that. Already told him I'd be right out—"

"You didn't tell him that you'd rent him one of our horses. Tell him to come back come mornin'."

"All right, all right," the beleaguered man said. Karl turned from the door, not waiting for the inevitable. When it came down to a decision between a woman like that and him, he knew who would win, no matter how much extra he paid. He was walking down the stairs when the man peeked out the door. He looked sorry and embarrassed. "I take it you heard."

"Yes, sir. I appreciate you trying." He turned to walk up the street again.

"Where ya headin'?"

"The Third Street graveyard."

"The graveyard? This time of night?"

"I have an old friend…it's been too long. I have to take care of this tonight."

The stable master looked twice as guilty upon hearing this new revelation. "It's not a far piece. About five blocks north and two west."

Karl raised his eyes in surprise. "Guess I didn't need a horse after all."

"All the same, I wish I could let you one. It's not a night for a walk."

"Good night," Karl said, turning away. As the rain fell again over his shoulders and the light from the stable master's house receded, he shivered. He passed saloon after saloon, his steps becoming more leaden by the moment. He needed something to warm him from inside, a little liquid courage. At the next saloon, he turned and walked straight to the bar.

"Whiskey," he ordered from the bartender as he pulled off his hat.

The bartender poured, and Karl downed it in one swallow. "Again," he ordered.

Obediently, the man poured a second, a third, and a fourth before Karl waved him away. Slapping a bill on the counter and his hat back on his head, he stood and immediately felt the dizzying effect of the alcohol. *Stupid,* he thought, hating himself. *Weak. Can't even do this one last thing for Peder without a little false help, can you?* He concentrated on trying not to weave as he made his way back out into the Seattle night.

Somehow, he made it to the graveyard a half-hour later. He struggled with the flint and lamp in the rain, but finally got it lit. Peder's grave was easy to spot, being so close to the wrought-iron fence. He saw the anchor Elsa had mentioned, and knew it was his. Silently, he made his way into the burial grounds and knelt in the mud by Peder's grave. Over the mound was a soft layer of new grass.

For a long time, he felt nothing but emptiness as he remained on his knees. "Peder," he muttered. "I made a mess of things, didn't I? You and I were going to conquer the world together. We were going to be there for each other until we were old men. But I left you. I deceived you. And then I didn't have the guts to face you again."

He reached to trace the marker at the head of the grave. Rain sizzled and steamed as it hit the hot glass of the lamp, but still the flame flickered on, giving the scene an otherworldly feel. Karl smiled and spoke. "If anyone saw me here, old friend, they'd think I was crazy." He talked to the headstone as if Peder sat there instead. He could see his face, his hair, his shoulders.

"I'm sorry, Peder. I wish I had come to you earlier. I wish I had asked your forgiveness. I wish—" His voice broke as he wept. "I wish we could have had another chance to be friends. To be brothers. You meant so much to me. Forgive me, brother, forgive me."

Karl sank his fists into the muck around the grave and flung it to the sky. "Why, God? Why?" he screamed. "Why couldn't you have given us one more chance?"

He stared upward, trying to see the sky as if, in his fury, he could face God himself. "Why?" he screamed again. And then he gave in to weeping, curling up in a ball as the rain beat down upon his back.

He awoke to the creak of wagon wheels and the suspicious stares of the few passersby about at this hour. The rain had stopped, but it was barely light and bitterly cold. Stiffly, he rose from the grass of Peder's grave. He dimly remembered going to the saloon the night before but precious little afterward.

What was he doing here? What was he doing with his life? Where was he to go? He knew something had to change. He could not go on as he had. He was on the edge of a revelation—a new phase in his life journey—but he had not a clue of where to begin. He stared at Peder's grave marker and wondered again about the anchor. Who chose that? Elsa? Why? Because he was a sailor? It seemed a shallow reminder of the man…Peder was much more than that.

Peder Ramstad had been stalwart and strong, faithful, unmoving at times. Like…an anchor.

Like…God in a way.

How long had Karl been sailing without an anchor? Ever since he had given in to his desire for Elsa over what he knew to be right. Sailing without an anchor, without Peder, and more important, without God. Once again, it was as clear to Karl as the northern lights on the North Sea. It was the reason for his listlessness, his weakness for drink, his overwhelming sense of loss, the desire to gain possessions about him that might help him feel anchored.

Karl smiled for what felt like the first time in a long while. "Thank you," he whispered, looking up at the gray clouds that were moving south. Once more, he traced the anchor on the gravestone. "Thank you too, friend. I'll always miss you, brother. There was no one like you, nor will there ever be again."

Karl did several things upon returning to town: he stopped by the telegraph office to wire Brad and tell him he was going away for some time; he purchased a Bible at the nearest store, since he did not remember where he had left his old one; and he ordered a bath. Feeling clean and forgiven, refreshed as if he had had a full night's sleep instead of an hour in the rain, he spent the day reading his Bible and praying. He ate downstairs at five o'clock and returned to his room to pray. Not on his knees, but spread-eagle on the floor before his God until sleep overtook him.

He awakened the next morning early, packed, and walked to the docks. He signed up to serve as a sailor on the first schooner he saw, never mentioning his prior experience to the captain. To Karl, it felt like he was reborn. Starting over again.

And never had he felt the exhilaration he did that October morn the *Silver Sea* was towed out of the sound and set free upon the Pacific's waves.

t w e l v e

*Elsa found that Kaatje's tiny home was soothing to her soul, a cozy, healing balm to her grieving heart. Thoughts of returning home depressed her. She could not imagine climbing back into the huge four-poster bed without Peder. Tomorrow was Thanksgiving; thoughts of previous holidays together brought her even lower. When she had been in Seattle for the funeral, it was as if she had been in a stupor, a deadened, dreamlike world that held such memories at bay. Now her grief was sharp as a knife, each memory as clear as if it had occurred yesterday. *Oh, Peder, Peder,* she found herself saying to the ceiling, *what am I to do without you?*

While the reality of his permanent absence sank in with each day that passed, Elsa had a difficult time understanding what her place in the world was now to be. For years she had been the captain's wife, Kristian's mother, an occasional columnist for the *New York Times*. Now it was as if everything but her role as mother had receded like the tide, leaving her with scattered, shattered shells that, if she could just pick up and make sense of them, would tell her what to do next. She felt so utterly alone, it chilled her. Only Kaatje's warm, loving ministrations and the children's antics kept her despair at bay. But she had to face the truth; the five of them were painfully cramped in the tiny house and she would soon need to go home.

"Elsa!" Kaatje called as she opened the door. "Elsa—"

"Yes?"

"Where have you been?"

"I was just finishing up these dishes—"

"I've been calling you! Didn't you hear me? We have a new baby in the family!"

Elsa smiled. "A baby?"

"Yes, that old Mr. Goat turned out to be a Mrs. Goat young enough to bear another!"

They laughed together, and Elsa grabbed her coat. She shivered as they left the house, still toasty warm from the morning's baking and the fireplace embers. It was cold enough for snow, surely, and the ground was frozen solid beneath their feet. Before them was the glorious new barn that Karl had had built for Kaatje, with the understanding that the ancillary railroad he was building could store supplies there. No supplies had arrived yet, and Elsa doubted any ever would.

And she doubted that the extra material that arrived by "mistake" was anything of the kind. Karl had insisted that Kaatje use it to build another room on her house. When he stubbornly left the lumber out in the rain as if he truly was never going to return for it, she had hired a local man to do as he had bid. It was that extra room that Elsa now shared with Kaatje. Elsa was deeply thankful for Karl's generosity. Kaatje deserved every kindness that came her way.

She wondered at the woman who walked beside her. Although larger in stature than Kaatje, Elsa felt like a mouse compared to her lioness. Kaatje had come through abandonment, a lost farm, another trek west, and establishing a new homestead, to get to where she was now. Where had she found the strength? As Kaatje opened the door to the new barn, an aromatic wave of fresh-hewn lumber wafted about them.

"Kaatje," Elsa began. "How do you do it? Day after day, you make this farm work, you prepare food for the girls, you remake old clothes into new for them. Where do you find the strength?"

Kaatje smiled and looked down, as if a bit embarrassed. Then she looked at Elsa tenderly. "You'll find the strength too, Elsa. I promise you. Look at you now. You've made it this far, three months after you lost your sweet Peder. Day after day, you put one foot in front of the other, and pray that God will make a path for you. And hasn't he done just that?"

Elsa thought for a moment and nodded. "He has. He has been faithful."

"And he will continue to do so." Kaatje drew her in so she could close the barn door. In the far corner, they could hear the children squealing in delight and laughing. "No doubt you're feeling terribly lost. That too will wane. Gradually, life begins to feel all right again, even without your spouse. It's like losing a limb. You just have to get around without it, and eventually it somehow feels all right again."

At Elsa's horrified expression, Kaatje patted her arm. "Not all the time, of course. Sometimes you remember, and you ache for that limb. But in the day-to-day living, God teaches us how to do it in a new way. And somehow, that's all right. It becomes all right."

Elsa felt her furrowed brow relax a bit. She followed after Kaatje, wondering at her wisdom. Surely she would never forget Peder! The thought of not being able to remember his smell, his embrace, his laugh pained her. But right now, it was practically all she could think of. Perhaps one had to forget, just a little, in order to live without constant pain and grief. *But I am not ready,* Elsa thought, shaking her head. *I'm not ready to let my beloved go.*

She joined her friend on the rough-hewn bench that had been moved into the new barn. They were far enough away from the children to speak frankly, but close enough to enjoy watching them with the mother goat and her tiny, bleating kid. "Is that how you've done it?" she asked Kaatje. "Forgotten Soren, so you can move on?"

Kaatje smiled gently. "I didn't forget him on purpose. It's just that gradually, the minute-by-minute memories fade into hour-by-hour memories. Eventually those fade into day-by-day, and those in turn go to week-by-week. That is where I am now. I remember Soren—and you probably think I am crazy—but I still ache for him once in a while. But it's only once in a week that I do so. Life," she said, waving before and around her, "takes over. God heals the pain. And clears the way for a future."

"Which will be...?"

"I don't know. Lately, I've felt the urge to head north; to see if I can find out what happened to Soren. Like you still hoping that Peder somehow miraculously survived that storm, I still wonder if my husband is alive."

"But if he is alive..."

"Yes. If he is alive, he has abandoned us. If I know that for sure, then I can say good-bye to a marriage that was apparently never as important to him as it was to me. And if he is dead, I can bury him in my heart. But if he is alive—" Her words faltered.

"If he is alive..." Elsa encouraged.

"If he is alive and he sees me and the girls, there might be some chance of reconciliation."

Elsa swallowed hard. How could Kaatje desire reconciliation with such a man? She was certainly a better woman than Elsa to pursue such a dream.

"You don't approve," Kaatje said softly.

"I don't understand."

"Because of Tora?" she whispered.

"Because of her and all the affairs that went on before her. How can you love such a man?"

"You think I am weak?"

"I simply don't understand."

"At times, I do not understand myself. I seem to have this undying hope that Soren will see the light, to live as we have been taught, and to cherish his family—whether by me or another—as the gift of God it is. I want to look him in the face once more and give him that chance.

"I have grieved for him as you grieve for Peder now. I don't believe it will hurt as it did once. But I have to give him one more opportunity to redeem himself. If he turns from me, so be it."

They were silent for several long minutes. "And what happens when he sees Jessica?" Elsa asked at last. "He doesn't even know she exists."

"Unless he received one of my letters."

"Do you think that is why he disappeared? He could not confront the evidence of his own sin?"

"I do not know. That is why a part of me wishes to go, I suppose. To find out."

Elsa took Kaatje's hand. "I am so sorry for the burden Tora laid at your feet."

Kaatje looked at her quickly, as if surprised and a bit offended. "Look at her, Elsa. Look at your niece! Isn't she exquisite?"

Elsa looked across the room at Jessica, so lovely, so natural with the baby goat and its mother. "She is beautiful. From the inside out, thanks to you."

"She is a gift. At first I could not believe the injustice of it all," Kaatje murmured. "And then I realized that in the darkest moments of life Christ bestows upon us the grandest presents of all."

Kaatje and Elsa prepared their contribution for Thanksgiving dinner the next morning—pressed cod and cabbage in sour cream—and bundled up the children for the ride to church and then to the Gustavsons', who were hosting the meal. It was during the service, as they sang a hymn of thanks together, that Elsa nudged Kaatje in the ribs. Kaatje gave Elsa a puzzled look and silently reminded her to keep still in church.

Instead, Elsa leaned over and whispered in her ear. "Why don't you and the girls winter with me in Seattle?"

Kaatje smiled, thinking over the outrageous possibility. What about her farm? Her animals?

"Einar would take care of the place," Elsa whispered again, as if reading her mind.

Kaatje fought the urge to giggle, caught an older woman's disapproving stare, and felt like a young girl again in Bergen. Elsa was forever getting her in trouble in church there, too. She shot Elsa a look that said, *We will talk about this later.*

Elsa nodded, smiling, and went on singing, obviously proud of herself for planting the seed. It would be good to get off the farm for the winter, Kaatje thought, to see the city and experience life with Elsa again. Elsa's visit had brought back the sisterhood they had shared as children, and the thought of her leaving left Kaatje feeling a bit down. If Einar would care for the animals, what was to stop her?

After the service, Matthew greeted them outside and handed Kaatje a well-worn letter. "Postmaster asked me to give this to you a couple days back," he said offhandedly.

Elsa took one look at the postmark and retorted, "So why didn't you? Two days ago? Can't you see it's from Alaska?"

Matthew looked stupefied and backed away as if Elsa and Kaatje were two caged cougars about to escape. Elsa pulled her to the wagon, ignoring their friends' curious stares. "Open it, Kaatje. Open it."

Kaatje felt dizzy, bewildered. Her hand shook. "I cannot."

"Do you wish to do so later?" Elsa said, apparently wondering for the first time if Kaatje desired more privacy.

"I do not know." She placed one hand to her forehead, feeling the dampness of perspiration even in the cold afternoon air.

"Come on, ladies!" Nora called. "Dinner's waiting!" Her face was so jubilant that it felt distantly interesting to Kaatje to watch as it fell. Obviously, her own expression screamed that something was wrong.

"What is it?" Nora asked. "What's the matter?" She murmured something to Einar and scrambled down off the wagon without waiting for assistance, then hurried over to them. "What?"

"Kaatje got a letter from Alaska," Elsa whispered, conscious that others were staring at them curiously.

"Oh—" Nora said, covering her mouth with a gloved hand. "From…"

"It's not Soren's handwriting," Kaatje mumbled.

"Come," Nora directed, taking charge as usual. "Come to the house, and you can go the back bedroom and have some privacy," she said loudly, looking about them, "to read the news. Good or bad, this is Thanksgiving Day, and you have your friends about you, Kaatje."

"Thank you, Nora," she said. She looked up at Elsa. "Let's do as she suggests."

Quickly, Elsa gathered the children and they headed out to the Gustavsons' farm. "Stay out of those pies, Kristian," Elsa warned over her shoulder as they drove, but Kaatje heard her voice as if through a layer of dirt. It was muffled, distant. Her mind was in the Dakota Territory, the last time she had seen Soren. He had been so beautiful, so full of life. Was this the letter that would end it?

All the way to the farm, Kaatje remembered one day after another she had shared with Soren. None of the bad days, of course. All the good ones. And they were so sweet. He had been dear to her heart, and she supposed she held out more hope that he lived than she admitted. All at once, they had arrived at the Gustavsons', and huge Einar easily lifted her to the ground. "You can go on in, Kaatje," he said tenderly.

Nora waited at the door and took her coat, even as she waved down the hall. "Now you go and read your news. Do you want some company? Elsa?"

Dear Nora always did have an uncanny sense of what people needed. "Elsa. It would be good to have her with me."

"Elsa! Elsa!" Nora called.

"I'm coming, I'm coming," Elsa said. "I had to get the pies." She took one look at Kaatje and immediately handed the pies and her coat to her hosts. "Come, Kaatje. Let's get this over with."

Feeling as if she were on a dreamwalk, Kaatje moved down the dim hall and into a bedroom with a window. Nora and Einar had done well for themselves here in the valley, and their home showed the benefits of prosperity. It would have been nice to have a window in her new room, Kaatje thought.

"Kaatje?" Elsa asked carefully.

Kaatje's mind came back to the present and what was at hand. "I...I have waited for a letter for so long."

"Open it, Kaatje. I'm here. Together, we'll face whatever's inside."

Kaatje nodded and sat down on the edge of the bed with Elsa and tentatively tore open the letter. She read aloud in a voice that she was not quite sure was audible. It didn't matter; she read more for herself than Elsa anyway.

12 August 1886
Dear Mrs. Soren Janssen:

I have conducted a lengthy investigation of your husband's whereabouts as you requested. He was seen about this time last year around Forty Mile, but hasn't been heard from since. Got a letter from the sheriff in Kenai who said he staked a claim there a year or so back, but not striking gold, took off for my part of the territory. The Indians say he was trapping last winter, but haven't seen him since spring. Now I do not want to alarm you, ma'am, but these are harsh lands. Trappers come up for air at least twice a year, since most need some supplies. Nobody's seen hide nor hair of your husband for these last seven months, I'd say. There's a good chance that he either has left the territory and is heading home or has met some other dire circumstance. If I hear any other news of him, I'll be sure to pass it on. I wish you the best as you seek to find him and remain cordially yours—

Sheriff Jefferson Young

Kaatje let the letter fall to the bed. "Maybe… Perhaps he's coming home."

"To Dakota?"

"I don't know. Perhaps. If so, they'll tell him where we are."

Elsa looked down, not meeting her gaze. "Or he is not coming home at all." She dared to glance up at Kaatje. "Winter's soon upon us. Don't you think he'd be here by now? Even if he went all the way to Dakota and back?"

"It depends." She rose and paced before the window. "If he was on horseback, the journey could take months."

"Horseback? You don't think he would load his horse on a train and come that way?"

"But I've heard of trappers coming through the Yukon Territory, over into British Columbia, and down. If he was that far east—"

"Kaatje—"

"I know what you're going to say! You do not want me to get my hopes up." She looked up at Elsa suddenly, knowing by her expression that she believed Soren was dead. Kaatje shook her head slowly. "How could he be dead? I'd know somehow, wouldn't I?" Elsa looked at her helplessly, and Kaatje remembered her talking about still thinking Peder would appear, miraculously alive. "You don't know that Peder is dead either," Kaatje said flatly, sitting again on the bed. "Perhaps we'll never know."

"Perhaps we'll just have to live with that," Elsa said gently. "Or maybe, just maybe, Soren will come riding into town. Does this mean you won't come to Seattle with me?"

Kaatje shook her head, staring down at the letter. "No. I've waited half my adult life for Soren Janssen to come around. If he is alive, and he does come to me, he can take another journey and find me in Seattle. I'll not put my life off until I know for sure. I want to live it."

"You always were better at *hardunger* than I was," Elsa said much later that evening as the two sat by the fire. She picked at her knitting, but her mind buzzed with a thousand thoughts that distracted her from her counting.

"You do not concentrate," Kaatje said quietly, still staring at her tiny needlework.

"I was thinking about Tora, wondering where she is tonight," Elsa dared. "I wonder if she had a decent Thanksgiving. If she even knows she should be thankful for what she has."

Kaatje set down her needlework and stared into the fire. "Tonight, as I tucked Jessie in, for the first time I was truly grateful to Tora for giving her to me. Not that I haven't appreciated Jess before this," she amended quickly. "It's just that for the first time, I was really glad in my heart that Tora chose me to leave that precious girl to."

"You realize, of course, that she probably thought of it as justice. A way of punishing Soren."

"Sure, sure. But still, isn't God good? What she meant for evil, he has used to bless me."

"Jessie was blessed to get you as a mother, Kaatje," Elsa said, reaching across to squeeze her friend's hand. "Perhaps someday her real mother will realize what she lost."

"Or perhaps not. Some people never see the error of their ways."

"Like Soren?"

"And Tora. How many others have we known? If I'm ever that stubborn, promise me you'll slap me across the face."

"Kaatje!"

"Promise me."

Elsa guffawed, but seeing her earnest expression, nodded once. "And you do the same for me. Just the thought of it is enough to keep me straight."

Kaatje's face melted into a grin. "You had better walk the straight and narrow." She glanced back at the fire. "You're sure you want us in Seattle for the winter? Will it not be too much?"

"It will ease my heart considerably. Going back to the house alone with Kristian makes my heart ache. Your presence—and the girls'—will make it much easier to tolerate."

"We cannot stay forever. The farm—I'll get Einar to care for the animals and look in on the house. But I'll need to return come springtime. I was thinking we should leave in a couple of weeks."

"Grand! Just grand!" Elsa came out of her chair and knelt by Kaatje. "Thank you, friend, for this. I know it is not easy to leave your home."

"And come to yours? Yes, I guess it will be a sheer sacrifice," she said, amusement in her tone. "The girls will think they've died and gone to heaven."

thirteen

*I*t was only as Tora awakened on Thanksgiving Day that she felt the depths of her despair. Her new job and the new challenges before her had buoyed her up, given her a false sense of importance, and taken her mind off her immediate circumstances. But with the day off from teaching, she had time to ponder her true condition. Winter was fast approaching, she thought dismally, shivering as the frosty air met skin. What would a long winter as a schoolmarm in a shack be like? And what was there in life to look forward to now? She had no friends and had been treated as an oddity in her new surroundings.

The children were off today on holiday, but the cantankerous schoolteacher had not received one invitation to Thanksgiving dinner, Tora mused. She was alone for the first time, left to her own devices. Suddenly, she longed for the warmth of her mother's kitchen, and even her father's gruff voice. She longed to return home, snuggle deep into a feather comforter with Gratia's careful design stitched to its cover, and listen to the sounds of her Bergen home. Even seeing Elsa and Carina wouldn't be all bad, she supposed. What was her alternative? Eating cold beef and hard rolls. That was her day.

She groaned and turned over, thinking of last Thanksgiving. She and Trent had had a nice reunion in Helena the day before, and had hosted over twenty people for the holiday dinner. It had been a bois-terous, loud event, after which Trent had claimed he wished they had spent it alone. At the time, his words had irritated her. Now, she wished she could hear them again, and relish the loving heart from which they emerged—the desire to be with her alone. How could she have jeopardized that love? Her chance for a future?

Tora flipped back over, agitated by her thoughts. Trent had been more than her future. In the beginning, that was how she saw him. But the years and the distance taught her more. She had loved him, with her whole heart. She had loved the way he moved, the way he held her like a precious, fragile doll, the way he had given her room to grow and to show the world what she could do. She had loved talking business with him, making plans, building something together. And now she had nothing of him. The tears were gone from her eyes, but the ache still built within her gut.

Frustrated, she pushed back the covers and sat up. Nothing would be accomplished by lying in bed and mooning over a man who had banished her not only from his life, but her own world as well. She threw on some more clothes, her breath clouding in the cold morning air, and hurried to the potbellied stove to get a fire going. Today she would stuff the cracks in the wall with strips from an old dress, and at-tempt to make her shanty a worthy shelter for winter. And her piled luggage would form a nice wall of insulation on the north end of the shanty, the direction from which most of the valley's wind came.

But as she worked, memories of Trent kept entering her mind, memories of happy times and all she had lost. What did she have to be thankful for this year? she chided herself, attempting to take control of her self-pity. A roof over her head, a bed, a meal—sad as it was— and a means to support herself. But what about the other things in life, things like family, friends, love…? Again, an overwhelming sense of loneliness entered her heart. Working to find inspiration, she grabbed a sheet of paper and pen and sat on her bed with a book. She did not stop to think. She merely wrote what was on her heart, deciding that she would consider later whether or not to send it.

> *25 November 1886*
> *Dear Trent,*
>
> *You have been in my thoughts constantly since the day we last parted. I owe you an apology for my actions. First, for hiding the truth of my child from you. Second, for using your name to get ahead in my own enterprise while jeopardizing yours. I was a woman scorned, and acted in haste, not wisdom.*

Tora paused for a moment, wondering what to write next. Although she truly felt regret, could she actually convince herself to send such words to him? She pressed on.

> *I was wrong, Trent, and I am deeply sorry. You meant the world to me, and I tried every which way to make you love me too, all to no avail. It is only now that I realize that we had the love I so desperately sought, but risked it for my own gain. You never deserved to be betrayed, nor to be deceived. I hope you will find happiness someday. I am in search of it myself.*
>
> > *Always yours,*
> > *Tora*

The words, when she reread them, felt frightfully honest and frank. Trent would probably laugh as he read them. But something inside her drove Tora to leave them as they lay, to fold the paper, once dry, and seal it inside one of her last French envelopes. She addressed it from memory, feeling as if she were running a hand over Trent's cheek instead of the smooth stationery. "I miss you, Trent," she whispered.

Her teacup, sitting on a warming tray above the stove, suddenly rattled, and Tora looked up. It became silent, so she again considered her letter. But when it began rattling again, it did not stop, and then Tora felt the rumble under her floor. What could be making such a commotion?

She peered out the window, and could not see anything out of the ordinary for a long time, but the ground trembled more and more even as her trepidation grew. When the first head of cattle came into view, Tora breathed a sigh of relief. It was merely a cattle drive. A cattleman taking his stock to the railroad, or overland himself. It made sense they would come this way, by the schoolhouse. It was on a strip of land that ran for miles without fences, whereas most of the homesteaders had erected barbed wire to keep cattlemen from razing the land on their way through.

A horseman cantered by her window and pulled the stock to a halt. Probably thirsty, Tora thought, rushing to grab her pail and her coat. She opened the door, glad to have a little company on this lonely day, when she saw the first cowboy's face.

Instinctively, she knew he was trouble. His eyes were deep set and constantly shifting, and his posture reminded Tora of a mountain lion on the prowl. He was large, strong, menacing. She took a step backward.

He whistled and looked her over appreciatively, obviously enjoying her alarm. "Now, I had heard the schoolmarm out this way was something to see."

Tora looked quickly at his two companions to see if they approved of him. Both looked as trustworthy as the first.

The leader dismounted and strode up to her with confidence. "Going to offer me some water, miss?"

"Certainly," she said, pretending to feel more at ease than she felt.

As she bent to pump the water, she could feel him edge nearer to her than was proper. Sudden laughter from his cohorts made her look up with suspicion, but he smiled innocently. "Here's your water," she said, handing him the pail without offering a scoop. She stepped away.

"Much obliged," he said, his eyes never leaving hers.

"I am glad to help."

He set the bucket down and took a step closer. "Helpful women are difficult to find this far west."

"Not if you look hard enough," she said lightly. "My man and I plan to marry in the fall." It was a desperate statement that she hoped would fool them. "Whose cattle are you running?"

The man's scarred face slowly widened in a lazy smile. "You tryin' to lose me? Tell me the truth. You don't have no beau." He took another step closer, merely inches from her body. "Why make up a fantasy man when I'm right here? That's right, we haven't even been properly introduced. Have to be introduced if we're to get to know each other. Name's Decker, at your service." He took off his hat and bowed low before her, setting his cohorts to chuckling.

Tora stepped away before he could reach an arm around her. "You boys get your water and get on your way. I'm expecting my ride for Thanksgiving dinner any minute." She hoped her voice sounded more confident than she felt. To her, it sounded like a blatant lie. She went to close the door behind her when Decker pushed it in, his friends laughing as if they were watching a circus clown.

"You can't come in here!" Tora yelled, suddenly desperately afraid.

"On the contrary," Decker said, peeling off his huge jacket and advancing toward her. "There ain't no man around to protect you. And as I said, we should get to know each other better. I'm a lonely cowboy. You're a lonely schoolmarm. I think we should take advantage of our situation."

"Get out. Get out!"

"Don't worry, sweetheart. I'm here. I'm here to be your man."

When Mr. Crosby's news of Tora's absence reached Joseph Campbell upon his return from his Helena holiday, he immediately hurried from Spokane to the schoolhouse to search her room. Outside in the yard were the tracks of a herd of cattle. It being long after midnight, he lit a second lamp from his wagon and studied the tracks further. He could see evidence of three horses. He moved inside, tentatively opening the door with his foot while holding the lamps in his hand. "Miss Anders?" he called, his voice sounding thin and quiet in the night.

The room was a mess. There had been a scuffle, judging by the overturned chair and by the bed. Then he noticed the drops of blood. Joseph looked around grimly. She had taken none of her luggage, if he counted right. And she had disappeared a couple of days ago. Thanksgiving Day, probably. The only people who had left their homes for anywhere besides church had been some cowboys driving a hundred head of cattle through town. Was she crazy enough, desperate enough, to take up with one of them and leave everything she had behind?

Joseph shook his head. Tora Anders loved her things. It had been hard enough for her to leave her home. There was no way she would willingly leave the few things she still possessed. What had caused her to depart without her clothing and possessions?

Then he spied the letter addressed to Trent. He picked it off the floor, wiping away the dirt that smudged its surface. *Mister Trent Storm,* she had written in a clear, concise script. Joseph decided to open it—perhaps it would give some clue as to her whereabouts. It was critical to know where she had gone and if she was in trouble. And it was critical to know right away. Swiftly he read the letter.

These were not the words of a woman who was saying good-bye. They were honest words written from the heart, a heart's apology, a heart that was missing Trent. Had she turned a corner? Some corner Trent had been waiting for? Joseph knew, deep down, that something monumental had happened to Tora before writing these words. And after.

He turned to go. He would send a messenger with the letter directly to Mr. Storm. And he would track down Tora Anders.

Decker used Tora until they reached the railroad days later. He offered her to his friends, but they declined, apparently embarrassed. *Thank heaven for small mercies,* Tora thought distantly. She no longer felt as if she inhabited her body, so tired and abused was she. She did not know when her trial would end, and when Decker hustled her aboard an empty railway car, she despaired that he was coming with her.

"I'm afraid I'm headin' in a different direction, Tora," he said, tipping his hat as if he were a gentleman suitor saying good-bye rather than her abductor. "I want you aboard this train so we can gain some distance. Don't think about squawkin' to the sheriff. I'll be long gone, and you'll just be a used-up prostitute as far as he's concerned. Not that I didn't appreciate your favors."

Tora scrambled to the other side of the car, receding into the darkness as Decker stood in the doorway, his massive silhouette visible against the moonlight. She trembled from the cold, but more in fear that he might use her one last time. She couldn't believe that he was leaving her, letting her escape from him!

"Don't get off this car, Tora," he said quietly. "It'll leave in an hour or so. Going straight to Seattle, you are! You strike me as a city kind of girl. You'll like it. If you get off here, I'll kill you. And if you tell any tales about me, I'll hunt you down and kill you later. Understand me?"

Tora nodded, her throat dry.

"Understand me?" His voice rose. "I'll find you again."

"Yes. I understand you," she said, with a voice that came from the depths of desperation.

Decker straightened and nodded again. "Good. Happy trails, Tora. Maybe we'll meet again."

"Only if I have the pistol and you're at the other end," she said, suddenly fiercely angry.

Decker laughed uproariously and hopped off the train. "Now you do as you're told and stay in this car. I swear, if I see your pretty head peek out I'll have to shoot it off."

Tora did not respond. Decker disappeared from the doorway, and Tora did not dare to look out. She did not know how far they had traveled by horseback in the last few days, but they were a good distance from Spokane. When she thought about it, she could not care. All she could think about now was the relief of being away from her kidnapper and how utterly, completely lost she was.

Days later, a railroader found her half-frozen body in the car and yanked her out, practically dumping her on the tracks. She groaned and winced at the aches in her body.

"Tramp," he spat out and turned to walk away.

Tora's throat was so dry she could barely speak, but she attempted to do so anyway. "W-wait. Wait!"

The man turned around in dismay, obviously disgusted at himself for speaking to such a woman.

"Where are we?" she asked, flinching at the ache in her throat.

"Seattle. You're in Seattle, Washington Territory. Not that you paid for your passage here. Now get out of here before I call the sheriff and have you locked up."

Numbly, Tora found the will to stand. It was late afternoon, judging from the slant of the sun, and if she spent another night without a blanket, she knew she might die. Looking down at her dress, she closed her eyes. She did look like a tramp. Her dress was in dirty, stripped rags. With aching arms, she felt her head. Parts of her chignon still held, but most of her dark hair was down around her shoulders. From what she could see of the long strands, it was full of barbs, knots, and straw. She started to laugh, a small giggle that built to a doubled-over, hysterical laugh. Another railroader passed by, shaking his head, which made her laugh all the harder. They thought her a tramp. A crazy, no-good vagrant with no place to go. And what was she other than that?

She wiped the tears of laughter from her eyes and made herself start walking. She needed a bath and a roof for the night. She needed sanctuary. Where would she find that in such a large, bustling city? She was terribly weary, weak from lack of food and water. Tora decided water would be first on her list to find. Forcing herself to take step after step, she made her way off the train tracks and toward the throngs of people. She wove through them, searching each face to ask for a bit of water, but none would look at her. Eventually, she was past the station and wandering the streets, looking blankly at sign after sign, hoping that someone would tell her where to go. Give her some food.

It was getting dark, and Tora was growing more chilled by the minute. It was clear that no one was going to help her. Knowing she could not walk more than a few steps without collapsing, she looked up at the nearest building. A stable. She turned and walked in as if someone were guiding her. The stable master was talking to a client. She walked right past the two of them, to the very back, where there were several empty stalls, and went into one with fresh hay. She paused only twice, once to scoop her hand into a startled horse's bucket of water and allow the cold, fresh liquid to flow past her aching throat and then to steal a half-rotten apple from a table nearby, no doubt meant as a treat for one of the stallions.

Hearing the stable master finish his business, she scurried into the stall, wincing as the rough wood squeaked on its hinges. She paused there for a moment, half waiting for him to call out "Hey! You there!" but no call came. Tora managed to take the three remaining steps toward the back and cover herself with hay as she swallowed the apple practically whole, rot and all. Seconds later, she was asleep, feeling safe for the first time in days.

Tora was jolted awake as the enraged stable master grabbed her by the hair and began dragging her out of the stall. Then he grabbed her arm and pulled as she struggled to get to her feet. She wondered if she had just fallen asleep, since it seemed to be about the same time as when

169

she had curled up in the hay, but dimly surmised that she had slept for more than twenty-four hours since the horses were in different stalls than the night before. The stable master threw her out on the street, where several ladies stopped to gape at her.

"Stay out of my stables, tramp! This is no hotel!"

Tora would have died of embarrassment a month ago at such treatment. Now, all she could think about was what she would do next. She crawled to the nearest lady. "Please. Please. I have nowhere to go. Please help me."

Stiffly, the woman pulled her fine silk skirt from Tora's dirty hands. "Come, Sara," she said to a younger lady by her side. "I do not want you seeing such sights." The younger woman did as she was told, but a third lady remained.

Tora turned to her. "Please." She searched her tired mind for a stronger word, a word that would get through to someone, anyone. It came to her. "Mercy."

The woman, who had turned to follow her companions, visibly faltered. She searched her purse for a coin and threw it at Tora's knees. "I do not know what has happened to you, miss, but pull yourself together."

She walked off and Tora fought off another urge to laugh hysterically. As if she had the means to pull herself together! She picked up the coin and rose, dusting off her skirt. A penny. Perhaps it was enough for another apple, not a rotten one stolen from the beasts. She had to eat something and soon, or she would not be able to think at all.

She went to a corner store and hungrily looked at the foodstuffs. But the merchant threw her out, saying, "Get out! Get out!" as if shooing away a stray cat.

"I have money!" she yelled, waving the penny before him. "I simply wanted to purchase an apple!" How could people be so unjust? So unfair? So unchristian? She checked herself. How often had she treated people the same?

An apple dropped at her feet. "There's your apple. Use your

money for the good sisters at Our Lady of Hope. They'll give you a bath and help you get on your feet again."

Tora bent to pick up the fruit, uncaring of its dusty condition. "Our Lady of Hope?" she asked in confusion. Hungrily, she took a bite, dimly aware that she would have once frowned upon others for doing the same in public.

"Up the street," he said in obvious irritation. "Are you stupid as well, woman? Get yourself to the Catholics. They have a mission for people down on their luck."

Tora sucked in her breath and knelt at his feet. "Thank you! Thank you! I tell you, I just need a bath and a night's sleep—"

"Yes, yes," he said, his voice a little less gruff now. "Get on with it, then, and away from my storefront."

She nodded. "Thank you, sir. Thank you." She turned to wander up the street, ignoring the lewd comments from men entering and exiting the saloons, and the contemptuous glances of the more sophisticated crowd. At the end of the road sat a brick cathedral, its tower standing straight to the sky. In the doorway was a warm light, and as she drew closer, there was a sign—"FOR ALL GOD'S CHILDREN IN NEED OF ASSISTANCE." She did as directed and followed the path around to the kitchen in back of the building. There, more than twenty people who had obviously been living on the street waited in line. A heavenly smell filled the air.

"What's that?" she asked in wonder of the man nearest her. "What's that incredible smell?"

"Why, that's soup, sister. You new here? They feed us every night. You being a woman and all, they'll give you a bed tonight, if there's room."

Soup and a bed, Tora thought dreamily. *Surely this is of God.*

fourteen

December 1886

*K*aatje quickly settled into Elsa's elaborate home with the girls, feeling as if she were on some dream holiday. Here in Seattle, she had her own four-poster bed and an indoor lavatory at the end of the hall. On each floor, no less! The house had been wired for that modern miracle of electricity, but each hall lamp also was connected with the house gas supply, to be used when the electricity failed. Which it often did. But even the luxury of lamps that never needed re-filling was a marvel to Kaatje. How could she ever go back to her dimly lit, modest home and be content again? she wondered.

Yet when she thought about it, she yearned for her house in the Skagit Valley. It was cozy, warm, and sufficient for their needs. This winter would be a good experience for her and the girls. And return-ing to the place they belonged would be a good lesson as well. *There is a place in the world,* Kaatje thought, *for the haves and the have-nots. For now I'll enjoy pretending I'm one of the haves!*

She leapt out of bed and hurried to her robe and slippers, pro-vided by Elsa of course. Since arriving, Elsa had purchased three new dresses for her and each of the girls, as well as underclothes, new shoes, and other necessities for city life. When Kaatje had protested, Elsa whispered, "It's my way of helping. It makes me happy, Kaatje. Would you rob me of such joy?"

Looking into eyes she had seen filled with tears too often of late, Kaatje had acquiesced. *God has given me friends who give generously,* she decided. *I will give back in other ways.* With that in mind, she hurried to the door and down the grand staircase. In the kitchen, she found Mrs. Hodge just pulling fresh rolls from the iron woodstove, filling the house with heavenly, yeasty smells. "Those look divine," she said, stooping to sniff over the pan.

Mrs. Hodge shooed her away, reminding Kaatje of her dear aunt who had raised her in Bergen. She smiled back into Mrs. Hodge's falsely disapproving face. But Kaatje knew the woman took delight in pleasing Elsa and her guests. "You'll not be having one until everyone else rises," she said.

"Then I'll go and roust them immediately."

"Under no circumstances!" Mrs. Hodge said, genuinely alarmed. Her frown faded to a grim smile when she figured what Kaatje had done. "Well all right, just one. But you'll wait until I have a proper cup of coffee brewed for you."

"Of course," Kaatje said, sitting at the rough kitchen table. "Mrs. Hodge, how long have you been working for the Ramstads?"

"Since five years back. Worked for them in Camden when my dear husband—God rest his soul—was killed on board a Ramstad ship in a freak accident. I was beside myself, not knowing what I and my two boys would do. Then dear Peder—God rest his soul—convinced me to come to Seattle with them. Wanted someone trustworthy in the new house, you know. We knew enough good folk in Camden-by-the-Sea to find a suitable replacement, and I jumped at the chance for employment."

"They were blessed to find you."

Mrs. Hodge blushed to her hairline. "You're kind, miss. I'd say the same thing of you. God knew what he was doing to send you to the valley for Elsa to go to in her time of need."

"I need her just as much as she needs me." Then, "You've never been tempted to remarry?"

"Ach, no. There never was anyone like my Phil, and never will be again, I'm afraid. Got my two boys raised, and they're off to find their fortunes."

Mrs. Hodge poured two cups of steaming coffee, pried out a sticky roll from the pan, and sat down with Kaatje to watch her eat.

"You're not having one?" Kaatje asked, taking a bite immediately. It was full of caramel, pecans, and cinnamon, and the dough was decadently rich. "Mmm, Mrs. Hodge, these are incredible."

"An old recipe," she dismissed. "I'll have one later. There are plenty more."

"But none right out of the oven!"

"There's something to be said for delayed gratification."

"And immediate gratification."

The two smiled at each other. Kaatje decided to take a chance. "Mrs. Hodge, when you all moved west, did the Ramstads bring any Christmas decorations?"

The housekeeper smiled ruefully. "You've noticed it too, then. Elsa can't seem to make herself get out and purchase any this year."

Kaatje nodded, chewing, thinking. "It probably feels unfair to her to be celebrating anything in the wake of Peder's death."

After a moment, Mrs. Hodge said, "I have some household cash for such things. Elsa brought none of her decorations from home, leaving them there in case they returned for the holidays. Perhaps you and I…"

"That would be marvelous!" Kaatje enthused. She had been trying to figure out how to scrape together enough money for decorations and still be able to purchase presents for all. If Elsa could not find it within herself to prepare for Jesus' birth in suitable fashion—making the house and hopefully the occupants festive—then Kaatje and Mrs. Hodge would take care of things.

"I've been thinking of pine swags for the staircase," Mrs. Hodge said conspiratorially.

"Beautiful! And a huge wreath for the front door!"

"My nephew can get a tree."

"Get a huge one. One that will near the ceiling of the parlor!"

"Why, that's nearly fifteen feet!"

"Don't you think?"

"Yes, you're right. It would look foolish to have anything smaller. And you and the children should go downtown to find decorations. We'll string popcorn and cranberries here, of course, but a tree in a house such as this deserves some city baubles and lots of candles."

Kaatje smiled and clapped her hands. "Oh yes, lots of candles! On the tree and throughout the house! They'll love it. It will look just grand!"

Two days later the house was transformed. The tree was in place, the swags hung from the staircase rail, and a wreath graced the door. Elsa, for the first time in months, was laughing and singing with the rest of them, apparently forgetting for but a moment that Peder was missing. *And so it begins,* Kaatje thought, remembering how it startled her when she first stopped noticing that Soren was not present.

The children ate more popcorn than they strung—as well as too many of Mrs. Hodge's Christmas cookies—and Kristian and Christina were sent to bed early to tend to their aching bellies. The others stayed up, talking about the Christmas cantata and past celebrations. The distraction and hubbub were good for them all, Kaatje decided, smiling at the shine on Jessie's face. The girl was relishing this time with her aunt and cousin, though she didn't know Kristian was a blood relative. She had taken to the boy much as she did every animal that entered their barn, carefully tending to the younger child's needs and joyfully playing with him from dawn until dusk. They would miss one another once the Janssens left for home.

When the children and Mrs. Hodge had turned in for the night, Elsa and Kaatje were left to sit beside the crackling fire, a more quiet, relaxed atmosphere for stringing. They enjoyed the compatible silence for a while, each in her own private thoughts.

"I couldn't have done it without you," Elsa said, letting her hands rest on her lap. "It would not be much of a Christmas this year for Kristian, had you and the girls not come."

"It's the best present of all for me to be here," Kaatje returned. "You know how dear you are to me, Elsa. And you have treated us like royalty since we arrived. We'll never want to go home!"

"That would be fine with me," Elsa said, carefully studying her next piece of popcorn for a suitable place to puncture. "Why don't you stay?"

"And leave my farm? Let the ground lie fallow?"

Elsa shrugged. "Perhaps. For a time."

Kaatje waited until she looked up again. "Elsa, our place is there. This is a dream of a holiday for us, but it cannot be forever. You need to find your own walk again too."

Elsa looked away and into the fire. "Where? I wish I was as sure as you! You have a place. Someplace to return. Someplace where…you're sure of yourself."

Kaatje shifted in her chair and said, "When your man is gone you're forced to look only to yourself. I sometimes think that I let Soren pull too much of me into him. It was as if he sucked half of my life into his own body so that when he disappeared, part of me disappeared too. As if he left me leaning over, trying to find my other leg again. Just so I could stand."

"Exactly!" Elsa said, eyes wide. She considered her words for a moment and then said, "I never thought I was so dependent upon Peder that losing him would feel like I died too."

"It's impossible to love and not give of yourself, Elsa," Kaatje said. "It's the risk of life. Each time we choose to love, we choose to risk a part of our heart. But how much would we be missing without taking that risk? I think it's worth it. You simply have to let yourself have some time to find your equilibrium again."

Elsa rose, letting the popcorn in her lap fall to the ground, and walked to the window. "Right now, Kaatje," she whispered when Kaatje came up behind her and placed a hand on her shoulder, "I wish I had never risked it. I wish I had never loved Peder. It's too painful."

"I understand," Kaatje said. "But what would you have missed? You must concentrate on that, Elsa. Dwell on all the joy you shared, all the laughter, the love, the peace. Otherwise, the darkness and pain of your mourning will overtake you."

Elsa turned to embrace her, weeping again for the first time in weeks.

"Elsa," Kaatje said, backing away after a minute. She stroked her taller friend's lovely face, wiping away the tears. "You have so much to be thankful for. I know that you miss Peder horribly. But he'd want you to live, to celebrate. He'd want you to take every moment for the gift that it is from God. Cling to that. And do not feel guilty for living when he had to die."

Tora had come within a block of the Ramstad home nearly eight times. Never had she been able to force herself to walk the last block and face her sister. Today a light, wet snow was falling, chilling her to the bone and almost convincing her to go, if for no other reason than to seek warmth and shelter.

"Go on, why don't ya?" Magda said, shivering behind her. For some odd reason the older woman had attached herself to Tora as soon as she had entered the Catholic shelter. Magda seemed drawn to Tora, no matter how poorly the younger woman treated her. Tora had grown to accept her as though she had no choice about it; she felt strangely comforted by the batty woman's presence. "You know you want to," Magda urged again, seemingly unable to stop herself from repeating her words, "Want to. Want to. Want to. Go see her. Go see your famous sister."

At least Magda never doubted Tora's word—that her sister was the Heroine of the Horn. One day, while cleaning one of the mission's rooms, Tora had discovered an old newspaper, opened to the obituaries. When she saw Peder's name, Tora had sunk to the ground, her hand over her mouth in shock. Magda had found her. "What? What is it?"

"It's my brother-in-law," she said, waving vaguely at the paper. "He's dead. Elsa's alone as I am."

"You should go to her," Magda had said. For a woman who frequently raved like a creature riddled with madness, Magda could sound terribly lucid for moments at a time.

"You don't know what has happened between us. You don't know what I've done. Elsa will never forgive me."

"There is nothing done that is beyond forgiveness, child," Magda had said. Tora studied her, thinking that an unearthly, holy light seemed to emanate from the woman. It was moments like this, when Magda seemed to have a toehold in eternity, that Tora found her fascinating. But a moment later, Magda was yelling, "Heroine of the Horn! Heroine! Heroine! Tora is sisters with the Heroine of the Horn!"

Her announcement at the mission left Tora open to hushed jeers and sarcastic remarks from the others. Only Magda and the sisters continued to treat her with anything akin to respect. Days after arriving, she had secured enough work from the home to pay for her food and lodging, but nothing more. She existed on thin soup and day-old bread donated by the baker, and slept on a hard cot amid a hundred other sleeping, snoring women. She frequently spent hours, when not working, spying around town, trying to overhear any news of her sister. Eight times, she had come as close as this to facing her sibling but never closer.

"What holds you back?" Magda asked again, shivering in the late afternoon breeze that blew the snow at a slant.

Tora laughed, a hollow sound. "Pride, I suppose. I wanted to face her again. But I wanted to arrive in a fine carriage. In fine dress." She turned, angry at Magda because it was easier than being angry at herself. "Look at me! A trollop living in a Catholic shelter. I haven't bathed in a week."

"We're blessed to get a bath each week—"

"In lukewarm, used water?" Tora shivered at the thought. Was there much more she had to bear?

"Still, it's something…"

"Magda, why do you cling to me so? Why don't you live your own life and leave me to mine?"

Magda studied her with rheumy eyes. "'Cause you've been touched."

"Touched?" Tora shook her head. "You're mad. Perhaps it's spreading."

"No. Jesus has come near."

"And run away as fast as he could," Tora said with another hollow laugh.

"No. He's here now."

Tora studied the woman, observing again a light that seemed to shine within her. It took her breath away. "Why?" she asked unsteadily. "Why would he bother?"

"Because you are loved."

"Impossible. No one loves me. I have driven them all away."

Magda looked from the sky to her. "I love you, Tora. Your sister loves you. Jesus loves you more."

Tora turned and walked away. "You know nothing. You should take your love to someone more worthwhile," she called over her shoulder. "I am undeserving of even a madwoman's love." She continued walking, not watching where she was going. In a few moments, she bumped into a young woman, making her dump all her packages—presumably Christmas presents—across the boardwalk.

"I'm sorry," Tora muttered, stooping immediately to pick up the nearest package, wrapped in brown paper and tied with string. How many similar bundles had she brought home last year in Helena? she thought.

"No trouble," the woman said, stooping nearby. Something in her voice made Tora look up. She could not look away. It was Kaatje. Kaatje Janssen.

"Here, Mama," said a girl, rushing up behind her. "Christina and I'll help you."

Tora felt dizzy, as if she would faint at any moment. Still, she could do nothing but stare. At Kaatje. At Jessica. At Christina. At Jessica again. She looked similar to Letitia Conner in Spokane, she assessed, as if safely viewing her from a hidden spot, but she looked different. Her mother's intuition was dead-on. Tora would have recognized the girl anywhere.

"Are you okay, miss?" Kaatje was asking. "You seemed to be—" Tora met her eyes. Her recognizing, understanding gray eyes. The last time she had seen them, she was depositing Jessica at Kaatje's feet. Then they had been angry, disbelieving eyes. Now they were only disbelieving. "T-Tora," she said simply.

Tora, coming to her senses, scrambled to her feet. Everything in her told her to run. *Run. Run. Run.* She ran past a cackling Magda, past the cemetery, past the Catholic mission to the waterfront. It felt as if she never could run far enough.

At the wharf, on an abandoned dock, she walked to the end, conscious that the rotting planks could give way at any moment and she would plunge into the icy waters below. But she did not care. It would be fitting, she thought, to drown in the murky waters, held down by broken planks, her lungs filled with cold. She deserved nothing more. What was she thinking? Attempting to see Elsa? And now Kaatje and Jessica? She was not worthy of them. Of any of them.

It was still snowing. Giant white flakes wept into the Sound, disappearing on contact with the water. It was as Tora felt she herself should do, to allow herself to slip into the water and out of life forever. If she took one step, it all could be over. The misery. The striving. The ache. The pain. "Dear God," she mumbled, looking up to the sky and watching as the snow came down, making pinpricks on her face as ice met warmth, "dear God in heaven, what do you want?" Her voice grew louder. "What do you want from me? What do you want?" she screamed.

"He wants you," a voice said behind her.

Tora whirled, almost falling. "Magda. How—how in the world—?"

"He wants you," the old woman repeated.

Suddenly, Tora knew the truth. Knew it in her heart, in her bones.

Magda was not a madwoman at all.

Magda was a seer.

f i f t e e n

*oy to the world! the Lord is come. Let earth receive her King!" Karl smiled as his smooth bass joined the other voices in the congregation in this final hymn of the evening. In the magnificent cathedral in downtown San Francisco, their celebration seemed all the more joyous. Even the thought of returning alone to his modest rented cottage a mile south failed to dampen Karl's spirits. He was here to worship his Savior; nothing else mattered.

To be able to travel back in time and see the babe in the manger! Karl thought, glancing at the nativity scene at the front of the church. *What would it be like to look upon the face of Jesus?* His God in infant form! The thought overwhelmed and warmed him at once. How good it was to be again in companionship with the One who mattered. It all made sense to him now. His despair. His loneliness. His very soul had been crying for the Christ child.

As the pastor dismissed his congregation calling "Merry Christmas! Go and serve the Lord!" people mingled and chatted as they walked down the center aisle. People Karl had never met stopped him to introduce themselves and wish him a blessed holiday. Just as he was nearing the door, a burly man in a fine overcoat turned and smiled at him. "Good day, sir. I'm Gerald Kenney. Merry Christmas to you!"

"And to you! I am Karl Martensen," Karl rejoined as they shook hands. He watched as Gerald pulled out a pocket watch and glanced at the time. On the face of it Karl could see an anchor. "Are you a sailor by chance?" Karl asked.

"Ah, I love the sea," Gerald said, placing a hand on his shoulder with all the familiarity of an old friend. "I'm afraid my good wife has convinced me to stay ashore from now on. I merely invest."

"I see," Karl said, following Gerald's gaze to a portly woman he supposed was Mrs. Kenney and to his two young daughters. "I've just returned to sailing myself. Docked last week from Seattle."

"Seattle? Were you on the *Silver Sea,* by chance? Serving under Captain Stover?"

"Aye. He's a very fine captain."

"That he is. I believe he was actually here at this service. Have you been a sailor long?"

"Just returned after a bit of an absence. To be honest, I cannot wait to get back to it."

"Understood," Gerald said, his eyes brightening. "Nothing like the sea, and the anchor," he added meaningfully, gesturing toward his watch, "to remind a man of what is important."

Karl met his glance, wondering if Gerald was possibly talking about his faith as well as the ocean. One look, and he recognized a brother in Christ.

"Hayden!" Gerald called, motioning for Karl's captain to join them. The two men shook hands, clearly old friends, and shared Christmas blessings.

When Captain Stover turned to see who else was with him, he smiled, and said, "Why, Martensen! Good to see you! Merry Christmas!"

"And to you too, sir," Karl said, returning the captain's firm handshake.

"This man," Captain Stover said, speaking to Gerald Kenney

while placing a hand on Karl's shoulder, "signed on as a common deck boy but could've been running my ship."

Karl shifted uneasily under the praise.

"Where'd you get your experience, son?" Gerald asked.

"Sailed for some time out of Boston Harbor, then later for an operation out of Camden, Maine. Of late I have been making my own investments along the interior riverways in steam and the like."

"Ah, I see," Gerald said.

"Got to Seattle last month and found that God wanted me to take a new direction. At least for a while," he said uneasily. Speaking overtly of his Lord still was a bit awkward to him. "The sea is the place for me; I was born to be on the water. I've taken a leave of absence from my regular duties. My business partner will carry on without me until I decide to stay ashore."

"When do you ship out again?" Captain Stover asked him. "Will you be rejoining my crew?"

"It would be a pleasure, sir," Karl said. "I simply have not decided where I am to go next."

"Well, you're welcome anytime, Martensen," the captain said. "If I didn't have a first mate that was like a brother to me, I'd hire you on as such."

"That's high praise, sir. Have a very merry Christmas."

"And to you." He turned to Gerald with a nod. "Kenney. Don't eat too much turkey."

"Only until I cannot move a muscle." Gerald turned and motioned toward his family. The ladies walked toward them in genteel fashion, and Karl smiled at all three, making the young women blush. "Mr. Martensen, may I present my lovely wife, Rosalind, and my daughters, Nina and Mara."

Karl bowed slightly. "So pleased to meet you all. Merry Christmas."

"And to you, Mr. Martensen," Rosalind said warmly.

"Mr. Martensen just docked from Seattle," Gerald said. "I thought we might have him join us for dinner—"

"Oh, that's very kind, but—" Karl interrupted.

"Nonsense," Mrs. Kenney said, hearing no excuses. "There's no friend like a new friend, and we'd be pleased as punch if you would join our Christmas celebration." The girls giggled in unison and ducked their heads when Karl looked their way.

"Well, this is truly a surprise. Thank you. Shall I come to your home later?"

"No, no. Our celebration begins now," Mrs. Kenney said. "Follow us, if you're free to do so."

"Of course. Again, I am humbled by your generosity."

"It's Christmas!" Gerald said. "No time like the present to follow the example set by Christ himself."

Trent had spent Christmas morning with his great-aunt and was relieved when he could excuse himself by noon. The woman was tiresome, never doing anything but complain, and to make things worse, she ate to the point of gluttony, often allowing crumbs to spill out upon her lips and her breast. They had nothing in common. She even refused to attend church with him that morning, wanting nothing to do with "those hypocrites" at Duluth's First Presbyterian, or any other church for that matter. Her life was empty and angry, and Trent wished he had more family than her. He longed for his dead wife. He longed for the children they never had. He longed for Tora Anders.

For all her foibles and grand ambition, Tora was filled with the spark of life. He felt drained just thinking about it. Had he made the mistake of his life in letting her get on that train to the Montana territory four years ago? Had he made a bigger mistake closing her out and shutting her business down last summer? Sickened at the thought, he roamed through the tall, silent grand hall of his home and to his office. There, on a massive mahogany desk, under a brass paperweight, was the letter he had read a hundred times.

25 November 1886
Dear Trent,

You have been in my thoughts constantly since the day we last parted. I owe you an apology for my actions. First, for hiding the truth of my child from you. Second, for using your name to get ahead in my own enterprise while jeopardizing yours. I was a woman scorned, and acted in haste, not wisdom.

I was wrong, Trent, and I am deeply sorry. You meant the world to me, and I tried every which way to make you love me too, all to no avail. It is only now that I realize that we had the love I so desperately sought, but risked it for my own gain. You never deserved to be betrayed, nor to be deceived. I hope you will find happiness someday. I am in search of it myself.

Always yours,
Tora

He was still there, standing quietly, struck numb by conviction, when a knock sounded at the front door. The servants had been dismissed for the day, cozily tucked into their homes and surrounded by family. The sheer emptiness of it all hit Trent once again, and he wearily headed to the door. Who could be out and about on Christmas Day?

The front door came open with a creak at its massive hinges. A small boy was outside, shivering in the cold. He stretched out a tiny hand. "A message for you, sir. Urgent from the telegraph office."

Trent dug in his pocket for two bits. "Thank you, son. Merry Christmas."

"And you, sir!" he exclaimed, looking at his palm and the coin.

Trent did not wait to see him out the gate. He closed the door, ignoring the irritating squeak that usually drove him to distraction. Curious, he opened the telegraph envelope before returning to his study.

25 December 1886
FOR URGENT DELIVERY TO: Mr. Storm

Mr. Storm:
Have found subject in question. Situation dismal. Living
in Seattle. Exact location is unknown. Will establish con-
tact shortly. Please advise as to next steps. Campbell

Trent sat down heavily, suddenly feeling every hour of his forty-two years. Tora was alive. Not in good condition, it appeared. But alive. When Joseph had reported his suspicion that she had been kidnapped by some cowhands passing through, Trent had become physically sick. It had all been his fault. To what had he exposed her? Why hadn't he been more understanding? Why hadn't he married her when he had the chance? Perhaps if…

He stopped himself right there, knowing that God had answered his questions long ago. There had been a reason that Trent saw no way other than to let her go. It had been so clear to him at the time—that she had to go her own way to discover what was truly important, what was vital in her life, before they would ever have a chance together. She had been deluded, chasing empty dreams, and she had to see that for herself, since she would have never heard it from him. He clung to that truth, that understanding in his heart. For every day he doubted it. How could God have led her to such a dangerous path? How could he have taken her from the safety of Trent's wing to the streets of Seattle? Was she ill? Would they ever have a chance again?

Quickly, he reached for his pen and dipped it in ink to draft a return telegraph message.

25 December 1886
FOR IMMEDIATE DELIVERY TO: *Joseph Campbell*

*Locate subject immediately. Secure room and board. Seek
medical assistance if necessary.*

He paused to pull out a drawer and consult a train schedule, then
returned to his missive.

Will arrive on 2 January. Meet at the Butler Hotel.
Storm

Karl smiled happily as he exited his rented coach. Life was an adventure! One never knew what the next turn in the road would bring, what friend he would meet next. He was amazed at the instant camaraderie he had felt with Gerald Kenney, and breathed a silent prayer of thanks for an entire new family he instinctively knew would become dear friends. There was something about them all that reminded him of the Bergensers. And the feeling made him jubilant.

Mrs. Kenney opened the door, welcoming Karl inside. "Come in, come in, Mr. Martensen. You may give your overcoat to Ronni, here," she said, gesturing toward a diminutive maid beside her. "Then my Mr. Kenney is awaiting you in his study. He'll be pleased to share some refreshment with you while I oversee the kitchen staff. My girls have retired for a bit."

Karl smiled at the tiny, round woman who reminded him of a tough sea captain thinly disguised in feminine ways and garb. No doubt Gerald had his hands full with this one. It was just what Karl sought in a wife—a mind of her own, strong ways, but never losing the charm of womanhood. A woman like her would be a true helpmeet. A friend. A mate for life. He sighed, dismissing the question that crossed his mind every once in a while: When would he meet the right match for him? Perhaps it was never to be. And perhaps it would not mean emptiness for his life, if he could fill it with people he enjoyed like the Kenneys. Surely there were other ways on God's fine earth to find peace, fulfillment.

Gerald turned from a map of the Northern Territories on his wall. "Ah, Martensen," he said, reaching out a hand to his guest. He nodded toward the map. "A gift from my daughters. You've seen much of it, I suppose?"

"Yes," Karl said, envisioning each place as if he were there again. "There are many beautiful sights."

"And plenty of business opportunities, yes?"

"Indeed. The West is full of opportunity. But then I like to think the entire world is our Creator's richest blessing. We have yet to see but a tiny portion of what he has to offer us."

Kenney smiled, looking as pleased as if he had come up with the concept himself. "A fine idea," he enthused. "Has it been your thought for long?"

"A most recent idea, actually," Karl said. "You see, I was away from my Savior for some time." It amazed him how the words came from his mouth effortlessly now. Heretofore, speaking of Christ made him vaguely uncomfortable. But now, it was as if something significant had shifted within him, making him feel as if talking about Jesus and his lead were as easy as speaking of the beauty of San Francisco Bay. A major reason had to be Gerald's own openness, he decided.

"Astounding news," said Gerald. "I am so glad you've found your way home, son."

And as Karl stared back into his eyes, he had the distinct feeling that Gerald too felt something like kinship.

s i x t e e n

When Kaatje had fantasized about seeing Tora again, she had imagined experiencing many feelings, many reactions. Mostly frustration and fury. Never had she anticipated fear. But it was the first thing she thought of upon seeing Tora, upon seeing Tora look at Jessie. Fright. In all the years she had held Jessie to her chest in comfort, wiped away her tears, laughed with her, played with her, fed her, tucked her in at night—never had she considered that Tora would want her back. When Tora had turned and left the babe on the dirt road in a basket, Kaatje decided she was truly never returning. No mother who loved a child could do such a thing.

But what she had witnessed six days before was the face of a woman in pain. Tora not only loved Jessie, but longed for her. It was as plain as day. What would happen now? No matter that the woman was plainly in desperate straits. She was Jessica's mother! What would Tora do? Would she steal her daughter back? The thought of it had kept Kaatje awake at night, listening to the cracks and groans of the settling house and making her rise to check on the girls each hour.

It was three in the morning on Christmas Eve when Elsa found Kaatje in the parlor, staring at the dying embers of the fire. "Will you tell me what has been bothering you now?" Elsa asked gently.

191

Kaatje turned to glance at her through the darkness of the room. "I'm afraid I have a confession to make, Elsa."

Elsa sat down on the edge of the sofa, waiting.

"I've seen Tora."

"Tora, my sister?"

"Yes. I ran into her. Literally. She was but a block from the house, standing with an old woman, staring this way. She turned suddenly—"

"But, where is she?"

Kaatje shook her head and paced a bit. "I'm sorry. I do not know. When she recognized me and the girls, she ran. I called after her but she just kept running. There was no way to catch her." She rose and walked over to her friend. "Elsa, she was not well. She's terribly thin. She looked like she was living on the streets."

"The streets? Tora?"

"It is my guess that that is why she's here in Seattle. She's at the end of her rope, so she's come to you. And yet she cannot face you. Let alone me and Jess."

Elsa was silent for a moment, then walked to the window. "Why did you not tell me immediately?"

"I don't know. I've been frightened."

"Frightened? Of what?"

"That she'll want Jessie back," Kaatje said quietly. "If you could have seen her eyes, Elsa. It was with a mother's eyes that she looked upon Jess. I was afraid you'd want me to give her back."

"Give her back?" Elsa scoffed. "To a mother who willfully abandoned her own child? For nothing more than spite and a desire for personal gain?"

"So much has happened to her. We may never know. She may have changed since then."

"What could have happened? Last I heard, she was being courted by Trent Storm and was a successful businesswoman in her own right. She's made the papers more than I!" Elsa walked to the fire, clearly irked at the memory of her sister's indulgences, and how she had tossed her family aside with little thought. "Do you know that I was even interviewed by a private investigator? He let it slip that Tora claimed her family was dead. *Dead.* Can you imagine?"

"I don't know," Kaatje said. "Whatever happened, it must have been ugly, to make her fall so far. She's in rags, Elsa."

"Rags?" Elsa asked, disbelieving. She strode back and forth across the room.

"Yes. Her eyes—you know how she always had that look in her eye? As if she could see the future and knew where she was going? There was never a time that I could see doubt in her. She was always so…sure. So dead-on."

"And?"

"She's lost, Elsa. The look is gone."

"I have to find her," Elsa said dully.

"I know," Kaatje whispered.

Elsa paused. "You are Jessica's mother, Kaatje. More than Tora ever will be."

Kaatje could do nothing more than nod.

"Trust me in this. My loyalty lies with you. But she's my sister. I have to find her. No matter what has transpired, I need to make sure she is all right."

"And I'll have to tell Jessica the truth."

"You would have had to do that eventually."

"I know. She just seems so young. How do I tell her something so foul?"

"You tell her she is loved and always will be loved," Elsa said, taking Kaatje by the shoulders. "You tell her she will always have her Auntie Elsa, and you as her mama. But you have to tell her about her real mother."

"O God," Kaatje muttered heavenward, her breath taken away at the thought. "How am I to do that? How am I to bear it?"

After running into Kaatje and considering suicide on the old docks, Tora had left the safety of the mission and made her way in the streets of Seattle. If Kaatje told Elsa of seeing Tora, and her obvious despairing condition, the mission was the first place Elsa would look. Tora wanted to see no one. Especially her sister.

Tora was starving, but she didn't care. Again, she thought of her desire to die. She wanted to melt away, to end the pain and despair that God had brought upon her. She laughed mirthlessly. There was no need to die and go to hell; she was living in hell now. She had no home, no job, no friends. She had distanced herself from her family. And when she looked to herself, Tora did not like what she saw.

By lying to the whores on Washington Street, she was told of a woman who could give her some medicine to end her life painlessly. After stealing enough to barter for two bottles of the murky green liquid—twice that necessary to do the job—Tora went to her, feeling as if she were removed, reading her own story from a book rather than living it out. She sneaked into the town stables for the night and sat staring at the bottles she held in her hands, sealed with corks and wax. *Am I ready to give up my life?* she asked herself.

I am better off dead. She peeled off the wax and uncorked the first bottle. It shimmered in the faint light of a nearby lantern as the stable master walked by. She gazed into the bottle, making her wonder again what it contained. Tora's heartbeat did not even pick up at the sound of the man's footsteps. She cared little if she was discovered and thrown out yet again. Perhaps the stable master might even call the sheriff, as he always threatened. At least she would then have a cot and a blanket at the jail. Maybe some food.

She sat up to cover herself better with hay, making it more difficult for anyone to see her and warmer at the same time. Tora had no idea what would happen once she drank the liquid. Only that it wasn't likely to be pleasant. Feeling she had no other choice, Tora drank the foul concoction down in five big gulps. She winced at the bitter after-taste in her mouth, immediately feeling sick to her stomach, but forced herself to swallow the other bottle too before she lost courage. Moments later, bile rose in her throat and she retched, quietly at first, then more violently.

It was impossible to keep back the sound, or her coughs, and it wasn't long before the stable master found her and dragged her to the street, calling her every dirty name he could think of. "Comin' here, after drinkin' away your money," he derided as she writhed before him in the street. She felt as if her stomach were coming apart, it hurt so badly. "Stay in the mud and filth, you louse! You don't deserve to sleep among my horses' manure!" he yelled, kicking her thigh.

Tora gasped for breath, wondering how long it would take for it all to be over. She was alone on the abandoned street, shivering with cold, curled up in pain. Her cheek scraped against the rough brick of the street. "Help me," she whispered in spite of herself. She had not been prepared for the excruciating pain of death, and it made her weak. "Help me!" she called feebly, wondering if anyone, anyone at all, was around.

"It's my only way out," she chanted to herself, wincing at the pain that rivaled childbirth. She was no longer able to think of anything but the knifelike sensations in her gut. "My only way out."

You will live. There is another way.

Tora looked around, wondering if there was indeed help about. She wiped sweat and tears from her eyes, trying to see better. "Magda?" she whispered.

You will live. There is another way.

"No. I'm going to die. Tonight. It is the best way."

It is the wrong way.

Tora winced and looked around again. "Magda? Come out. I need you."

You need Me.

Tora stilled, listening harder.

You need others.

Tora laughed mirthlessly, bearing through another pain. "I need no one. Haven't I proven that?"

Have you?

Again, Tora could think of nothing for a while but the pain. "I am going to die."

You will live.

"For what reason?" she whispered.

For Me, if for no other.

"Who are you?"

You do not know?

"Who…are…you?" she ground out.

I am the Alpha and the Omega. I am the Source. I am the Christ.

All at once, the pain was gone, and warm hands were lifting her, cradling her. "Don't worry, child," Magda said. "It will be all right. I've come to take you someplace safe."

"Merry Christmas," Magda said when Tora awakened the next morning. Tora looked around in confusion, trying to get her bearings. There was a cracked window covered in newspaper and peeling paint on the rough-hewn walls.

"The abandoned warehouse," Magda said, as if reading her mind. "I know you didn't want to go back to the mission—to the mission—mission—on account of your sister. You have to make that choice on your own." She patted Tora's hand, and moved to take a can of beans from a nearby shelf. "Here," she offered.

Tora turned away, grimacing. "I almost died from retching last night. I cannot eat…those."

"Suit yourself," Magda said.

Tora raised a hand from beneath a pile of filthy blankets to press at her temple. "How did you find me?"

"The Lord led me to you," she said simply, stuffing her mouth full of beans.

"You heard him last night too?"

"Heard what he had to say to me, at least. Told me where to go and collect you."

"Did he tell you that I want to die?" Tora spat out. "That I had hoped it would happen last night?"

Magda stopped chewing. "Life is not something we should give away."

"God doesn't care about me. Look at me! What I once was..."

"God's ways are mysterious."

Tora laughed. Had God ever seemed mysterious to her? Not at all. She had hardly lived as Amund and Gratia Anders had raised her; certainly God was angry at her, and this was her punishment. So why save her? Why not let her die? She searched her mind, relishing her fury. But after a while her thoughts came to rest upon Jessica. And moments later, the vague idea that she was secretly glad to be alive. Somewhere, deep within her, was the tiniest glimmer of hope.

"It's a second chance," Magda said, again as if reading her mind.

"For what? I cannot find a way to live like this. I cannot find a way out. I'm trapped."

"You must surrender," the older woman said, rising and walking to the window. "All your life, you've never surrendered, have you, Tora? Tora. Tora. Tor—"

"To whom? Why should I?"

"Because. Life is easier when you do. To the One who loves you more than any other."

Tora was still, listening to Magda, thinking about how her words sounded so familiar, so similar to the Voice that spoke to her last night. They were words her mother would have used.

For a long time she was silent. "But why?" she whispered. "Why would he want me? Why me?"

But Magda was gone into another realm again, lost in mad giggles.

"Dear God," Tora whispered, staring at the ceiling. "You had to send me a crazy woman as my angel?"

Later that day, Tora felt healthier than she had in years. Aware that it must be a delusion, that she truly had faced death the night before, she walked on leaden feet down the now-familiar path to Elsa's home. For a long time, she stood outside. It was terribly dark from the gray clouds overhead, but at least it wasn't snowing or raining.

She made her aching fingers open the front iron gate. As she approached, she could see a family around the dinner table, a fat golden turkey at its center and Scandinavian dishes surrounding it. She identified Elsa, and a boy who must be her son, then paused. She stepped closer to the window, feeling as if she were a phantom, invisible to the people inside. There was Kaatje, with a girl to her left who must be Christina, and to her right

"O God," she whispered. *O God.* She felt as if she could not breathe. Sitting there was Jessica, so beautiful, so perfect. Her Jessie. The pain of a thousand nights flooded her soul, and Tora sank to her knees in the wet snow underfoot. The movement drew Kristian's attention, and he pointed her way. Ducking as if avoiding a snowball, Tora rolled from the window and on aching legs ran for the gate. The front door opened behind her and Elsa called, "Wait! Can I help you? Miss! Tora? Tora, wait!"

But Tora kept running. It was enough for now. It was enough just to see them.

seventeen

January 1887

Elsa sighed into the mirror as she watched Kaatje pull out long sections of her golden blond hair to wrap into an elegant coiffure. "I do not know how you do this to your own," she said despondently. "Another reason why you can't leave. I'll be left to my same old out-dated chignon."

"It's beautiful any way you do it," Kaatje said with a small smile.

"Perhaps. But if all the ladies in town saw me without an elaborate hairdo and pearl comb, they'd deem me unworthy of any invitations."

"Really, Elsa! Such a thing to say!"

"I cannot help it. They're all so catty, the way they talk and talk of nothing."

"I'm probably fodder for their rumor mill," Kaatje said. "The poor relation come to visit."

"I don't care. I have half a mind to invite old man Yessler's wife over to tea. The women have practically ostracized her. She wouldn't be invited to anything if she weren't married to a founder of the city— whose business is it that there's such an age disparity between the two of them?"

"My goodness, who put a bee in your bonnet today?" Kaatje asked, stopping to stare at Elsa in the mirror.

"I suppose it is Tora," Elsa said, idly picking up a pearl-handled brush from Japan and twisting it in her hands. "I cannot get her out of my mind."

"We have scoured the city. She'll have to come to you when she's ready."

"And you," Elsa added.

Kaatje nodded and continued her work on Elsa's hair, adding delicate ringlets around her face after the knots were done.

"Well, now you have my hair ready for a ball," Elsa said. "But I can't get into anything but my shift. Mrs. Hodge says there's no room to let out my dresses anymore."

"Showing more with this one, are you?" Kaatje asked, gesturing toward Elsa's waistline.

"I think it's twins."

Kaatje dropped her hands to Elsa's shoulders. "I know what would cheer you! Let's visit the dressmaker. Get her to make you some decent maternity dresses! The girls will love it. You remember how they played with her scraps and buttons for hours?"

"While Kristian moped about."

"Perhaps Kristian can find another playmate for the afternoon. Come, Elsa, you need to get out. I need to get out, for that matter."

"Very well. I believe you're right," Elsa said, rising to try and find something suitable to wear about town.

Kaatje breathed a sigh of relief as the carriage pulled up outside the house and the girls and Elsa climbed in with her. Since the elation of Christmas had faded away, they had all slowly succumbed to a "funk" as Mrs. Hodge called it, withering like the pine swags about them until everyone felt a bit brittle and irritable. The constant, drenching rain, so common this time of year, did not help matters. Getting out was just what they all needed. And new dresses for Elsa might raise her spirits as well.

Elsa was stunning, Kaatje admired from across the carriage. Despite her hardship, mourning, and pregnancy, she was still one of the most beautiful women she had ever seen. Even in black.

She looked out the window and thought about her own appearance. Despite Elsa's generously purchased dresses, she still felt like a brown church mouse next to her dearest friend. If she had only been a bit prettier, perhaps Soren would never have gone. Yet some days when she awakened, she half expected to hear that he had arrived, tracking them down from the Dakota Territory to the valley. But he remained absent as ever, and she fought off her disappointment and faced the new day.

Maybe that was why God was calling her north. So the nagging question of where her husband was, what Soren wanted from her in the future, was laid to rest. *Alaska,* she thought, visualizing the word written on paper. It seemed terribly wild and untamed to her. An unlikely place for a farm maid from Bergen. But if she had made it this far, could she not go farther?

"Kaatje? Kaatje!" Elsa was saying. "Are you with us?"

"Oh. Yes. Sorry. A little daydreaming, I'm afraid." The girls giggled at each other, happy to see their mother caught for once.

"I was saying we ought to have luncheon out. Just us ladies out and about on the town."

Kaatje smiled. "That would be lovely."

"Then it's settled. We'll get some suitable clothing for my increasing girth and then go fill my stomach with some delicious eats!" she said, tickling Jessie.

Kaatje looked back out the window. As they passed through downtown, past Our Lady of Hope, an old woman caught her eye, and Kaatje struggled to place her. Where on earth had she seen her before? When she finally knew, they were several blocks past, and Kaatje decided not to stop the carriage. "Elsa," she said, still thinking.

"Yes."

"I've had a thought. Tomorrow, let us check in with the good sisters at Our Lady of Hope. Perhaps we and the girls could do some

charity work there. Helping prepare food, serve, whatever the need."
She stared into Elsa's eyes, making her understand her true purpose.

Elsa nodded, clearly comprehending. "It is a good idea. Today we play. Tomorrow we get to work."

"This is just wonderful," Elsa scowled into the mirror as Madame de Boisiere took her measurements. "Could not bustles be out this year? That's just fine, madame. Simply give me a bustle in back, *and* in front."

Kaatje covered a smile and moved to face her friend. "You'll look lovely, I'm sure."

"Then add to that every shade of black one can imagine and I'll look like a rotten potato."

"My, you're cantankerous!" Kaatje chided. "If Madame de Boisiere cannot make you the most beautiful expectant mother in town, then no one can."

Madame de Boisiere smiled demurely and went on measuring. "You will be a pleasure to drape, Madame Ramstad, with child or no. We will merely add more ruffles up front."

"No, please. I prefer long lines to help disguise my stomach, or soft drapes of fabric."

"Good," the dressmaker replied. "We will do as you suggest."

The woman had a soothing manner, and Elsa relaxed as the session went on. Jessica and Christina, dressed in their own finest frocks for the outing, were deep into a pail of buttons, wrapping scraps of material about their heads in what appeared to be their attempt at an elaborate coiffure. It did feel good to be out, Elsa admitted to herself, and to be doing something about her desperate clothing situation. None of the maternity dresses she had worn when carrying Kristian were suitable, since none were in black. She didn't know if she could've borne the idea of wearing them again anyway. Each dress would remind her of Peder, of where they had traveled together, of the way he had looked at her in it, anticipating their first child.

Ever since proclaiming to Kaatje that she had no sense of *place* as Kaatje obviously did in the Skagit Valley, her words had come back to pound at her like heavy waves upon the beach. It wasn't completely true. While she enjoyed her time in Seattle and Camden, she had been happiest on the ocean. She missed the sea. It was where she was meant to be, just as it had been for Peder. But the thought of traveling alone frightened her. Peder had been her protector on the waters, her captain. She had simply gone along for the ride. She couldn't imagine how she would do it without him, but she knew she needed to. For herself.

"I am going back to sea," she said, abruptly voicing her thoughts.

Kaatje sat down and smiled. "I had wondered when you would come to that. When?"

"This spring, I suppose. When I get the nerve up to try it on my own. Truly on my own again."

"What about the baby you're expecting?"

"I'll wait until she is born. Or he."

"You had thought Seattle would bring you comfort."

"And it has," Elsa said, turning to face her. "As you have. But over the last few days, I've realized that my future is where I found my foundation with Peder. At sea. I need to travel, to discover new sights, to uncover new business opportunities on my own. Start building new memories."

"You'll sail with Riley?"

"I'll captain my own ship."

Madame de Boisiere paused almost imperceptibly, then resumed her work.

Kaatje's eyebrows shot up. "With Riley as your mate?"

"Riley has his own ship now. I will find a suitable, trustworthy first mate." Her tone brooked no discussion.

"Already the captain," Kaatje commented wryly.

Elsa ignored her comment. "You think it unseemly that I go to sea myself?"

"I think it irresponsible if you don't have someone at your right hand whom you would trust with your life."

"Of course. I will choose my mate, and the others, very carefully."

"What would Peder say?" Kaatje asked quietly.

"He would be glad I was on the waters he loved so well. And he would be furious I was out there on my own." She turned toward Kaatje. "But he never did understand—truly understand—that I loved it nearly as well as he. And I learned so much! By the time we docked here, I felt I could round the Horn myself, should the opportunity ever arise again."

She turned back to her mirror image as Madame de Boisiere went on measuring and draping fabrics. "In some ways it would be carrying on Peder's legacy. Teaching Kristian the art of seamanship. Exposing our children to new lands, new cultures. Could there be a better education for them?"

"You sound as if you are arguing with yourself."

"I'm thinking aloud." She smiled for the first time, looking mischievous. "Do you think I have the tenacity to actually go through with it?"

"No doubt, Elsa," Kaatje said with a grin. "There is no doubt."

Later that evening, poor Kristian was paraded through the parlor, the victim of the girls' attempts at their own dressmaking. Kaatje and Elsa laughed until they cried, until Kristian cried himself at being the target of their good humor.

"Forgive me, darling," Elsa said, gesturing him toward her and unwrapping him from the faux dress, and wiping her eyes. "We so appreciate the laugh, though. Let me give you a big kiss for bearing it." Kristian grimaced and scooted away from his mother, not at all appeased by a buss on the cheek for his tolerance.

"I'm going to play in my room," he announced regally. "With my *trains.*"

The women could barely hold in their laughter until he had exited. They returned to a small table and their game of chess—a game each endeavored to master. Peder had taught Elsa the basics aboard ship and Elsa had taught Kaatje. "That's yet another good reason to return to the sea," Elsa said. "Kristian will need male influences in his life."

"But of what caliber?" Kaatje asked delicately.

"Well, I see your point," Elsa said, studying the board before making her next move. "But there are many fine men aboard Ramstad ships. Some are more coarse than others, but most have a good heart. I believe it is good for a child to be exposed to all kinds of individuals—within reason, of course—to prepare them for this great big world we live in."

"And what about men like Mason Dutton?"

Elsa glanced up at Kaatje quickly, then back to the board.

"They never did catch the man, did they, Elsa?"

Elsa shook her head ever so slightly.

"Are you ready to encounter him again? On your own? Without Peder or Karl at your side?"

Elsa's mind flew back to Honolulu, to spotting Mason in the mercantile. Simply seeing him had struck terror through her heart. Even Peder had run. And since her column had been printed, the American and British navies had doubled their efforts to catch the vagabond.

"I read he is not truly an officer of the Royal Navy." Kaatje had obviously been keeping track of the news too.

"No," Elsa said, finding her voice again. "He was, once. Then went astray. Apparently, the uniform simply helps him get what he wants."

"I read that he has been operating like the pirates of old," Kaatje pressed on. "Slipping through the law's fingers time and again. He has raided more than five ships this year, Elsa." She waited until Elsa looked her in the eye. "You have made a powerful enemy. To expose his enterprise to the entire English-speaking world—"

"There are dangers wherever we go," Elsa interrupted. "I always wanted Peder to face him. Expose him. Get others to track him down and turn him over to the authorities. He never would." She lifted her chin. "He will not make me run."

Kaatje shook her head. "Peder Ramstad was one of the wisest, strongest men I knew. Why would he run? The only reason I can think of is that he feared for you. For Kristian. Don't you see the wisdom in that?"

"I do not see the wisdom in backing away from a fight," Elsa said. "Again, I tell you I will choose men I trust. And men who can protect me and our ship. I will choose wisely."

Kaatje stared at her for a long moment. "Then God go with you, my friend. I can see your mind is already made up. But please. Please search your heart for wisdom in this. I fear for you already on the seas. Add a shark like Dutton to the mix and it terrifies me. He will not treat you well should he get his hands on you again, Elsa. And you have the children to think about now."

"Do you think I'm not a good mother? That I care not for their safety?"

"Of course not. No one loves your children like you. But I'm not sure you're thinking through all the ramifications. Yes, there is the incredible opportunity to show your children the world. But they could die as you try to pass the Cape of Good Hope, or be taken prisoner by Mason Dutton. It is a glorious world out there, on the sea. It is also incredibly dangerous."

"Life is full of risks. Our greatest gifts come when we face those risks and get to the other side. You yourself have said so."

"But God has given us the wisdom to analyze those risks, and choose when we should take them. Peder opted not to risk Mason Dutton again."

"I realize that," Elsa said, her irritation growing. "I know that! Don't you think I debated before I filed that column on Mason? But look what has happened. Efforts have doubled to catch the rogue."

"And all have failed. In the process, Mason probably is doubling his own efforts to find you."

The thought struck Elsa dumb. "You think…you think he would actually dare to come after me?"

"I think, my friend, that a man as ruthless as he is capable of anything. And it is time, should you wish to be captain, that you think as he does. Wise as serpents, harmless as doves."

Kaatje left Elsa by the fire with that, satisfied she had raised the questions that needed raising. As she walked up the stairs, she wondered how many of her questions were simply queries she had asked herself should she actually go to Alaska. What dangers would lie in *her* path? Was it completely irresponsible to risk her life, as well as her daughters', to go? For the oceans were no more dangerous than the mountain frontier. For every shark there was a bear. For every shoal there was a river to cross. No, Elsa and she both headed to dangerous places.

But instinctively, Kaatje knew they had no choice but to move forward.

eighteen

*I*t was a cold, drizzly, wintry day that January in San Francisco, but nothing could put a damper on Karl's mood. He stood beside the proud iron frigate—the *Tempest*—just christened from a fine yard in Boston in which Gerald Kenney had a stake. She had been abandoned by her captain once he made it west. It seemed he had obtained a touch of gold fever while rounding the Horn and was heading north to the Alaska territory. When Gerald had come to Karl with the opportunity to captain her, Karl had leapt at the chance. To be at sea again! And at the helm of a ship on the cutting edge of modern technology! He could not seem to stop praising God for smiling upon him. If it went well, he would build his own ship in the coming year.

Mrs. Kenney clucked around him as his mother used to do, fiddling with his coat collar and his sleeves, fretting that he might not be warm enough. Her daughters, Nina and Mara, still did not treat him as a brother as he wished they would; instead they threw him coquettish glances, staring at him until he met their gazes and then dramatically lowering their lashes. He laughed at their girlish attempts to win his heart, playing the role of an elder brother with whom they could test their feminine wiles without being held responsible for their actions. They were young, and neither was the type of woman he sought for his bride. At least not yet. Perhaps in a few years, he thought, giving Nina a second glance before shouting an order to Lucas, his first mate.

"She has a first-rate steam engine, and is fully rigged for square sails, should you need them," Gerald said for the tenth time. Clearly the man yearned to at least set sail with Karl, if not see distant shores again.

"Yes," Karl said. "It will be a pleasure to have the power of not only sail, but a steamer's triple-screw propeller at my fingertips."

They looked up together at the *Tempest,* studying the four masts and huge boiler tubes on what otherwise looked like a normal frigate. "You think she might be a bit unwieldy in heavy seas?" he asked.

"The first mate reported a propensity to heave to port in swells of over fifteen feet," his friend said gravely. "I've been puzzling over that all week. I cannot imagine the reason."

"I'll figure it out, Gerald," Karl said forcefully, wanting him to have no reason to doubt his captaincy. "I've designed over twenty steamers and plenty of sailers with Peder. Give me some time on her, and we'll solve the problem."

"He'll do just fine, Gerald," Mrs. Kenney said, nudging her husband. She faced Karl. "He only pesters you because he wishes he were going with you."

"You can take the man off the sea—" Karl began.

"But you can't take the sea out of the man," enjoined Mrs. Kenney. "I told him he could go. You've become like a son to us, Karl. I think he'll miss you as much as the voyage."

"Oh, pshaw," Gerald put in.

"He said he couldn't leave me and the girls. Thought we might get into some mischief." Her eyes twinkled with merriment, before she continued, "Do an old sea captain's wife a favor, will you?"

"Anything."

"Send word soon on your progress?" The girls were now at their mother's elbows, hanging on every word.

"Every port."

"You are a true gentleman, Karl Martensen," Mrs. Kenney said smugly, as if she were indeed his mother. "We'll look forward to your return."

"As will I. But now I should see to the ship. Mrs. Kenney, Nina, Mara." Mrs. Kenney nodded her head, beaming with pleasure, as the girls dissolved into giggles and blushes.

"I'll walk aboard with you," Gerald said, gesturing toward the gangplank. And Karl wondered momentarily if he would end up setting sail with them after all.

"Very well. Good day, ladies."

"Go with God, Karl."

Once aboard ship, Gerald turned to him. "Son, I wish to give you a small gift."

"Gerald, you've done so much for me already—"

"Nonsense." He reached into his pocket and pulled from it a gold watch, an anchor on its face. "I saw that you were in need of one."

Karl smiled. "Mine broke some time ago." He shook his head. "A fine captain I am, eh? What sort of man sets sail without a way of recording the time?"

"I'm sure you would have managed. The anchor," Gerald said, placing the fine timepiece in Karl's hand, "is to remind you of what is important. So you never stray from our Savior again."

"I'll think of it on every occasion I check for the time."

"Very well," Gerald said, lifting his chin and clapping Karl on the shoulder. "Blessings on your voyage, Karl. Treat her well."

"I will, sir. Thank you for entrusting her to me."

"It has been a long time," he said, staring Karl in the eye, "since I met a man I would ever trust more. We'll see you in a few months."

"Very well." He paused and cast a glance over his shoulder. "Last chance, Gerald," he said, raising a brow. "You're sure you won't come along for the ride?"

"No. My place is here with my family. Perhaps on another trip."

"I'll look forward to it," Karl said, shaking his hand. "Now I had better see to the ship or we'll never get under way."

Trent stood before Elsa's house, wondering what he might say to the sister of the woman he loved. He had read Elsa's columns, and consequently felt as if he knew her in part. What would she say when he told her who he was? How would she react? He paced outside the wrought-iron gate, searching for the right words. Would she think him mad? What kind of man came to a woman's door and asked about her sister, a sister who had seemingly disappeared from the city within days of arriving?

Shaking his head, Trent forced himself on. There was nothing to say but the truth. Flat out. Removing his hat as he reached the door, he knocked twice and waited. A middle-aged woman answered his knock, and after eyeing him suspiciously, led him to the drawing room before seeking her mistress.

Moments later, Elsa appeared. Upon first inspection she seemed very different from Tora, as fair as her younger sister was dark. But when his gaze alighted on her eyes, he found it difficult to breathe. For in them he saw the same shade of turbulent blue that Tora's were. It was a color he had not seen before meeting an Anders woman, and had not seen since.

"Mr. Storm?" Elsa said in concern when he did not speak. "You look ill. Please. Sit down," she said, gesturing toward a settee nearby. "May I get you a glass of water?"

"No, no," he said, shaking his head in embarrassment. "Forgive me. I am Trent Storm. You are Elsa Anders Ramstad?"

"I am." She sat down and gestured again to the settee. "You have come about Tora," she stated.

"I have. You see, I had a detective trace her path to Seattle. Apparently, she has been living here for some time."

"Yes," Elsa said, looking sorrowful. "I have looked for her as well.

She has come close, as near as my window," she said, nodding to her left. "But when I saw her, called to her, she ran." She studied Trent with intent eyes. "She is not well, Mr. Storm."

"I am aware of her condition."

"You are aware she appears to be without a home? In rags?"

"Yes."

They sat in silence for a moment. "I am in love with your sister, Mrs. Ramstad."

She sighed. "Elsa. Call me Elsa. Do you know how many men have fallen in love with my sister, Mr. Storm?"

Trent nodded. "I imagine quite a few. But I believe we had something remarkable together. Something I should never have let go, but found I could make no other choice."

"She wronged you," Elsa stated flatly.

"In some ways." He studied Elsa's expression. Clearly, she was someone who knew Tora—and her patterns—well. But did she know how Tora had changed? What had begun, as evidenced in her letter to him? After all, it had been years since the sisters had seen each other or spoken. "You should see this," he said, taking out Tora's well-worn letter from his pocket. "It might explain why I've come after her."

Elsa took the letter from him and leaned back against her seat to read it. She was silent for a long moment afterward. "You think she was discovering what was right, what was true? After all this time?"

"It is my hope."

She rose and paced before him, clearly split between excitement and skepticism. "You don't know my sister. You don't know what she's capable of."

"On the contrary. I know her very well. I've seen all she's capable of. More important, I see all she's capable of becoming."

Elsa paused and sat at the edge of her seat. "She wronged you. That is why you parted ways."

"She did," he admitted. "Consequently she lost everything. I wanted her to learn that she could not always take advantage of others and win. I forced her to lose her business, her home. I walked away from her." He looked at Elsa, his eyes beseeching her to understand. "I had no choice, you see. I loved her desperately. But things were desperately wrong between us."

Elsa surprised him by reaching out a slender hand and squeezing his briefly. "I understand. I know what it is to love Tora. You did what you had to." Her look betrayed the anguish that she herself had felt over Tora.

Trent shook his head. "But she's gone now. Disappeared. What if I'm too late in returning to her side? What if she's dead now?"

"She is not dead. I saw her not two weeks ago. Tora is biding her time, trying to find whatever God is seeking to show her. She'll come to us when it is right. Believe me, I have turned this city upside down trying to find her."

"Everywhere?"

"Everywhere. She can't be found because she doesn't wish it."

"So we wait?"

Elsa shrugged. "What else?"

Trent suddenly laughed. "How is it," he began, laughing even harder, "that Tora is able to keep us on edge even when she's at the end of her rope?"

Elsa laughed with him, her voice soft and welcoming. "That is my sister," she said. "That has always been my sister."

Karl inhaled deeply, relishing the sting of rain against his cheek as it spread across the Pacific before him in sheets. Never had he felt more alive, more sure of his path than now. The *Tempest* was performing marvelously, and she was at full steam ahead now that the winds had died and only rain prevailed. What might once have set him back a day or two with sail was now overcome. He grinned, fighting to look up into the sky. "You see, Peder? There was a way to do what we both wanted!"

Lucas, the first mate, joined him at the rail, studying him for a moment as if he were batty. "Sir? The second-dog watch is in place, and we may retire. The crew will alert us if this rain becomes anything more serious."

"Good enough, Lucas. See you at sunrise."

Lucas left his side and Karl laughed out loud. Let him think his captain was on the edge of lunacy; it would keep him on his toes. There would be time enough to show him that Karl Martensen intended to be the finest captain on the seas of God's great creation. Until then he was satisfied to rest in his captaincy. There was nothing left to prove. God was again first in his life. And his Creator had given him his life's dream—a ship to command and a world to explore. Surely, all the rest of his dreams would be handled as efficiently. Until that time, he would rest in the peace that surrounded a man who was where he was supposed to be.

Karl laughed again. Why hadn't he thought of returning to sea years before?

nineteen

January 1887

*E*lsa liked the man who was in love with her sister. Time and again she found herself shaking her head, unable to quite believe that Tora had snared the heart of an honest, decent man, regardless of their difference in age. She refused to allow herself to hope that they might indeed reunite; that Trent Storm would one day become her brother-in-law. It was too much to ask for. Immediately, he had connected with Kristian and the girls like a doting uncle who truly enjoyed the antics of children. It was a delight to watch them interact and play. She paused in the doorway of the parlor, unseen, to study Trent as he built a tower of blocks with Kristian. Peder would have liked him too.

"I've brought tea," she said, setting down a silver tray laden with imported teacups and Mrs. Hodge's famous cookies. It had become a daily tradition for Trent to join them midafternoon. Over the last two weeks, they had talked about the search for Tora, Trent's business, his association with Karl, shipping, opportunities in the West, and eventually matters as personal as his relationship with Elsa's sister and their shared loss of spouses. She found the idea that Trent had recovered enough to love again comforting; perhaps if another had done it before her, she too could find her way out of the quagmire of grief to happiness.

"That will be perfect," Trent said, smiling at Kristian as he placed yet another block on a precariously leaning tower.

Kristian giggled and reached for another.

"Sure you want to do that, young man?" Trent asked with a raised brow. "She's looking pretty unstable."

Kristian eyed the tower and then Trent again. Pursing his lips, he resolutely turned back to his project. Concentrating, he licked his lips and delicately placed another block on top. The tower wavered, leaned an impossible quarter inch farther, but remained upright.

"Outstanding!" Trent said, clapping Kristian on the shoulder and smiling broadly. He rose and joined Elsa, who sat across the coffee table from him. "I believe you have a capitalist on your hands."

"He won't be the first in his family," Elsa said, pouring from the silver teapot. "Kristian, would you care for some tea?"

"No thank you, Mama," he said. "May I go join the girls?"

"If they'll have you," she said with a laugh. They had been playing in the attic since lunch with some old dolls Kaatje had brought home from a street vendor. Kaatje was back at the soup kitchen, filling in for Doris Mitchell, who had taken to her bed with the influenza. "If they want to play alone, come back and sit with us."

"All right!" he shouted, launching his small body toward the stairs.

"Slow down, Kristian. Slow down!"

"All right!" he responded, still running up the stairs as fast as he could go.

Elsa laughed and met Trent's smiling eyes. He was such a gentleman, kind and peaceful. Distinguished. She could see what had drawn Tora to him. Although he was probably over forty, there was a hint of childish delight in his eyes. Perhaps that was what had drawn Trent to Tora: While her childish ways were often irritating and still needed corralling, she too was inexplicably alive in ways that few others were. There was a vivaciousness, an inherent charisma that drew people to her like lava to the sea. "If only we could find some way to turn that flame into a burning ember," she muttered.

"Pardon me?"

"Oh. I'm sorry. Just talking to myself. Please. Tell me how your search went this morning."

Trent's face fell a bit. "She's here. There's no doubt. But she doesn't intend to be found. By now she must know I am in Seattle. She obviously doesn't wish to see me."

Elsa paused over her teacup. "Why would she not want to see you, Trent? You've put out the word that you'd like to see her?"

Trent stared back at her. "Our last meeting was not pleasant. Perhaps she is afraid."

"Of you?"

"You forget. I drove her from her home, her business. From any place that was safe." He looked miserable.

"Do not let yourself forget that you had no choice."

"How can you be so sure? You barely know me!"

"I know enough of you to see that you did what I would've done. Tora has a certain spark…we're all drawn to it. But she needs to learn how to harness that spark, that charm. She needs to learn that life and the people she encounters are not hers to bend every which way. She's a manipulator, Trent. Or was. I pray each day that she's discovered the path to God, the path that could bring her more happiness than she can imagine." Elsa rose and paced, wringing her hands. "That said, please understand I miss her terribly. How I wish that we could be close! She is my only relative here in America—do you know how lonely I am without her?"

"I understand your feelings wholly. Nevertheless, I fear she does not remember me with fondness. While the letter I showed you gave me hope, it appears that all manner of trouble has befallen her since then. What is to keep her from hating me? For blaming me for not protecting her? I had thought that she might have to fall, to lose what was dear to her to understand what *ought* to be dear to her, but this…"

"God," Elsa said, setting her teacup down gently. "God will see us all through this. I've agonized over Tora's choices for years. And still, I've missed her. I long for my sister as much as you long for your lost love, Trent."

Trent turned a pale shade of gray at the mention of love. He rose and leaned against the fireplace mantel, staring into the flames. "I lost my wife, Elsa. I cannot imagine losing Tora for good too."

"I understand," she said softly. "It is difficult for me to fathom risking my heart again. It is almost too much for one soul to bear." Dimly, she heard the front door open and close, but her attention was focused on Trent, for he was crying softly.

She rose and went to him, placing a hand on his shoulder as he wept. Suddenly, he turned and enveloped her in his arms. It was not the movement of a lover, but of a man in need. Instinctively, she wrapped her arms around his waist and bent her head to rest against his shoulder. It was not what propriety demanded. It was the compassion of a Christian for another in pain.

Elsa did not know how long they clung to each other before she heard Kaatje cough gently at the doorway. She moved quickly away from Trent, embarrassed when she noticed that someone was with Kaatje.

Tora.

Her sister looked ghastly, with an expression of shock and disbelief on her face as she gazed from her love to her sister in each other's arms.

"Tora," Trent gasped, wiping tears from his eyes.

"Tora, you're here," Elsa said, taking a step toward her. "I'm so glad. Won't you sit with us? It has been too long."

"Not long enough," Tora said, chin rising slightly. For once, her eyes were full of pain, not defiance. It sent a chill down Elsa's spine. Her glance went from Elsa to Trent and back again. "Your husband has barely been buried, Elsa. You must go after the man I loved?" She turned halfway, as if to go. "Not that I have any claim on him. Do I, Trent? Our love died long ago for you."

"No, Tora—"

"I know I did everything to drive you away," she said mournfully. Somehow, she managed to hold a dignified form, despite her attire and words. "I have learned much since my days in Helena."

"I know, sweetheart." He moved toward her but paused when she raised one hand.

"No. Do not come near me. I am not worthy of you any longer." She looked at Elsa again and nodded once. "It makes sense that you and my sister would come together. She is the one with whom you belong."

"You do not understand!" Elsa said, moving to grip Tora by the forearm. "He is mourning you! So much that it brought him to tears! I was only comforting a man in pain."

Tora glanced hopefully at Trent and then at Elsa again, her eyes dropping to the carpet. "You see?" she whispered so only Elsa and Kaatje, standing beside her, could hear. "I still bring him pain. I do not deserve him."

"It's not true. Tora, wait," Elsa begged as Tora flung off her hand and moved to the door.

"Tora!" Trent called, right behind them.

She turned and raised her hands. "Enough. I cannot handle any more. You both wished to see me. I am here. I am alive. And I will continue to survive. Please cease searching for me."

Both Elsa and Trent moved to follow her, but Kaatje held them back. "Wait. Let her go," she said softly.

Confused, they did as she bid, watching as Tora once again slipped out the door of their lives. They returned to the parlor and their cold tea. Trent sat and held his head in his hands. "What have I done?" he asked, sounding sick at heart.

"You did nothing," Elsa said. "You did only what you could."

"If I were a stronger man, Tora would have never seen us in such a…compromising situation."

"You are such a strong man that you are not afraid of turning to a woman for comfort," Elsa corrected. "Kaatje, where on earth did you find her?"

"I was in the soup kitchen," Kaatje began, searching her mind for that incredible moment when her eyes again met Tora's. "I filled in today for Doris. We've been there, how many times? Three times a week for a month now? Tora clearly came to see me."

"And what happened?"

"I was serving soup, when she was suddenly the next in line. She held no bowl. She just looked at me as if she wanted to be anyplace but there, yet could not be anyplace else." Kaatje looked from Elsa to Trent. "I had prepared myself to feel so many things. Anger. Fear. Frustration."

"And?"

"All I felt was this sweeping, abiding sense of openness…forgiveness. It was as if our Lord was present, directing me."

"What did you do?" Trent asked.

"I opened my arms. I stopped right there and then stepped away from the line and opened my arms to her."

"And she?" Elsa asked, holding her breath.

"Came to me directly." Kaatje giggled a bit, glad for the release of emotion. "I'm sure we were quite a sight, standing there."

"What did she say?"

"She said nothing," Kaatje said, her eyes filling with tears. "That was the majesty of the moment. She said nothing, only reluctantly received my embrace."

"Tora?" Elsa asked in wonder.

"Tora," Kaatje answered. She felt her face heat with embarrassment as she related the intensity of the moment. "I told her I needed to take her home. To see you, Elsa." Kaatje glanced at Trent. "I didn't know you were here. I would never have—"

"No, no," Trent said, holding his hands up. "You did nothing wrong." He looked rueful. "She simply picked the least opportune moment to reenter my life." He laughed a little. "Isn't that just like your sister?" he asked Elsa.

Elsa joined his laughter. "Yes. Tora always has liked making a grand entrance."

"The question is, has she made a final exit?"

Kaatje pondered his concern, then said, "I don't think so. I think she was taken aback, a bit bewildered to find you two…as you were. She probably spoke the truth. There is something different about her. Monumentally so. Let's trust that God is at work on her. We'll know soon enough about the outcome."

"You are a remarkable woman, Kaatje," Trent said. "To come through what you have. To bear the burden of what Tora laid at your feet…and still be able to forgive."

Kaatje shook her head. "It was not me. As I said, I've imagined feeling many emotions upon seeing Tora again, but none of them held a trace of forgiveness. I asked for it, I begged for it, but until today, I could not conjure up one smidgen of forgiveness within my heart for Tora Anders." She glanced at Elsa, then Trent, feeling hesitant to say what she had to say, yet unable to say anything else. "This is bigger than all of us. Never have I felt the Holy Spirit as I have today. He is here. He is present. And he is at work in Tora."

Magda took one look at Tora's face as she fled the Ramstad home and seemed to know just what to do. The old woman had followed Tora and Kaatje at a distance, and Tora had allowed it, feeling comforted by her presence. Now Tora followed her lead, unable to do anything else. She felt limp, exhausted, and worthless. She was empty, inside and out, and incapable of making another move on her own.

The old seer led her up the hill and down another. They made so many turns, Tora lost track of where they were in the city. Not that she cared. It would have made perfect sense to her to lie down and die there in the muddy tracks of the street, so tired was she. Suddenly, before them was a small clapboard church. Wearily, she climbed the steps behind Magda and entered the white building. It smelled of newly sawn lumber and candle wax. At the front was a small altar and beyond it, a picture window that framed an incredible view of Puget Sound.

Magda led her to the second pew, and Tora sagged into it. Moments later, she reappeared with a glass of water and a man who followed her into the tiny sanctuary. He gave Tora a tiny smile, turned, and knelt in front of the altar. Idly, Tora gulped down the water and watched as the man prayed for a good five minutes. Magda slipped into the pew behind her, uncharacteristically silent. Tora remained still.

The pastor rose from his knees and came to sit in front of Tora, his arm over the back of the first pew. "Tora, I am Pastor Mellinger. Thank you for coming here."

"I did not choose to. Magda brought me here."

"For good reason."

Tora's eyes flew upward, meeting the young minister's clear gray gaze.

"Once in a while, Magda brings me very special people."

"I am afraid this isn't one of those times, pastor," Tora mumbled bitterly. She was angry at his supposition, at Magda for bringing her here. And just as quickly, she was incredibly sad. Tears came unbidden.

"You are brokenhearted," the man said softly.

"Do not believe my tears, pastor. I'm capable of working them up at a moment's notice." She looked down, to the side, anywhere but into those clear gray eyes that seemed to see all as clearly as Magda did in her more lucid moments.

He studied her for a minute before answering. "Perhaps once. Perhaps once you used tears to your advantage. No longer. You have seen too much."

He reached out and wiped one cheek, then the other. Tora remained motionless. His touch, obviously born of utter confidence and love, stunned her. There was no hesitation on his part, no reluctance to touch a filthy woman of the streets.

"You are different now, Tora. Because of the pain you have suffered."

"Yes. I am a bitter old woman of…twenty-three." She laughed, the sound hollowly echoing in the tiny chamber. When had her birthday come and gone before?

"You cry the tears of Christ's chosen. You are dear to his heart."

Tora snorted. "Impossible. I have denied him too often for him to care about me any longer."

"Do you want him to care?"

Tora glanced up at the pastor, studying his kind eyes. She wanted to shock him, stun him, shake him out of his assumption that he understood her. "I had physical relations outside of marriage. With a married man. I bore his child and left the babe at his wife's feet. I abandoned my baby. And why? Because I wanted more! Why would Christ care about someone capable of such deeds?"

"Because he loves you. He died for you and your sins. His entire goal in life was to bring you back into accord with God. This is your chance."

"Did he have to take everything from me to bring me back to him?"

The pastor considered her words and then asked, "I don't know. Did he?"

His question surprised Tora. Had it taken losing all for her to consider returning to God again?

"Did he take it all from you? Or did you do it all yourself? In any case, it matters little. We are all sinful people. What matters is where you are now. Sin's eventual penalty is death. We are all dying. All I see in you is emptiness and despair."

"I tried to kill myself. I wanted to die. To end it all. To end the pain."

"Jesus can fill that void inside you. He can make you whole again. He came and died for you—your penalty has been paid. He wants you to live. For him. For you. Are you hungry for the Christ, Tora?"

Tears flowed freely now down Tora's face. How could she hope for such promises again? She had tried her best to be all she could, and what had it gotten her? Now this minister in a lonely church wanted her to trust that God could give her all her heart desired?

"I have nothing. What use can God have for me?"

He stared back at her, seemingly unperturbed. "You have your life. He will use you in ways that will amaze you."

Tora laughed. "If you had known me, pastor…if you had seen me a year ago, you'd think it was laughable too. I've never let anyone use me. I've used others."

"Perhaps, then, God *has* brought you to this place. To find a new path, a new direction."

"He arranged for men to kidnap me? To be raped and thrown on a train to this place?"

As if she had slapped him, pain shot across the pastor's face. It occurred to her that the old Tora would have used this moment to play her hand. To manipulate him to gain something for herself. But she was tired. She wanted no more games. She wanted answers. She wanted rest.

"No. Our God is one of love. Sin runs rampant across our world. You got in the way. Perhaps it was sin that led you to that crossroads. God wants to save, not condemn. But he uses these painful moments in our lives to show us how we can walk more closely with him. He uses these moments when we are weakest to build us up, to edify us. You will see. I promise. Someday, Tora, you will look back on these days and be glad for them."

"You are joking."

"I am not."

They sat in silence for several minutes. The afternoon was wearing on, the sanctuary becoming darker. Pastor Mellinger rose and stretched out a hand in invitation to Tora. After hesitating a moment, she took it and followed after him to the altar. He struck a match and handed it to her, nodding at the two thick candles that were on either side of the table.

Unable to do anything else, Tora lit the candles, watching as a warm glow lit up the front of the room. She stared past them to the view beyond, filled with the heavily forested curving shoreline of the Sound. The water was gray, almost black, under the dark, cloudy sky. She didn't know how long she had stood there when the pastor spoke again.

"What holds you back, Tora? What holds you back from the God who saves?"

"Sin. The darkness that resides in my heart. The emptiness. I have nothing to give."

"Ask for it, and forgiveness is yours. He fills you with what you need."

"How can that be? I am unworthy."

"No one is worthy to take from the hand of Christ. Still it is his gift. We cannot do anything else. He wants us to have it. But we must believe in him. You must ask him to be the Lord of your heart. Then, the gift is yours."

She remained where she stood, moving her eyes to one of the candles and its sputtering flame.

"Sometimes, Tora, the hardest part of forgiveness is forgiving ourselves. Ask it of God, and he'll fling your sin as far from you as east is from west. Begin with God. Then allow yourself time to forgive yourself."

Tora glanced at the gray-eyed man for a second before nodding once. Instinctively, she knelt where he had when he first entered the room, in front of the altar. Pastor Mellinger took one candle from its brass holder and placed it in her hands.

"You have been baptized?" he asked her softly.

She nodded. "As a baby. And later confirmed."

He left her side, and Tora stared again at the candle and its flame.

A moment later he returned, standing on one side of her as Magda stood on the other. "Tora," he said softly, nothing but kindness in his voice. She raised her eyes, seeing that he carried a small basin.

He dipped his fingers in the basin and reached out damp fingers to trace a cross on her forehead. "Tora, remember that you were made a child of Christ, and that the Holy Spirit is always with you. Remember that the Christ died to free you from your sins."

"I remember," Tora whispered, staring at the candle as water dripped between her brows.

"Remember that all you have to do is ask, and forgiveness is yours. But you have to ask. You have to change your ways and ask him into your heart. You must be willing to live as a new creature."

"I ask it." She closed her eyes, hesitantly choosing words long forgotten. "Father…forgive me of all I have done. Forgive me for how I have failed you…and the others who loved…me." Her voice cracked on the last word. Then she whispered, staring into the flame, "Make me…whole again. I have never followed you. Show me how."

"You are different now. You are part of the bride of Christ, his church."

"I do not feel different. Only broken."

"You know where your family is, Tora?"

"I do."

"Go to them. Go to your child, the child you left behind. Go to the woman who accepted your child as her own. Ask their forgiveness. Ask to serve them."

Tora wept at the idea. "I cannot. Not yet."

"When it is time, then. And when they offer you their forgiveness, accept it. It is your path. That is why you were brought here, at this time. Accept the gladness that he has given you. Give it an opportunity to flourish in your heart. Pray for vision. For understanding of where you are to go next."

"Right now? Here?"

The pastor laughed, the sound warming her heart. "What better place? Magda and I will wait until you are done."

She did as he bid, repeating the words she had spoken aloud silently. They came easier by the second, like a floodgate that had been opened upon a dry prairie field. *Dear Jesus, come near me. I need you. Not for the first time, but for the first time I can remember recognizing the fact. I am sad and I am empty. The pastor says you can fill that. You can fill the emptiness inside me. Please, Father, fill me. Enter me. Make me yours as surely as I've wished to be my own.*

Suddenly, true contentment and happiness flooded into Tora's heart. It was crystal clear, as if God has made the candle speak out loud to her. It was not about wealth and stature, as she had thought all along. It was about being saved by God, and forgiven, and basking in the glory of his creation, regardless of her social stature.

It was about being his. And his alone.

Springs of Living Water

twenty

January 1887

ora laughed aloud as the Salishan Indian paddled his dugout canoe to the distant shore, looking over his shoulder at her as if she were crazy Magda. Tora understood at last that God had a sense of humor. She liked that about him, and felt closer for the discovery. After her visit to the Seattle chapel, Pastor Mellinger and Magda had conferred and the next day announced they had found a job for her. The job her friends had found for her was cooking at the Kenai Peninsula lumber camp of Ramstad Lumber Yard in Seaport.

Of all the lumberyards that bordered the Sound, she *would* end up working for her sister! The inner peace she felt over the matter surprised and amazed Tora. It was as if she knew all would be well, regardless of the circumstances. What would have once eaten her alive—working for Elsa of all people!—now seemed to make perfect sense. Whatever was to be, would be. God would take care of her. For now, she had a purpose, a clean bed and food.

I just hope there will be adequate opportunity to get dry, she thought, shivering as the dense sheets of mist continued to rain down upon them. Mato, her Indian guide, seemed to think nothing of it. He ignored the driblets of water that collected on his crown, then ran down his black hair to the middle of his back. He was clean and respectful, the first Indian to whom Tora had been in close proximity outside of those who stood in line with her at the soup kitchen.

"Do you do this all day, every day?" she called to him. "I mean, do you paddle between the lumberyards, delivering people?" She had taken a steamer to the peninsula, and been directed to Mato from there.

"When I'm hired," he said over his shoulder, still paddling with long, deep strokes. He was clearly familiar with English, but just as clearly not interested in chitchat.

Tora's eyes followed the swirl the paddle left in the water as her end of the canoe passed it by. Tiny bubbles outlined its path, and beyond it, the water was an emerald-green-to-black color and fathoms deep. The sun, when it dared to peek out, sent a stream of light down into its depths, as if attempting to pierce the darkness with its hope. Tora found comfort in the knowledge that the ocean was big and wide, larger than she could truly imagine, deeper than any ray of sun. Had she not ridden at the *Herald*'s bow, observing the horizon and seeing nothing but sea? It was like God, that way; bigger than one's dreams, deeper than one's imaginings. Would she ever see her Lord as she ought?

Her eyes traveled around Puget Sound, watching frigates, grand schooners, and old brigantines head in and out of the harbor, industrious steamers carrying passengers of greater wealth than she, tiny lighters bouncing on the waves, fishermen at work. Perhaps this vision of God was not entirely inappropriate. Just as this harbor would give her comfort and work and food, so too would God provide for her as the deepest harbor of all. There was simply much, much to explore about him. So much to know!

Tora's hand went to the Bible in her small bag, which held a change of clothes and a brush, gifts from Pastor Mellinger. She knew not where he had obtained them. Nor did she care. All she knew was that she was in the right place at the right time. And the future held a dim but unmistakable hope.

Elsa gasped and reached for the banister of the stair as a contraction knit her womb into one large knot, held, then released. Kaatje paused before her and stared at her in concern. "What?"

"Oh, nothing. Just a practice run at the real thing. Reminds me to prepare myself for the big day."

"Ah. When do you suppose that day is?"

"The doctor and I are guessing it will be toward the end of February." Elsa finished climbing the stairs and glanced at her friend. "Can you stay that long?"

"Of course! I wouldn't miss this child's birth for anything in the world."

"And it helps that you needn't return yet to the farm."

"Yes, that does help make the decision easier. But Elsa..."

"Yes?"

"I'll be here as long as you need me."

Her words moved Elsa to tears. Where would she be now if Kaatje and the girls had not come with her last fall? Their company had done her and Kristian a world of good. But soon, she knew, they would need to part ways. Elsa needed to be on her own again, to prove that she could go on without Peder and survive on her own. "Thank you, Kaatje," she said, reaching to squeeze her friend's hand. "Have you heard from Einar lately?"

"Just two days ago, in fact. You must have been at the soup kitchen. He reports that all the animals are doing well, in typical Einar fashion. Then Nora added all her news of the Bergensers. Matthew's wife is expecting! And Nels—the man, not our horse—he's courting a neighbor girl."

"Norwegian?"

"No, Swedish! Can you imagine? The *scandal...*" Her eyes held a merry look. Ongoing rivalry between the Swedes and Norse seemed to have followed them all the way to America.

"He always did have a mind of his own." She turned before entering her bedroom. "You're sure, Kaatje? You do not mind staying here for another month?"

"Not at all. The girls are having a marvelous time! The only thing that concerns me is how they'll feel about returning to our little house on the farm after all this," she said, waving her hand around.

"They'll be fine. It's their home. It will probably feel comforting and warm to them to return."

"Yes, well, we'll see what transpires. But here with you is where I want to be."

"And what about Tora?"

"I leave it to God. One day I fret over it, the next day I'm as peaceful as a Jersey cow chewing her cud."

Elsa laughed at that description. "This is a cud day, I take it?"

"A nice, spring-grass-meadow-all-to-myself kind of day. Now you go and rest for a while. I'm going to write a letter and then do the same."

"Good enough." She turned to do as Kaatje had directed when a knock sounded at the door below them. Elsa paused to listen as Mrs. Hodge answered it. "Why, Mr. Storm!" the woman said, welcoming him in as she would one of her nieces or nephews. "And, Mr. Campbell. Come in, come in. I'll go and find the mistress. Won't you make yourselves at home?"

Elsa puzzled over why they had come. Trent had distinctly told her he would not be over today for tea, since Mr. Campbell had found a new lead to where Tora had disappeared, and Trent had business he wished to see to. She descended the stairs. Trent and Joseph stood in the parlor, having not removed their coats or hats, and obviously not intending to do so.

Trent came toward her, a light in his eye. "He's found her, Elsa. She's in good hands."

"She is?" Elsa moved to the couch, gladdened by the news, eager to hear more. "Where is she? What is she doing?"

Trent grinned. "She's working for you."

"What?"

"She's working at the Ramstad Lumber Yard over in Seaport. As the camp cook. She appears to be in good shape—well, I'll let Joseph tell you."

"Please, gentlemen. Let me take your coats," Elsa said.

"I'll see to them," Mrs. Hodge said, bustling in from an unseen corner of the room. "And I'll fetch a pot of tea too."

"Yes, yes," Trent said, pulling off his coat and hat as his detective did the same. "I'm sorry. I was simply so delighted when Joseph came to me with the news." He sat down on the edge of the settee, and Mr. Campbell perched on an armchair, looking too small in its generous expanse. "Tell her, Joseph. Tell her everything you know."

Joseph glanced at Elsa and smiled like an elf at Christmas. "She appears to have had a conversion. A true anointing. I had a long conversation with a Pastor Mellinger, minister to a small flock just on the outskirts of town. He refused to give me many details, just told me that Tora has made a distinct choice to follow a different path."

Elsa leaned back against the chair, feeling faint. Could Tora be coming to know the Lord? What a difference it would make in her life if it were true! "And? You said she's working for me?"

"Yes. Pastor Mellinger knows the foreman of your lumberyard. Says it was providential. The day he attempted to secure a job for Tora, a future, he ran into his friend—"

"Ian McBride."

"Yes. That's his name. A good, upstanding sort. Well suited to watch out for Tora in a man's world."

Elsa nodded. "And she is cooking, you say?"

"Six days a week, breakfast, lunch, dinner."

Elsa shook her head. "I bet she's never worked so hard in her life."

"I don't know," Trent said with a smile. "Storm Enterprises wasn't easy on her at first."

"But she's a *cook*," Elsa said, meeting his glance with a meaningful look. "A cook, Trent." She turned to Joseph. "You visited the yard?"

"No. I sent another. She knows me. I rented her home in Helena, and found her a position as a teacher in Spokane."

Elsa glanced from Trent to Joseph. "You've had her followed all that time?"

"I was worried," Trent said, shifting uncomfortably in his chair.

"For good reason, it seems," she said, wanting to put him at ease. "And the report from your man?"

"She appears to be healthy and—this is the most surprising part— happy."

"Happy as a camp cook?"

"It appeared that way," Joseph said with a shrug.

Elsa looked away toward the window, thinking. "I haven't visited the yard since Peder died. It's time to do so. Do you think she's ready to see me?"

"Perhaps," Trent said. "I have some business over in that part of the Sound. May I accompany you?"

Elsa considered his suggestion. "You think she might be ready? To see us both?"

Trent raised one brow. "What if we merely showed up? If she is ready, she could seek us out. I'm worried about her, an attractive woman in a camp full of lumbermen."

Elsa nodded. "I can understand your concern. But Ian will watch over her. And if she's truly made a change in her heart, perhaps her outward actions have changed too." She nodded again and then shook her head with a rueful smile. "I can't explain it. I feel an uncommon peace over it all."

"I want to be sure this time," Trent said, kneeling at her side as if begging Elsa to allow him to go to Tora, to rescue her. "I'm afraid she's been through abuse no woman should ever go through. Joseph's report...It's nothing I'd want a lady to hear, let alone bear."

Elsa again leaned back against the couch. "Trent, this is out of our hands. We can't push Tora to do anything." She took his hand and looked into his eyes. "You deserve a woman who comes to you of her own volition, ready to love you with her whole heart. That is why you let her go in the first place. See this through. Give her time to heal—from whatever she's gone through. I hope you are wrong. I hope she hasn't had to face the worst. But if she has, she has. We need to leave her with God to heal. Leave her at the Lord's feet, Trent."

His face went gray. "You don't know what you're asking of me."

"I do. I've ached, worried over my sister for years. I love her too. I *do* know. I do."

It didn't take long for Tora to settle into life at the lumber camp. Ian McBride, the camp boss, while notoriously rough on the men, treated her like fine china, doing all he could to make her living quarters comfortable—a tiny but sturdy canvas tent—even while showing new male arrivals to their bunks with a curt "That's your bunk and if you want it softer get yourself some spruce boughs."

Her job was simple. From morning to night, she cooked. While the men still slept "like stunned sheep," as one put it, she would rise in the dark and begin mixing flapjack batter and brewing coffee. By the time Ian rang the morning bell, Tora was prepared to feed a hundred men. They came in as a trickle in the morning, never eager to begin their day, as a steady stream by noon dinner, hungry after a morning's work, and as a torrential, ravenous mass at supper time.

They were from Norway and Sweden, Finland and England, Ireland and elsewhere. They were hired as swampers, fallers, sawyers, hook-tenders, bull punchers, or teamsters. And all, married or no, professed love for Tora. She received ten proposals of marriage a day from the start, if she got one. Their proposals came as idle banter, meant to fill the time and entertain after a long day of sweat, dirt, and wearying work. But generally, she felt a camaraderie with the men, a respect that made her feel safe and cared for, as if they were all a gaggle of brothers, rather than potential suitors. And Tora did her best to give them food, and a lot of it. The temptation to flirt left her. She was truly a new woman. All she wanted was to work and be left alone, to think and pray and think some more.

She had no choice as to what she was to cook. The supplies were set before her with quick instructions: flapjacks and molasses in the morning, corned beef and cabbage at noon, and salt pork and potatoes at supper. Apparently, variety was not a concern to lumbermen, Tora surmised. She soon knew why. All that mattered was that there was food, hot and plenty of it. Never in her life had she seen food consumed in such quantities, even during her roadhouse days.

The mill, purchased from another company after their own mill had burned down, had grown threefold in the years under Peder's ownership, and they were experimenting with steam-powered donkey engines, log flumes, corduroy roads, and two-log trail chutes to get to the deeper forests and bring the timber to the mill. The sawmills, now three in a row, were situated on a river that had been diverted to power the saws and bring the logs over the final distance.

At one end of the camp, railroad ties were stacked over fifty feet high. The pile went on and on, and even with the ever-expanding railroads, Tora wondered how they would all get used. On a Sunday afternoon off, some of the men took her to a place in the woods where eight men could stand in the undercut of a giant fir. A high climber named Wesley, eager to show off for her, donned spurs and rope and shimmied to the top of a nearby tree to demonstrate how they took down a tree, forty feet at a time.

The others in the group moved back a safe distance, watching and hollering taunts at the lanky young man. After sawing for some time, Wesley braced as the first portion came hurtling down. Tora gasped as he clung to the top of the tree as it bucked and swayed like a wild bronco. The men cheered and Tora clapped, feeling like a child at a circus. When had she ever felt so at ease, so free amid so many men? Most of her life, she had used such an opportunity to her advantage, she pondered. Five years ago, she might have pretended to faint in order to play on the men's affection for her.

But no longer. Her life was different now. *I am different,* Tora decided. Something monumental had shifted within her heart and soul in the last year, and for the first time, she was able to smile over it. God was good. And he was gracious.

At least, that was what she thought before Elsa and Trent appeared in camp one day.

Trent shifted uneasily beside Elsa as the steamer pulled up alongside the rough dock. Before them was an enormous lumberyard, and Trent whistled under his breath. "Small little enterprise, Mrs. Ramstad."

Elsa smiled demurely and took his proffered hand to stand up beside him. "Are we doing the right thing?" she asked under her breath.

"I hope so."

"What if she thinks we're here together? I mean to say...*together.*"

"Then it's high time we straighten it out."

"All right. Let's go and review my holdings in lumber," she said grandly.

"Perhaps, dear lady, there are indeed some business opportunities we could explore together," he said.

"We will see," she responded. "I need to make sure you're a trustworthy sort." She made her way out of the small steamer passenger compartment, uncomfortably aware of her growing girth. The baby, due in less than a month's time, seemed ready to come sooner rather than later, in her opinion. Surely Kristian had not been this large!

"Are you feeling all right?" Trent asked delicately.

"Fine, fine," Elsa answered, flushing at the obvious reason for his question. "Although I am not sure I'll be up to riding the flume today."

"No?" Trent asked in mock surprise. He walked down the gangplank and turned to reach for her hand. "You'll miss out on all the fun."

"Part of the joy of motherhood, I suppose," she quipped. She turned to the steamer captain. "Please wait here. We'll be docked for about four hours, I suppose. If you need anything, see the bull cook."

"Yes, ma'am," the young man said with a curt nod of his head.

"Trent? Let us see the foreman, shall we?"

"Indeed."

The camp was in full swing at ten o'clock in the morning. Elsa had wondered if she would have to search for Tora to make sure she was seen, or put out the word that the owner was there, hoping the news would spread through the lumber camp like wildfire. As it turned out, Tora emerged from the cook's cabin just as they were passing by. She stopped, obviously surprised to see them there, and wiped at a flour smudge on her cheek, just making it worse. She looked lovely, and from the look on his face Elsa was sure that Trent's heart was pounding.

"Tora," she said, deciding honesty was the best tack. "I had heard you were working here." She avoided *working for me,* thinking that such an inference might be humiliating to Tora. "When you have the chance, would you care to sit and visit with us?"

Tora looked from Trent to Elsa. "You have news for me?" she asked in a dignified manner.

"Oh! No! Nothing of the sort. Trent is here to see to business matters—"

"And to see you," he said, his voice deep and intent. He took three strides over to her, staring at her tenderly. "I wanted to wait for you to come to me, Tora. But then I was afraid you might never—"

Tora ducked away, turning back toward the cabin. "I really must see to the noon dinner. The men will soon be in—"

"And afterward, Tora?" Elsa intervened. "Could we steal you away for a few minutes once the men are served? Perhaps there's another who could help you—"

"No! No. I don't want any help." She glanced from Elsa to Trent again. "I'll see what transpires. Perhaps for a few minutes, after the men are served…"

"We'll look forward to it," Trent said longingly. Elsa half feared she would have to drag him away before he would leave Tora's side again.

When Tora had first seen her sister and Trent outside, it had taken her breath away and she had struggled to regain her composure. It made sense that it wouldn't be long before Elsa discovered that Tora was on the payroll. But to see Elsa together with Trent just brought back all the pain of seeing them embracing in Elsa's parlor. How could they *not* fall in love with each other? Trent was a brilliant, handsome, successful widower. Elsa, obviously not without means herself, was a beautiful, adventurous widow clearly in need of a husband, a father for her children. They would be the toast of Seattle.

Tora tore her eyes from Trent's and tried to make it back into the cook's cabin without giving herself away. She backed up against the wall, breathing hard, fighting tears. How she had missed him! His hair had grown more gray, but it only made him more dignified. Her hands went to her hair and her threadbare, secondhand dress. Even Elsa, in her advanced state of pregnancy, looked more glamorous and enticing than she! In spite of his words, Trent probably had dismissed any lingering fantasies about Tora as soon as she had left his side. How could he possibly still care for her?

Longing for another glimpse of him, she edged toward the window and peeked out through the curtains. Trent still stood there, staring at the doorway as if willing her to appear. After a moment longer, he turned resolutely and followed Elsa's path to Ian's cabin. Tora's eyes followed his every manly, sure step. Was he truly there on business? No doubt his association with Elsa had given rise to many new ideas to expand Storm Enterprises. When he disappeared into Ian's cabin, Tora turned to the dark room before her and wondered if she would dare to see them again. It would be easy enough to avoid them, claiming a lack of time. But a large part of her wanted to know the truth; why they were there, what they wanted from her, if they were in love with each other.

Smoothing back her hair, she returned to cutting the cabbage and mixing biscuits. She wished there was something more she could put on the table today, something to impress Trent, but there was little from which to choose. Tora sighed and looked heavenward. "Whatever is in store, be with me, Lord," she mumbled, then squared her shoulders and concentrated on the lunch before her. As best she could, anyway.

After the men were served and there was nothing else they could possibly want, Tora left the dining hall and walked to Ian's cabin. Upon seeing her, Ian smiled and rose, excusing himself with, "I'll let you three catch up. I need to talk with the men and grab some grub." He paused beside her. "You didn't tell me you were the boss's sister."

"Didn't want you to hold it against me," she quipped, meeting his glance.

Ian smiled and went on his way, leaving her standing in the doorway.

Trent rose and motioned vaguely toward an empty chair. "Please, Tora. Join us."

"I will stand here, if you don't mind," she said, wishing she could sit down. At least they couldn't see her trembling legs underneath her skirt.

Elsa rose and came toward her. She looked as if she wanted to reach out to Tora, to embrace her, but was hesitant. A part of Tora wanted to do so herself, but pride kept her from it. "What is it, Elsa? Why have you come?"

"Please. Please, Tora. Come and sit with us." She motioned to the three chairs at the table.

"All right," Tora said, making it sound as though she only did so to please Elsa.

Once they were all situated again, Elsa began. "Trent came to me, in search of you. He had tracked your progress from Spokane—"

"Progress?" Tora said, unable to keep back a sarcastic tone. "I suppose you could call it that."

Elsa's eyebrows knit in concern. "We gathered that you were taken from your home there by force."

Tora swallowed hard. "Yes," she said, staring at a knot in the pine table.

Trent and Elsa were silent.

"But as you can see, I am fine now. I've found my own way. If you have a problem with me working for your yard…"

"No, no, not at all. I am glad that you have found satisfactory work."

"Would you rather come back and work for me?" Trent put in eagerly.

"No!" Tora said forcefully, and then embarrassed, softened it. "No. Those days are over, Trent."

"Why? Because you felt pushed to be with me? To see me because I was the boss?" Trent asked, pain evident in his tone.

"Of course not," Tora said quietly, meeting his eyes. "Those were the best times of my life. I wanted nothing else than to be with you." She swallowed hard, pushing back the lump in her throat. "But my life has changed. I have changed."

"In what way?" asked Elsa.

Tora considered her words carefully before speaking. "All my life, I've had everything I wanted laid at my feet. When it was all taken away, I had to work again for something of value and substance. Along the way," she said, glancing at her two companions, "I discovered there was much more to life than wealth. I have my health, I have a newfound faith, and—" She glanced up again. "I have hope. In something more basic. In life, in Christ."

Her news did not seem to surprise them. "What will you do?" Elsa asked quietly. "You can't stay here forever."

"I do not know. Ian says I'm doing well. I can stay on as long as I'd like."

"It doesn't," Elsa began, clearly feeling awkward, "it doesn't make you feel ill at ease, being around all these men? After what you went through?"

"Surprisingly, no. They're good men. Rough-and-tumble, a lot of them, but generally courteous. They treat me like a kid sister."

Trent rose and paced. "Tora, for years I've waited for you to come to this place. To understand what was important in life." He glanced at Elsa as if self-conscious. "You are the woman I've sought, the woman I've longed for all this time. I can see it in your eyes. We can be together now. Come away with me. We'll marry on the morrow if you want."

Tora gave him a sad smile. Her heart pounded at his words, but she knew this was not the right time. She shook her head. "Too much has gone on, Trent. I need time. Time to let it all sink in. Time to sort out what it means."

Trent's mouth twisted up as if in frustration, and he turned and walked out the door in silence.

"What does he expect of me?" Tora asked her sister. "Surely he didn't think I would pack up and leave with him? After all that has transpired?"

"A part of him hoped it would be so, I suppose," Elsa said.

Tora's heart leapt at her words. Did he truly still love her? Was it more than a grudging sense of duty that brought about this marriage proposal—a proposal she had so dearly wanted to hear from him for a year? "Does that make you sorry?" she dared ask.

Elsa frowned at her. "Not at all. I, too, would love to pack you up and take you home. But you seem determined. And I must say, I like this change in you, Tora. I respect it. Trent, although worried, will come to respect it too."

Tora toyed with a splinter in the rough-hewn table before her. "He never asked me to marry him before. I wanted it. With all my heart."

"But with all the right reasons?"

Tora paused. "No. Probably not. But it was love I felt for him."

"Maybe it was simply not the right time."

"So...you are not in love with him?"

"No, Tora. I have come to love him as a brother. He is a fine man. And I am so happy that he fell in love with you. Yes. Don't look so surprised. He is in love with you. That is why he is here!"

"I had thought..." Tora remained silent as she considered her words. "I had thought he was here with you, and concerned for my safety because we once meant something to each other and now that he was to be my brother-in-law—"

"Tora! Peder's been dead merely five months. How could you think such a thing?"

"I'm sorry. I don't know what I was thinking."

They sat together in silence for some time. Then Tora said, "I should get back to the cook's quarters. The men will be gone by now, and I'll need to begin supper." She rose. "Thank you for coming to check on me. You and yours are well?"

"Well enough."

"And...Kaatje?"

"Kaatje, Christina, and Jessie are all fine. They'll stay to attend me at the birth of my child and then return home to the Skagit Valley."

"Ahh."

"You are truly happy here, Tora?"

Tora considered the word *happiness* and all it had once entailed for her. "I guess I am. Or I would say I am contented. It's where I am to be."

Elsa nodded. "You know you are always welcome in my home, at any time, for any reason." She reached out to take Tora's hand. "We could begin again. You could even travel with me, see the world. I intend to set sail again soon after this babe is born."

Tora nodded once. "Thank you. One day, I think it would be good for us to...become closer. But I will stay here for now."

"Then I will too," said Trent from the doorway. Tora's eyes flew to his silhouetted form.

"What?"

"Then I will stay here in the Sound and pursue business options for a while. I will stay here to get to know you again, Tora. To court you."

twenty-one

February 1887

*K*arl sailed the *Tempest* around the windward side of Kahoolawe toward the port of Honolulu. Between the reefs that surrounded the Hawaiian Islands and the whales that were migrating in countless numbers and the whalers that pursued them, porting in Honolulu demanded he remember every nuance of captaining a ship. "Whales ho!" called his man from the crow's nest for the tenth time that morning. "There she blows!" he yelled, pointing. Karl followed his direction, observing a pod of whales through a telescope, and smiled.

A huge blue whale crested after her baby, spouted a shower of water, and then dove, ending with a tremendous show of tail and a splash as she dug in for the deep. Such majestic animals inhabited the depths that God had created! Karl longed to dive into the water himself, to follow the whales, and see what their world looked like.

What had happened to him since he had again taken to the seas? It was as if his eyes had been opened, as if he had been sleeping all the time he remained landlocked. His heart, his soul, called for him to explore the oceans of the world, the waters his Creator had made. This, this was where he belonged.

"Steamer tug approaching," reported his second mate, Clayton Rogers.

"Good enough. Signal him forward, Clay," Karl said. This time of year, the harbor was carefully organized by a British harbormaster, anchoring each ship that arrived in a spot conducive to the traffic that continued to enter and exit the harbor. It was a gorgeous day, hot and sunny. The breeze off the water cooled the sweat on his brow, making it just about perfect. He took off his captain's hat and ran his fingers through his hair, which he allowed to grow a little longer now that he was out of polite society. He fancied the idea of longer hair at the nape of his neck and, at some point, an earring. A new look was the physical manifestation of his new life, he decided.

He placed the cap back on his head as the tug drew near. Yes. The earring would happen today. "Luke!" he called to his first mate. "You said you had your ear pierced here in Honolulu, right?"

"Aye, sir, but if you're interested, I could do it for you sure enough."

Karl returned his smile. "That's generous of you, mate, but I think I'll leave it to a professional. I need an earring anyway to hold it open."

"Suit yourself. My fee's free. Part of the package of first mate," he said, proudly placing his thumbs in his suspenders. All the men, with land in sight and visions of wine and women, were in high spirits. Karl had sailed with Lucas Laning on the *Silver Sea* from Seattle, and immediately connected with the man. He was a fine sailor with good experience, and an upstanding Christian. And since Luke knew many other fine sailors in the Bay Area, he helped Karl handpick their crew.

"And it's a fine package indeed," Karl bantered back. "But we won't be needing your skills as an ear piercer just yet."

"You can pierce my ear!" said the cabin boy excitedly. Charlie Woodrow was all of eleven years old and followed Karl like a shadow. An orphan who had taken to the docks at nine, he had been largely ignored by a less indulgent captain than Karl over the last two years. When that man keeled over in a wharf tavern, Lucas had brought

Charlie to Karl, hoping his captain would take the lad on as cabin boy. Karl was glad to have him. Ever eager to do whatever Karl bid, Charlie was tall for his age, with sandy brown hair and eyes.

Karl smiled. "I do not think so. Luke, didn't you say that any boy under thirteen caught with an earring was hanged by it from the lanyards?"

The boy paled, looking quickly from one man to the other. "You're joshing."

Lucas pursed his lips and tapped one finger on his chin, as if exaggerating the thinking process. "Let me see. I do believe you're right, cap'n. Last I saw of little Jeremy Halloway, he was hanging by his ear from the lanyard—about that high—" he said, pointing to one twenty feet above them, "and then his ear clear ripped apart and he fell into the seas." Luke sighed heavily. "Tremendous loss, that one."

Karl turned to cover his smile and went to meet the second mate at the stairs. "Tug is alongside, cap'n. Harbormaster is asking to speak with you."

"Of course, Clay. Nice work. Lead the way." He turned toward Lucas. "Reef all remaining sails!" he ordered.

"Reef all remaining sails!" the mate called out. The men scurried about, eager to carry out the command, get settled closer to shore, and feel land beneath their feet. They had been at sea for over eighteen days. Many had never set foot on Hawaii, but had heard about such luxuries as dramatic, delicious luaus and mesmerizing dancing maidens. Karl smiled again. It was a fine port in which to restock supplies and consider his next steps. He could speak with other captains ashore and find out what the best cargo would be for Kenney, Bradford, and himself in Japan. Prices and availability made it an ever-changing option, and it was wise to gather any information he could.

An hour later they were situated in about fifty feet of water, the sea floor visible to them from above. The water was an incredible turquoise green, and once in a while a sand shark or a school of fish would scurry past along the creamy bottom. The anchor descended with a great splash, and after a nod from Karl, all men not on the first launch toward shore appeased themselves with a dive into the tropical waters. They shouted and dunked one another, swearing and laughing. Karl laughed with them. It was a good crew, all in all, that he had found in San Francisco.

Out of deference to his men, Karl waited for one of the last launches toward shore, reaching land just in time to find some supper. Accompanied by Lucas, he followed the harbormaster's directions to a tavern with the best meals and, therefore, the most sea captains with whom he could swap tales. The two men strode jauntily down the busy street, observing shopkeepers closing up for the night and less virtuous ladies just beginning their evening racket. The men carefully averted their eyes.

Seeing the disreputable ladies reminded Karl of Charlie and his life on the streets. The boy had seen too many unsavory sights in his short life, and Karl felt protective of the lad. With an odd sense of being followed, Karl turned and looked back down the street. Sure enough, the cabin boy trailed them by twenty feet, flirting with the women, who patted and coddled him. "Charles!" Karl roared. The boy blanched and sidled up to his captain and the mate. "I thought I told you to stay aboard the ship," Karl said, placing a firm hand on the boy's shoulder.

"Oh, but Captain, everybody was coming ashore."

"And you will also. When I can give you proper supervision."

"But Cap'n, this isn't anything I haven't seen already," Charlie said, surveying the street with a worldly, bored glance.

"That's a shame, son. I aim to change your views. You work for me—you do as I say. Go directly back to the ship. Tell the man on launch duty that I commanded he take you back aboard."

"But Cap'n—"

"Now."

Charlie kicked at the dirt of the street with bare feet and then turned to go back as directed. Lucas remained silent at Karl's side as they watched the boy reluctantly walk back toward the beach. "Think I can make a change in the boy, Luke?"

"He's seen an awful lot for an eleven-year-old," Lucas said.

"It's never too late for redemption, right?" Karl asked, looking him in the eye.

Lucas cocked his head and nodded once. "I hope you're right."

They turned together and continued walking. "Remind me to get that boy a Bible."

"Sure, Cap'n. You'll have to teach him to read first, though."

Karl groaned. "No schooling at all?"

"Not that I can gather. Clayton said he's been on his own since he was a wee tyke."

Karl had been so intent on keeping the *Tempest* on track and shipshape that he had spent little time with his cabin boy. Clearly, he needed to focus some attention there. He pursed his lips and then laughed, thinking. Imagine him, a role model for a child! And yet it was a welcome weight of responsibility.

Karl and Lucas had been in the tavern for an hour, talking and eating with other captains and their first mates, when Mason Dutton strode in. Karl would have recognized him anywhere, despite the beard and fine apparel. Karl stood, his eyes never wavering.

Mason met his glance, and nonchalantly pulled his jacket from his shoulders and set it upon a chair back. "Karl Martensen?" he asked, as if testing his memory of names.

The other men, inherently sensing the tension, grew quiet.

Karl's mind flew from memories of the island and Dutton's attack to what he should do now. Elsa had told him she had seen him here a year ago, but Karl could hardly believe the man dared to walk out in the open after her column appeared in the *New York Times* and was syndicated worldwide.

The words came quickly, Karl's tone low and menacing. Everything in him wanted to lunge at the man who had dared to attack

Peder's ship, his ship, and Elsa. But something deep within held him back. Only his words flew freely.

"You are a pirate and a scoundrel, Mason Dutton," he growled.

"Why, Karl, we haven't even exchanged greetings, yet," Mason said, one eyebrow cocked. Two large men moved to stand behind him. "And here you are, calling me scandalous names that might sully my reputation."

Lucas rose to stand at Karl's side. "I am surprised you dare to show your face," Karl said.

"Oh, because of that silly Elsa Ramstad's article?" He laughed and sat down, an obvious move to try and put Karl in his place. "I have an understanding with the locals. And with my fellow sea captains," he said, his eyes roving around the room. "Elsa Ramstad will eventually pay for her attempt at blackening my name. But that's another matter."

Karl followed his glance around the room, incredulous. The sailors had grown quiet, avoiding his gaze. How could the pirate have bought off all these men?

Mason laughed again. "You will soon see that you should join my comrades, here. I will not attack your ship if you agree to steer clear of me."

"I will not. I will go to the local authorities. And I am not afraid to face you again in battle."

"Karl, Karl. I take it you are a captain now? You are a merchant-man. Your ship would never hold up against mine. I come fully armed."

"The military surely does not allow you to roam these waters free, menacing others with an armed ship."

"Oh, they do their best to find me and eradicate my presence, but I am good at what I do."

"For how long? They must be planning a full-scale attack soon," Karl bluffed.

Mason rose, all good humor leaving his face. "I suggest you refrain from challenging me, Martensen. As I said, they've tried to take me, but failed. Why, the last time, I slit the commander's throat myself." His eyes narrowed, menacing.

"Is that where you obtained the British uniform?"

"Ah," Mason said, his smile returning. "So you have spoken to the lovely Elsa Ramstad since I glimpsed her here last year. Yes, I enjoy dressing up in the folderol of my countrymen. It has afforded me impressive entrée to places you wouldn't believe."

Karl shook his head. "You are a dead man in our midst. Your days are limited."

"On the contrary, Martensen. I consider that a challenge. Your days—and your ship's—are limited. But let's get back to Elsa Ramstad. I hear her coward of a husband drowned. A pity. Do you know where I might seek her to offer my condolences?"

Karl moved forward, unable to curb his fury, but Lucas held him back.

"Ah. I've hit a nerve." He tapped his chin. "Very interesting. Elsa Ramstad is a handsome, admirable woman. Perhaps I'm not the only man in this room who has had certain…feelings toward her?"

Karl felt the heat rise in his neck. "Elsa Ramstad would spit in your face if you ever managed to get near her."

"I think not. If I ever manage to get near her, let's just say there will be more interesting activities on my mind."

"I'm warning you, Dutton. Steer clear of her."

Mason laughed. "My, my. I never knew you were in love with her."

Karl pulled himself up short. He was giving Dutton ammunition he did not care to hand over to the pirate. "She has been a friend to me from childhood. I would give my life for her. Take her on, and you take me on."

Dutton pretended to shiver. "That is indeed frightening."

Again Karl moved to lunge at the man, but Luke held him back. "No, Karl. Do not do it," Luke said.

"Good day, Captain Martensen," Mason said, taking his coat

from the chair back. "We will not settle our disagreement here. We will meet on the high seas, yes?"

"Who is cowardly now, Dutton? You refuse to fight me man to man?" Luke's hand pressed harder on Karl's shoulder, but Karl ignored it.

Dutton's hand went to the scabbard at his waist. "Not at all. Shall we—?"

Just then, the men behind Mason waved like palms in a storm as someone pushed past them.

"You fight my captain, you'll have to get through me first!" Charlie called out as he faced off with Mason, a tiny blade in his hand.

The tavern erupted in laughter.

"Sure, boy. I'd be happy to teach you a lesson," Mason said, his eyes never leaving Karl's. Now he knew he had him. It infuriated Karl.

"Charles! Get over here!" Karl thundered.

The boy glanced back, unsure.

"Charles! Now, or I'll whip you raw!"

The cabin boy turned and came to Karl's side, standing just behind him and to the side as Lucas had done.

Mason laughed. "Another day, Martensen. Another day." With that, he placed his cap on his head and left the tavern.

Karl stood there shaking, a long time after Mason left the building.

One captain said softly, "Give it up, Martensen. You'll live longer if you come to a gentleman's agreement with Dutton."

Another said, "Aye, son. He's taken many a ship in and around these waters. Every time the military has any kind of presence, he hightails it."

"He's slippery, that one," said still another.

"The best of the last pirates."

"Protect your ship and your men, Martensen!" called the first. "For a small fee, Dutton will let you pass without fear."

"How can any of you go along with this?" Karl exploded. He felt supercharged, enraged. "How can any of us 'pass without fear'? You trust a man such as that? He is the lowest of the low. Why, the only way we can beat him is together!"

"They've tried that. Five ships together surrounded and attacked Dutton in his lair. They thought they had him. But they were severely outgunned. Dutton's been stockpiling for years. In the end, their crews were hanged from the lanyards, and all five ships were burned to the waterline. One eyeful of that is all a man needs to make him turn tail."

"And the local authorities?" Karl asked, incredulous.

"They turn a blind eye and open their pocketbooks. Dutton lines them well."

Karl shook his head. "This cannot go on."

"It's been going on for years."

The first captain spoke up again. "He must have moles within the British and American naval forces. It's uncanny. Each time they arrive, Dutton is away."

"Or he's got the luck of the devil," said another glumly.

They were all silent.

"There is nothing I can say to sway you," Karl stated, looking around the room. Few dared to meet his eye. "A tavern full of fine captains, men, and you refuse to stand up to one man who menaces us all? What does he charge you? A flat fee? A portion of your profits?" He grabbed the nearest man by the collar for an answer. "What?"

"Fifteen percent. The deal is fifteen percent. After delivery to the Orient, you port here again. Together you look over your logs and come to an agreement about what you'll earn in the States on your cargo. If he misses you, he'll come looking for you, or he'll bring it up next time you're around. He keeps records. Very businesslike."

Karl shook his head again. "He's a hoodlum. A no-account hoodlum. If you were living in your home, you would meet him at the door with a rifle pointed directly at his head."

"And he'd come around with twenty men, pointing rifles at our heads," said another grimly.

Clearly, Karl was getting nowhere. Frustrated beyond belief, dying to punch a hand through something, he grabbed Charlie and hauled him out of the tavern, Lucas following close behind.

From the window of a whore's room across the street, Mason watched Karl and his men exit the tavern. She stood behind him, her body pressed against his, her hands roaming. But Mason's mind was elsewhere. He smiled, watching the man's angry, frustrated gait. Clearly, Mason had gotten to him. It would be a pleasure taking the man's cargo or forcing him into submission as he had the other captains who frequented these waters. Perhaps he would charge him twenty percent rather than the customary fifteen. For his impertinence. He chuckled. Or as a tax for his friendship with a sworn enemy of Mason's, Elsa Ramstad.

The pirate's eyes shifted to the sea. How long would it take for him to find Elsa Ramstad again? He had searched for the Ramstad ship when he had seen them the year before. But the coward had fled like a mouse from a burning barn. Perhaps if he had found them, she never would have written that piece for the *Times*. She had made a deadly mistake in filing that article. Before that, she had been a distant memory that intrigued him. Since she had published her words, setting the naval dogs on his heels, Mason's interest in her had become a burning desire to get even. He would make her pay for the torture she had put him through, forcing him to post extra guards and lose precious income wherever he went. He just needed to find her; then he could get his restitution. What would be appropriate punishment for Mrs. Ramstad?

Mason thought for a while and then smiled. It was too good. Yes, it was just too good. And he could not wait for the day to put his plan into action.

twenty-two

February 1887

Kaatje awakened to find Jessie at her bedside, staring at her in- tently. "Why, Jess, what has you up so early?"

"I had a bad dream."

"Oh? Come here, sweetheart," she beckoned, spreading open the sheet and down comforter. "It is cold out there this morning." She shivered. Jessica nodded. "Want to tell me about your dream?"

"I dreamed you went away. That I had to find a new mother."

Kaatje fought to keep herself from reacting. "And what hap- pened?"

"I don't know. I woke up before I found her. All I knew was that I was so sad to be away from you." She stared at Kaatje, her Soren-blue eyes never leaving her mother.

Kaatje pulled her close, her small body snuggling against her. She was cold. How long had she stood beside Kaatje's bed? "No one will ever take you away from me," Kaatje promised. "You are mine and I will always be your mother. But there is something I have to tell you, Jessie."

"What?"

"I've tried to find the words, the right time..." She stroked Jessica's

hair, trying to soothe her own shattered nerves. "You know that Auntie Elsa has a sister."

"Miss Tora."

"Yes," Kaatje said, surprised that the girl had gathered so much. "Yes, well it was Tora who gave you to me."

Jessie sat up slowly. "Gave me to you?"

"Yes." Kaatje pasted on a smile. "I was so blessed to get you. Tora couldn't care for you the way she wanted. She came to me in Dakota when you were just a tiny baby. I decided right then and there that I would try my best to be your mother, if Tora could not."

"So...so you aren't my real mother."

Kaatje fought back tears. "I am your mother in every way possible except for one. I didn't carry you in my womb." She reached out to stroke the child's cheek. "But I have always been there for you, and I always will be. I love you as my own."

"But Tora is my mother."

"She gave birth to you."

"She didn't want me?"

"I think she loved you deep down, sweetheart. She just couldn't care for you at that time in her life." She hoped the answer would suffice.

"What if she decides she wants me now? Will I have to go with her?"

"No! No. I am your mother now. She can't just come in and lay claim to you, Jessie."

"You won't let her?"

Kaatje pulled her back down on the bed for another embrace. "I promise you, Jessica. You are my daughter in every way. And I would fight to keep you safe with me as much as I would for Christina."

By late afternoon, her early morning conversation with Jessie was still haunting Kaatje. When Elsa called for tea, Kaatje decided she had to know where her friend stood. Elsa had affirmed her belief that Jessie

belonged with Kaatje, but now that she'd seen Tora…seen Tora on a better track, in a different light…

"Elsa, I had a most troubling talk with Jessica this morning," she said in low tones, not wanting the children or house staff to overhear.

"Oh?" Elsa asked, looking up from her sketching. "About what?"

"About Tora."

"Oh. I had wondered when and if she might come up."

Kaatje stood to pace the room. She wrung her hands, searching for the right words. "You have been so kind to me and the girls. I don't want anything to come between us."

"Nothing ever could, Kaatje," Elsa said, her eyes staring into Kaatje's.

"Yes, well, I know that is what you say. But this is what concerns me. Jessie had a bad dream last night. A dream in which I was gone and she had to seek a new mother. If anything happened to me, would you take in the girls?"

"Of course. Without question."

"You wouldn't give them to Tora?"

"Tora? I hardly think she's in a position to—"

"No. She's not in a position now to take them on. But you said yourself she's made a remarkable change. Perhaps she's getting her life back in order. And if that is the case, what would stop her from coming to get Jessie?"

"If her life is back in order—" She paused as Mrs. Hodge arrived with the tray of tea and cookies. After the woman left, shutting the door behind her, Elsa continued, "Even if she gets her life back in order, she's hardly in a place to take on two girls."

"But what if she was? What if Trent continues to pursue her, to court her? And they marry? She'll have every luxury. Any servant she wishes to hire. And how can I compete with that? She is Jessie's real mother." Kaatje felt frantic, at odds within.

Elsa calmly poured a cup of tea and offered it to Kaatje. "Here. Drink some tea. Then let us play a game of chess."

Her manner irritated Kaatje to no end. She whirled and struck the
china cup from Elsa's hand, sending it flying toward the fireplace and
shattering. "I don't want tea! Nor to play chess! I want to know where
you stand!"

"Kaatje!" Elsa exclaimed, rising.

An apology crossed her heart, but Kaatje was inexplicably angry.
Elsa was clearly going to side with Tora. Didn't she already love Trent
as a brother-in-law? Every night, that was all Kaatje heard. "Trent said"
this…"Trent said" that. If he married Tora, how could Elsa turn them
away?

"They're family!" Kaatje said, pressing the back of her hand to her
sweating brow.

"What?" Elsa asked, looking utterly confused.

"Trent! Tora! If they come to you together, intent on getting Jessie
back, how could you not support them?"

Elsa sighed and pointed toward the couch. Kaatje began to cry.
"Sit down, Kaatje. Sit down, right now." When she had done so, Elsa
knelt near her feet, looking as precarious as a teapot with a rounded
bottom. "Kaatje," Elsa said, taking her hands and waiting until she
met her gaze. "I will never let Tora take Jessie away from you."

Kaatje wrenched away from her friend and went to the window.
"I cannot find it within me to entirely believe you."

"Why? Have I ever deceived you? Wronged you?"

"No. It's just that there's this feeling within me that tells me it will
only be a matter of time."

"A matter of time before I betray you?"

Kaatje considered the madness of her words. But it was true. It was
how she felt. "At some point, Elsa, we all fail. Isn't this a likely way for
you to fail me?"

Elsa came near her, a hand at the small of her back. She frowned
at Kaatje's words. "Just because Soren failed you, betrayed you, doesn't
mean I will. Just because Tora sliced open your skin and poured salt
on the wound does *not* mean I will!"

Kaatje was silent for a moment, staring out at the gray skies. "He was so rotten," she whispered.

"Soren?"

"Yes. I'm still so angry at him. For his indiscretions. For leaving us. He never even gave me a chance to yell at him! He left me with a small child, and then Tora..."

"It was bitterly unfair."

"Yes!" It felt good to give in to the pity she felt for herself in her heart. "I deserved better!"

"Yes."

"It was not fair of God."

"It was life, not God, that dealt you such a rotten hand. Life is difficult, but God is not. Soren was not following the ways of the Savior."

"So I had to suffer for it?" Kaatje asked, glancing at her.

Elsa winced again and sat down. "You chose Soren."

"Ah. So it's all my fault."

Elsa sighed and reached out a hand. "No. Not all of it is your fault. But we choose our paths, Kaatje. You know that. We make choices, good and bad."

"And Soren was a bad one."

"Perhaps. But look at your beautiful daughters. Christina and Jessie. They're yours and you have plenty to be proud of. And Kaatje..."

"What?"

"I will *never* ever let Tora take Jessie from you. She is yours, as much as if you had borne her yourself. Tora has no right to her. I'll tell her so. I promise you."

Kaatje studied her, relaxed enough to finally observe her pale, clammy skin and quick breathing. "Elsa? Are you all right?"

"Yes," Elsa gasped, placing a hand on her abdomen. "Just preparing to bring yet another babe into this world."

Kaatje mumbled her profuse apologies all the way up the stairs, calling for Mrs. Hodge as they went. The children came running, their eyes wide as they saw their mothers' tear-stained cheeks. "Elsa is about to have her baby," Kaatje said, curbing their countless questions. "Be good children and stay with Mrs. Hodge. Do what she tells you."

Elsa concentrated on reaching the master bedroom and on the contractions that grasped her body every few minutes. "The doctor," she reminded Kaatje.

"Oh yes!" She turned toward the stairs again. "Mrs. Hodge! Send for the doctor!" Then she turned back and continued to support Elsa as they moved toward the bedroom. "I am so sorry, Elsa. I don't know what got into me."

"Stop apologizing," Elsa said. "You obviously had to get it out of your system."

"But heavens! I even broke a teacup!"

"Probably what you feel like doing to Soren," Elsa said. "Just remind me to keep the crystal away from you if it ever happens again."

"I don't think it will," Kaatje said, sighing as they sat down together on the massive four-poster's mattress. She rose immediately to help Elsa change into a loose nightshift, then lifted her legs onto the bed. "I suppose you're right—I just needed to work it through. All that worry. All that anger. I feel worlds better."

"Terrific. I wish I did," Elsa quipped.

Kaatje laughed and bustled about, gathering linens and a basin for some extra water. She paused by Elsa's side. "I'm truly very sorry. You've never given me reason to doubt you."

"Enough. You're forgiven. As long as you track down the doctor for me."

"Even if I have to go searching for him myself," Kaatje promised. She left the room then, and Elsa was left to her own thoughts. She rolled on her side as another contraction gripped her center, from the small of her back all the way around her belly, and clutched at what had once been Peder's pillow. All at once, the longing for him over-

whelmed her. She pulled the pillow toward her, wishing she could remember exactly how it felt to be in Peder's arms. How could she do
this? How could she bear another of Peder's children without him
waiting in the next room? The melancholy quickly brought tears to
her eyes and dampened the pillow beneath her face.

Elsa missed him for more reasons than the birth. She knew he
would know what to do with Tora and Trent. What to do for Kaatje,
to appease her fears. He did not always know just what to say, she
mused with a mirthless chuckle, remembering how he used to nettle
her by blurting out something captainesque rather than feeling her
fears. But he had gotten better at it all…The tears came faster as she
thought about his deep green eyes and the sunlight in his hair.

After a moment, she rose and padded over to her desk, lighting a
lamp beside it. Outside, an uncommon late-winter storm sent fat
flakes floating down past her window. She opened a portfolio and dug
down to the bottom, where she had hidden illustrations she had been
unwilling to see for months. Peder on deck, at the wheel, staring out
to sea, in the ratlines, up in the crow's nest. They were pictures that
had been printed in the newspapers, pictures that made "Captain
Ramstad" as famous as his wife. She supposed a nation of women fell
in love with him along with her, she mused silently.

"Oh, Peder," she mumbled. The tears ran off her cheeks and
dripped onto the canvas, making a smeared spot on his shoulder. How
she ached for that shoulder, those arms!

A contraction ripped through her body, making her gasp. It was
stronger this time and closely followed by another. Mrs. Hodge came
in and scolded her for being out of bed. Nearing Elsa, and seeing her
drawings, her tone softened. "Ah, child. He is here," she said, taking
her by the shoulders and leading her to the bed. "He's here in spirit,
waiting to welcome your child to the world."

The baby was born four hours later. She didn't cry, which concerned Elsa at first, but she took to the breast without hesitation and
the doctor confirmed that all seemed to be in working order.

Later, everyone gathered around the bed to admire the child. "Maybe she just knows you needed some peace in the household," Kaatje said gently.

"Or maybe she'll blow all at once," Kristian said, gazing at his sister in awe. "Like a steam engine."

The adults laughed.

"What will you call her?" Mrs. Hodge asked.

Elsa considered her daughter, so tiny, so perfect. She had Peder's wavy brown hair, and lots of it.

"Eve," she said. "Since she was born on the eve of a new day for me. A new life for us all. Next month, we sail."

twenty-three

As March wore on, Kaatje grew more and more restless. When Elsa's precious tulip bulbs began to emerge in their bright spring green foliage, Kaatje longed to see for herself how the land looked in the Skagit Valley. She was kneeling one day by the tulips, her hands in the dirt, checking to see how thawed the ground was, when Elsa opened the front door. Kaatje picked up a handful, held it, then released it in a clump. "Perfect for planting," she said.

"You'll need to go soon," Elsa said, Eve on her shoulder.

"If your soil here is any indication, I need to get back shortly to break up sod and plant."

Elsa nodded somberly. "I will miss you."

"And I you," Kaatje said, rubbing the dirt from her palms as she stood. "I feel better though, since Eve seems to be doing so well. You'll leave yourself in what? Two weeks?"

"Yes. If I can get our affairs in order."

Kaatje climbed the steps and shivered a bit. "Still nippy for spring, don't you think?"

"Yes. But I am so glad for the sun you will not hear a complaint upon my lips."

Kaatje laughed. It had been a particularly damp and gloomy

winter. Today the skies were a deep blue with white, fluffy clouds. The children were out playing at the park under the watchful eye of Mrs. Hodge. The woman had been such a blessing to Elsa in this difficult time. Kaatje was glad for her presence. After much cajoling, Mrs. Hodge had agreed to accompany Elsa on her first voyage without Peder. If it went well, she said she would consider others. Without her help, Kaatje doubted that Elsa would have actually moved forward with her plans to captain the *Grace*, newly christened from Ramstad Yard and brought to Seattle by Riley. Part of her wished Elsa's plans had been hobbled—that she hadn't convinced Mrs. Hodge to join her; for the risk she was taking frightened Kaatje. Yet what could she say? She herself was considering Alaska!

The two friends went in the house and settled in the parlor. "I'm a bit afraid of going home, you know," Kaatje confessed, returning to her earlier thoughts.

"Oh?"

"Yes. I've gotten used to your soft life. I can already feel the aching muscles I'll have after a few days' work."

"I can understand that. Life aboard ship isn't exactly the same as that of a Seattle socialite, either."

"You can't mean you'll do manual labor."

"Anything I can. It's important for the men to see me doing tasks alongside them. If I didn't, it would be difficult to garner their respect."

Kaatje shook her head. "I don't know how you'll do it. Even with Mrs. Hodge's help. How can you mother two children and captain a ship?"

Elsa smiled. "The same way you've mothered two children—without assistance—and managed a farm."

Kaatje returned her smile ruefully. "It'll be easier now. The girls are getting older and becoming more of a help." For the thousandth time, her fears resurfaced and she wondered what her life would be like without Jessie. How Christina and she would miss her! A part of her, when she was honest with herself, longed to leave Seattle and place more distance between Jessie and Tora. Not that Tora would be unable to find her. It was just something Kaatje could not explain, an urgency to *escape*. Somehow, once she was out of the city streets, the blocks of two-story homes and storefronts, and into the broad, open skies of the Skagit Valley, she felt she would breathe easier. As if Tora would be less likely to seek them there than at her sister's home.

Eve fussed on Elsa's shoulder, and Elsa moved to turn her around so the baby could see the light from the window. "She could sit still for hours, watching the trees and sunlight through that window," Elsa said.

"She'll like the sails and sounds of the ocean."

"As will I," Elsa said. She paused, obviously thinking. "When Peder died, I couldn't get off that ship fast enough. Now, stepping aboard the *Grace,* it's as if it's another world for me."

"Perhaps you only needed some time ashore. Time to grieve for Peder before you could see what he loved about sailing again."

Elsa nodded. "My heart still is heavy each time I think of him. But it is getting better, I must admit. I only think of him a couple of times a day, rather than every hour."

"Time is a welcome balm," Kaatje said, remembering how gradually her thoughts of Soren lessened to only once or twice a week. Now, it was only once or twice a month. It seemed crazy, really. How could someone so dear, so important to her, slip from her mind like that? "It is God's way of healing us. Unless we are allowed to think of other things, other people, it is difficult not to ache for our loved one."

Elsa closed her eyes. "I am not ready to give up on Peder's memory. I'm not ready to stop missing him."

Kaatje nodded. "I understand. Eventually, your heart will want room for other memories. Not that you shouldn't always honor and cherish Peder and who he was…It's only that we have to move forward. If we're stuck in the mud of yesterday, it's hard to enjoy the cleansing baths of today."

"Eloquently put." She stared at Kaatje. "I will miss you so much."

"And I, you. We knew it was coming."

"Yes. But I didn't want to think about how hard it would be."

"We'll have our letters."

"Ah yes. Our letters. I suppose I'll have to get back into the habit again."

"Speaking of letters, have you heard from the Bergensers in Norway of late? Or those in Camden?"

"Just that letter from Mother last month I read to you. I have half a mind to take the *Grace* to Bergen and bring her here."

"Carina would never forgive you."

"Still. She could see America. Where two of her daughters have made a new life. Meet her other grandchildren."

Kaatje felt she included Jessie, making her feel ill at ease again.

"How about the Skagit Valley Bergensers?" Elsa asked.

"Not much in the last few weeks. It is part of why I want to return home and see for myself. I miss all of them." She paused, choosing her words carefully. "And Tora? What have you heard from her? Or Trent?"

Elsa met her glance. "Nothing. I have not heard a word from either of them since I left Seaport a month ago."

Kaatje nodded, trying to look nonchalant. But she knew Elsa knew her better than that.

It was an uncommonly warm, dry eve for late March, and Tora was glad for it. After finishing the supper dishes, she washed her face and then patted it with a flour-sack towel, looking out her tiny cabin window for Trent. As usual, he awaited her beneath a giant fir to the left of the cabin, staring out at the Sound. In the golden light of the spring sunset, he looked magnificent. She gazed down at her sad, secondhand dress, wondering that she and Trent were more in love than ever, yet she had nothing that she once thought would draw him to her. There was that sense of humor from God again, she mused, smiling.

She grabbed a shawl and walked toward him, green pine cones scattering away from her boots as she stepped. He smiled at her—a warmer, friendlier grin than she had ever seen on him—and offered her his arm. She gladly took it. "You look relaxed," she said.

"I am. I'm in a beautiful part of the country, courting the woman I love again."

Tora looked down at her feet, relishing his words, but wondering if she should say something to halt their progress. She did not know where God would take her, but she knew she had to follow his direction for her life. She hated the idea that Trent would not be a part of it, but something in her heart niggled at her, warned her that it might just play out that way. Surely God would not be so unfair!

They walked down to the beach in companionable silence. The tide was out, and the sun had just sunk over the horizon, leaving a pink hue in the sky that darkened to a lavender around the edges of the few clouds above and cast a purplish glow over the still waters.

"Feels like summer is on its way," Trent said, bending to pick up a rounded turquoise rock and examine it.

"It does. I suppose you'll be heading home soon."

He looked at her quickly. "Not at all. I am enjoying this. This time with you, Tora. We were always so rushed before. I think it was one of our mistakes. No time to simply get to know each other. This month has been invaluable."

They walked a bit farther. Tora said, "Perhaps if we had had time together before, you would have dismissed any notion of a relationship with me."

"Perhaps. But you are different now."

"In fundamental ways." She stopped to peer at him in the growing shadows. "I must know something, Trent. You know that I have made a commitment to Christ, one that still feels odd to talk about, yet right in my heart. Do you consider yourself a Christian as well?"

Trent looked out to sea, at her, then to the trees beside them. "I find it very interesting that as God was at work in you, he was at work in me as well. I have always been a Christian man, although I have frequently allowed my work to get in the way of regular worship. In my concern for you…" He paused to stroke her cheek and jawline. "I had no other place to turn. I was sure that he had given me no other option but to leave you. But when you disappeared…when your note was found and I read that hint of a change in you…when I could not find you—" His voice cracked, and he took a moment to gather himself. "Once again, God was giving me no choice but to lean on him, to trust in him. And then I come to find out he was holding you close all along."

Tora stared at him, wondering at the care and concern in his voice. She smiled a little. "I am glad that God has drawn you closer too." She began walking again, concern speeding her heartbeat more than the exercise. "There is another thing we must talk about."

Trent took her arm and strolled beside her, waiting for her to speak.

"You have been here a month, and we've talked of so much. But never have we spoken of my child, my daughter, Jessica. Kaatje is a good mother to her—she loves Jessica with all her heart. But I'm still struggling…"

He stopped her and turned her toward him, then took both of her hands in his. "That is the most amazing part of the change in you that I see, Tora. What was done with Jessica is done. I know you will find a way to try and make amends as best you can. And I will stand beside you."

He sounded confident in his words, but Tora wanted to be sure. She turned away from him, unable to bear watching his kind expression. "Knowing how I lived, the mistakes I made, the heartless way I acted…I would understand if you wanted to walk away. I do not want you to be with me out of some sense of…obligation."

"Tora," he said, coming around her so he could see her face. "God is in the business of making ugly things beautiful. He's done it with you already. I can see it. I want to marry you. You've told me that you are a new creation, and I believe you. How many times have I made my own mistakes? How many times have I made decisions for my own personal gain that hurt others? I shudder to think about it. I want your second chance to be our second chance. Let's begin again."

Tora smiled through her tears as she looked up at him. "We will see, Trent Storm. We will see. Let us wait for a while, shall we? All my life I've been in such a rush. For now, I want only to wait for the Lord's direction."

When Trent looked downcast, she laid a gentle hand on his chest. He glanced at her. "I am praying that God will have marriage in our future. I am praying specifically for that," she said.

Trent only nodded.

Elsa saw Kaatje and the girls off on the train two weeks later and boarded the *Grace* the day afterward. She grinned when she saw Riley at the top of the gangplank. They shook hands formally, their eyes conveying more emotion.

"It's good to have ya back aboard, Missus," Riley said, moving to ruffle Kristian's sandy hair. The boy moved into his arms with delight, wrapping his legs around Riley's waist and clinging to him like a lost monkey to his newly found master.

"Where's Cook?" Kristian asked in excitement.

"Here, young master," said the short Chinese man softly from behind them. Riley turned, and Kristian dropped from his arms to the deck and ran to Cook, fiercely embracing his leg. If Elsa was not mistaken, there was a tear in the stalwart Chinaman's eye.

Of all her old crew, these two were the only ones she had shanghaied from other Ramstad ships. On her first voyage out, she had bowed to Kaatje's advice to seek their support, if no one else's. "Thank you, gentlemen, for agreeing to serve me on the *Grace*," she said assertively, looking at one and then the other. Of the two, it had been a greater sacrifice for Riley, who had captained the *Grace* from Camden-by-the-Sea, and the *Eagle* to Camden after leaving Elsa and Kristian in

Seattle. Yet Riley had come up with the idea, claiming it would be an honor to serve as her first mate on their voyage to Japan. "I'll no' take any other position," he had insisted upon their encounter three weeks past.

"Stubborn man," Elsa had jested, while inwardly thanking God for his fearsome loyalty. "I'll be honored to have you stand by my side as I regain my sea legs."

"Aye, Cap'n," he said. "By your leave. I'll look into potential cargo from Seattle to the Orient."

"Very good. I'll assume we'll haul wood from Ramstad Lumber Yard, unless you come across something more profitable," she directed, feeling the power of command for the first time in a long while. She felt stronger, more vital for it.

"Captain?" Riley asked, bringing her mind back to the present. "I'd like to introduce you to our second mate, Eric Young."

Elsa shook the man's hand, observing his broad shoulders and reddish-blond hair. His eyes were a light blue, his complexion ruddy. But mostly she studied his eyes. There she could see good humor and a hint of challenge. A hint was to be expected. It was a full-blown challenge she would rather not face. How would he feel about serving a female captain, and a new mother at that? She knew that some men would have a difficult time taking orders from a woman. But there would be time enough to show Eric and the rest of the men that she was not some soft socialite taking on a ship's duty as a lark. She meant this to be the first voyage of the rest of her life.

"Where do you hail from, Mr. Young?" she asked.

"These last ten years, I've been sailing for an operation out of San Francisco."

"And what brought you to us?"

"Got into a bit of a scrape last time we came out of Caracas. A storm landed the remains of my ship on the coast of Trinidad. Lost all I had and most of my crew as well."

"Terrible," Elsa said, careful to not seem too moved by the traumatic story. "You were her captain?"

"No, ma'am. I was the second, just as I'll be for you."

Elsa nodded. "So why did you not ship out again for the same operation?"

"It was a small operation. Changes in management over the years had not endeared them to me. I figured it was God's way of turning me in a different direction, so when a Ramstad ship came by, I signed on as a crew member and got to know our first mate here en route."

Elsa nodded again, glad to hear that Riley had had some experience with the man. She trusted his judgment. "I hope you'll be pleased with this new direction God has taken you."

Eric smiled appreciatively at her. "It will be interesting, to say the least, ma'am."

There was a glint in his eye that reminded Elsa of Stefan, her wayward first mate who had been placed in chains for making unwanted advances on her. But she dismissed it. Her heart told her he was merely playing, flirting in the idle fashion of all sailors. There would be time enough to show him she meant business, from launch to landing.

"Gather the men, Mr. Young," she commanded, beginning her duties in earnest. "Introduce them to your captain and then we shall be under way."

"Aye, aye, Cap'n," he said.

Elsa turned and greeted Mrs. Hodge, showing her the way to the captain's quarters, which were made up of five rooms on the main deck: her own stateroom, a study, the dining room, a quickly altered nursery, and another bedroom for Mrs. Hodge. It was lovely, Elsa thought as she ran her hands along the woodwork she knew her friends in Camden had labored over. They were turning out first-rate ships for Ramstad Yard, and Elsa smiled. Peder would have been proud.

Mrs. Hodge took Eve from her as the men gathered outside and

Elsa hurriedly changed into dungarees and a loose-fitting white blouse. She belted the pants at the waist and smiled at herself in the mirror. Most of the men outside would be surprised, but she needed every nuance to help convince them she was as capable as the next man to run the *Grace*. Squaring her shoulders, she left the stateroom and, looking down, resolutely walked up the outside stairs to the platform above her quarters.

There she turned, placed her hands in A-fashion on the banister before her and looked each man in the eye as Riley called, "Gentlemen! Meet your new captain, Elsa Ramstad!"

They paused for a moment, then collectively nodded toward her in deference. All in all, it was a warmer reception than she had anticipated. But when one lone man started clapping from the back of the crowd and others joined him, she was taken aback.

She glanced at Riley in concern.

"It's all right, Cap'n," he reassured, and cocked his head to one side. "I told 'em what you did the night Peder was swept overboard. Thought it might pave the way a bit." He glanced at her nervously.

Elsa nodded slightly, glad for the explanation. She motioned for the men, ninety-eight in all, to settle down. "Good morning, men. Thank you for your welcome. As you have gathered, this is the first time I have been aboard ship since I left the sea to mourn my husband. There is no doubt that I have a lot yet to learn, but I think you will find me a fair and decent captain. Having traveled with my husband, Peder, and our first mate, Riley, here, for several years gave me the opportunity to learn a lot about running a tight ship. Being female does not mean I will be soft. When discipline is demanded, I will see to it. Do not cross me, and we shall get along fine."

The men shifted under her gaze. "I know it is unusual to serve under a woman," Elsa said, her tone never softening, never giving an edge to any doubt they might be feeling. "But there have been many fine, honest female captains, and some dishonest female pirate captains as well. Be glad I am of the first variety." The men laughed.

"Mr. Riley will see to your duties. I say make this a profitable excursion for Ramstad Yard, and I'll see to it that you are all rewarded with bonuses that will surpass those of any other sailor. Done?"

"Done!" the men roared.

"Man the capstan!" Elsa commanded.

"Man the capstan!" Riley echoed.

"See to it that we're under way in short order, Riley."

"Aye, aye, Cap'n. Haul in the anchor!"

She turned to the crowd and nodded once, dismissing them. Within the hour, all sails were unfurled and the *Grace* was riding the high seas again. Elsa breathed a sigh of relief and retreated to her quarters to check on her children.

That night, after Kristian and Eve were in bed and fast asleep, Elsa donned a warm coat and left her quarters to walk the deck. She paused at the bow, relishing the stinging, salty spray of the ocean as the waves passed beneath the *Grace's* hull. She did not grab the rail, wanting to feel the pound and pull of the ocean's momentum as her ship danced upon it. Her sea legs had returned quickly.

They headed in a southwesterly direction, so it was only as she turned back toward her quarters that she spied movement in the north skies. She picked up her pace, making her way to the stern. This time, she gripped the rail as she looked heavenward. There, blue and purple lights danced in the sky.

Quick tears laced her lashes. For in seeing the northern lights, it was as if the hand of her father was on one shoulder behind her, and Peder's hand on the other. Above her, God himself was casting an artistic composition of nature's most miraculous lights across the canvas of his sky. Surely, this was reassurance that she was on the right path. She had not seen the aurora borealis for many, many months. Her heart soared. "Thank you, Lord. Papa, I miss you. Peder, I miss you as I would my right arm. Nothing seems right without you here," she whispered. "Thank you for being with me. For watching out for me."

She stood there until the cold got the better of her, then returned to her quarters. Unable to sleep, she entered the study, took pen, ink, and paper from her desk, and prepared to write her first column for the *New York Times* since her hiatus. She began by doing a quick self-portrait of herself on deck addressing the men, a rare perspective. Most of her illustrations for the *Times* had been of others, but she felt it important that her audience see her as her crew had seen her today. It would give them a sense of being there that Elsa knew would thrill her editor. Later, she dipped her pen in the cobalt ink, blotted it, and paused over the paper, choosing her words carefully for the accompanying article.

24 March 1887

Today I am captain of the mighty schooner Grace, newly christened from Ramstad Yard, Camden. I leave my home in Seattle with some hesitation, fretting that I will lose a part of my beloved Peder in leaving his graveside. But here on the Pacific, I feel closer to him than I have in many months. This was the life he loved, and I intend to introduce his children to the same. Through it, they will come to know a part of their father they would otherwise never know.

Last month I bore a daughter, Eve, and both she and Kristian are traveling with me on this voyage to Japan. It is unusual for a female to captain a ship, and a new mother at that, but I am blessed with good men to serve me and a loyal nanny who will care for my children as her own when I am not about. This is something that my God and my heart have called me to. Having left our last ship with not as much as a glance over my shoulder, so eager was I to rid myself of the horrible memories of losing my husband aboard her, this calling comes as a surprise.

Yet I find we live with a surprising God, do we not? I was welcomed today by a crew who applauded my return to the sea, although they do not yet know me. It warmed my heart but made me eager to justify their high regard. It is my hope that I will be half the captain my husband was, and that will be enough.

Tonight, the northern lights danced in the sky, an Easter brigade of purple and green bands. I took it as confirmation that I am on the right track. So forward we move, across the Pacific, porting briefly in Hawaii, and then onward to Japan. More later.

Captain Elsa Ramstad

twenty-four

May 1887

*W*ord of her arrival had obviously preceded her. By the time Elsa reached Honolulu, she found a stack of invitations from the island socialites, including the Lady Bancock. Elsa fingered the fine linen stationery and tapped it to her chin, thinking. She did not have time to see them all, but perhaps if she accepted Lady Bancock's invitation to her estate, she could see many of them at the evening ball on Saturday. The opportunity for a walk among the governor's fabled gardens and white beaches, as well as a stay on land, was more than she could pass up. She sent a man with a return correspondence the day after making port, and was soon met by servants from Lady Bancock's estate in a skiff, there to escort her and her family to the grounds.

Elsa hurriedly finished packing and followed her luggage, Kristian, and Mrs. Hodge over the edge to the skiff below. Eve was carefully lowered in a basket and, as usual, she slept through the entire escapade.

"That child is the most relaxed thing I've ever laid eyes on," Mrs. Hodge exclaimed, wiping a sheen of sweat from her brow. Clearly, climbing the lines was not her cup of tea. Kristian bounced up and down in his seat beside her.

"God knew we had our hands full with that one," Elsa said,

nodding at Kristian. She turned to the servant in charge. "Carry on, gentlemen. I believe we're all here."

The man, dressed in elegant attire despite the sweltering heat, nodded and turned to the two native oarsmen. Without another word, they dug deep, carrying the group toward a distant point on which Lady Bancock's estate lay. In half an hour, they had arrived, and Lady Bancock met them on the edge of her green, manicured lawn, just beyond the white sand beach and tropical foliage. "My dear Captain Ramstad," she exclaimed, reaching out to Elsa. "What a pleasure and privilege it is to have you here in my home!"

"It is my pleasure," Elsa said. "It is good to see you again. Thank you for your invitation. May I present my children? Kristian and Eve Ramstad, as well as our nanny, Mrs. Hodge?"

"A pleasure, a pleasure," the lady smiled, clearly delighted that she had snagged the elusive Elsa Ramstad for her party. Elsa knew a female captain was something of an oddity. She was bound to draw attention; it had to be the reason for all the invitations awaiting her. When she had passed through Honolulu on many occasions previously she had received perhaps two or three invitations to call. Peder's death, news of her public accusations against Mason Dutton, and her recent choice to captain a ship herself, had apparently tripled her fame. But Lady Bancock had always been kind to her, so she didn't fear being exploited by her as she might be by others. It was primarily for that reason that Elsa had accepted her invitation.

"Let me show you the way to your rooms," Lady Bancock said. She was dressed in the superior linens of a proper lady, and wore a fine-gauge straw hat that could only have come from France on the latest ship through the islands. She had little shape, just the rounded lines of well-to-do maturity, and she had merry eyes that Elsa wanted to draw.

"Right behind you," Elsa said. She took Eve from the perspiring Mrs. Hodge and followed Lady Bancock up the stone path toward the house. Two greyhounds ran circles around them, glad for the unexpected company.

"We will get you situated and then share a refreshing glass of tea on the lanai," her hostess said.

"It sounds delightful."

"Yes, well, you take all the time you need to get settled, dear," she said, opening the koawood doors to a grand suite that could easily have housed half of Elsa's crew. "Here you all can have your own rooms," she said, opening door after door. The house was decorated in fine island Victorian style. While the walls were a pale ivory from the floor to the edge of the tall ceiling—where they met a massive molding also painted eggshell white—the furniture woods were rich and dark hued. Linens were soft and gauzy, beckoning her to retire to the huge four-poster bed that reminded Elsa of her own bed in Seattle. Each bed had a mosquito net over it, giving it an exotic air, and once again Elsa congratulated herself on accepting this invitation.

"Kristian, get off there at once!" she hissed, seeing her son bounce on his bed.

"Ah, boys will be boys," Lady Bancock said. "We went through five beds getting our two sons raised to manhood."

"That's very gracious," Elsa said, her eyes commanding Kristian to get down anyway. He slid off the bed and came to her, taking her hand. "We are guests in this fine lady's home," she said to him. "I expect you to be a little gentleman."

Kristian said nothing, and the tour went on. In their suite's private room were a massive porcelain tub on clawed brass feet and an indoor water closet and bidet. There were two freestanding sinks and a mirror edged in gilt that crossed an entire wall of the room. And the floor was of huge white marble tiles, streaked with gray.

Elsa followed her hostess to the next two rooms, situating the slumbering Eve on a bed between four feather pillows and then Mrs. Hodge in a smaller room that would have suited Elsa just fine. At each stop, she nodded to servants, motioning at the bags to be left there. At the main door, Lady Bancock turned and asked, "Is there anything you'll need immediately?"

"No. You are too kind. This is just lovely. I'll simply rest for a few moments, freshen up, and join you on the lanai."

"Only if you are up to it, *Captain*," she said, obviously relishing the use of the word. "If you'd prefer to wait until supper—"

"Not at all," Elsa said. "I will join you within the hour."

"Very well," Lady Bancock said, clearly pleased. She reached for the knobs of the double doors and closed them behind her, leaving Elsa alone in the giant suite's hall.

"Can I go swimmin', Mama? Can I?" Kristian yelled, tearing out of his room as fast as he could. "I saw a pool on the way in here."

"It is a fountain," Elsa said with a smile.

"Well, then, can I go to the beach with Mrs. Hodge?"

Elsa glimpsed Mrs. Hodge through her bedroom door as she lay down on her bed. "Perhaps. Let her rest for a moment. I'm going to lie down as well. You, young man, need to keep still. There are toys in your trunk, as well as some books."

"Oh, Mother," he whined.

"Kristian," she warned. "Give me half an hour to settle in. I'm sure Lady Bancock has an afternoon's worth of entertainment for you without a swim. But give me half an hour. Yes?"

"Yes," he agreed reluctantly. "But *hurry.*"

Elsa smiled. "Just as fast as half an hour can be hurried." She watched as he returned to his room and dug in his trunk. Satisfied that he was sufficiently distracted, she retreated to her own room, lay down in her luxurious bed for five minutes, then rose to feed her suddenly squalling daughter. Afterward she pulled an afternoon garden gown in pale gray from her trunk. It was a bit mussed, but she doubted if Lady Bancock would hold it against her.

Eve lay on her bed, moving her arms with delight as the island breeze swept through the room and made the mosquito net dance in the warm afternoon light. In minutes Elsa was dressed and her hair was redone in a graceful knot at the nape of her neck. A servant had come to collect "Young Master Ramstad" to visit the toy room, which—if it was anything like the rest of the house—was no doubt extensive. Yes, being a sea captain had certain advantages, she mused, quietly leaving the snoring Mrs. Hodge behind to attend Eve, who would tire of the mosquito net and demand more attention shortly. Until then, Elsa would let Mrs. Hodge rest.

Two days later, Elsa smiled into the full-length mirror. Outside, the sounds of surf and sliding waves on the evening breeze came floating through the suite. The rumblings of a gathering on the lanai, where Lady Bancock's party was to begin, could already be heard, punctuated with laughter and the faint smell of cigar smoke.

Tonight would be Elsa's first formal evening occasion since her mourning had begun, and although she was still draped in black, Madame de Boisiere had done a marvelous job in combining faille and lace to make an elegantly sedate but still flattering gown just days before her departure. From twin rosebuds at her shoulders, the gown tapered to a narrow waist. At her breast was a fan of material that modestly covered any cleavage. The skirt had a small bustle and cascaded to the floor in a simply fluted pattern with a small train behind her.

She worked on her hair for an hour, wishing Kaatje were there to assist her, but finally managed to create a simple yet elegant French twist with two fine ebony combs Peder had given her the year before. She dabbed some light pink color on her lips and pinched her cheeks. *Who are you dressing up for?* she silently asked her mirror image, frowning. Peder would have celebrated her beauty tonight, but Peder was gone, never to return. As she thought about it, Elsa decided that she simply enjoyed the ritual of preparing for such an event with or without someone to dress for. There was an inherent excitement, a pleasure in anticipating what might lie ahead.

"Peder would be proud of me," she whispered at herself. "It's been nine months since I buried him. He would want me to laugh. To try to get on with my life in this arena as well." Having decided to make the best of it and not feel guilty for the enjoyment, she laced up her evening slippers, pulled on long gloves, and then grabbed her mourning handkerchief and black fan from Japan. Although the breeze was cool, and her arms and shoulders were largely bare, she felt more comfortable holding something, even if she didn't need the fan. It gave her a sense of security, not that she could truly hide behind it. But she felt nervous. How long had it been since she had attended a party without an escort? she wondered. Not since Bergen. Not for years.

As she bid good night to Kristian and Mrs. Hodge, she fretted about whom she would speak with and what all she should say. Kristian said, "Mama, you are beautiful."

Elsa smiled and bent low to kiss him. "Thank you, dearest. You helped me." Turning, she walked straight toward the double doors and opened them with as much confidence as she could muster.

Awaiting her on the other side was Karl Martensen.

He was dressed in a finely seamed double-breasted coat of black with bound edges, with a crisp white shirt and cravat at his neck. He winked at her and then bowed. "Captain Ramstad," he said.

"Karl!" Elsa exclaimed, finding her breath at last. "Whatever are you doing here?"

"I was due to ship out three days ago, but Lady Bancock insisted I stay for the gala. Told me it was my duty to remain and escort you to the ball. I gladly agreed."

"You've been here all this time?" she asked, taking his proffered arm and swatting him playfully with her fan. "Why haven't you come to call?"

"I assumed you had been as busy as I in gathering supplies and preparing for the next leg of your voyage. And I had other…responsibilities that needed attention."

"You are at sea again?" she asked in wonder.

"Aye," he said with a wink. "Captain Martensen, at your service. Made the acquaintance of a fine fellow in San Francisco, and the path was laid out before me." They neared the noisy banquet hall, in which refreshments were being served. Karl pulled her to a stop. "I am sorry I haven't come sooner, Elsa. We have much to talk about." He glanced around and bent nearer to her. "You must be warned. Mason Dutton frequents these waters."

Elsa frowned. "Dutton? *Still?* He still manages to roam these waters freely?"

"It is uncanny. He is as slippery as an eel. Each time the military attempts to curtail his efforts, Mason escapes. And he's bought off most of the local authorities, as well as any captains who sail Hawaiian waters. It's even rumored that King Kalakaua frequently entertains him here at the palace." He glanced up, spotting Lady Bancock coming to collect her prize guest. "We must speak again. Later on this evening?"

"Yes," Elsa said seriously, staring into his gray eyes. He had let his hair grow out a bit and she spotted a glint of gold in his left ear. Karl Martensen was wearing an earring? Obviously, he had much, much to tell her.

Although he was her escort, she saw precious little of Karl as the evening wore on. She was introduced to guest after guest, and soon the dancing began. Although her slippers were elegant and up to the minute in fashion, they were killing her toes.

She was just wishing someone would rescue her when Karl suddenly appeared, took her in his arms, and confidently danced her straight out onto the lanai. Once safely there, they were served drinks and went for a walk on the Bancock grounds. Near the crashing waves, they found a secluded marble bench nestled in a copse of swaying palm fronds. Elsa sat down with a sigh, raising her skirts just enough to release her aching feet from the strapped slippers.

"Captain Ramstad!" Karl said in mock surprise.

"Will you quit calling me that? I've heard enough of it tonight. And these shoes are as pleasurable as wearing a crab on each toe."

"That nice, eh?" Karl said, sitting beside her. She liked his jovial, confident mood.

"What has happened to you, Karl?" she asked in wonder.

"What do you mean?"

"You are different somehow. Happier. Are you in love?" she asked with one eyebrow raised. She did so hope that he would find the right woman someday.

"No, no. Well, yes. I am in love with the sea. I am happy because I am on the right path again. The path that God would have me take. I had no idea how my heart yearned to be on the sea. I guess I was missing it all that time. More than that, I made things right with God." He turned toward her. "And as best I could, with Peder. After that, with myself."

Elsa met his intent gaze. "I am so glad, Karl. Peder would be glad too."

Karl nodded. "He was the one who led me to Christ. Although he was quite angry at me, I don't think even he would have wanted me to suffer over it for so long." He smiled suddenly. "Realization of that, and what I was missing in not following my Lord, set me free." He thumped his chest two times. "I'm a new man, Elsa."

"I can see that," she said, finding his smile contagious. She felt a deep camaraderie with him, and was glad he had stayed around to escort her tonight. "So, your ship comes from San Francisco?"

"Yes. And you'll love this—she's a steamer with sailing capabilities."

Elsa laughed, remembering Peder's long debates with Karl over the use of steam. "Perfect! How does she handle?"

"Fairly well," Karl said, his head cocked to one side, his eyes again on the sand at his feet. "She's difficult in rough waters."

"Oh, Karl, do be careful."

"Always. At least on this run from San Francisco to Japan, there is no Cape Horn to face."

"Thankfully."

Karl sobered. "But as I was telling you earlier, Elsa, there are other dangers to face. Last time I was here, I ran into Mason. I challenged him in a tavern on the wharf. We had to leave under cover of dark, and hightailed it to Japan. I haven't seen him yet, but expect him at any moment."

He turned to better face her, intent on making sure she understood the danger Mason represented. "He'll hide for months at a time, and just when everyone considers him gone, he appears and attacks. Elsa, you made an enemy of him with your column. Because of you, both British and American naval forces have doubled their efforts to find him. If he finds you first, it will not be well. And he's looking for you."

"He told you that?"

"In so many words."

Elsa shivered. Her stomach tied in knots, thinking of Mason circling her like a shark. And she had her children to think of too. For the first time since setting sail, she had doubts about what she was doing.

"Who is your first mate?"

"Riley," she said, staring out at the surf.

"Your men carry weapons?"

"Whatever they brought aboard and was approved by Riley."

"Double them. Here on the island. Do not leave without adequate ammunition. And tell Riley to rig extra sails. From here to the Far East, Mason roams the waves and strikes with little conscience. It is my fear that he will hunt for you."

She remembered the night Mason and his men attacked Peder's ship, sending her diving for the water and swimming for her life. Had it not been for Karl, she would have been taken as part of the bounty, and who knew what Mason would have done with her. Elsa was so scared her heart was in her throat. "What have I done?" she whispered, wringing her hands. "I have the children to think of now. Kaatje tried to warn me."

Karl took her trembling hands in his own large, warm ones. "You are a captain now, Elsa. You must face these dangers with God. Wise as serpents, and harmless as doves, right? You need to show your men that you are aware of the danger and prepared to face it with valor. It will win their devotion, and their respect."

She looked at him steadily. "You think I can do this? You really do?"

His mouth was set grimly. "If any woman can, you can, Elsa Ramstad. Take courage in your position. You run one of the finest shipping yards in the world. You have means. I have had little luck speaking with the local authorities. Perhaps they would respond better to you. Use every means you have—money, feminine wiles, the power of the press. Use all of it, Elsa. You have the best chance of anyone to put a stop to this madness with Dutton. Before he finds you."

twenty-five

As it turned out, the Skagit Valley's soil was not ready for plant-ing when Kaatje returned to it in May. She spent the time waiting for the final thaw to arrive, spring-cleaning the house from top to bottom, preparing her home and heart for another year's work on the farm. Each time she looked at the dusty plow in the barn, and at tired old Nels, she felt weary. How could she again manage to break the earth's crust and plant more than twenty acres? It was hard, heavy work, but she had little choice.

Or did she? The question came to her as it did on any given day that she allowed her soul to search for God's lead. He clearly wanted her to go to Alaska. To seek out Soren. To find the opportunities that remained for them there. Kaatje stared out her small, square kitchen window. But surely it would be no easier than this. Yes, farmwork was grueling, but she knew her way with it. What God asked of her was impossible—he wanted her to face the unknown, to take on people, animals, and land she knew little of. And to take her children with her!

I am going mad, she decided. There was no sane woman in the West who would do what she contemplated. The girls had a solid home life—a home at all for that matter—here in the Skagit Valley. They knew the Bergensers as if they were an extended family. What could possibly be waiting for them in Alaska but the skeleton of Soren's broken, unmet dreams? Why, going to Alaska might well be the same as committing murder, setting her children up for utter disaster. The mining camps were not meant for women, let alone children.

Do not ask this of me, she prayed. *Do not ask it. Take me elsewhere, Father. Anywhere. I cannot do what you ask alone.*

You will not be alone.

Kaatje frowned and clasped her hands, kneeling. *Even with you at my side, I cannot do this, Jesus. It is too much. It is simply too much. Please, please, take this burden from me.*

She was met only by silence.

"You cannot mean that," Trent said, pacing before Tora. They had taken a long walk into the woods, and Tora sat on a giant, mossy log, staring back at him.

"I do. I don't know why. It frightens me. But I must. I must go."

"Kaatje Janssen doesn't want you there, Tora. Jessie has only known Kaatje as her mother, all her life. Kaatje has done a fine job raising her. She doesn't deserve to have you walk back into her life again now."

Tora winced at his words. "Do you not think I've thought of that? This is not an easy path for me. You've proposed marriage twice—the thing I've always wanted! But God wants me elsewhere. I owe him, Trent. I've failed him in so many ways, I owe him this. We can continue to see each other—"

"But not in the way I wish!" Trent said, pacing. He ran his hand through his hair, his eyes desperate, pleading. "We've finally found our way back to each other, back home, and now you're telling me you're leaving."

"For a while."

"For how long? A week? A month? A year?"

"I don't know. However long it takes."

Trent sank to the log beside her and placed his face in his hands. "Why? Why do you suppose he wants you to go to her? What do you think will be accomplished? You'll tear up a young girl's heart, her understanding of who she is."

"I won't tell her without Kaatje's permission, Trent," she said, turning toward him and taking his hands in hers. "All my life I've planned and schemed, making my own path. This is clearly of God, and it is not easy for me to meekly follow when I've always wanted to make my own wide swath. Surely you know enough about me to understand that."

"Yes," he said, placing an arm around her shoulders with a sigh. "I suppose it is my own test from God—I finally found the woman I love, and she's ready to love me the way I love her. And now she wants to go away again. If I trust you, and our God, then I must let you go."

"Yes."

"Then I will be near. Just as I have been here. I will set up business wherever you go, Tora."

Tora smiled through her tears. "I would love to have you close by…But for a time, I need to go alone."

Trent released her from his embrace. "What? I cannot even be nearby?"

"This is something I need to do on my own." She stood and brushed off her skirt. "There is nothing I would like better than to have you escort me to Kaatje's house, to stand by my side in case she slams the door in my face or laughs when I tell her why I'm there. But I have to do this alone, Trent. For me. For God. For Kaatje. And for us."

Trent stared back into her eyes for a long moment, saying nothing. Then he nodded, almost imperceptibly. He looked older, and weary. Tora's heart pounded. How long would he wait for her? Would he tire of her and the path God had laid out for her? Or would he tell her, "Fine, go on your path, but don't expect me to be here when you return"?

But then Trent opened his arms to her, and she entered them, relishing the sanctity of his embrace and the feel of his chest beneath her cheek. She listened as his heart beat, sound and strong. Thoughts of leaving him again brought more tears. Trent leaned back, wiped the tears from her face and traced one finger along her lower lip. After a moment's hesitation, he bent to kiss her, long and deep, as he had done years before. But it meant more this time. It was the kiss of love and devotion. Regardless of where God took them. Never had Tora felt closer to a man. Never had she known love could be like this.

Tora stepped away, a bit dazed at the intensity between them. Trent grasped her face between his two large hands, his eyes never leaving hers. "I love you, Tora Anders. I'll love you until the end of time. You come to me when you're ready to be married, and we shall do so at once."

Tora cried harder and nodded. She felt as if her heart were tearing in two, leaving the man she adored to face the unknown. "I love you too, Trent. I love you too." She had expected the words to sound odd on her lips, but they were so sure, so right, they came out with all the heartfelt emotion she held within her breast. Before she had claimed love for Trent in an attempt to finagle the marriage she sought. Now she knew love for real.

He pulled her into his arms again. "God help me," he whispered. "God help us all."

It was a late May afternoon. Kaatje unhitched the strap from Nels's belly and slapped him on the back to let him saunter back to the barn for dinner. That was when she saw her. Tora stood at the edge of the field, Christina and Jessica on either side of her. Yet she only looked toward Kaatje.

Kaatje was too stunned to move. When she had returned home, she had felt safe, separated from the chance that Tora might again seek them out. What did she want? Kaatje thought. What was she to say? All the kindness and sympathy that Kaatje had felt for her that day in the soup kitchen, the day she had brought Tora home to Elsa, was gone. All she felt now was fear and dread. "God help me," she whispered.

The girls followed Tora as she picked her way down the row toward Kaatje. Then seeing their mother's expression, they drew together and stopped. Tora continued and stopped before Kaatje, never speaking. Somehow Kaatje sensed that the Tora who stood before her now was a new person. No longer the flashy girl who pushed for her own way, she seemed humble, a plea for forgiveness clearly written in her eyes.

Kaatje looked at her and noticed that Tora was covered with soot from the train and dust from the road. Even though she herself was just as grimy after a day in the fields, her first thought was for Tora. Gently, she took Tora's hand and led her to the well in front of the house. Still they had not shared one word. The girls followed, but kept their distance. Once they reached the well, Kaatje pulled up a fresh bucket of water and offered Tora the first dipper. She drank deeply, then Kaatje did the same.

Then Kaatje took a rag from the side of the well and dipped it in the cool water. She wrung it out and gently washed Tora's cheeks, chin, and forehead as the younger woman wept. Words came at last. "I am undeserving of your kindness, Kaatje."

Kaatje turned to wash her own face and take another drink, examining every feeling in her heart. Nowhere could she find the hate and fury she once felt toward Tora. Its absence stunned her. She turned back to Tora. "We have needed to make peace for some time," she said.

Tora looked down at the ground and then back toward Kaatje. "Can you ever forgive me?"

"I forgave you awhile ago, I guess." Kaatje looked toward Jessica and then back at Tora. "Come inside, Tora. Girls, go and milk the Jersey cow. You can get to know our guest this evening." Reluctant to leave the drama unfolding before them, the girls turned to walk toward the barn, their heads together as they whispered back and forth.

"Come in, Tora. Let us talk inside."

Tora followed Kaatje into the tiny house and finally said, "I have come to serve you, Kaatje. For as long as it takes. God has sent me here."

"You need not serve me, Tora. I have forgiven you."

She met Kaatje's gaze and repeated, "God has sent me here. He told me you would need help."

"We manage on our own. Have for five years," she said pointedly.

"Let me stay," Tora pleaded. "Just for a while. Until we determine what is right."

Kaatje studied her pained expression for a moment. "You may stay in the hayloft until we decide what to do next."

"You mean before we leave?"

"Leave? We are not going anywhere."

"I am sorry…I had somehow understood…I'll go and fetch my satchel." Kaatje watched her through the window as she went out to the field and knelt by her satchel. She stayed there for a moment, apparently weeping into her hands. She could see that this was as difficult for her as it was for Kaatje. And yet what was that talk of leaving? *Before we leave.* Did she have hopes of taking Jessie away?

The girls hurried past Tora with a sloshing bucket of milk, eager not to miss anything, yet clearly unnerved by the crying stranger.

"Mama, who is that?" Christina asked as soon as they entered the house.

Kaatje's eyes did not leave the huddled form outside. "That is Tora. She is Auntie Elsa's sister. She will stay for a while." Her eyes went with dread to Jessie. The girl stood stock-still, then gazed back out the open doorway.

"She is my mother?"

"What?" Christina asked crossly.

But Jessie only looked at Kaatje.

"Yes, Jessica. She is the woman who gave you to me."

The four of them shared a torturous dinner in near silence, then eagerly went their separate ways. Kaatje did not know where to begin with Tora, how to help her to find her peace so she would leave them alone. Yet Tora's eyes did not betray any desire to steal Jessie away from her, just a hungry curiosity about the girl. And Jessie was the same.

Kaatje tossed and turned in bed, sweat dampening the sheets although the evening was cool. How could they find their way through this? Why had God sent Tora here? A form in her doorway caught her attention. "Jess?"

"Yes, Mama. Mama, I'm scared."

Kaatje opened up the sheets to her daughter. "Come here." She held the thin girl's form close to her own, discovering that Jessica trembled.

"You won't let her take me away?" Jessica whispered.

"I promised. Somehow, I don't think that's why she's here."

"*Why* is she here?"

"I think to find forgiveness. To make amends. To get to know you a bit. She knows we're a family, Jess. The last thing she wants is to cause you any pain."

Her daughter said nothing.

"Go to sleep, Jessie," Kaatje said gently, kissing the back of her head. "It will all look better in the morning." Her words were meant to reassure herself as much as the girl in her arms.

It was much later that Tora's words came back to her. *Before we leave.* The Lord's words also came, shouted in her head, not allowing her to think of anything else. *You will not be alone.*

Stunned, she sat up, rubbed her face, trying to make sure she was not dreaming. With Tora, she might be able to handle the wilds of

Alaska. She was another adult, capable of bearing a portion of their required load over the Klondike. Perhaps she could even help with the financial load. Together, they'd have a better chance. *Before we leave.* Was that the reason God had sent Tora to her? So she could go to Alaska? For a moment she felt hopeful, but then her old fears resurfaced.

Could she risk having Tora Anders near her for that long?

twenty-six

July 1887

ince there was no pier where ships could discharge cargo or passengers could disembark in Yokohama, the vast array of sailing ships, steamships, and warships of many nations were serviced by sampans and small steam launches. These launches transported people and goods to and from the Bund, the wide waterfront street that faced the harbor, all day long and often into the night.

If the expatriates in Hawaii had treated her as a novelty, the Japanese made Elsa feel like royalty. Once the men understood that her morals were not lacking simply because she captained a ship, she was swept up into their world without further ado. But Elsa found trading in Japan to be as painfully slow and as tedious a process as Peder had. If it had not been for the Japanese people's reception of her, she might have given up the whole idea. Since her last visit with Peder, the harbor had become muddled with more red tape than she cared to wade through. Passing the responsibility off to Riley, she took the children and Mrs. Hodge and accepted any invitation that came her way.

Throughout June and July they had seen those cities heretofore opened by treaty: Yokohama, Kobe, Osaka, Nagasaki, Niigata, Hakodate, and Tokyo. But the Saitos gave her access beyond those familiar cities' borders. They traveled by jinrikisha to the interior, visiting

Japanese inns that served unfamiliar food that Kristian balked at eating, to say nothing of Mrs. Hodge. Although privacy was nearly impossible to obtain and Western-style sanitation unknown, Elsa relished the opportunity to see the native people in their natural setting. If one were to stay in the well-known Western-style hotels that most captains frequented in the treaty cities, she reasoned, it was impossible to absorb the true culture of Japan. "Why, that's as exotic as a London hotel," Elsa had chided when Mrs. Hodge suggested they stay at the Grand Hotel in Yokohama.

Her adventuresome spirit had attracted the attention of the most prestigious people of Japan. The legend of the tall Norwegian-American Heroine of the Horn grew larger, and word that she stayed within their borders spread across the countryside. Therefore, when she again returned to Yokohama after a two-day excursion to Kamakura and Enoshima, she was deluged by swarms of people who had heard of Elsa Ramstad. They came at her from all directions, wanting to touch her champagne-colored hair and her creamy skin. As the jinrikisha attempted to reach the Bund across the macadam streets, they came to a halt in the midst of the frenzy. At first Elsa was amazed and amused. Then she grew frightened. The Japanese women passed Kristian around as if he were a doll, fascinated by his light hair. After a few minutes, he began to cry, calling for Elsa. She had just gotten him back into her arms when Mrs. Hodge screamed, slapping away hands that reached for Eve. Elsa had had enough. She stood and pulled a pistol from her waistband. "Go away!" she shouted, in English and Japanese. "Let us through!"

Her sense was that these people did not intend to hurt her and her family; they were merely curious. But the intensity and number of them unnerved her. Still, her gun did little more than quiet briefly the furor that was growing around her. More and more people arrived, adding to the madness.

Suddenly, the crowd calmed and parted for a small group traveling in an elaborate open carriage. Upon seeing them, Elsa gasped and sat down abruptly. The people all about them bowed as low as they could get to the ground. It was Emperor Meiji and his mistress, the Empress, as usual, conspicuously absent. The Emperor wore a modern-style military uniform while the girl was still robed in the traditional dress of the day. In contrast, the Empress had abandoned the blacking of teeth and shaved eyebrows that had formerly marked married women, and instead favored western dress. A servant hopped off the back of the carriage and hurried over to Elsa.

"His Highness wishes for you and your children to accompany him to the Imperial Palace," he said in practiced English with a British accent. "We shall go from here to the train station and be there by nightfall. There you shall be well fed and entertained."

Elsa fought to conceal her surprise. "Why, thank you. Please pass along my most high praise for his generous offer. But I must see how the men of my ship are faring before I leave on leisure again."

The servant listened intently and then turned to translate for the Emperor. The older man smiled and gave her a little wave, nodding over and over again.

"His Highness agrees to your terms," the servant said formally. "You may go to the station at your convenience. There the royal car shall be waiting to take you to Tokyo."

"It is most kind of Emperor Meiji to offer such a generous invitation," Elsa said, keeping her eyes low to the ground. "If my ship is ready to sail, would it be acceptable to His Highness if we would sail to Tokyo Bay rather than travel by train?"

Again the servant turned and discussed it with the Emperor. He turned back to Elsa. "The Emperor will expect you, in three days' time, by train or by sail. For you, he will have a formal reception on the evening of the third day."

"In three days," Elsa said with a nod. "I will be honored to accept."

She watched as the servant and the Emperor again conferred. The servant said, "His Highness wishes to know why you tarry so long in Yokohama."

Elsa blushed and searched for the right words. "Please tell Emperor Meiji that we had hoped to sell our American wood here, but find the trade laws have again changed. Apparently, the week before we arrived, it was made law that nothing other than kerosene or cotton could be off-loaded. We came such a long way that we had hoped to—"

Again master and servant conferred. "He says to tell you that if you haven't sold your wood by the end of the day to bring it to Tokyo. He will see to it that it will be sold there at a good price."

"Splendid. Please tell him that is most kind and gracious of him." She bowed low.

The servant returned her bow while the Emperor looked away, as if bored. "In three days, Captain Ramstad."

"In three days."

In her absence, Riley had made no progress in persuading the locals to buy their hardwoods. Even with a bit of "lining their pockets," as he put it, no inroads were made. "This month lost at harbor and in fruitless negotiation has cost Ramstad Yard a pretty penny," he said, his face churlish. Elsa felt guilty for a moment, thinking of her frequent jaunts through the countryside and to the nobles' homes while Riley labored on. But that was his duty as first mate, she reasoned. And she had the children to think about. Excursions within foreign lands were one of her reasons for bringing them along, to broaden their experience. If they got to know exotic places now, they would never fear exploration later in life.

"Well, I think I can resolve it," Elsa said, peeling off her gloves and placing them on the desk.

Riley crossed his arms. "Just like that? I've been workin' my tail off for nigh on to six weeks, and you think you can fix it like that?" He snapped his fingers.

Elsa did not react to his irritation. She supposed she would feel the same if their roles were reversed. "I met the Emperor today," she said quietly.

"Emperor Meiji?" Riley asked in wonder, sinking to the settee across the table from her.

"Aye. One and the same. He arrived in a carriage, just as I shot my pistol so we could get to the Bund again. We were swamped with well-wishers."

"I told you, Elsa. I told you you shouldn't be going about without an armed guard. You don't know—"

"I told him we were having difficulty selling our cargo since the trade laws changed the week before we arrived," Elsa smoothly interrupted his well-known tirade.

Riley paused. *"And?"*

"And he said that if we hadn't sold our cargo by the end of the day to come to Tokyo. There, he would see to it that we get the highest amount. We're to attend a reception in three days, apparently in my honor."

Riley's face was a mask of relief. "Well, I'll be..." His apparent exhaustion evolved into a smile. "I suppose it pays to travel with the Heroine of the Horn," he quipped. "Peder's ugly mug never got us anything."

Elsa returned his smile. "I still miss that ugly mug."

"As well you should, missus. But I do appreciate the fact that traveling with a female captain has suddenly made my job a good sight easier."

"I take it we'll weigh anchor and leave for Tokyo in the morning?"

"Aye. And I won't be sorry to leave these choppy, unfriendly waters." He rose to leave.

"Riley?"

"Yes?"

"I do appreciate all your efforts on behalf of the *Grace* and Ramstad Yard. On my behalf. I hope you didn't feel…abandoned."

"Not at all. I'm glad you and the children were able to travel while I messed wi' those…*gentlemen* at the trade house. Gave me the freedom to concentrate on what I had to do. Not that it did much good."

"It must be frustrating for you. But at least we know we can unload and be off for the States again within the week."

"Aye. That is good news." He rose to go and then paused. "I don't mind telling you that I have an uneasy feelin' about being here."

"Uneasy?" Elsa asked with a frown.

Riley shook his head. "Can't shake it. I'll just be glad to set sail again and be off for the States."

They arrived in Tokyo two days later. Elsa left her children in Mrs. Hodge's care and dressed in the gown she had worn to Lady Bancock's ball. At the wharf, she and Riley went to talk with the trade-house officials, who greeted her warmly and seemed to know all about the special agreement with the Emperor. Seeing that all was in order, she placed a hand on Riley's elbow. "Thank you for seeing to the business of this, Riley. I intend to hail a jinrikisha and go to the palace now. I will see you there later?"

Riley held up a hand to a man speaking poor English to turn toward her. "Elsa, I think you should wait for me. You're not expected for another few hours. This will take no more than an hour or two."

"Or perhaps three or four. I'm dressed for the ball and liable to draw more attention than we want," she whispered back, remembering Yokohama and the mob. "I think it would be much better to get along to the palace."

"Yet it is unseemly for a woman to travel alone—"

"Nonsense," Elsa said, lifting her chin in the air in jest. She cocked one eyebrow and leaned closer to his ear. "They expect nothing less from the Heroine of the Horn."

Riley sighed. "I don't like it. If you would simply—"

"I will see you at the palace," Elsa said firmly. "See to it that you are not late for supper." With that, she turned and walked through the crowd of grinning, filthy men to the welcome fresh air outdoors.

Just outside the trade house was a dark, covered carriage that bore the mark of the Emperor. A short, squat Japanese man in a pristine uniform bowed deeply toward her and opened the door. *The Emperor has sent a coach!* Never in her life had Elsa felt so honored. She bowed back toward the footman, accepted his small hand, and climbed the tiny gold steps into the luxurious carriage. Once seated, she could see that she was not alone. She smiled as her eyes adjusted from the bright midday sun to the darkness of the carriage, assuming it was another guest of the Emperor, or perhaps his emissary. He smelled of vanilla and soap, a vaguely familiar combination. Where had she noted that scent before?

A second later, a scream lodged in her throat.

"Good afternoon, Captain Ramstad," came his silken voice. "It has been too long, has it not?" Mason Dutton tapped on the roof and the carriage lurched to a quick pace.

Elsa lunged, ready to jump out of the moving carriage if necessary, but Mason was too quick for her. He grabbed her from behind and pulled her to his side, covering her mouth. She noted that the shades had been drawn, preventing anyone from seeing her plight. *How had he commandeered a royal carriage?* she wondered.

"You do like to travel in style, do you not?" he whispered in her ear. "It is nice that you were unescorted. Much easier for me, all in all. Where is your husband now? Oh, that's right, poor dear. He's dead, correct? Pity I couldn't kill him myself. Someday soon I'll catch up with Karl Martensen. I'll simply have to extract justice from him instead. And you."

Elsa writhed, aching to be away from the scoundrel, but she was inhibited by her tight bodice and long skirts, and he easily held her back.

Mason let out an exaggerated sigh. "Yes, it has been too long, my dear. We have so much to catch up on. So much to settle. And it will be delightful settling accounts with you alone." His other hand moved from her waist upward.

Furious, Elsa elbowed him in the stomach and lurched to the other side of the carriage. Mason laughed. "That is fine. Play hard to get for now, my dear. There will be time enough for us to become… close."

"Never. I will never allow you to touch me. I'll die first."

"Perhaps," Mason said, raising a brow. "But it might not be up to you to decide." The carriage hit a bump and both braced themselves. "Whoa," Mason said with a delighted smile. "You see? Even now we've left the civilized streets and are making our way to my secret little harbor. We are surrounded by my men, and the carriage will not be missed for some time." He pulled out a pocket watch and checked the time. "You are not expected for what? Another three hours?"

Karl Martensen pulled his pocket watch from his vest and frowned. She was late, by more than an hour. He glanced at Emperor Meiji, who was now openly scowling in frustration. His guests shuffled in their places at the edge of the ostentatious receiving hall, getting tired and hungry. Never had Karl known Elsa to be tardy anywhere, especially for an event such as this, in her honor. It had been providence that brought Karl to Tokyo the day before with a load of cotton. The *Tempest* had made incredible time, allowing him to bypass Hawaii altogether on the way back east. The first trip had been so profitable, Kenney had proposed they ship back out in two days' time. It was tight, but now he was here, in Tokyo, the same day Elsa Ramstad was to be honored by the Emperor. He grinned. *Won't she be surprised?* he wondered for the hundredth time. But where on earth was she?

Just then a man moved through the crowd. The people parted, ladies gasping and men stepping forward in a motion that said, "Explain yourself." It was Riley, dressed in common street clothes. Two guards grabbed him and held him back. "I am the first mate to Captain Ramstad!" he called over their shoulders, his chest heaving for breath as if he had run all the way. "Let me through!"

Karl came forward and shoved the guard nearest him back. "Let him pass!" he said through gritted teeth. "Riley, where is Elsa?"

Riley looked at him in wonder at his presence and then gripped his hand fiercely. The other guard let him go and the crowd took a step back as the Emperor waved them away. "He's here, Karl. Here in the vicinity."

"Who?"

"Mason Dutton."

Karl closed his eyes. *O dear God. O Father in heaven! Help us! Protect Elsa! Give me wisdom!* Knowing what he had to do as if God had directed his thoughts in response, Karl strode down the great hall and knelt at the Emperor's feet. When he was acknowledged, Karl looked him in the eye. "Emperor Meiji, I have bad news. Your royal guest, Captain Elsa Ramstad, is missing. And I think I know why." The translator hurriedly did his work.

"There is a pirate that roams your waters. One with a personal vendetta against Elsa Ramstad. His name is Mason Dutton." A hush went through the room. Even in the Far East, the people had heard of Elsa's narrow escape from the clutches of Mason Dutton. The Emperor rose. He spoke softly, assuredly.

"Your Western navies apparently have not the capabilities of ours," the translator said, his face betraying no emotion. "It is time that this man be stopped. He has dared to enter my waters and take my royal guest hostage. He will pay for it with his life."

The Emperor nodded at two men in full military regalia and they moved forward at once.

"Do you know where this man hides?"

Karl looked to Riley, and Riley shook his head, grim faced. "They cannot be far," Riley said. "They took her in a royal carriage. I spotted a man I recognized as one of Mason's crew, clinging to the back as they left. I ran after them, tracked them for a time, but they got away."

Emperor Meiji's face darkened. "They dare to abscond with one of my carriages?"

Karl faced him. "I know this man. Captain Ramstad is in imminent danger. He is a man of no moral account."

"You will accompany my naval commanders," the Emperor stated. "You will know how he works and will be best at coming up with a plan for capture."

"Yes," Karl said.

Riley stepped forward. "I would like to go along also, your Grace."

The Emperor nodded. "Go," said the translator. "Find this leech and bring him back to me. I shall have the skin flayed from his back."

"If he lives that long," Karl said under his breath.

The pirates aboard Mason's ship hooted and hollered as Elsa was unceremoniously hauled aboard in a basket and dropped. Her wrists were tied and she lurched one way and the other, trying to escape the daring hands of all those on deck. "Gentlemen, gentlemen," Mason chided. They parted, clearing the way from him to her. "This is not some parlor maid I brought back for your enjoyment. Can you not see from her dress that this is a lady?"

A man nearby tilted Elsa's skirt with the tip of his cane. She slapped it away as the men laughed. "The lady's legs look as good as any parlor maid's, Cap'n," he said. He drew near and Elsa spat in his face. The men roared with laughter.

"Enough, enough!" Mason intervened, stepping between the two. "She has gumption. But surely someone aboard recognizes the lady." He looked around as if interviewing a harmless group of schoolchildren for the answer to an elementary question.

"Why, that's Elsa Ramstad!" shouted one.

"I'll be! The famous Cap'n Ramstad!" exclaimed another.

"Heroine of the Horn, right here on our ship!" said still another.

Elsa's heart sank. Never had she felt so helpless. Last time she had encountered Mason Dutton, it was at Peder's side. The time before that, Peder's sailors had fought valiantly for her, Peder, and their ship. Here she was alone. Entirely alone. Only one thought consoled her. At least her children were not in danger. Wildly, her eyes searched the crowd, looking for one decent man who might dare to stand by her side and fight. But all she saw were villainous, ravenous looks. She lifted her chin, nostrils flaring, daring them to touch her.

"Elsa?" Mason beckoned from the doorway to his quarters. "Shall we retire to a place more...private?" His inference was clear. She glanced from him to the others. Regardless of the danger he posed, she was outnumbered among his crew. Perhaps if she cooperated, she could buy some time and figure out a means of escape. In a hidden pocket of her gown was a tiny pistol with one round of ammunition. In another was a small knife in a slender sheath. She had not gone out entirely unprepared; she simply could not get to her weapons. Elsa had to choose her timing carefully. Even armed with those basic weapons, she would not be able to hold an entire crew at bay.

She raised her chin and strode to his cabin with all the grace she could muster among the catcalls and whistles of the crew. Once inside the captain's quarters, she looked about the overly decorated room. Above seats with many pillows were walls covered by rich fabrics from distant lands. In the corner was a solid gold statue of a Greek goddess. In another, a giant china vase. "Spoils of your robberies?"

"I prefer to call them excursions," Mason said benignly. He poured red liquid into a crystal goblet. "Wine?" he asked, roughly shoving her down to perch on the edge of the bed.

"I think not," she said. "Do you mind unbinding me?"

"Will you promise not to run away?"

"To where? Into the arms of your waiting crew? They're a bunch of savages, Dutton. Not that you're any better."

He eyed her over the edge of his goblet. "You and your husband have caused me much grief, Elsa." He spoke with the tone of a pained parent.

"Nothing you didn't bring on yourself, Dutton. It is only a matter of time before some navy corners you and blows you to smithereens."

"You had better hope it is not soon," he said, grinning. "Then your children would be left without a mother and a father. Orphans."

She stared back into his eyes. "I knew you were evil, Mason. I did not know you were cruel."

He strode over to her and caressed her cheek. She forced herself not to pull away. "I don't have to be cruel. I can be very, very kind to you, Elsa. I admire you, the Heroine of the Horn. Think of what would happen if we joined forces. Think of the new twist in your column for the *Times!* The public would go mad for you."

Elsa snorted and shook her head. "You are the one who is mad."

He pushed her back on the bed and closed tight fingers around her neck. She had not seen it coming. "Your life is in my hands, darling," he said softly. She writhed, trying to pry his fingers from her larynx before she suffocated. He bent closer to her ear and whispered, "I'd be more careful in choosing your words."

Mason eased away from Elsa then, observing her. She gasped for breath as she sat up again, unable to hide her fear. He stood beside her and moved his hands to her hair. His touch made her want to scream, but she knew she had to bide her time, gain some semblance of Dutton's trust. Slowly, he took the combs from her hair and pulled the knot loose. With agonizing tenderness he pulled out one thick section of hair and laid it over her shoulder. Then he took the other half and fanned it over her back.

"Lovely," he whispered. "Welcome to the lion's den, Elsa. You chose the wrong cat to cross."

The *Tempest* moved under sail only, not wanting to make any sound that might alert the pirate that trouble was afoot. Karl winced as he checked the time. Eight hours Elsa had been gone! It had taken four for Riley to make it past the palace guards and seek help. It had taken the remaining four to garner the Emperor's forces and pay enough sources to discover where Mason's ship was harbored. He was but fifteen miles up the coast! The plan was for Karl and his men to attack, and if the pirates fled, eight navy ships would keep him at bay. One way or another, Mason had backed himself into an inescapable corner.

At the edge of the tiny cove, Karl motioned for all sails to be furled and their momentum halted. Silently, as had been discussed with his crew earlier, three skiffs were launched, each holding eight men. Working as quietly as natives on the warpath, they entered the cove and sought a place to land their skiffs. From there, they sank into the water, swimming toward Dutton's ship as the pirates themselves had attacked Peder's ship in the West Indies. Karl had wrapped two pistols in oilskin and strapped them to his chest. In his teeth he clenched a bowie knife.

They swam the last fifty feet underwater, keeping the guards on duty from mounting any intruder alert. Karl was proud of his men. None of them had been spotted! In minutes they were next to Dutton's ship, clinging to the ratlines that dragged in the water. Their only chance was to take some of the pirates out quietly before the rest were alerted. Slowly, eight of his best men climbed the lines to begin the process as half of their group trod water around the ship to the port side.

God was smiling upon them. The pirates had obviously grown lackadaisical and overly cocky with their success.

Elsa rose and looked pointedly at the chess board. "You like games, do you not?" she asked, one eyebrow raised.

Mason came over to her side of the table and lifted one lock of hair. He inhaled deeply, and Elsa struggled not to turn and slap him away. "I do," he said softly. He traced one finger across the bare skin of her neck. "I think it is time you leave your mourning black and wear colors that befit your beauty again."

Elsa ignored his comment. "I see you have taken to chess."

"It is not a new pursuit," he said, his eyes still roaming her uncomfortably. "All my life, I have studied the art of it. It has served me well in my current vocation."

"Ahh," Elsa said, pretending to appreciate his supposed mastery of the game. "Why don't we play?" She walked a few steps away as if to idly peruse his shelf of leather-bound books.

"A game?"

"Yes. If you win I shall join you at your side, as you suggested. I'll wear colorful dresses again, when I am not in a blouse and dungarees." She turned back to him. "But if I win, I shall go free."

Mason pursed his lips, studying her. "Those are high stakes. I've spent years waiting to cross paths with you again."

"They are high stakes for me as well."

"So they are," Mason said with a nod. "Very well. I am attracted to the idea of a willing woman at my side rather than a captive bride." Her heart pounded at his words. He actually expected her to marry him?

"Bride?" she spat out in utter surprise.

"Of course!" Mason said with a sly smile. "I assumed you would expect nothing else. After all, how would it look if we were to travel together, in one cabin?"

Elsa turned away, trying to gather her thoughts. "You expect me to abandon my children? My ship?"

"I have no place for children here. Surely you'd agree that my men are not the finest of influences. You do not have someone in the States who could care for them?"

It took her breath away, even thinking of such a preposterous option. Yet he had to trust her for a game such as this to work. To stall for time. To give her a chance at escape. Were she to lose the game... *no, I cannot think of such an option. I will win. And he will let me walk away.*

"Elsa, I assume you are a woman of honor and not gambling idly. I expect you to live up to your end of the bargain."

She met his eyes, not allowing them to waver. "As do I. I shall win this game, Dutton, and walk off your ship and turn you over to the authorities."

"Very well," he said with a chuckle, pulling out a chair for her in front of the elegant, white-carved game pieces. He reached down and slit the bonds that held her wrists. "White moves first, Elsa. Are you certain about this?"

"Are you certain about giving me the white side of the board?" She locked her eyes on the figures set before her, already planning her strategy.

Mason snorted and sat down. "Of course," he said, leaning forward over the black rows of chesspieces. "I am, after all, a gentleman."

"That," Elsa said, making the first move, "I seriously doubt."

twenty-seven

$\mathcal{K}$arl held on to the ratlines with gritted teeth, shivering as the Pacific waters washed him and his men against the ship's starboard side and then sucked them out again. They had been in the water for more than an hour. He grimaced, not from the cold, but from the sight of a dead pirate's lifeless eyes, floating just before him.

The eight soldiers above him—six a part of the Emperor's elite guard—waited for what seemed hours, looking for just the right opportunity to snatch yet another sailor from the pirate ship. Already, twelve men had been slain and lowered to the water's edge without raising an alarm. It was imperative that many more be taken care of before Karl and his men attacked. He hoped their forces on the port side were faring as well. Certainly it was only a matter of minutes before someone above noticed that fewer and fewer sailors roamed the decks.

It was a moonless night, and for that Karl was thankful. But every inch of him itched to climb the net and charge Mason Dutton's door. It was eerily quiet above, except for the drunken singing of a group at the bow. Where was Elsa? Was she in imminent danger? He knew he had no choice but to swallow his anger and remain where he was, but the fury burned. If Dutton harmed Elsa at all...

"Martensen!" whispered a sailor to his left. *One from the port side,* his mind registered. "We've taken care of ten of them," he went on, treading water until he could grab hold beside Karl.

Karl nodded once. "Have you been able to account for the others?"

"Most are belowdecks. There's a group at the bow."

"Aye. I hear." His mind whirled, trying to think of the best plan. He turned back to the messenger. "Tell your men that the first aboard are to silence the rowdy sailors at the bow. The second group aboard shall join ours and stave off any that might climb up, as well as see to Captain Ramstad and Dutton. As soon as Captain Ramstad is safely off, we are to abandon ship and swim back to the skiffs. We are severely outnumbered. No one is to stay and fight unless the bilge rats swarm us before we can retreat. You understand?"

"Aye, Cap'n."

"Good. We move in five minutes. Begin counting on my mark."

The man nodded again, his profile a mere shadow.

"Mark."

With that, the man slipped back into the water and moved around the bow of the ship, directly under the group singing a rowdy song with lyrics that would have made his mother blush. It mattered little, Karl thought grimly. Soon, they would never sing again.

"Your move, Elsa," Mason said, her name slipping from his lips like a treasured memory. He set the captured knight next to his wineglass.

Elsa said nothing, merely stared at the board before her. Mason had mounted a chaotic and aggressive offensive, but Elsa knew that behind the chaos could lie a fatal trap designed to draw out her choice pieces…He was either very good at the game or he knew virtually nothing. He seemed to be employing a variation of the Delphi attack, but it was impossible to be sure. Perhaps the board and polished ivory pieces were merely for show, raided from the ship of a better man. Elsa did not want to be there long enough to find out. She pushed down her fear and focused her attention on a large pocket of open squares near the far left corner of the board. Mason had quickly moved several pawns, both knights, his rooks, and one bishop into a lopsided battalion bearing down on the smattering of pawns standing before Elsa's king. In his rush to confront her minor pieces, he had left a huge gap along his rear flank.

She moved her queen quickly, hoping he would mistake speed for recklessness. He ignored the move, took one of her pawns, and sat back, gazing across the table at her. She hoped she looked puzzled, concentrating on the board, and inched her queen forward a few more spaces into the gap.

As Mason studied the board again, she reached down to pull the tiny ivory-handled pistol from her skirts. He looked up at her, and Elsa stilled her hand and smiled, even while her heart felt as if it had taken up residence in her throat. He looked from one eye to the other for a moment, returned her smile, and then looked back at the board. "Of what are you thinking?" he asked, not looking up at her again.

"Of winning the game, of course," she said lightly.

"Not of finding your way out of here?"

"This game is my way out."

Mason drew his lead rook back four spaces and looked up at her. Had he seen her slipping into the unprotected area or was he moving to make a final run at her king? Her hand was on the pistol, but she had not yet extricated it from her hidden skirt pocket. "If you win," he said. "It is more likely that you will lose. I'm afraid we'll have to ship out at dawn. No doubt there will be some sort of alarm sent up since the Emperor's guest has disappeared."

"You are not overly concerned about that," she commented. "Would it not be prudent for you to depart right away?"

Mason sat back in his chair and sipped his wine, staring at her. Slowly, Elsa released the pistol. There was no way to get it from the folds of fabric without gaining his attention. "You seem concerned about my welfare, Elsa. I am touched."

"Touched in the head," Elsa snapped, bringing her hands to the table and reviewing the chessboard again.

Mason laughed. "I love your spirit." He stood and clapped, suddenly galvanized by the confidence that he would win the game. "I cannot wait to sail these seas with you. It will be a new adventure!"

"I do not intend to sail with you. I intend to win this game."

He returned to her side and fingered her hair, his voice growing husky and low. "You will not win, Elsa. Not this time. At least in the way you might think. Eventually, you will come to see the beauty of what we can have together."

Elsa watched the pieces on the board, then laughed aloud as the solution presented itself to her like a horse emerging from a foggy field. Slowly, delicately, she reached out and moved her queen into the corner. "You seem to 'see' much, Mason, but you do not understand any of it. Checkmate."

Mason's rook was now wedged in front of his king, and two dark pawns stood at attention next to the rook. The king sat pinned behind his own men. Elsa's queen gazed down the long empty corridor of space between them. There was no move to block. All of Mason's key pieces were out of range. The king could move one space in either direction, but it would not be enough.

Mason let go of her hair and went around to the other side of the board. "Impossible," he muttered, staring at his side of the board. Just then, the door opened behind him, and Mason glanced over his shoulder. "I told you we were not to be disturbed—"

Elsa gasped as Karl and three others slid into the room, pistols drawn. Karl! He was here! How on earth had he managed to get on board unnoticed? He motioned for her to rise as he glanced over the board and smiled.

He stared right into Mason's eyes. "I think she's won."

On shaking legs, Elsa rose and went to him. He moved in front of her as the others searched the rest of the captain's suite. They came back, indicating they were alone.

"You realize, of course, Martensen, that this is a declaration of war."

"You'll be the first casualty," Karl said. "Go ahead, Dutton. Declare it. It will be a pleasure to place a bullet between your eyes."

"And call my men to their posts with that shot? I think not. Your only hope is to swim for shore and hope we do not pursue you. You will meet a painful death, I assure you." He looked over Karl's shoulder at Elsa. "And Captain Ramstad, there will be no more games. You will be mine."

Karl nudged her farther behind him. "Be quiet, Dutton. Your threats are no longer a concern to us. We will leave your ship now, and you will drown as the Emperor's cannon blow your ship to pieces." Karl nodded at his men. "Tie him up."

Just then, a shot was fired. It was merely seconds after that that the group inside the cabin could hear an alarm sounding. "Get in that room!" Karl yelled at Mason, nodding toward the dining room. "Go!" He turned to Elsa. "Get out of here. Get rid of those skirts, dive into the water, and swim with all you have in you!" Two of the men took her arms and hustled her out of the cabin.

"Karl—"

"Go!"

They were just outside when Elsa heard another shot, this time from inside Mason's cabin. Had Karl shot Mason? Or had the pirate secured his own weapon and killed Karl? "Karl!" she yelled, but the men pushed her onward, past the fellows who were barricading the doors from belowdecks. More shots were fired, blowing holes in the deck and narrowly missing Karl's men above. Only thoughts of Eve and Kristian kept her from resisting her escorts and returning to Mason's cabin. Grim-faced, and without a thought of modesty, Elsa reached for her knife and cut away the cloth from her legs so that she might not drown.

She reached for the two men at her side, guarding her. "I will go. I will go if you will go see to Captain Martensen. You have done your duty. Please be sure that the captain fares as well as I."

One nodded and she looked to the other. As soon as she secured his silent promise as well, she climbed the rail and dove off, never feeling freer than she did as her hands and head met the cold water. Beside her, others dove in as well. Not knowing where she should head to, she followed the others blindly, hoping it wouldn't be far. Even with the skirts cut away, her outfit was not meant for such an exercise. The bodice was tight, and her corset chafed. She paused for a moment to look back.

Chaos reigned on deck. It was apparent even in the dim lantern light that the pirates had emerged and were fighting those left on deck. She could not see well enough to ascertain whether Karl and the others were among those who remained. Half of her wanted to return and fight them herself; the other half begged her onward toward safety. Gunfire grew louder, the shots creating eerie flashes in the night. Yet it was only as several shots sank into the waters nearby that Elsa turned and again followed the men who were growing distant. She had to live. If not for herself, or for Karl, for her children. The idea was as clear in her mind as if God had spoken.

I go, she prayed silently, swimming with everything she had in her. *I go, but please be with Karl.*

She continued swimming, no reassuring response coming to her heart. She reached the shore, and the men helped her into a skiff. Another was loaded and traveled beside them, intent upon giving word, she learned, to the waiting ships that they were clear to attack. "But what of Captain Martensen?" she asked.

"Don't worry, Cap'n, he'll be fine," said one.

"He'll be along shortly. We'll leave some men and a skiff for him an' the others."

With a sigh she looked on as the men rowed off among choppy seas to the point and then around it. She could not see anything in the black night until they were nearly upon the first ship, the *Tempest.*

"I need to get to the *Grace.* Is she a part of this convoy?"

320

"Aye," said one sailor. "But the captain wanted you aboard his ship. Wanted to know where he could find you."

"But my children—"

"Cap'n will be along shortly," said another, with utter confidence. Did they not know that he might lie dead in Mason Dutton's cabin?

Elsa agreed, for she needed to know about his welfare as surely as Karl had needed to know about hers. "But send word to the *Grace* that I am alive. Tell them to bring my children to me." She had not fed Eve since that morning, and the babe would not take more than a bottle or two of goat's milk before screaming for her. And Elsa needed to hold her children and know they were safe.

"Aye, aye, Cap'n," said the first sailor.

Elsa climbed the lines and stood, shivering, on the deck of Karl's ship. A man came forward and offered her a wool blanket, which she accepted gratefully. Elsa wrapped herself in it and turned back toward the water. At least she could no longer hear gunfire. Was it because they were past the point or because it had ceased?

Wearily she rolled her head and rubbed her neck.

A slender man in a white apron, who she presumed was the cook, came up beside her. "Cap'n will be along, ma'am. He's a good man."

"You needn't tell me so," she said. "I know."

"Brought you some tea."

"Thank you," she said, taking the hot tin cup from his hands. "How many in this convoy?" she asked, seeing only the closest ship off the port side.

"Eight. Come dawn we'll blow that bilge rat out of the water."

"But the *Tempest* is unarmed."

"Aye. But we'll stand by. If any are left, we'll pick them out of the water to be hanged in America or England, take your pick. That is, if the Emperor lets them get that far."

Elsa reached for the rail, suddenly shaky on her feet. "Is there someplace I might sit a moment?"

"Yes, yes, ma'am. Right this way. The cap'n would want you to rest in his parlor." She followed the man to Karl's quarters, feeling a bit odd at entering without him there. But the cook seemed to have no qualms about it, so Elsa told herself she was being silly. Who cared at that point where she rested and waited?

The cook looked hard at her. "If you're weary, you could rest in there," he said, nodding to what Elsa presumed was Karl's bedroom.

She shook her head. "No, I couldn't. Not that I could sleep. I will wait until Karl—Captain Martensen arrives safely."

"Should be soon, ma'am. I'll leave you be. Flag down any of us, should you be wantin' for anything."

"Thank you," she said, sinking to a wooden chair. The door closed behind the cook, and Elsa looked around the room. It was Spartan and clean, typical of how she imagined Karl would decorate. There was not one hint of a feminine touch, and only two pictures on the walls. She rose to see them. One was of a schooner like the *Sunrise* that they had first sailed out of Camden. Another was a steamer like the *Tempest*. Elsa walked through the room and into Karl's study. This room was warmer, more masculine, more apparently Karl's. There was a fine wooden desk which was open, papers strewn every which way. She walked over to it and idly looked over the pages, not snooping necessarily, she told herself, merely reviewing what was there. A corner of a newspaper clipping peeked out of the secretary above. Looking around guiltily, Elsa pulled it out. It was from her column, a picture she had drawn of Peder, shortly before his death.

She gave it a sad smile. Because Peder had been so handsome, so alive. Because they had been so happy together. And because Karl and Peder had never made amends.

With one last glance at her beloved's picture, she slid it back in the secretary where she had found it and looked at the maps on the wall. Karl's log was open, notes written in his clean, manly script and small emblems artfully drawn. She had never known he could sketch so well. Peder had always enjoyed keeping his own logs, so Elsa had never seen

Karl's work. She paged backward through the volume, pausing over drawings of other ships, whales, and dolphins, as well as coastlines and the like.

The main door opened with a swollen shudder. Guiltily, Elsa turned back the pages to where she had found it opened and then went to the study door. Karl stood there, dripping wet and grinning. She raced into his arms, feeling as though she had never been happier to see anyone in all her life.

"Oh, Karl, Karl! You're well! You're safe!" She pulled back to make sure there was no blood, no wounds, then embraced him again. His arms wrapped around her, and he closed the door on a dozen smiling sailors' faces. Elsa blushed, but she did not care. All that mattered was that her friend was alive and well. Or was that it? Suddenly she remembered what had happened the last time they had encountered Mason Dutton together. Their kiss. She dropped her arms from him and stepped away, fighting to meet his gaze, but uncertain. What did he want from her this time? She was no longer a married woman, and he had saved her life.

"Thank you, Karl. Thank you for saving me," she said, going to the chair and sitting on the wool blanket that she had left there. She watched as he retrieved a blanket for himself and dried his shoulder-length hair. His clothing clung to his well-formed body, making her aware of the muscles beneath.

He came to her with a guileless smile and knelt before her. "Elsa, Elsa," he said, placing a roughened hand on her cheek, and waiting until she met his gaze. "I could not do anything else. I could never be anywhere else. I am your friend." Gently, he dropped his hand.

Friend. She shook her head at her stupidity and nodded. She returned his tender touch by placing her own hand on his cheek as he had done before her. "You are indeed the finest friend a woman could have. Thank you, Karl. If you had not come, I doubt that I would have left Mason's ship alive."

Karl grinned and rose. "I don't know about that. The Heroine of the Horn has made a name for herself as a captain known for bravery and valor."

Elsa grimaced. "I grow tired of the legend of the Heroine of the Horn."

"We cannot stop the forces that have begun."

"No, I suppose we cannot. Karl, did you lose many men?"

"Two of the Emperor's men died. I have two wounded." His look was jubilant. "I never expected that God would smile so clearly upon us. All went just as planned."

Elsa shook her head and returned his smile. "And Mason? I heard a shot, just as we left the captain's quarters."

Karl turned away, as if to brush off the memory. "He made a move. I shot him in the thigh." He turned back toward her. "If the Emperor's navy does not kill every man aboard, it is likely that Dutton will die before the day is done anyway. He was losing a lot of blood."

Elsa looked down, surprised at the shame that flooded through her for being jubilant at such news. What kind of Christian was she to rejoice in another's death, regardless of what he had done? "I cannot help myself," she said lowly. "I am glad that he will no longer be a threat."

Karl walked over to her and lifted her chin. "He threatened you."

"He did. He told me he would make me his captive bride."

Anger flooded Karl's face. "He deserves a painful death."

"Let us not concentrate on that. Let's not celebrate another's pain. Let's celebrate being free."

Karl met her gaze and nodded. "You are right. But we will not celebrate until we know Mason Dutton will never threaten us again."

t w e n t y - e i g h t

August 1887

The Bergensers had no idea what to do with Tora Anders. She had once been a part of them, but as a snobby child. Now she was again among them, but as a woman with a much quieter spirit. The change in her seemed too dramatic to believe, and thus the Bergensers, while treating her civilly, were still rather cool in their approach to Tora.

"It's distrust, plain and simple," Nora said one day, under her breath, to Kaatje as they watched Tora struggle to make conversation with Eira Nelson across the churchyard. "Can't say I blame them, though. While I'm glad for you that she's of some help, I don't understand why she is here. Is she just using you, biding her time until she can go off and chase her dreams again?"

Kaatje swallowed hard, feeling guilty that Nora was merely voicing her own thoughts, her own doubts about Tora's sincerity. How dedicated was Tora to her new path in life? "She says she was called to be here," Kaatje said simply.

"The only call Tora Anders has ever heeded is a siren's call."

Kaatje turned toward Nora. "She has changed. I have seen evidence of it. And she's been a tremendous help to me."

Nora snorted and eyed Kaatje. "Perhaps. But for how long? I don't trust her. Not as far as I can throw her, anyway. Which isn't all that far these days."

Kaatje understood her friend's harsh judgment as she smiled at Nora's burgeoning belly. She expected their fifth child in a month's time. Indeed, Kaatje could not remain angry over anyone's reaction to Tora. This summer had torn down her own preconceived ideas of who Tora once was and rebuilt them with the knowledge of what she knew to be true about the young woman now. Yet it remained a constant battle. Old thoughts and fears haunted her mind and preyed upon her at weak moments. Everything would be going fine, and suddenly Kaatje would remember that Tora had once been her husband's lover. She'd be tucking Jessica in at night and it would strike her that Jessie was Tora's child, not hers. Would Tora grow to love her as Kaatje had, with the love of a mother? Would she come to Kaatje, wanting Jess for her own?

Still, they had managed to forge an uneasy camaraderie over the last ten weeks, slowly finding common ground and walking it, each trying to stay away from the edges. They found common ground in the land they farmed—thirty acres this year with Tora's help—the weeds they plucked, the ditches they dug, the water they hauled, the animals they fed, the children they cared for, and lastly, their plans for the fall.

For in September, they would sail for Alaska.

"You must be joking," said Birger Nelson, when they told the Bergensers.

"It is insane. Two women and two children, heading to the Alaskan wilderness!" said Nora.

"Why go?" asked Matthew. "You have a good farm, a good home. An enviable crop this year! Why strike out for the unknown?"

"It is inviting disaster!" Einar announced.

"It is where God would have me," Kaatje said, silencing them all. "It is where God has called me. And apparently, Tora is willing to accompany me. I could never have gone alone. But with her help, I think we can make it. Look at our farm! That extra ten acres planted this year will help us put away a nest egg that will see us through the toughest Alaskan winter."

"And it won't necessarily be tough," Tora said quietly. "I know how to run a business. From what I hear, there is more than enough room for new businesses up there. We could earn much more than Kaatje ever would get alone on her farm."

The Bergensers listened to Tora's quiet, confident speech, but said nothing. They still distrusted her, like a stranger in their midst, the crazy cousin that everyone tolerated, the distant relation of whom everyone was ashamed but no one would admit to it. Kaatje knew Tora sensed this; it was part of the reason Tora tried so hard to be nothing but admirable. But she also knew with certainty that Tora's entire goal remained to serve Kaatje. Never had she wavered. And gradually, Kaatje's trust grew. Gradually, her appreciation of the change God had wrought in Tora grew as well.

The thought made Kaatje's hands perspire in excitement. Never had she considered that plans to sail to the Alaska territory, hike the infamous Chilkoot Pass, and enter the interior of the roughest country known to man, would be part of God's plan for her. She stood outside one hot August night and stared at a full moon. That was part of the beauty of God, she told herself. Just when she thought she had figured out what she was to do and how she was to do it, he took her to a new path.

Tora interrupted her thoughts as she pulled the cottage door shut with a familiar scraping noise and joined Kaatje beside the well. "The girls are asleep." Then, "It is a beautiful night, is it not?" She nudged Kaatje's elbow, indicating she had brought her wrap out to her.

Kaatje shook her head. "No thank you. I'm still hot after this day," she said. "And yes, it is beautiful. Do you think it will look the same in Alaska?"

Tora gazed upward before answering. "It looked the same in Bergen, and in Camden-by-the-Sea, and in Duluth, and in Helena. It is like God. Never changing. But always showing us a different aspect of himself."

Kaatje smiled and glanced at Tora in the moonlight. "You amaze me, Tora. You constantly surprise me."

Tora returned her gaze. "But do you trust me?"

"I'm beginning to."

"How long will it take to forgive me?"

Kaatje thought about her words. "As I told you the day you arrived, I'd forgiven you a long time ago. But it is like an old wound. Do you understand? Every time you move in a new direction, it pains you, and you have to stop and acknowledge it. But eventually, it hurts less and less."

Tora nodded, and they stood staring upward for some time. "Kaatje, what if Soren is alive? What will it be like if you find him there, living, but never writing to you?"

Kaatje cocked an eyebrow. "I think he is dead. Somehow, I think it is true. He went on a packing trip and never returned to his cabin." Surprisingly, uttering such frank words did not feel like a laceration of her heart. Perhaps she was getting over Soren.

"But what if he—?"

"I'll cross that bridge when I get to it. I suppose I'd first take a switch to his behind."

Tora laughed in surprise.

Kaatje tensed, needing to voice difficult words. "Are you still in love with him?"

Tora didn't respond right away, apparently choosing her words. "Kaatje, I'm sorry. I was never in love with him. I know that sounds horrible."

Kaatje paused, then said, "Yes. Yes it does. But it does make it easier if he lives, does it not?"

Tora let out a little breath, as if laughing. "Yes. That is true. I am in love with another. Not your husband."

"Trent Storm."

"Yes."

"He has not come to see you."

"By my request. He waits in Seattle. I hope to see him before we go, but I knew we needed this time to…find our way."

Kaatje nodded, discovering yet another surprising angle of Tora Anders to admire. She had forsaken her love, and obviously was prepared to walk away from him, all to go with Kaatje to Alaska. Would she have been as strong had their situations been reversed? "Does it not pain you to leave him?"

Tora sighed. "It feels as if my heart is about to tear in two. But it is the right path. If Trent and I are meant to be, we will marry when I return from Alaska." She reached out to take Kaatje's hand and waited until Kaatje met her eyes. "It is right."

"I know," Kaatje whispered. Finally she understood in her heart what Tora so clearly knew from the start—God was leading them. They didn't know exactly where it would take them or what they would discover along the way. But they both knew they had to go, and trust that he would meet all their needs. "Good night, Tora."

"Good night."

"And Tora?"

"Yes?"

"I am glad you came to me when you did. I am glad you are going with me."

"As am I."

Tora left Kaatje's side and made her way to the new part of the barn, in which they had made her a makeshift bedroom. Ever the hostess, it had clearly bothered Kaatje at first to have her sleep in the barn. But Tora had been firm. It would be for the best if she had her own space, and they had theirs. She had not come intending to disrupt the family's life, but to help in some way. And it would not be of help to move in on their private time.

With some work, the space was all Tora needed. It was warmer and drier than her tent at the lumber camp, and the straw tick was more comfortable than the lumpy mattress she had at camp too. In the corner was her only trunk, a gift from Trent. In the other was a hastily built table and chair. She sat down at it now, pulled a clean sheet of paper from the pile in the corner, and uncapped the ink. How she missed Trent! She hoped writing to him would ease her pain.

> *10 August 1887*
> *Dearest Trent,*
>
> *Thank you for honoring my decision to remain apart these long weeks. Now I ask if you can come to me, and soon. In September, Kaatje and I will travel to the Alaska territory.*

She paused over the paper, knowing that this news would surprise and anger Trent. He undoubtedly hoped that her sojourn to the Skagit Valley would soon end and they could marry. It would come as a rude awakening to discover that Tora intended to go farther along this path she had chosen.

> *I understand that you will find this news disappointing, my love. It is not my own desire to go farther from you than I already have. It is distressing and worrisome, and yet, I can do nothing else but this. For it was to Kaatje's side I was called and with her I must stay. I sensed from the start that we would not remain in the valley. I had little idea we were to go so far. But if I am to follow my heart and my Lord as my soul begs me to do, what can I say but yes? Perhaps it will be for but a season. Perhaps it will be longer.*

Again Tora paused, agonizing over her word choice. Was she truly ready to do what she was about to do? Deciding, she put pen to paper again.

I feel I must give you the opportunity to leave me and this relationship forever, Trent. Make no mistake. I am in love with you. More clearly now than ever before. But God has taken me on a path that does not bring me toward you, but away from you. Your home, your business, is in Minnesota. The Alaska territory is so far. No doubt you tire of follow-ing me about the country, waiting for me to come to my senses. Hopefully, you understand I walk this path solely out of a desire to be within my newfound God's will. With his help, you will understand why I do what I must do. But simply because I have been called along this path does not mean you shall be also. If your heart takes you elsewhere, I will endeavor to do my best to understand, and to let you go as you have let me go.

Tora closed her eyes in anguish, wondering at the pain that seared her heart. What if he did as she bid him? What if he left Seattle and returned home to Minnesota? What if he gave up on Tora Anders and their fragile dream of what they might be together? *Dear God,* she thought, *I have wondered at the pain I have survived. I have rejoiced at what you have brought me through. But what you ask of me is killing me. Is this truly of you?*

She opened her eyes and stared at the script drying in blotches be-neath her pen. What would Trent say? What would he feel? And how on earth were they ever to reunite if God kept sending her farther and farther away from him?

Trent walked up the Butler Hotel's marble steps, nodding at the door-man. It had been weeks since he had heard from Tora, yet still he hoped to hear this day. He had gone for a walk downtown as he did every morning, enjoying the sounds of the city awakening to a new day. In a few minutes, he was to meet with Bradford Bresley, with whom he had been doing more and more business. He liked the man, and therefore looked forward to their meeting. Moreover, it would help to distract his attention from the lobby desk, where the mail often arrived midmorning.

Brad was early and stood up from his armchair as Trent moved forward to greet him. "Brad! Such a pleasure to see you again!"

"I'm glad as well, Trent," Brad said, shaking his hand with a friendly smile. "I see there is a men's meeting room," he said, indicating the dark-paneled drawing room behind him.

"Yes. Would you care to meet there? We could have a cup of coffee and catch up on things."

"Fine, fine."

Trent led the way with Bradford just behind his left shoulder. He spoke briefly to the host, and the distinguished servant led them to two velvet-covered armchairs that flanked a vibrant fire in the marble fireplace. "Perfect," Trent said, placing a bill in the man's hand.

"Thank you, sir. I will be back shortly with your coffee."

Brad sat down, legs spread, ever confident and relaxed. Trent liked the way the younger man made him feel the same. "Business in the Skagit Valley continues to boom," Brad said. "We have three steamers up and running out of the harbor there, bringing goods to the valley, and returning with the harvest. It is just beginning. Rest of the year, we'll haul people to and fro and still do well for ourselves."

"Fine, fine," Trent said. "What brings you down to Seattle?"

"Well, now that that operation is up and running, I'm considering heading north."

"North? To Bellingham? Or Anacortes?"

"Alaska. The Alaska territory."

Trent chuckled. "Don't tell me you have gold fever."

"Nah. I'm not that foolish. But my wife is itching to join me out west, and rather than bring her here, where I have a business established, I'm thinking I'd rather take her to the new territory, where we can build a home and where there is more than enough business to pursue. I hear if one goes with resources," he paused as the servant returned to pour them both coffee, "one can make quite a go of it."

Trent raised an eyebrow and nodded. "I have heard the same. How will Virginia feel about you hauling her to places unknown?"

Brad shrugged. "She's a strong, adventuresome woman. What's the difference between moving her to Seattle or to Juneau?"

"A civilized city, amenities, social life…"

"The important thing is that we're reunited, right?"

Trent smiled and cocked his head. "You know your wife far better than I."

"So how about it?"

"How about what?"

"Well, seeing that my current business partner has reestablished his love for seafaring, and I have enjoyed our partnership in business, I was wondering if you would care to join me in heading north."

"Me? North?" Trent shook his head. "I have ties here," he said softly. "I might be open to investing, but—"

"Don't get me wrong, Trent. I'll take your money," Brad said with a cheeky grin. "But there's something about having a partner physically present that works well for me. You can talk things over daily, check each other's figures and projected numbers. You understand."

Trent sipped his coffee. "Yes. I'm beginning to. For quite some time I've run Storm Enterprises on my own. It has come as a pleasurable surprise to find the benefits of joining forces with others. Particularly others one can respect." His intonation was clear. Both men had had run-ins with less reputable businessmen. "You're thinking you'd like to continue investing in steam? Rail?"

Brad set down his coffee cup with a clatter and threw up his hands. "I hear that the world's an oyster up there. When the people there have nothing, every new thing is bound to boom."

Trent nodded, considering his friend's words. What would it be like to head to such a rough-and-tumble territory? As part of a railroad operation, he had seen town after town opened up and civilized. But

Bradford was talking about land that wouldn't see train or steam for years. Goods had to be packed in. Lumber had to be hand hewn. It was an entirely new challenge. And it appealed to him, made his blood flow faster.

But he couldn't leave Tora. He loved her and he would wait for her to return. They had been apart for far too long. If she wouldn't go, neither would he. "Brad, I'll have to think this over," Trent said carefully. "I'm intrigued, but my responsibility lies with a certain woman…"

"Tora Anders."

Trent looked up at him in surprise.

Brad beamed, cocky with his knowledge. "Karl filled me in. Where is she now?"

"The Skagit Valley."

This news took him by surprise. "And you're here because…?"

"She needed to do something on her own."

"Ah," Brad said, after another sip of coffee. "Another independent woman. Tell you what, Trent. You convince your gal to head north, and I'll convince mine. At least they'd have each other."

Trent smiled, finding Brad's enthusiasm contagious, as always. "We'll see. But I think that moving again is the last thing on Tora's mind."

twenty-nine

September 1887

$\mathcal{K}$arl entered the Butler Hotel in Seattle, and immediately ran into Brad and Virginia Bresley in the lobby.

Brad turned to him and said, "Well, if it isn't my ol' seafaring partner back from the dead!" He shook his hand joyfully and clapped him on the back.

Karl returned his greeting and then turned to greet Virginia with a kiss to her cheek. "It's good to be back in the States."

"Staying home for a while?" Brad asked.

"Just picking up a load from Ramstad Lumber Yard and then heading south to San Francisco. I'm not sure where we'll go after that."

"I gather you're just in from Japan?"

"Just. We docked not three hours ago."

"Things went all right?"

Karl grinned. Where would he start? "As well as could be expected. Let's just say I have enough news to fill a dinner conversation."

"Excellent! Can you join us tonight?"

"I'd be honored. But I need to see to—"

"No, no excuses," Brad said, shaking his head. "We won't be around for long."

"What do you mean?"

Brad and Virginia shared a meaningful glance and then Brad turned back to him. "We're heading out. North. To Alaska."

"Alaska?" Karl asked, looking from one to the other. "Sounds like we have enough to fill two dinner conversations!"

"And then some," Virginia put in.

Brad put an arm around her. "We're expecting," he said, in a quieter, conspiratorial tone.

"Congratulations!" Karl exclaimed. "My, this is a bit much to take in. Shall we meet here at around five?"

"That will work for us. Looking forward to it, friend," he said, sticking out his hand again. "I've missed your ugly face."

"No more than I've missed yours," Karl said, pumping his hand up and down. "Until tonight, then."

They parted ways and Karl checked into the hotel. He found several letters waiting for him, one from Gerald Kenney, one from Elsa, and one from Kaatje. He could hardly wait to get to his room and tear them open.

When he got upstairs, he threw his valise on the bed and went immediately to the writing desk by the window. Deciding to save the best for last, he opened Gerald's letter first. It was full of good news and encouragement, going on and on about their success in placing his first load from Japan and anticipating similar response for the load of wood that he was to bring from Seattle. They expected him home in the Bay Area this month, when his business was complete in the Washington Territory.

He turned toward Kaatje's letter.

22 August 1886
Dear Karl,

I pray this letter finds you well and happy. I'm assuming you will stay in your usual hotel by sending this directly there. I wanted you to be the first to know that I am going north.

Karl opened his eyes wider. Was everyone he knew heading north?

As you know, I have felt a pull to go northward for over a year now. I'm assuming it's so I might have a chance to find out about Soren once and for all, then get back to the business of life in full. However, I won't put any limitations on what God can do. We've seen much, have we not? The wilds north of us are bound to teach me many more lessons than I have in mind. Please pray for me and the girls.

We do not travel alone. In May, Tora Anders came to reside with us. With her help, we were able to bring in a sizable crop that covered thirty acres. It will sustain us well through the winter, regardless of what we might encounter. I will rent out the farm here in the Skagit Valley until we return or decide to sell. Tora and I have found our peace, and I think she has become a remarkable young woman. You wouldn't recognize her, I'm sure. She has a devout heart for the Lord, and it shines through her, making her all the more lovely. She's determined to travel with us and stay with us through the spring. I am glad for her company; I do not think I would have had the tenacity to see this through without her, to say nothing of the funds.

I will write soon after our arrival to let you know our exact whereabouts. I hear from Elsa that you are again traveling the high seas and loving it. I am so glad for your newfound freedom and happiness. Please pray that I find the same, will you?

All my best,
Kaatje

Karl sat back in wonder. Tora was with Kaatje! With Jessica! And they had obviously found a way to forge a new friendship. What had taken Tora there, of all places? Obviously, God was as heavily at work in her as he had been in him. Karl's head swam with all the information that buzzed through it.

He turned toward Elsa's letter, examining her clean, sophisticated script on the envelope. He sliced this one open more thoughtfully, taking care not to tear it.

12 August 1887
The Hawaiian Islands
Dear Karl,

I have just put my children to bed and as I stare at their angelic faces, so content, so peaceful, in the dim light of the candle, I can only think of you and what you have done for me. If you had not come to my rescue, it is very likely that I would not ever have seen their darling faces again. You have made me appreciate them all the more, and acknowledge that they are far too young to lose a mother as well as a father.

With that in mind, I return to Seattle for the fall and winter. The Bergen, a new ironclad schooner, is soon due to arrive, and she might tempt me to attempt winter sailing, but until then I will weigh my options. For now I am happy to be alive, captaining my Grace, and with my children. Thank you, thank you, dear Karl, for your part in that. Should you find yourself in the Northwest come Thanksgiving time, do look us up. We'll be in Seattle or the Skagit Valley to spend it with the Bergensers. It is so much like being with family that I find it difficult to resist.

We are mending a broken mast here in Hawaii, so I'll send this along with another ship due to head out shortly.

*Faced a terrible storm coming in. If only we were near
Ramstad Lumber Yard! I guess the sailor's life is not one of
convenience.*

    I pray that this finds you well after a successful voyage.

            With a grateful heart,

            Elsa

Karl smiled wistfully at her friendly manner and stared out the window. Below him, the street was alive with carriages and wagons pulled by horses, men on horseback, pedestrians, and shopkeepers. But his thoughts were of Elsa. Where was she now? Soon home in Seattle? Who would ever have believed that he and Elsa would reestablish their friendship? It filled his heart with a gladness he could not explain. *Thank you, Father. Thank you for this peace, this freedom.* Perhaps he would still find himself in the Northwest come November. He would see. And if he was…He shook off the thought and rose.

Still mulling over the news he had received from his friends in the lobby and then from the letters, he unpacked his valise, hanging up his suit in the armoire so the wrinkles would fade a bit, and carefully set up his razor edge and shaving soap cake on the sink in his room. While the water closets and bathing facilities were down the hall, Karl appreciated the individual sinks in each room. It allowed him much-needed privacy that was part of the reason he stayed here each time he came to town. The other part was that many sea captains stayed here as well, giving him the opportunity to share stories and swap information.

As he ran the water to give himself a clean shave before dinner, he thought of Peder. Once in a while, the pain of Peder's death was so acute it left him breathless. It seemed impossible that he would never see his best friend again. Yet, he considered as he lathered up the brush and swiped his cheeks, chin, and upper lip, something monumental had changed for him. Just as it had when he had sought Elsa out for her forgiveness and when he had visited Peder's grave. It was as if in freeing Elsa from Mason he had paid some sort of debt. Something wrong had been made right.

Karl reached for the blade and carefully scraped his cheek. He paused and stared at himself in the mirror. Was it merely the act of saving her, or their reunion afterward that brought him this peace? He'd never forget how she looked as he entered his cabin. Her face had been a mix of relief and excitement. Even with her hair hastily dried in matted coils, she still had been lovely. Yet all he had felt was the same relief and excitement that her face exhibited. Relief that his friend was alive. Excitement that she was well. The last time they had been in such close proximity, he had kissed her. And that kiss had changed everything.

This time it had gone as it should. Their reunion was warm, friendly, but completely chaste. He smiled at his mirror image. God had truly done a great work in him. He was finally free to be what Elsa needed most: a trusted friend.

Karl finished shaving and then dressed for dinner. Downstairs, he found Brad and Virginia waiting for him.

"Shall we go to the cafe down the street?" Brad suggested.

"Anywhere there's fresh food and plenty of it," Karl said. He offered Virginia his arm and she took it gleefully. "I must say that motherhood is becoming to you. You're more beautiful every time I see you."

"Karl, you flatterer," she said, giving him a sly look. "How is it that you haven't made a girl fall in love with you yet?"

"Guess I haven't met the right one. Now how did my scoundrel of a friend convince you to go to the Alaska territory?"

"At first I told him no. Told him if he was going someplace so godforsaken, he could go on his own."

Karl shot Brad a surprised glance. "You were in dire straits, my friend. How did you escape?"

Brad let Virginia answer for him. "Soon enough I knew that I was expecting. It made me put my priorities in order. I figured we would be a family in one place or die trying."

"Well, bully for you," Karl said, patting her arm. "It takes a courageous woman to head north. It so happens I know another who's intending to go soon too."

"Kaatje Janssen and Tora Anders?"

"Why, yes! How did you know?" He looked over her head at Brad in wonder.

"We're all going together."

"Together? Seriously?" Karl shook his head. "How did this transpire?"

"Well, Trent Storm is deeply in love with Tora Anders."

They had reached the cafe, and Karl could hardly stand the interruption of being seated. As soon as the menus had been distributed and the waiter had departed, Karl said, "Please! Go on! Last time I talked with Trent, he had tracked Tora to the Seattle area, but had not seen her."

"Well, he found her all right," Brad said.

"He found her and they reestablished their relationship. Tora Anders is a different girl now. You wouldn't recognize her," Virginia said.

"No joking," Brad added. "The woman's had some sort of transformation."

"Reformation," Virginia amended. "She's come to Christ and he's remade her. I like her a lot better than I ever did in Minnesota."

"So anyway," Brad cut in, "Tora decided to go to Alaska to help Kaatje find out about her husband that disappeared way back when. Sam, or Saul—"

"Soren," Karl supplied.

"That's right. Soren. And she writes Trent this letter telling him that she needs to go with her, and she hopes they can find their way to be together again, but if not, she would understand if he had to forget their relationship completely."

"Tora Anders wrote *that?*"

"She's a different gal, I tell you," Brad said.

"But anyway, that was right after I asked Trent if he would consider doing some business with me up in the new territory, seeing that you have this newfound love for the sea…"

"I understand. So Trent took it as God's way of confirming that it was the right thing for him to do?"

"Right."

"Can you believe it?" Virginia asked. "It's a miracle."

Karl nodded. "Our God works in amazing ways." He turned his attention back to his menu, but his mind was again spinning. Who could have planned it this way other than their Lord?

"I'll want in on the shipping end," he said to Brad.

"I was counting on it. Can't stand to be left out, eh?" he taunted.

"Out of something lucrative that involves the sea?" Karl said.

"Stick around," Brad said. "Trent should be back soon from sending a telegraph with his happy news to Tora, and then we'll be shipping out of here on a passenger steamer. We could discuss our options."

"I don't know. I need to get back to the Bay Area. Perhaps I can go there, drop my load of lumber, pick up a load of goods and head to Juneau. We could meet there. No doubt the new arrivals are hungry for anything I could bring in."

"Most likely."

Karl nodded and turned back to the menu as the waiter approached them again. "Waiter," he said, feeling celebratory, "I'll have your finest, biggest steak, and all the trimmings."

t h i r t y

⚜

$\mathcal{T}$ora and Trent, Bradley and Virginia, and Kaatje and her children all gathered at the docks, huddling against the cold as they waited to board the steamer to Juneau. There was an icy wind off the Puget Sound's waters that morning, and Tora was glad they were on their way. Winter would soon be upon them, especially as far north as Alaska. She bent over Kaatje's girls, tucking their hoods more firmly around red, chapped cheeks.

She glanced up to see Trent moving nearer, smiling. He had taken to the girls as he did to all children. She was certain he would be a wonderful father someday. Tora too felt a new desire to begin a family with Trent, but a sudden fear overtook her. What would happen if they never had children of their own? She had heard of other women who'd borne children early in their lives, only to be barren when they wanted more children later. Her glance went from Trent to the girls, and then to Kaatje.

Kaatje looked back at Tora as if she could read her thoughts, kindness in her eyes. As soon as she had heard that Trent was coming north, that he wanted to marry her, she had begun her campaign to convince Tora of the wisdom of a wedding. But Tora had remained steadfast. It was enough that he was coming with them. She was sure this was how

343

it was supposed to be; for her to remain free to support Kaatje through this transition. When the time was right, she would know. There was a peace about it all; as if she knew, deep down, that it was all going to work out right, regardless of their dreams and desires and decisions. For now she had to concentrate on what the Lord wanted, first.

Christina leaned toward Jessica and whispered something to her. They giggled together conspiratorially, and Tora smiled. She felt a genuine love for them both. There had only been hints of it with Kristoffer's boys and Jessica in the short months she had spent with them in Camden. At the time, all she had allowed herself to think about was the future. She hadn't allowed herself to truly care. Now she knew that the present was the most precious moment of all. One never knew what was behind the next corner.

"Now boarding!" called the captain from his deck. "All first-class passengers proceed to the aft deck and hand your carry-on luggage to the steward as you board!" Trent had insisted on purchasing tickets for Kaatje, her girls, Tora, and himself, so they were all traveling with Brad and Virginia in first-rate accommodations. He and Kaatje and Tora had spent the last several evenings talking about different business options in Alaska, and Trent had chalked up the steamer tickets to "an advance on my investment," obviously assuming he'd buy into anything Tora and Kaatje decided upon, so great did he consider the opportunity spectrum in the new territory, so strong was his belief in the two women.

A man collected their tickets from Trent as they passed him, and Tora helped keep the Janssen girls from leaning too far over the edge, herding them up the gangplank like excited rabbits. To them, this was an adventure; there was no fear. What was it about childhood that allowed such fresh perspective? She wanted to remember it, feel it herself. Because it was how she wanted to proceed, with the faith of a small child. Regardless of what had transpired, regardless of what had happened to her to this point, she always wanted to remember to step forward with the grace, excitement, and assuredness that the girls exhibited before her.

"Ready?" Trent asked, taking her hand as she stepped onto the ship, his look meaningful.

"Ready," she said.

Elsa could not explain why she was feeling the way she did. She was restless, irritable, unhappy. Ever since she had returned to Seattle, she had struggled with a vague sense of disappointment, as if she had organized a party and no one had attended. She supposed it was because she had been met with the news that her friends and sister were heading north. She chided herself for being childish. Her mother's words came to her often: *It's always easier to be the one going than the one left behind.*

Was that what she considered herself? Left behind? Since marrying Peder, she had largely been the one waving good-bye to those at home. After she convinced him to let her travel with him, that is. But could she not bear it with greater grace? Surely there was some deeper reason for her disquiet than that.

If only I had had a chance to say good-bye, she thought, staring out the window at a brilliant Seattle fall day. The leaves were in full regalia, reminding her of those in Camden-by-the-Sea. Even that thought made her more melancholy, wishing for friends she had not seen in over two years. Briefly she considered a transcontinental trip by train, but then immediately discounted it, unwilling to put her children, or Mrs. Hodge, through such an ordeal.

If only I had had a chance to say good-bye, she thought again, picturing Kaatje's face, the two girls, and lastly Tora's. She was a bit jealous, she decided, that Kaatje and Tora had forged a new friendship strong enough to take Tora northward with Kaatje, when she herself and Tora were more distant than ever. What kind of sisters were they? If Carina were here, then…"Uff da!" Elsa muttered under her breath, turning away from the window. Since when had she started feeling so sorry for herself? She went to her desk and sat down with Kaatje's last letter.

20 September 1887
Dear Friend,

I ache with sadness that we are not to see each other one final time before we leave for Alaska. Word has reached me that you have been waylaid in the Hawaiian Islands with a broken mast, and your homecoming has been delayed. I had so hoped you might join our harvest celebration and see us off. Perhaps your shipping excursions can soon bring you to the Alaska territory.

Please celebrate with me, Elsa. I am so sure this is the right direction. Although Soren is most probably long gone, it will bring me peace of mind to at least attempt to find out the truth. And I am certain that God takes me there not only to gain this knowledge, but also to explore a new phase of my life. While farming has its rewards, perhaps there is a more genteel way of making a living in such a new, rough place. Please pray that we all remain safe. It remains my chief concern.

Tora continues to surprise me. She shores me up when I begin to doubt, and we grow closer by the day. Almost like the sister I never had—aside from you, of course! Knowing that she will at least travel by my side and be my companion through the winter gives me the confidence I need to get there. Never did I anticipate that my rallying forces would come from such an unexpected sector. But our God is one of surprises, is he not? It heartens me to think of him smiling over our simple expectations and how easily he outsmarts us for our greater good.

Tora has sent word to Trent Storm that she intends to go. I assume we shall see him here before we depart. Her relationship with Jess is one of a doting auntie. Each knows who the other truly is, but it has not disrupted our family life a whit. This, in itself, is a small miracle.

We head north in ten days' time, and make our way toward Juneau. It is the biggest town of consequence where we can safely winter and begin to make inquiries about Soren. I will write as soon as I can.

> *Until then I remain*
> *Your devoted friend,*
> *Kaatje*

A tap at the door interrupted her reverie. "Come in," she called idly.

Mrs. Hodge hauled in a canvas bag full of letters over one shoulder and Eve on the other. "Mail call," she said drolly. "More response from your last column in the *Times*. And a child in need of her mother."

Elsa shook her head and smiled. She took Eve and cooed at her daughter's pudgy, smiling face. "I am amazed that so many take the step to wish me well. I guess there are a few people out there pleased to know that Mason Dutton is no longer a threat." When the Japanese ships had moved in, they had made short work of Dutton's schooner, although they lost two of their own in the battle. Mason had managed to slip ashore, but he had been captured and sent to Britain. He was due to hang in a month's time.

"Any personal letters?" Elsa switched Eve to her other shoulder.

"I didn't sift through them all," Mrs. Hodge said.

Just then, Kristian edged past her legs. "Mama!"

"Hi, love," Elsa said, ruffling his hair. "Want to look through the letters with me?"

"Yes!" he said in delight. He sat down by the bag and began to dump handfuls to the floor. When Mrs. Hodge moved to stop him, Elsa shook her head. "I'll have to go through them all eventually. We might as well let him have some fun with them."

"Suit yourself. I'm going to see to supper. You'll be all right with the children?"

"Just fine," said Elsa, smiling at each. She should have gone to get her children earlier—she could never remain melancholy with them about. "And Mrs. Hodge?"

"Yes?"

"The children and I will travel north to the Skagit Valley for Thanksgiving. That should give you some time off to concentrate on your own family."

"Very well!" she said, looking pleased at the news. "When do you intend to leave?"

Elsa thought for a moment and then said, "Midmonth. I'll send a wire to Nora and see if she and Einar can put us up."

"Very good, Mrs. Ramstad. I'll see to the arrangements once you get me the specific dates."

After the children were down for their naps, Elsa donned her overcoat and, using an umbrella, set off for the cemetery. It was time to pay Peder's grave a visit. She thought it might bring her some semblance of peace, some understanding for her disquieted heart. She passed by the three blocks quickly and turned into the somber place, the ground already soggy and giving way beneath her feet after all the recent rain. Pulling up her skirts in one hand, Elsa wrinkled her nose and trudged on. She was alone in the graveyard. Here and there, bits of fog hung about the stones.

Peder's grave site remained exactly as she had left it. She pulled away the dead flowers beneath the stone and replaced them with marigolds she had cut from the garden before departing. That done, she stood and sighed. Elsa gave the stone a melancholy smile, picturing Peder's face instead of the anchor.

"I suppose you'd have a thing or two to tell me," she began. "No doubt you're displeased with me taking to sea alone. But even you would have to admit that I've done all right for myself, love. Even faced down Mason Dutton and made it out alive."

She shifted her umbrella to the other hand. "I still have a lot to figure out. Such as how to be both a mother and a father to our children." Elsa listened to the raindrops fall on the canvas of her umbrella for a moment. The ground smelled of freshly turned peat. "No, you're right. I'll just have to be a mother to them and hope it's enough." She smiled again, but this time there were quick tears in her eyes. "It's getting better, Peder, it really is. I just miss you so. And I ache for the void your departure leaves in our children's lives. I wanted them to know you." The last part was spoken in a whisper, her voice cracking.

Elsa wiped her eyes and smiled with new resolve. "So I'm moving forward the best way I know how. Apparently the way everyone else does it. You wouldn't believe Tora these days. I don't know if I'd recognize her as the same girl. And Karl has become a fine friend." She pictured his longer, curlier hair and earring, his bright teeth when he grinned at her, then pushed away the image. "Kaatje's heading off for Alaska, and here am I, alone for the first time."

Alone for the first time. The thought struck her. That was it. That was the reason for her restlessness. Yes, she had the children. But when was the last time she had ever been truly alone as an adult? Kaatje had come to her as a companion last fall. Her spring and summer were spent in the company of Riley and the men, her attention drawn to the next horizon as the *Grace* sailed on. "It's because I'm home, alone. I'm forced to deal with the quiet," she whispered.

Elsa sniffed and wiped her eyes again. "I am forced to deal with the fact that you're gone, and never coming back."

The rain came down more steadily now.

"I will make it," she announced, then looked around, a bit embarrassed at how loudly it had emerged from her mouth. Fortunately, she was still by herself. She stared at Peder's stone, the cutter's marks, the anchor. "With God by my side, I shall make it."

Unable to tolerate the silence any longer, she kissed her fingertips and bent to touch the stone. "Good-bye, Peder. I miss you. I love you." And with that, she turned and walked away.

thirty-one

As Elsa flicked the reins over the gray's back, taking her rented carriage west to Nora's home, she looked about, wishing she was soon to see Kaatje and the girls, as well as the others. It was a sunny afternoon, but the air held the crisp heartiness of fall. The ground lay fallow beside the road, Kaatje's crops already borne by railroad to the nearby granaries and cities to be distributed. In the year since he had begun operations here, Karl and his associates had made great changes for the valley. It was obvious that a newfound prosperity was upon them—new homes were completed, the church expanded, and the roads graded.

Elsa used one hand to tuck Eve in amid her blankets and bassinet. Kristian held on to the side rail and grinned as if he were on a carousel rather than a buggy. "Faster, Mama, faster!"

"I think this is fast enough," Elsa said with a smile. "This old gray will pass on to heaven if we go any faster."

"Like Papa?" Kristian asked soberly.

Elsa's grin faltered. "Yes," she said, too brightly, "like Papa."

"Who are we going to see again, Mama?" Kristian asked, his mind moving past Peder much faster than Elsa's could.

"We're going to see all the people who came to America with us, people from Bergen."

"Do they all talk funny?"

Elsa laughed. "Some of them still speak Norwegian, but most speak English with an accent. Some talk just like you," she said, poking him in the tummy. "Now hold on, Kristian. We're turning here."

"Whoa!" Kristian said, overly dramatic for the calm turn.

"Nearly lost it, eh?" Elsa asked with a grin.

"Almost overboard," he said. Elsa winced at the comment, but he continued, unconscious of the reminder of his father's death. "Mama, when will we ship out again?"

"I haven't decided, love. It could be as long as four months."

"What's a month?"

"A long time." Nora's house came into view. "Here we are!" Elsa exclaimed. In her heart, she knew this was just the place for her to come. Even though Kaatje and the girls were gone, she knew that simply being with her old family friends would bring a measure of healing. Had it been over a year since she had come with the news of Peder's death? She shook her head. Time had crawled at first, but the last six months had flown by.

Nora emerged and stepping-stone children followed her out, circling her skirts. "Five of them!" Elsa exclaimed, pulling the gray to a stop and hopping down. She turned to help Kristian, but he had already jumped out the other side. She reached instead for Eve. "I'm afraid I'll never keep up with you," she said to Nora, moving into her embrace even though she held her youngest.

"Ah well, two are enough, by anyone's standards," Nora said, embracing her with a fleshy hug. She had grown quite rotund in the last year. "How are you, friend?"

"As well as can be expected," Elsa answered, looking into her eyes. There was no hint of melancholy to her tone, just truthfulness. "And you?"

"Fat and happy," Nora said with a smile.

Elsa shook her head and laughed.

"Come in, come in," Nora said, taking Eve from her to introduce the babe in her other arm. "Eve, meet Jahn. Master Jahn, Mistress Eve." Elsa trailed behind them, smiling. Already she felt worlds better. The last month had been good for her. She had fasted; she had prayed. She had concentrated on being alone and finding a place in her heart that made it all right to be so. But it was great to be among family again.

As if reading her mind, Nora glanced at her and asked, "What do you hear from your mother these days?"

"Not a lot. It's been several months. She has moved in with Garth and Carina."

"That'll be good for her. A body can only take so much solitude."

Elsa nodded, knowing exactly what she meant. "So you'll be hosting a tiny little crowd here on the morrow?"

"If you call forty-two tiny, yes."

Elsa laughed. "I suppose it's difficult to host fewer, with the way your families grow like weeds out here."

Nora joined her in laughter. "Ja. But I'm glad for the difficulty. It's a happy burden to bear." She turned at the door. "Now come in, come in. I'll show you to your room so you can get the children settled."

"Thank you, Nora," she said, hoping her eyes conveyed the gratitude her heart felt.

Nora waved it off. "In you go, miss. We'll have time enough for the sentimentalities."

That next afternoon, it was raining "like cats and dogs" Einar said, using the American expression. The men had constructed rough tables and benches in the barn, and the women had brought their best linens. Elsa was amazed. With the linens and candlelight, the stalls mucked out and fresh hay applied, the barn was transformed. The tables were set in the middle of the main room of the barn, with hay stacked high all around to help to keep it warmer. With hot bricks at their feet and the combined body heat of over forty people, the room would serve them well.

She left the barn after setting out the silver and ran to the house in the rain, splashing through puddles. She had to remove her boots in the room just off the kitchen, and briefly wished for more practical clothing here in the country. Before leaving Seattle, Elsa had picked up her first dresses denoting she was out of mourning. Nothing radical, she thought, but the subtle gray-blue, light green, and pale yellow gowns lifted her spirits upon sight. Tonight she would wear the gray-blue. It was the sturdiest and most subtle of her gowns, more fitting among her countryfolk who did not pay much attention to the latest styles in Paris, as did Madame de Boisiere.

Smells of steamed carrot pudding and spices filled her nostrils as she unlaced her boots. Elsa smiled, salivating a bit at the thought of the heavy dessert, covered in a rich, sugary sauce. What a treat to be with friends, eating meals that reminded her of her mother. *Mother.* How she wished she could see the dear lady again! A thought struck her and she smiled. What was to stop her? Why not take a load of lumber this winter and head to Norway? The cargo would probably be a wash, but would pay for her voyage. She could return to the East Coast with a load from Europe. After seeing Mother.

What joy it would be to introduce her children to their grandmother! And to see Carina and Garth...married. And it would be good to see Peder's parents. How they, too, would cherish the chance to meet Peder's offspring. She slapped the bench at either side of her waist. She would do it. She would take the new ironclad schooner and travel to Norway after the holidays, arriving in time for Easter. It was befitting, she supposed. Easter was a time of rebirth, renewal, celebration of their Lord's resurrection. So too would she renew her familial ties and celebrate what she did have, instead of focusing on what she did not.

She rose and entered the kitchen, in a higher mood than she had felt in months.

"Ach," Nora muttered, peering into a steaming pot.

"Can I help?" Elsa offered.

"No, no. You go and get dressed. I'll be needing you in an hour." She turned to peer at Elsa. "You're leaving your mourning black behind today?"

"I was thinking so..." Elsa said, suddenly uncertain. "Do you think it's been long enough? I've been in black for over a year—"

"Oh yes," she muttered, turning back to her pots and stirring. "You do what is right in your heart. Your people will support you."

Elsa nodded. She felt ready for the color of clothing, for life in general again, yet parting from her black was like leaving the last vestiges of Peder behind. *I'm not forgetting you, love,* she thought. *I'm simply moving forward.* Knowing how Peder loved her in glorious gowns of amazing colors, she determined he would be glad for it. Thanksgiving, like Easter, was a time of being thankful for what one had been given. She was alive. She had her children. She had her friends. She would live.

After church services, the Bergensers hurried back to the Gustavsons' through the miserable weather. By the time they got back to the farm, Elsa's new gown was soaked from the trim of the skirt to the waist. She had no choice but to change into her light green. She hoped it would not seem showy to change when the others hovered about the woodstove trying to dry, but Nora had insisted. Sighing, she laid Eve on the bed and began the arduous process of changing clothes. After getting down to her lingerie, a quick look in the mirror told her that her attempt at a coiffure was a disaster, and her hair would need attention too. Eve squawked and rolled over, playing with a button on the down comforter of the bed as if it were the most transfixing item she had ever seen. She leaned to suck on it.

"No, you don't," Elsa said with a laugh, lifting the babe into her arms while she pulled the combs from her hair. Eve's attention turned toward Elsa's tresses. Elsa let her play with one strand while she brushed out the rest of her hair. It had grown long, to her waist, and she considered cutting it off to her shoulders, with just enough to do up in fashion, but not so much to deal with. Perhaps in time she would have the courage to take such an outrageous action.

"Ahyaa," Eve said.

"To have your hair," Elsa sighed, stroking the baby's nearly bald head. There were faint wisps of blond curls, but nothing of consequence yet. She put the girl back down on the bed, handed her the comb to play with, and returned to the mirror. Quickly, she swept her hair into a simple knot and secured it again with the combs. Then she shook out her green dress and pulled it on, using a button hook to bring the simple bodice together. Once done, she smoothed the skirt and took another look.

"Not bad, considering I can barely breathe," she muttered. Madame de Boisiere relished her small waist—not quite as small now after two children—and liked to accentuate it with the lines of the day. The green wool had darker green silk stripes of velvet ribbon, which followed her feminine curves. It had a high neck and long sleeves, and a skirt that dropped in large, loose folds over a straight skirt beneath.

"Ahyaa," Eve said again.

"You like it too, eh?" Elsa asked, knowing the girl still stared at her comb. She felt good in the dress, pretty for the first time in ages. Well, at least since Lady Bancock's ball. It was such a relief to wear color again, yet it felt a bit scandalous. The sensation gave her a thrill. It would all take some getting used to after so many months of somber colors.

A knock sounded at the door. "Elsa? Almost ready?"

"Yes!" She felt guilty spending so much time primping when the others had been in the kitchen, but as she left her room with Eve and entered the warm, low-ceilinged room, her fears were assuaged. The women still chattered around the stove and turned to admire her gown in earnest, in turn complimenting her and putting her at ease. Not one seemed to pass judgment on her.

"Let me hold the baby," Eira said, reaching for Eve. Elsa gladly handed her off. "Has anyone seen my son?"

"He's out with the other boys, playing in the haystack."

Elsa nodded with a smile. "Nora, put me to work."

"Here," she said, handing her a steaming plate. "Cover that with a dish towel to try and keep it warm and take it to the barn. Ladies, I'll need all of you who are available too."

They were all seated minutes later, an amazing feat with so many children in the mix. Everyone was hungry, she supposed. *That will help every time.* Gazing around the happy faces passing dish after dish, Elsa grinned too. Life was good. She had been given much. And she would give thanks until the day she died.

As tempting as Elsa's invitation to join them in the valley had been, Karl had to get back to San Francisco to deliver his load. When he knocked on the door of the Kenneys' home, he thought of Elsa and her children, surrounded by their loving neighbors and friends of the Skagit Valley. They would be well cared for. He was confident in it. But there still was the slightest pang in his heart, a vague sense of missing something…

"Karl!" Mrs. Kenney squealed, opening her arms to him as he moved past the maid. He was briefly enveloped by her voluptuous body and then released to face her giggling girls.

"Hello, Mr. Martensen," said Mara coquettishly.

"Mr. Martensen," flirted Nina, echoing her sister.

"Ladies," he said gallantly, giving them each a nod and a grin. In the months that he had been at sea, they had grown more lovely, but he was as sure as ever that his role for them would never be anything other than brotherly.

"Martensen!" Gerald said, coming out of his study to heartily shake the younger man's hand.

"Gerald, it's good to see you. Happy Thanksgiving."

"And to you, my boy. And to you. Come in. Let me get you some refreshment," he paused, looking pointedly at the maidservant, "and the ladies can join us in the parlor before dinner."

"After we freshen up, Papa," Mara said demurely.

"Yes, yes. Come when you can," he said, waving her off.

"I will get the hors d'oeuvres," Mrs. Kenney said. "Please, Karl, leave your coat and hat with Ronni."

As directed, Karl slipped out of his coat and handed it and his hat to the maid. He followed Gerald into the parlor, smiling at the crackling fire in the fireplace and candles lit about the room. It was warm and cozy, the perfect place for a man to think, on a day such as this, about what he had been given.

"You got the wood off-loaded," Gerald stated, sitting down and handing Karl a crystal glass.

"Yes. With little difficulty. Seems there's as great a hunger for quality lumber down here as there ever has been."

"Excellent. Excellent, my boy. Will you make some more runs for me?"

Karl smiled and hesitated. "Actually, Gerald, I've been meaning to talk with you about that." He edged forward in his seat. "Perhaps we should discuss it later, after dinner."

"No, no. Out with it."

"Well, you see, Gerald, you and I met at just the right time for me to accept captaincy of your ship. It seemed providential, right. And I have no quarrel with how you run your company or pay me," he said urgently, searching his friend's eyes. "The thing is that I'm not being a wise investor. I have enough capital to captain my own ship, and would like to have my own steamer built. My time sailing as a captain without more than a partial buy into the load was good, but it's not wise for me to continue doing so. Not when I could be sailing my own ship, and taking a hundred percent of the profit."

Gerald chuckled and sat back. "I had no idea. I had no idea you had the means to buy your own vessel. I suppose I should be glad I got you when I did, son. You've done well for me and my investments."

Karl cocked his head, a bit embarrassed. "It takes a while to have a ship built. And I've just finished a design that I'll order from Ramstad Yard in Camden. For the next year, I'll continue captaining your vessel, if you'll have me. Then we'll need to find a qualified man to take over."

"What can I say?" Gerald asked. "I hate to think of losing you at all, but I am glad that I had you for a while."

"Oh, you're not losing me, Gerald. I intend to be a friend to the Kenneys for a good long while."

"Oh?" said Mara, entering the room. She smelled of spicy perfume. Gerald grinned as he looked from one to the other.

"Yes," Karl said, shifting uncomfortably under her girlish gaze. Clearly, she had misinterpreted his words. But before he could say more, her sister and mother entered the room, and their conversation took another tack. Karl sighed. Surely, at some point, this too would have to be dealt with.

epilogue

‿✵◟

A knock at their door one late November evening startled Tora and Kaatje as they huddled near their tiny woodstove. "Who could that be?" Tora muttered.

"I hope everyone is all right," Kaatje added as she went to the door and opened it to see Trent Storm.

"Come on! You have to see them!" Trent practically shouted, unperturbed by the women shushing him. Christina peeked out from behind the curtain that separated their "kitchen" from the "bedroom" of their one-room home. Here in the new territory, there was precious little to choose from when it came to housing arrangements.

"What, Trent? See who?"

He grabbed her shawl by the door and wrapped it around her shoulders. "You too, Kaatje. Get your girls up. It's magnificent!"

"What? Trent Storm, what do you mean, taking us outside on such a cold night?" Kaatje demanded in a friendly, wondering tone. Still, she motioned toward Christina, who with a squeal went to awaken Jessica. After throwing on more clothes, they moved outside as a group.

Tora smiled as soon as they were away from the house. To the north, the aurora borealis was shining in such splendor that it took her breath away.

"Have you ever seen anything like it?" Trent exclaimed, placing an arm around Tora and another around Kaatje as they stared together. The girls stood in front of them, laughing and dancing at the sight.

"Not since—" Kaatje began.

"Bergen," Tora finished. "But even there, I do not suppose I ever appreciated what I was seeing." Over the mountains, streaks of purple and blue extended toward them, with red waves crossing the others as if a heavenly weaver were working on a fantastic loom.

"Do they appear often here?" Kaatje asked hopefully.

"On cold, clear nights, through April, I'm told," Trent said. "We could see them at times in Minnesota, but nothing like this."

"I'm so glad they're here," Tora said. There was something about the mere presence of the northern lights that gave her comfort, like a small hug sent from home.

"It is affirmation that we are on the right path," Kaatje said. "Regardless of what is before us." She moved away from the couple slightly and turned toward them, her face inscrutable in the near-darkness. "Thank you for coming with me, my friends," she said. "I could not have done it without you." Her voice broke a bit, and Tora moved nearer to her.

"No, Kaatje. Thank you for allowing us to come. I cannot begin to describe what it means to me."

Kaatje shook her head, as if embarrassed. "Well, it is clear that you belong together. You two should marry."

Tora smiled and took her hand. "Soon enough," she said over her shoulder to Trent. "Very soon. But first, let us move forward as one. When you have found out what you need to about Soren, when I am sure that you and Jessie and Christina are well on your way—beside me or on your own—then Trent and I will marry."

Kaatje turned to Trent. "I am sorry, Trent. You see how stubborn she is?"

Trent laughed and again placed an arm around each woman. "I recognize it. But for once her stubbornness is being used by the God who orchestrates nights like these," he said, looking upward. "For now, I am content to be simply near Tora, and to be your friend too. I have a peace about it all that I cannot explain."

"Then God go with us," Kaatje whispered, looking upward with Trent. In the silence, the northern lights created a holy atmosphere. So great was the sight and their momentum, it was surprising that there was not anything audible to accompany such a cacophony of motion.

"God be with us," whispered Trent.

"God *is* with us," finished Tora.

If you enjoyed Deep Harbor,
look for the third installment of

The Northern Lights Series

Midnight Sun

To be released Spring 2000

Kaatje has traveled to the most difficult territory in the west to find out if Soren is alive or dead. Surrounded by her friends and family, she feels ready, truly ready, to know the truth. Eventually Kaatje decides that all evidence points to the fact that Soren is dead, and she concentrates on building her successful business with Tora. Better yet, she allows herself to fall in love with a good man who has pursued her for years. Karl, Elsa, Trent, Tora, and the girls all celebrate her coming nuptials. But just as Kaatje's wedding draws near, she has to climb one last mountain. For only on the darkest of days, can she discover the truth and see her *Midnight Sun.*

Dear Friends,

Thanks for reading another one of my books. Writing is like tearing out your heart and placing it on a platter, and I appreciate that my readers are so tender with my offering! I hope you liked *Deep Harbor.* Tora Anders reminded me of Scarlett O'Hara in her determination and stubbornness, but also of myself. Although I have never wandered as far as Tora, how many times have I pained my Savior through sin? It makes me ache when I think about it and endeavor once again to try harder. Thank heaven for grace, or I'd be history. And for any who wonder, God's grace is as deep as the ocean. Praise him!

For all who have inquired, my second baby, Emma Reyne, was born in July. Her older sister, Olivia, adores her, and so does the rest of the family. There's nothing like a baby to remind me of how God feels about us; a moment of sweet, toothless smiles and cooing makes up for hours of crying. We thank God that she was born healthy and pray that we raise her with a heart for Christ.

Now I'm trying to reestablish a routine for our family and get crackin' on *Midnight Sun,* the third and last installment of the Northern Lights Series. It will really be Kaatje's story—is anyone more deserving than she is? Still, there are trials ahead for her, poor thing. But don't worry; I love her too!

I wish each of you every blessing in life. But most of all, I hope you can dive even deeper into the Word, knowing your Savior better each day. Always remember that he is our Living Water, our Stream in the desert, our safest Harbor in the storm.

All my best,

Lisa Tawn Bergren

Write to Lisa Tawn Bergren:
c/o WaterBrook Press
5446 N. Academy, #200
Colorado Springs, CO 80918